The

Coal Mine

Caper

By

Kenneth S. Murray

This book is a work of fiction. Names, characters, places, and incidents are either the product of the author's imagination or are used fictitiously, and any resemblance to actual persons, living or dead, business establishments, events, or locales is entirely coincidental.

ISBN: 1-4107-0956-6 (e-book)
ISBN: 1-4107-0957-4 (Paperback)
ISBN: 1-4107-6235-1 (Dust Jacket)

This book is printed on acid free paper.

Edited by Helen Cairns

1stBooks - rev. 05/28/03

Chapter 1

Hardin County, Kentucky, 1864

Lots of history happened in Hardin County. The first map of the area was published by John Filson in 1784 with the help of Colonel Daniel Boone. Both Daniel and his brother, Squire spent a lot of time in the area, attested to by the fact that the Boone family cemetery is located on Fort Knox, just north of Radcliff.

On June 1, 1792, Kentucky became the fifteenth state admitted to the union. Jefferson Davis, President of the Confederate States and Abraham Lincoln, sixteenth President of the United States, were both born in Hardin County.

"Yep. Seen a lot'a history this county has, Jeb. And I think we might be makin' history right now."

"Whose gonna remember us underground diggin' coal in this friggin' mine? You must be crazy, Luke.

You're sucking in too many fumes from that methane gas pocket we opened up. Damn near blew us to hell."

"No I'm not." Luke stood up and leaned on his shovel to catch his breath for a moment and stared hard at his friend. "We're diggin' coal for the trains that'll take the Union Army into the south and end this damn war. Americans killing each other! It don't make no sense."

Luke thought about his brother, two years younger than he was at twenty-one and his enemy, or so his captain told him. "This border state of Kentucky went union and we're part of General Grant's army," his commanding officer had said.

He hadn't heard from his brother in five months. Luke knew the people of Kentucky were much divided and his younger brother had joined the Confederate army and served under the famous Thomas Jonathan "Stonewall" Jackson, who confounded the northern armies with his brilliant tactics.

Luke turned his head as he heard some noise down the horizontal mine shaft. The light from his head lamp on the front of his miner's hat was the new safer type made with stearic wax. It was harder wax that didn't run much, put out little smoke, and did not smolder when blown out.

The candle gleamed off the shiny metal deflector behind it and illuminated the face of old Henry, the tired old mule that was pulling the coal car along the iron tracks to the front of the mine face. He stopped right in front of Jeb.

As usual, and as Henry anticipated, Jeb reached out and scratched Henry's huge ears. Henry promptly sneezed twice as if to say, "I shouldn't be down here with all this coal dust flyin' around."

His supervisor came around and unhitched Henry from one end of the car and pulled him around and hitched him back up to the other end. He pulled a bucket of water out of the empty car, poured some in a pan, placed it in front of Henry who sucked at it greedily.

Only then did he offer some to Jeb and Luke by setting the bucket down near them as he sat down on the flattest place he could find in the cramped mine shaft. He pulled off his hat and wiped the sweat off his face with a big dirty handkerchief, blew his nose in it, and then stuffed it in his back pocket.

"You think more of that old mule than you do us," Jeb fussed.

The supervisor was leaning forward, elbows on his knees, resting as he looked down along the coal seam, lit by his own lamp. "I guess so," he muttered back after he drank some of the cool water himself. "I remember what that cavalry officer told me. 'You take care to feed and water that mule. If he gets sick and dies, you ain't gettin' another one. That means you'll push and pull the coal car down that track yourself. You understand what I'm saying, soldier?'"

The supervisor looked up at Jeb and Luke. "I told the captain that I understood him real well," he said, "and that means you two come in third on my friendship list," and he straightened up and guffawed loudly, the sound echoing down the mine shaft.

They were working a slope mine. One that wasn't close enough to the surface to dig out from ground level and yet wasn't deep enough to shaft mine. This one was just thirty feet down so the miners cut an entrance with a gradual "slope," where a set of iron tracks could run underground and a coal car could be pulled by horses, oxen, or mules. Even big dogs were used like a dog sled team.

To support the ceiling from collapse, the room and pillar method was used where half the coal had to be left in the mine in the form of "pillars," a natural support system which reduced the time consuming use of wood beams.

Luke, Jeb, the supervisor, and Henry the mule lived through the coal mining operation along with many other miners who provided the coal for the steam driven locomotives that pulled railroad cars loaded with troops, guns, and equipment all over the United States during the Civil War.

None of them would ever know it, but Luke would eventually be right. Not for a long time, however. When they dug out that coal mine, and most importantly where they dug it out, would be forgotten for 135 years. But then in 1999, that coal mine would be talked about by every living person in the United States over eight years in age, and discussed by most of the intelligent people around the planet.

This momentous happening would make front page headlines in every major newspaper in the world. It would be remembered forever in school text books, non-fiction books, magazines, and novels. The guesses of what, who, how and when it happened would flood the bookstores. The "how," would eventually become all too clear and incredibly simple due to a myriad of very natural geologic events that occurred underground over several million years in addition to this man made change below the surface of the earth: The digging of coal mine number eighty-seven.

Chapter 2

Hardin County, 1935

Virgil Millier took a deep breath and cupped his hands over his mouth and nose. He blew lung warmed air out from pursed lips in long, slow puffs into his cold hands. He puffed hard enough to fog up his bifocal glasses that he now needed to wear at the age of forty-three.

Damn, it's cold, he thought. *Cold for November. Feels more like February weather.*

He had arrived early as was his usual practice when he was on a new job site. He decided that this one must be darn important. He was an engineer for the U. S. Army Corps of Engineers assigned to the southern district which included Kentucky.

The curled up construction plans he had taken out of the cardboard tube were spread out on the hood of his brand new Ford truck and weighted down carefully with a metal thermos bottle on one end and a cup of hot coffee on the other, which partly covered the classification stamped in large letters on each page of the plans. The word,

S E C R E T, meaning that under no circumstances was any one unauthorized allowed to look at these drawings.

He had already looked at the plans any number of times and he couldn't believe the materials required to construct the building. It was going to be a fortress, for Pete's sake, and for what? Out in the middle of nowhere.

He was here to meet with the owner of the construction company that had successfully bid the job under guidelines established by the Federal Property and Administrative Services, the precursor to the General Services Administration, formed by a congressional act passed in 1949.

Five hundred sixty thousand dollars. He couldn't believe it. In 1935 he couldn't think of any building far larger than this that cost so much. His face screwed up again as he studied the drawings. Its exterior dimensions only measured 105 feet by 121 feet, and it was only forty two feet above ground. *What a waste,* he thought, for a building with a two-story basement, a main floor and an attic.

He looked again at the required materials on the next page and slowly shook his head as he read in a low voice to himself. "Sixteen thousand five hundred feet of granite, four thousand two hundred cubic yards of concrete, seven hundred fifty tons of reinforcing steel, and six hundred seventy tons of structural steel." *It was an incredible list,* he thought.

He turned to the next page and saw what was required on the front of the structure. Over the marble entrance above the huge, thick double doors, would be the inscription, *United States Depository,* with the seal of the Department of the Treasury in gold. It would become known as the Fort Knox Bullion Depository.

Millier rolled up the plans, poured some more hot coffee into his cup, and stepped back to look at his beautiful nine month old vehicle that he had saved so long to buy. It was a pure white 1934 Ford 2 door Roadster Pick-Up S/R with a chrome and stainless Superbell assembly, chrome Halibrand rear end, tweed interior, removable chopped Carson black padded top, polished Americans, with a billet and wood truck bed.

The long hood over the engine gave it a rakish look, especially with the tall vertical grill in the front, he determined. Smiling to himself, he climbed back into his truck, turned his heater on, and waited ten more minutes. At eight o'clock sharp several dull brown colored Chevrolet cars with *U S Army* in white letters painted on the sides pulled up to the site and a group of people got out.

Millier walked over to them and said hello. He had met most of them before except for the architect, Archibald Pullman Montrose, whose appearance and demeanor was just as pompous as his name sounded or looked like on paper. His name was stamped all over his blueprints.

Got the job through family connections, Millier realized. The Pullman family, among other endeavors, built the first railroad passenger sleeping cars, the first dining cars with a kitchen, and the first parlor cars. The Pullman Company had a monopoly and there were thousands of railroad cars operating across the United States in 1935.

After preliminary introductions, the usual palavering about the unusually cold weather, and comments about current events in Germany involving Adolph Hitler and the new Nazi party, they got down to business.

After a half hour of discussion, Millier cleared his throat, snorted in disgust and just said it out loud. "Why the heck don't you put this building inside the grounds over there," Millier said, pointing to the Fort named after Major General Henry Knox, the first secretary of war.

"There's one hundred ten thousand acres in there surrounded by the Sixth Armored Division with all those soldiers, tanks and cannon. You could build this for one quarter of what this plan costs using concrete filled double block, one steel door, and a huge vault inside. It could be guarded by troops outside a high barbed wire fence with patrol dogs and inside the building with armed guards on three eight hour shifts. Nobody could ever break into it," Millier concluded.

The big pudgy architect turned his head quickly toward Millier. His double chin waddled back and forth, as fat eyes bulged outward and thick eyebrows raised at such a suggestion.

"This is one of the institutions under the supervision of the Director of the U S Mint," he said emphatically, "which in turn comes under the auspices of the United States Treasury, and accordingly will be guarded by their employees. This project has nothing to do with the army."

So the foundation was drawn with stakes and string to delineate the outer walls and a truck mounted drill was brought in to be sure the building would stand on solid ground underneath. They drilled ten holes. One at each of the four corners, one in the middle of each side, and two at random near the center of the foundation.

In each case they went down twenty feet until they hit the limestone bedrock at the same depth at every drill point.

"Excellent . . . couldn't be better," Millier said to the group. "The basement floors require that we dig out about twenty feet, which means we can pour the concrete almost on the bedrock."

What they didn't know was the fact that the limestone bedrock was only five feet thick and under that there were only two feet of bituminous, or soft coal. Below that there was nothing but twelve feet of empty space down to the floor of the coal mine.

If that group of architects, engineers, and construction company personnel assembled there on that particular plot of ground could see through the earth for some thirty feet, they wouldn't believe their eyes. The entire length of the new United States Bullion Depository was to be constructed exactly over the center of a Civil War coal mine dug out seventy one years before.

The old opening into the mine, which was some three hundred yards away, had been collapsed and destroyed by a farmer who had owned the land years before. He had lost a child in the mine. Several hundred pounds of coal had dropped on his son when the boy and his older brother were fooling around inside the dark horizontal shaft.

So the farmer dynamited the opening which was then covered with dirt. Eventually, field grasses, bushes and trees completed the cover up.

Ten years later the farmer sold the land to someone else and moved away. No one knew about it and there were no records left. The whole Hardin county area had any number of old abandoned coal mines.

The Fort Knox Bullion Depository was completed and opened in 1936. It would be sixty-three years later in 1999 before anyone again discovered the old mine. Before the end of that year the mine would become internationally famous and never forgotten again.

Chapter 3

Lexington, Kentucky, 1998

Floyd Richards felt like a million bucks. He folded the Lexington Herald-Leader and looked up at his pretty blonde wife and then let his eyes roam over their two children. One boy age six and one little girl, age four. *It's so perfect,* he thought smiling to himself about his wonderful family.

"Here it is in the university section of the paper, Doris. The announcement by UK that Floyd Richards has been awarded an associate professorship in the science department."

He looked up to make sure that Doris was watching him read, or at least listening. They lived in a rented duplex home that was in an older section of town filled with college professors and students. She was still at the kitchen counter making sandwiches for the kids to take to school.

She seemed to have a worried frown on her face and she hadn't been acting herself for several months.

Concerned, he continued to study her face. She had said that everything was all right. She didn't have any health problems that she hadn't told him about, and things were going fine at her work. She was a dental hygienist.

Richards loved her very much. He thought, *it must be some kind of unfathomable woman's thing that men are just not meant to understand.*

He looked back down and read more. "Mr. Richards holds a masters degree in Geology and is working on his doctoral thesis. When he becomes Dr. Floyd Richards, he will receive a full professorship. Congratulations to you and Mrs. Richards."

"Isn't that great, Doris?" He glanced up while she was putting two paper lunch bags in the kid's little back packs.

"I'm going to walk the kids to the bus stop, Floyd. I'll be right back."

She started out the screen door and suddenly stopped. Doris turned back to glance at her husband with an anemic, diffident smile.

"That's really nice, dear." She continued down the five wooden steps to the gravel path that led to the sidewalk as she buttoned her coat. Colder weather seemed early this year and there was a chill in the air.

As she walked the children were babbling away, happy as most kids that age should be. School was still new and fresh to them and they looked forward to every day. They would discover some wonderful new secret about life that they could come home and tell Mommy and Daddy about.

Doris glanced longingly at her children and hoped they would accept the changes that would be taking place soon.

It was mid-October and the leaves from the big maple trees that lined both sides of the street were dropping off faster now. Another big yellowy-gold maple leaf broke free with a gust of wind and sailed down to land on her forehead. It just stuck there for a moment, and her kids started to laugh out loud.

"Hey mom," her son said. "You could glue on a bunch of those and go out as a leaf pile on Halloween."

His sister thought that was hysterical and began yelling, "Leaf pile, leaf pile."

Floyd Richards stood outside the kitchen door on the wooden porch with the protective hand rail around it that led downstairs to the gravel path and watched his wife walk the kids to the bus stop with a concerned look on his face. *Something just isn't right. She's totally obsessed with other thoughts.*

He was a big man at six foot four and weighed well over two hundred pounds. But Richards had a mild temperament. He was gentle, kindly, and considerate of others around him. Like many big men, he was wired differently than the skinny little guys, who were usually jumpy and quick moving, like they were amped up all the time from an electric overload.

He would mull things over in his mind and might be slow to speak, but when he had something to say, you knew it was well thought out and it was the truth, as far as he knew it to be. He didn't make things up to hear himself speak or try to be the center of attention during every conversation. And he didn't talk in trivia about non-consequential subjects. That was the

14

inquisitive scientist in him. All things must be considered before a summation is presented to the public, even if it's talking to his young children.

Richards had sandy, light brown hair and a pleasant non-descriptive face that you could forget easily or lose in a crowd. He had no unusual facial defects or abnormalities. The forehead, eyes, nose, ears, lips, and chin were all just there, put together in no special way.

He walked back inside and checked the clock; 7:35 AM and he had an early class at 8:15 AM; time to grab his notes and get there a little early to review his ideas for the day.

He was a little annoyed at Doris, so he left before she got back, without the standard kiss and "have a nice day." He jumped in his five year old F150 Ford pick-up truck parked under some sweet gum and sycamore trees and drove onto the street, still puzzled by his wife's indifferent attitude.

When Doris returned from putting the kids on the bus and chatting with some of the other wives in the neighborhood at the bus stop, she noticed that Floyd's car was gone.

It's just as well, she thought. *He knows something is different. I just can't hide it well anymore,* she realized. She quickly cleaned up the breakfast area; brushed her teeth; checked her make-up; put on fresh lipstick; grabbed for her jacket, and ran out to her 1995 Honda Civic.

Doris arrived at the dental office of Dr. Kal Barakat in time to help make the office coffee and chat with the other technicians and the receptionist. Friday was always a half day and all the patients were checked in by 11:30 AM and Dr. Barakat finished with the last one at 1:00 PM.

All the other employees had left for the weekend and Doris went into one of the patient cubicles, adjusted some of her clothing, and flopped down in one of the elaborate dental chairs. She cranked it back level and closed her eyes. In a few minutes she actually dozed off. She was asleep. Doris needed the quick cat nap. She hadn't been sleeping well for the past several months.

Born in a more rural area in Kentucky to middle class parents, Doris had not been exposed much to life and had little experience in affairs of the heart. She had only a few boy friends in high school and had very little experience with sex.

She had never been to either the east or west coast. The longest trip the family had ever taken was to Disney World in Orlando, Florida. Most of their vacations were in and around the Appalachian states.

Doris had met Floyd Richards her last year in high school when he returned from college for his fifth year reunion at the May graduation in 1987. She then went to the School of Dentistry at the University of Louisville and after two years of dating they had decided to get married. She was only twenty at the time and now, at twenty-nine, she was still naive and immature for her age.

Chapter 4

Dr. Barakat came out of his private office still wearing the long white coat that he preferred to keep on during office hours. He liked his patients to think of him as a competent physician, which he was, and he felt that he should always look the part. He was forty-one years old, with a dark complexion, dark brown eyes, and going a little bald on the top of his short but solid body.

His family was Lebanese or Syrian, he wasn't sure which, but his parents had been born in Lebanon, as he had, and at the age of eleven, the family emigrated to The United States.

His parents had been worried about the civil war that broke out in the early 1970's between the Christian Lebanese and the larger population of Muslims, which was their religious group, who supported the Palestine Liberation Organization or PLO. There had been too much fighting and people dying on both sides with no end in sight as far as the Barakat family was concerned.

17

They had settled in the East where Kaled Barakat had excelled in school and went on to graduate from the School of Dental Medicine at the University of Pennsylvania. A few years later while working for another dentist in Philadelphia, he saw an advertisement in Dental Success, an industry magazine. A dentist in Lexington, Kentucky, wanted to sell his practice and retire.

It was the opportunity he had been seeking. His father helped him finance the business which was not too expensive; since really all the dentist had to sell was his office equipment and his lease. The patients may or might not continue with the new dentist, so the seller agreed to stay on for three months to introduce Dr. Barakat to his patients and assure them of the new doctor's ability, which was excellent.

He never used his given first name, Kaled, again. It was tough enough being Lebanese with the name Barakat in Kentucky, much less throw in Kaled. So everything in print for advertising only used the name, Kal Barakat. Kal sounded more like a good old country boy. It would fit in better.

He looked into each cubicle as he wandered down the hallway. There were four in a row and in the last one he saw Doris lying in a dental chair which was now horizontal. Her eyes were closed.

"Well now," Dr. Barakat said as he entered. "Did one of our patients fall asleep?"

There was no answer. He stepped into the room and leaned over Doris. Her eyes still remained closed and she was breathing regularly.

"I think our patient had too much nitrous oxide," he said.

Doris smiled and then giggled as if she were under the effect of laughing gas, the more popular name given to it by dental patients.

Dr. Barakat reached over and unbuttoned her white hygienist gown all the way down the front and pulled it open. He stood up and took a lustful look at her very voluptuous, naked body. She was a full figured woman and her large breasts fell slightly to each side.

"Why, Doctor Barakat," she said with a slight surprise in her voice. "What are you doing?"

"You need some very special treatment, young lady." Barakat leaned over and kissed her softly on the mouth.

Doris reached out with her right arm and felt up under his medical gown. Her eyes stared sensuously at Barakat as her hand found what she knew would be waiting for her touch. They had played this game before.

She moaned seductively as she felt his already stiff penis. He was also naked under his white gown. She fondled it some more as Dr. Barakat's mouth was now wide open, trying to take in as much breast as possible, and then firmly sucking and mouthing on her ample, large dark nipples.

He stood up, opened his gown, and stepped toward her with his erection aimed at her mouth. She had turned her head towards him expectantly as her lips parted to receive him. It was a perfect fit as the "patient" was exactly at the right level for oral penetration.

He closed his eyes as he slowly moved in and out. Her mouth seemed to be molded around his organ. "You're the kind of patient I love," he groaned softly.

Doris pulled away as she had to giggle at that remark. "Why don't we go into your office and finish this on your couch, doctor? We would be so much more comfortable," she added with a coy smile.

After they had made love, Doris went to the bathroom where she had left her clothes, freshened up, and returned to his office. Kal Barakat had fixed some fresh coffee and put some half and half from the office refrigerator in Doris' cup.

He poured and they relaxed for a moment with their own thoughts. Each one was reluctant to broach the subject that they had talked about many times before.

Finally Barakat broke the silence. He was nine years older than Doris and he had more experience in life. He had been married once before to a nice Lebanese girl just like his mother and father had always wanted for him.

He thought he had been in love with her and so did she. They were only in their early twenties but very soon it was apparent to her that it was not going to work. After only one year, she was looking to get out of the marriage, but it took her one more year and a court room scene to achieve the divorce.

Now after dating for many years, Barakat thought he knew what he wanted in a mate for the rest of his life and felt he had found it in Doris. She was a solid, level headed woman. Besides that she was quite lovely and very sexually active. That also helped make up his mind.

He had agreed to take her children, maybe have one of their own, raise them all with no partiality or favoritism on his part. Her kids were really good little guys and still very moldable.

"Look Doris. We've known each other for three years. We've been lovers for over one year. That has been too trying on both of us. All the sneaking around . . . and the situation is much harder on you. You're still married with two kids, so I understand your reluctance."

He reached over and took both her hands in his as he spoke lovingly to her. "It's tearing you apart, Doris. You've lost some weight and you're starting to get circles under your eyes."

He squeezed her hands. "It will be much harder on the kids the longer you wait. You are in love with me, I hope?" He said it with some sudden concern.

"Yes," Doris said pulling her hands away and reaching for a tissue. She dabbed at her eyes and blew her nose. "You know I am; so very much it hurts, and you're right. I just have to drum up the courage and do it. Floyd's not a violent man . . . never has been. So I guess he'll accept it without too many problems. What makes it tough, just like your last marriage, he's still in love with me." She dabbed at her eyes again.

Then she stood up and spoke in a very positive voice. "I'll call you at home sometime over the weekend, just after I tell him. If you're not home, it's all right to leave the message on your recorder, isn't it?"

Kal Barakat came over smiling, took hold of her arms, and kissed her on the cheek. As he pulled back, he said, "Yes darling, of course. I'm proud of you. Now you're taking charge of your life and our future."

She turned away and left the office. Barakat's face tightened perceptibly as he watched her leave. He had a hard look in his eyes. It was the worst part of his peculiar affliction. And Barakat didn't even realize it. The problem was starting already and they weren't even married yet.

Chapter 5

Eddie Cason watched the scenery slide past as he headed southeast on the Greyhound bus. It was only 255 miles, as the homing pigeon flies, to Bowling Green, Kentucky. His sister, Karlene, lived there.

He had started at Greenville early in the morning. They gave him a ride to the bus station. As he stepped out of the van, the driver stuck his head out of the window and said, "Hope we don't see you again, Eddie. Good luck."

Eddie Cason had just left the federal prison in Greenville, Illinois. According to the Federal Bureau of Prisons, Greenville was ranked as a medium security level, male prison. He had just done four years for defrauding the public in one of his better schemes. He sold stock in companies with names very much like those listed on the major stock exchanges.

And Eddie Cason's stock certificates looked much fancier, even prettier than most any printed for companies like IBM, General Electric, or Microsoft. They were printed on good, heavy, linen type paper, multi-colored, with eagles and lions all around the edges. In the middle of the certificate there would be depicted a scene that conveyed what the hell the company did, or at least what Cason told people that it did.

Of course, there wasn't really any company, just nice looking certificates, each for one hundred shares of a new and promising, and non-existent conglomerate that was the result of a merger between European and American software companies.

They had developed the expertise to put micro-chips in canned food that would signal when the food was no longer edible, or in baby diapers that would indicate when they got wet, or a real grabber for smokers, a chip implanted in the lungs that would send a signal to the brain when one more puff would trigger lung cancer.

In bars he would pitch those addicted to cigarettes about the product. "Smokers can suck on those 'cigs' right up to that final drag! That very point at which you must quit. No more guessing about it," Eddie Cason would say.

The list of miracle products were dependent on who was in his listening audience. He always remembered a quote from one of the greatest promoters of all time, Phineas Taylor, better known as P. T. Barnum, the circus developer who said, "There's a sucker born every minute." And Cason only needed a few of them every week.

Basically, he figured he could sell dark, bifocal sun-glasses to Ray Charles. He was a master of the "spiel," or "Hey man, money talks and bull shit walks."

All of his banter would come out of a mouth that produced such a broad smile while it exposed gleaming white teeth beneath wide, sparkling blue eyes. His was the voice of hope and enthusiasm and good old Eddie Cason was here to make you some money!

A few years before this jail term, he had done two years for a roofing and repair scam, better know as an R & R job. He'd talk several old couples into getting some work done inside, outside, or on top of their house, take a bunch of deposits, and then he'd go on R & R, or rest and relaxation. In prison the inmates that knew him called him Fast Eddie.

Cason wasn't a real bad criminal. He never did any strong arm stuff, use a gun, mug people, or pull a robbery. He figured those types of crimes were for stupid low-lifes. He was smarter than that. He considered himself on a par with the white collar type criminal and he was always trying to upgrade his trade or learn something new, trying for that one big score so he could retire from crime.

Fall sure was here in earnest, Cason thought as he saw the ground was covered with the autumn leaves of color along side the highway. *Well, Bowling Green, Kentucky is still a pretty little community,* Cason thought, as the bus rolled into town and found its way to the bus depot. He might be broke, but Eddie Cason always looked on the bright side of life. Things could only get better now that he had paid his debt to society and was off on a new start.

His sister, Karlene, was watching people get off the bus. Then she saw her younger brother as he stepped down holding a large satchel. *You can't miss him with that full head of straight brown hair and handsome features. The lean, wiry look,* she thought.

As the crowd thinned and he got closer, she noticed that Eddie was looking older this time. *Older than his forty two years,* Karlene felt. *This second stint in jail has aged him.*

Prison food must have agreed though, he's gained a little weight, she noticed. Karlene waved over the heads of the milling crowd and Cason spotted her. He walked towards her with a bounce in his step and that magic smile that made people trust him.

"You look good, sis," Cason said, pulling her into a big hug and a kiss on the cheek. "Don't B S me," she said. "I'm your sister, remember?"

"I'm not and I mean it, Karlene. The years have been good to you." He stepped back to take a good look while he produced that great smile again. "How's Bill and the kids?"

"Both in high school, now. They've gotten all grown up. Goin' to be losing them soon to the world, Eddie."

Cason noticed that she said it with real regret. She and Bill Owsley had been good parents. *Karlene in particular was a great mother, and she's doing her motherly thing with me right now,* he noted with a smile.

As a dedicated bachelor, his sister was the only person he really loved and he'd do anything for her and the kids. He had sent money on several occasions when they were in financial trouble with a note that read, "This is a gift. I owe you for a life time of kind things you've done for me. Love, Eddie."

Karlene and Eddie Cason were born to parents who generally neglected them. There wasn't any sexual child abuse, but both parents were alcoholics and their drunk father would smack them around on occasion. Split lips, black eyes, swollen checks, painful stuff but no permanent injuries. They learned to stay away when he tied one on.

And there was no real love either, even when they were sober. Hardly ever any hugs, kisses or much giving of themselves to their children. They didn't keep on top of them about their school work or see that they were involved in sports or academic activities.

There was nothing that bonded the children to their parents. Eddie had attention deficit disorder, which neither parent recognized or would have cared about anyway, and as a result, Eddie didn't do well in school. But he excelled at ingratiating himself to others, his peers, his teachers, or other adults. He had a special sense about people and knew what to do or say in almost any situation.

So as children, Eddie and Karlene bonded together and loved and looked after each other. And they were very close to this day. Karlene's spouse was a nice, considerate husband, and although he didn't like the thought of Eddie living with them for a while until he got on his feet financially, he didn't bitch about it because he remembered that Eddie had helped them at different times and that his wife had a special brother-sister relationship with him.

Even more important, the kids loved their Uncle Eddie. Whenever he came to visit he always thought of fun things to do with both of them. So it would be all right.

27

Chapter 6

Doris and Floyd Richards along with their two children, Robby and Karen, were just leaving the First Methodist Church parking lot in Lexington. After the Southern Baptists, the Methodists were the largest religious group in Kentucky. The National Baptists fit in there somewhere, but nobody outside that faith knew the difference between a National and a Southern Baptist. Most figured they must be some damn Yankee bunch.

The Richards had been devout church members ever since they started dating and had learned from their parents about the importance of God in their daily lives.

Their minister, Thomas W. Bramlette, had given a strong sermon about family values, togetherness, and that marriage was a double bond, both love and faith in each other and in God.

"Husband and wife, both together, have to work through the tough times, forgive each other, and treat each other kindly. Then the vows that each made to the other will stand the test of time and become even stronger; like a rope that ties two mountain climbers together must be fastened firmly with steel pins to the mountain they hope to climb."

Reverend Bramlette pounded his fist on the podium as his voice rose in pitch and volume to keep their attention and make his point.

"So too is your rope tied to God, your mountain that will always be there for you as you climb into a deeper faith and love with the Holy Father. Then let the heavy snows fall, let the stormy winds blow, let the earth tremble around you, but these forces can not pull you away from God, your own personal mountain of strength."

He stuck both arms straight out at his parishioners and with fingers pointed, swept over his audience. "As a result you will be more in love with each other than ever before and the thought of one leaving the other will never enter your mind."

Doris had squirmed on the hard wood seat of the pew during the entire sermon. Every sentence the minister uttered was like a stab in her heart. Several times Richards had taken her hand and squeezed it, as if to indicate that the two of them had experienced and lived through all that the minister mentioned and that he, Floyd, still loved her very much.

She kept glancing up at the twelve large, arched, stained glass windows, six on each side of the church that were so elegant and beautiful. Every Sunday, as the church filled, each parishioner who sat waiting for the service to begin was drawn to them.

They were like a beacon of faith, like a beam of brightness from a lighthouse on some rocky coast cutting through the foggy darkness of night that when seen, filled a sailor's heart with joy and brought him safely to shore.

Each window depicted one of the twelve apostles and Doris expected each one of them to suddenly speak in a booming voice, point a finger at her, and cry out, "You sinner, you faithless one, you deceiver, you're unworthy of being called a dutiful and loving wife!"

Never before had she been so uncomfortable in church. She glanced down at her blouse several times to see if the large, bright red letter "A" for adulteress had appeared on her front for all to observe.

"Forgive me Lord," she prayed. "I am living a dual life. I love my children but I also love another man. I have thought it over many times and I must do this. I can't live trapped in sin any longer. I must make this break. Forgive me." The tears had rolled down her cheeks and she dabbed at them with a dainty white handkerchief.

Floyd Richards had rolled his eyes sideways and peeked at her. The smallest smile appeared on his face, but inside he was beaming. *I'm a very lucky man,* he thought. He sensed that she must have been very moved by the minister and he felt contentment, twice blessed with health and happiness, and fulfillment in his work.

"Listen kids," Richards said as he drove them toward home. "What did you learn in Sunday school while your mother and I were in church?" He noticed that Doris was quiet. They dropped off Robby and Karen at a neighbor's house for the afternoon. Doris had said she wanted to go to a movie.

"Let's stop by the house for a few minutes, Floyd. I've got some laundry to put in the washer and then we can go. OK?" It was more of a statement than a question.

Doris came out of the little laundry room and saw Floyd sitting in his favorite big chair, a lazy-boy, where he could read or study, or kick-back to watch television, or flip almost level with the floor to take a comfortable nap. She put that last thought out of her mind. It reminded her of the dental chair, where she had done something else when the chair kicked-back.

She stood in front of her husband. Timidly, she said, "I've something to tell you, Floyd." He looked up. A quizzical look was on his face. *Her voice sounded different,* he thought. *Strained and thin,* would be a better description.

"I didn't plan this, Floyd," she started plaintively. "I loved you and I was happy with you. I didn't go looking for someone else. It just happened." Her voice quavered. "Happened over time," she added.

She watched her husband's face change as she spoke. His expressions went from concern for her at first, to incredulity, progressing to disbelief, and then on to a deep hurting pain, as if she could peer inside him and see her words twisting his heart.

"I'm sorry, Floyd." Her voice got stronger as she found the strength to be firm and resolute in her dilemma. "Sorry for what I am doing to you and our children. I know it will affect them too. But I've made the decision. I can't live two lives. I can't go on being unfaithful to you. It's not fair to either of us. I want a divorce, Floyd, as soon as possible."

Floyd didn't speak. His big head slowly drooped, his full shaggy brown hair shook slightly as he began to shiver or shudder. A chill, winter wind had swept through his heart, and he found himself suddenly cold and alone.

His eyes stared down at the carpet which he didn't see. What he did see was his beautiful world shattering, exploding in front of him. He couldn't believe what he had heard! What his wife had just said to him. Words that he had never expected to hear from her. He loved Doris so very much. He had been so happy.

He felt himself drifting, his body drifting out into the frigid void of space. Into unknown territory, a zone of lifelessness where nothing existed that he knew or understood. No one, no thing, no plant, no animal, no warm place in the sun would he ever experience again. Gone in an instant was his world.

He saw himself in a huge, bulky space suit outside the International Space Station two hundred miles above the earth making some repairs. But his lifeline had snapped, separated from the space platform, and very slowly he was moving away from all life, all warmth, the whole world, and everything that had meant anything to him was slowly receding out of reach and soon it would be out of sight. He was lost in time and space.

Chapter 7

Floyd Richards turned off his helmet light and sat up. He was fairly deep inside the earth and he felt at home for the first time in two weeks. This was the only part of his life that had stayed the same. His learning, his business, his work that would lead to a doctor's degree with the ability to advance in his profession.

This was his only way to get on with life. This was all that was left for him to do. This was something to keep him busy and allow him to keep his sanity in a world turned upside down by words, his going to be ex-wife's words, that she had spoken just two weeks ago on a Sunday after church, he remembered. He couldn't get it out of his conscious or subconscious mind. He had trouble sleeping at night thinking of it. "I want a divorce, Floyd, as soon as possible."

He forced himself to come back to the present. Where he was and what he was doing was the good part of his life now. Like a blind man, he opened his little back pack and felt for the thermos of hot coffee and the sandwich. He found them along with a paper napkin and he leisurely began to munch on lunch.

Richards was exploring a brand new part of Mammoth Cave system just recently found by some other cavers. The discovery was announced in the Lexington Herald-Leader last week and the explorers had said they could hear the sound of running water nearby, but hadn't found it yet.

The Mammoth Cave National Park covers 52,830 acres in the Mammoth-Flint Ridge Cave System some one hundred miles south of Louisville, Kentucky. Mammoth is the largest cave system in the world and from its first discovery in the late 1700's, the cave has been continuously explored and expanded to its current known length of 365 miles.

Richard's doctoral thesis was on *The Hydrology of underground water movement and the evolution of caves,* and this was an opportunity for him to do further research and inspect this new find.

"Damn, this is scary," said a voice.

"Don't get me thinking about it again. I'm trying to eat my lunch," said another voice.

There were other comments, boos, and whistles from other young students that accompanied Floyd Richards on this geology field trip. It counted as an extra credit for a science class and Richards was glad to have the company of young people. Thinking about his class and what he could teach them took his mind off his personal problems.

Tweeet, tweeet, came the trilling sound from Richard's whistle. It was a call to stop moving, stop talking and listen. That was an important signal in caving in the total dark except for head lamps and lanterns used for overnighters. Each one of the six pupils in his class had a whistle around his neck to be used in emergencies only.

"OK, thank you for responding correctly to my signal. We've been in the cave for three hours and it will be five more before we finish and retrace our steps to the entrance. Most of the time we've been moving, crawling, walking, and even sliding along flat on our bellies and talking to each other during our passage through the many turns, twists, drops and sloshing through water or streams.

"Now I want you to just listen to the sounds of the cave. Turn off all head lamps and just listen for the next ten minutes and tell me what you experience during that time. Keep track. Some will hear more than others and some will imagine things that they really didn't hear." He looked at his glowing watch. "OK. Start now. I'll let you know when the time is up and no talking."

He sat back against a sloping rock and closed his eyes. Even though they were immersed in total darkness, not even the slightest glow from anywhere, closing the eyes would eliminate even the thought of sight and thinking you saw something, or imagining you saw anything. Your mind said, *OK, now you've closed down one body function, the brain will just have to crank up the hearing a notch.*

Richards loved the feel of it. He liked having rock all around him, yet knowing there was an opening ahead and thinking I'll find some new, giant rooms, carved out by water and falling rock. A place never before seen by any human.

Spelunkers and cavers were a different breed. Climbers could stand at the base of a mountain and study how to climb it. They could see the trail ahead, or the cliff, and what equipment they would need at every turn. And most importantly, they could see the top of the mountain, their ultimate goal.

But cavers didn't know where they were going when they entered a hole in the ground. They didn't know where the many branches or tunnels would lead and they couldn't see anything without artificial light. How far they had to travel, how deep the journey might take them and what difficulties lay ahead were unknown. Most importantly, you had to remember how to get back out, and which of the three holes did you come through several hours ago?

Richards never had a sense of being trapped, lost, or struck with an attack of claustrophobia. He was totally relaxed. He also listened to the sounds. "Time's up," he said softly after checking his watch. Sound reverberated quickly in the tightness of most caves, even huge caverns one hundred feet high.

"Who heard what?" he asked.

All of the students heard water dripping, one said they heard a bat flutter by his head, but only two students got it right. Where the sound of the water came from. They turned on their head lamps as Richards, totally absorbed in his work, led them upwards, climbing up the cave wall some twenty feet where they found a shelf hidden from below.

They could move about ten feet further back into the side of the wall. Their head lamps illuminated a small opening, three feet across and only sixteen inches high at the very middle.

"The sound's coming from in there," one student exclaimed

"And it's much louder," another excitedly added.

"We're going in," Richards announced.

Chapter 8

Eddie Cason was at his sister's house. The teenagers were in school, her husband was at work, and Karlene had the day off. They were talking about his problem. He couldn't find a job.

Cason had checked the classified advertisements every day for the past two weeks and made fifty phone calls. He had gone to the Chamber of Commerce, the union hall, the post office, and even interviewed at an employment agency to help find him a job.

He'd had a dozen interviews, he told Sis, and of course there weren't any questions on employment applications that asked if you had been in a state or federal facility, the reason for incarceration, and the length of the prison sentence that you, the applicant had served.

"But the problem is, Sis, that I just haven't had much experience at any job. And where you give your employment history. . . I've got blanks in my life. You know, when I was behind bars."

Cason grimaced a little thinking about one particular job interview and then told Karlene. "This one guy was hiring for a drug store and I decided to tell him that I'd been in prison two different times. I wanted to see how he would react."

Cason glanced down and shook his head slowly from side to side. "It was like a movie scene. His mouth kinda' stuck open, nothing coming out, and I know he stopped breathing. It was like getting disconnected during a phone call. You know, nobody at the other end of the line. Or your server cuts you off in the middle of an email. Same thing. The guy definitely tuned out and changed channels. Then he looks at me with a sick smile and tells me that he just doesn't seem to have a place to put me.

"But I could read his mind like a sign in red neon lights. He was thinking, 'I'd rather hire a two hundred pound piranha to guard my bleeding goldfish, buster.'"

Karlene thought for a moment, and then said, "How about going to vocational school and learn a trade, Eddie? Plumbers, electricians, and carpenters . . . they make good money."

"You know about my attention deficit disorder, Sis. I found that out the first time I was in prison. I'm sure there are manuals to read and memorize stuff like that."

His sister encouraged her younger brother with a cheery smile. "Unfortunately it's the stigma attached to prison time. But the federal government says you've paid your debt to society and that can't be a reason not to hire you.

Kenneth S. Murray

It was only 9:30 in the morning. Karlene stood up. "Come on, brother. We're going to take a ride. I'll tell you about it on the way."

Karlene Owsley knew almost everybody on the payroll at the park. She had worked there for twenty years and had seniority as a civil service employee. She had some strings she could pull, favors owed to her, but nothing illegal. She had helped a lot of people there at different times and she figured that now it's her turn. Now she needed their assistance.

"The pay's not great to start, Eddie, but there are a lot of benefits working for the park system. Great hospitalization and major medical insurance, long paid vacations, sick time, and promotions come along from time to time."

She told him, "It's a place to start until you get your feet on the ground and people in town start to know you and then trust you. Plus you're good at talking to strangers, and you may impress some visitor who might want to hire you in his business."

Cason wasn't sure about working for the federal government, but he gave his sister a condescending look and a wink. "Thanks, Sis. If they'll hire me I'll give it a good try . . . see if it's what I want to do for the rest of my life."

He patted her on the arm and added. "I'm sure they've got good retirement benefits, too. In twenty years, I'll be pushing toward sixty five. Maybe it will work. And it will mostly be outside. That's better than being chained to a desk pushing paper or staring at a computer monitor all day."

From Bowling Green, it was just twenty miles driving northeast to the Mammoth Cave National Park.

40

Karlene told Eddie all about the cave system. "They've discovered five different levels underground down to a depth of 360 feet." She took state road 68 that paralleled Interstate highway 65 and turned north on 259.

Eddie read the street sign out loud. *Jesse James and Hundred Dome Caves?* "What the heck is that?"

Before she could answer he added, "Here comes some more . . . *Canter Cave, Diamond Caverns, and Sand Cave.*

"Oh, there's a lot more caves to see Eddie. Great Onyx Cave, and then to the north, Collins Crystal Cave, Horse Cave, and others in the area that over the past one hundred years have been linked up to Mammoth Cave. It's a whole underground network."

They drove onto the national park property and twenty minutes later arrived at the main one story building. Karlene took Eddie inside to meet the Mammoth National Park Superintendent whom she knew well. After filling out a bunch of forms the federal government is famous for, her boss told them that they would put Eddie near the top of the waiting list.

"It shouldn't be more than three weeks before you can start, Eddie," the park superintendent said. As they shook hands, he smiled and added, "You're lucky to have Karlene as a friend and a sister. If she says you're going to make a good park ranger, I'll take her word on it. In a few months, you'll be an old hand around here and familiar with most of the park activities."

Karlene drove her brother around the park for the balance of the day on a familiarization tour, and filled his head with more facts than anyone could possibly remember.

"You've just proved that old saying, Sis. It's not what you know, it's who you know to get somewhere in this world. Then to stay there, the smart ones just play along, fart and fake it."

Chapter 9

One month had gone by since his family had packed up and walked out of the door and as far as he was concerned, out of his life. It was a Tuesday in mid-November, and because of college scheduling that semester, it was a day when Floyd Richards had no classes. But he was at the university doing research for his doctoral thesis.

He couldn't stand to stay home alone at the duplex after his wife and the kids moved out. He missed them terribly. He was allowed to see his children at certain times and it was best to get the kids used to the arrangement even before the divorce, which he chose not to oppose, went through the court system.

He sat at his office desk in the science building surrounded by books, magazines, and other scientific material he needed for his research. But he was thinking about Doris. *What did I do wrong,* he agonized to himself. *I was attentive to her needs and the wishes that I could afford. Our sex life seemed to be good. I wasn't abusive. I loved and played with the kids all the time.*

"Damn it," he said out loud. He smashed his big beefy fist into the palm of his other hand that made a loud slapping sound. *I was a good husband.* "Why . . . why . . . why," he said in measured monotone as he banged his fist three times on his desk when each word was uttered.

Richards was showing a temperament that even surprised him. *I'm not myself.* He held his head in both hands and rocked slowly back and forth in his chair with eyes closed making a soft, grunting noise.

I've always been so easy going and relaxed. I liked that part of me. He leaned back in his spring loaded vinyl chair that allowed the seat to tilt and took a deep breath. He looked up and then slowly expelled it through puffed out lips. He sensed that his whole system, both mentally and physically, were now under pressure and he didn't like it. He wasn't used to dealing with such a dilemma.

Richards had enjoyed many aspects of life, one of which was his laid back ease about almost anything that happened. It came from a peace and calmness inside. He attributed much of that to his devout belief in God, in fairness in life that he thought would almost always prevail, and that circumstances would usually bring out the goodness in all people.

But Floyd Richards was much too simplistic and very idealistic about life. He would experience some hard knocks over the next year, but he would learn from it.

He thought for a moment that he had lost his balance in the chair; leaning as far back as it would go.

He leaned forward and put his feet on the floor. The chair still wobbled. He looked up as he caught movement out of the corner of his eye. The water in the glass on his desk was sloshing back and forth a bit. *What the heck is happening?*

Within seconds while he still sat there, his phone rang. "Hey, Floyd . . . glad you're in. This is Jimmy Garrard down at seismograph. We've just had a nice little tremor that showed up as a four point seven on the Richter scale. The epicenter seems to be west of here along the Central Kentucky Karst. I thought you guys in geology would like to know about it."

"Thanks, Jimmy; I'll be right down to take a look at those readings."

Richards went down a floor and into Garrard's laboratory. *You couldn't miss him.* It was like someone had taken a huge brush, dunked in reddish-brown paint, laid Jimmy naked on the floor and speckled him, letting little dots of paint fly all over his body.

Red freckles covered his entire skinny frame, and on top of his head, he grew naturally spiky, red hair. Perfectly round, wire rimmed glasses seemed to defy gravity as they balanced almost off the end of his long, thin nose.

"Micro quakes register very frequently in Kentucky, but bad ones occur too on occasion," Garrard said in his squeaky voice. That's how his students referred to him behind his back. . . "Mister Squeak."

"In eighteen eleven there was a real boomer. A nine point zero and a number of four point nines to six point zero in later years on the New Madrid Fault Line that runs along the Kentucky and Missouri border. But we haven't had one this strong in twenty-five years," he concluded.

Richards talked a bit more with Jimmy Garrard and then left. As he walked back up the stairs to his office, he decided he would take an exploratory trip over the coming weekend. There were several places in that karst area where he had found sinkholes and other indications of underground activity.

Chapter 10

It was Saturday. Richards loaded gear into the back of his Ford pickup truck and slid up into the driver's seat. He started the engine and locked on his seat belt. It was always the same procedure. Like most people, he had repetitive habits, although he was considered to be a little anal compulsive. But, that's what made him an excellent hydrologist, people said.

The third week of November was colder and Richards had on a warm, heavy jacket he used for geologic field trips. His gear included a sleeping bag, sterno stove, coffee pot, zip locked food, power bars, and a tooth brush. That was all he needed in case he decided to stay over night in the woods and pack back out to his truck in the morning.

His Ford 150 headed west on The Blue Grass Parkway to Elizabethtown, turning north on 31W past the small town of Radcliff where he turned west on a small two lane road that led back into a wooded area. To the East was the Fort Knox Military Reserve.

Richards was in a little inhabited area of dome-like knobs and interlaced flood plains. The knobs resemble volcanic cones and give the area its name, the Knobs Region. The light soils of the area wear away quickly, and the region has been left wooded to hold the soft earth together.

The flood plain was created by the Rolling Fork River flowing down from Indiana; the nearby Rough River; Rough River Lake; then to the south, Nolin Lake, and the Green River.

Richards made his way carefully down the embankment into an area of thick brush, woods, and swampy land. A place where only hunters occasionally wander through. He walked with the prior knowledge of where he wanted to go. He was heading for a series of sinkholes that he had discovered two years ago on another geology field trip with some of his students.

As a caver, Richards knew these holes usually meant unstable land, particularly in this Karst region where a large bed of limestone stretches down from Indiana and through into Tennessee. Over millions of years, water draining through the cracks in the sandstone rock dissolved the limestone below, creating an intricate network of underground passages, such as the Flint Ridge and Mammoth Cave areas just a few miles to the south.

Some of the sinkholes in the area were fifty feet deep and the going was tough. It was too dark by early evening to see clearly, so he found a dry spot, dragged over some soft pine limbs he had cut, put down his poncho to guard against water, and flopped the heavy water proof sleeping bag on top. He made a small fire to heat some food and make coffee.

Solitude, Richards thought. *Some people don't understand there's a big difference between loneliness and solitude. Either you have or don't have contentment within yourself.*

He leaned back against a big moss covered maple log, sipped the coffee and glanced up through tree branches that were now mostly bare of leaves. The night sky was clear and a full moon seemed to look back down at him.

Peaceful, beautiful, full of wonder. If only modern day kids could spend more time outside, experiencing a night in the woods like this instead of staring at a television set or a computer modem.

Floyd Richards had been born in eastern Kentucky and raised on a farm. His father was a sensible man. He had inherited the farm from Floyd's grandfather, who had only grown burley tobacco on a part of the seven hundred acres and had done well.

But those times were slipping away fast and in 1980, Floyd's father could see trouble coming for the tobacco industry and reduced the acreage in that crop while adding soybean, corn and wheat, plus planting fifty unused acres in peach trees. Diet and nutrition were the new craze and a crop of juicy peaches would fit right into that life style. It would also produce a nice profit.

The whole family was involved in the farm and the father taught young Floyd to respect all living things, both animal and vegetable. All life was to be revered and treasured. He spent a lot of time outdoors and learned to love the sky, rain or shine, the earth and all the critters on it.

Farming was a slower, easier life than meeting deadlines with the rush, rush, and hurry up life style of the city. You couldn't rush a crop to maturity. You had to watch it and see what it needed. Then you nurtured it and lived with it as it developed.

Richards learned about patience and tolerance, about compassion and kindness in his daily life growing up on that farm. It would stand him in good stead in the months ahead.

He slipped off his clothes and climbed into his warm, fleece lined sleeping bag. He worried some about his family, but the exercise of hiking around in the woods helped him drift off to sleep.

After a quick breakfast the next morning, Richards continued to find and study the sinkholes for any changes since the recent earthquake in this area that Garrard had told him about. Some of the holes were so steep that he had to tie a rope to a tree and repel down the side. After inspection, he then had to haul himself up. *Oh well, It's good aerobic exercise if nothing else,* he mused.

He was convinced that the numerous sinkholes in close proximity to each other indicated a considerable amount of limestone erosion below ground and there could be a honeycomb of tunnels and caves to be explored.

Richards had started at the furthest sinkhole from the road and was working his way back toward 31W. The second to last one was the steepest of all and again it required him to repel down. The hole was cone shaped maybe sixty feet in diameter, but it was also forty feet deep.

He noticed on the way down that a big oak tree had been uprooted near the edge of the hole and fell into it with its roots sticking up in the air and its branches pointing down. The tree had crunched up when it landed and the branches stuck in some bushes and long grass growing around the bottom. Richards walked around the tree, carefully looking for any openings in the sinkhole that would reveal a passageway or entrance into the ground. There were none. Again he started to climb back up the rope.

It had been overcast for most of the day and a light misty rain had been falling since early that morning. Suddenly the sun came out with a burst of light that entered the sinkhole.

Richards stopped his climb, braced his feet against the face of the hole and looked up. It was a clear sky almost everywhere. *Well, at least I won't get soaked before I can get to my truck.*

He glanced back down to place his feet for the walk up the wall when he saw it. It was hidden behind the tree trunk and if the sun hadn't lit up that side of the sinkhole he would never have noticed anything. It was a dark area. At first he thought it was a cloud shadow. But there were no clouds.

Richards swung over to the tree trunk and grabbed onto some branches so he could tie off the rope and stand on a limb. He lay down on the trunk and peered around it. To a caver, a spelunker, it was a beautiful sight. An opening into the side of the sinkhole about five feet across and two feet high.

He scooted around the trunk and walked out on a limb to the hole. It was black as a tub of tar in there. He took a flashlight from his waist-belt and snapped the beam on, pointing it into the hole. The light diffused across the black space into nothingness. It didn't touch anything solid. Richards' heartbeat elevated as adrenaline pumped into his system.

Reaching his arm totally inside the hole, he pointed the light down and the beam hit the cavern floor about twenty feet below. Now even more excited, he pointed the beam up and the ceiling of the room was close to ten feet above him. *The earthquake must have opened this entrance to the cave.*

Again he flicked the light down inside the hole and held it still. A lot of particles floated across the beam's light! Dust was stirring around in the pure clear air inside. The 4.7 earthquake must have shaken the limestone and some of it avalanched down and broke up on the rock floor.

Richards turned off the flashlight, grabbed his rope and repelled down to the bottom of the sinkhole again. Using his large knife, he dug up some still leafy bushes. He climbed back to the hole in the wall and carefully placed the bushes in the hole, making it look as much like it was growing there as possible.

He was so excited that he was talking to himself as he made his way back to the road and walked to his truck parked in a little turn off. He knew that he couldn't say a word about his discovery.

Cave wars had erupted many years ago when the biggest caverns in the Mammoth Flint Ridge area had been discovered and individually owned. Each owner would build a road to a parking lot near their cave, maybe build a small motel with a restaurant, and advertise it to the public as the best cave in Kentucky. They would all try to lure customers away from each other with ridiculous claims plastered on large road side billboards. For many of the cave owners it was a lucrative business.

Finally in order to protect its natural wonders the Mammoth Cave National Park was established in 1941 and government advertising on a national basis by the park system actually helped the other cave owners.

The area with its multitude of limestone caves, underground rivers, springs, and sinkholes, is known to be a Karst landscape.

Chapter 11

Eddie Cason had been on the job now for a month. He couldn't believe it. He was actually working for the federal government. He told them up front about his two terms in a federal prison and they still hired him. He'd gotten two pay checks already.

"You'll do just fine, Eddie," he was told after two weeks on the job. "You've got the gift of gab needed for a guide inside the caves, but you'll have to work up to that. Right now you're on duty in the general park area. Gotta' learn the ropes, you know."

His sister Karlene was glad they had hired Eddie. She only hoped that he would give it a good try.

Cason moved out of the Owsley's house after six weeks. At the outskirts of town, he had found a big double wide mobile home, completely furnished, and he could afford the rent. He knew that Bill Owsley was tired of seeing him around and Karlene was more quiet with him than usual, which meant, I love you baby brother, but it's time for you to move on.

Of course, he needed transportation. And of course, Fast Eddie Cason just had to have something a little special in case he had to get somewhere quick, or get away from someone quicker. *With his past,* he thought, *and who knew what in his future, one had to be careful and be prepared.*

So he financed a 1995 GMC Syclone, a two-door, two passenger sports car with a pick-up bed on the back. Eddie Cason walked around it at the GMC dealer's lot and took it all in without expression. He knew better than to grin or show enthusiasm. After all, he was the experienced con-artist. *Don't ever show your hand.* He grimaced at the sales representative.

"Well, it's not quite what I wanted." He made an even more sour expression. Of course it was just what Eddie Cason wanted and his mouth salivated as he looked it over a second time.

Air conditioning, power windows and door locks, AM/FM stereo cassette, tilt wheel, intermittent wipers, analog gauges, including a 140 mph speedo, cruise control and tinted glass. On the truck bed was a Lexxus TruxCover tonneau cover that snaps to the frame.

The sales representative cleared his throat. "The best I can do is take five hundred off the low price I've already offered you. This is a real cream puff."

"I just don't know," Cason whined slowly. He stuck his head inside to view the contoured sport bucket seats, a floor-mounted shifter, center console with cup holders, leather wrapped steering wheel and a Syclone insignia.

He pulled his head out and glanced at the truck's lamp black body with subtle red accents. He noticed the fat Firestone 245/50VR-16 rubber tires on 8x16 aluminum wheels. *Freeway handling will be excellent.*

The sales representative excused himself for a minute as he went in to see the boss about squeezing off a few more bucks. When he came out, Cason was ambling away from the truck looking around the lot with disinterest all over his face.

"Wait, Mr. Cason," he said raising the Syclone's hood. "Did I tell you that in nineteen ninety one, the factory put the new alloy pistons in this Katech race-ready five liter engine?" The salesman reviewed his notes. "It's a gasoline-fueled, naturally aspirated ninety degree V-Six."

He glanced up at his customer. "It says here they added the 'pow' to the Syclone's power with electronic multiport fuel injection, iron exhaust manifolds with a front-mounted exhaust crossover tube and a Corvette L ninety-eight throttle body."

The salesman smiled at Cason with satisfaction. He felt like he had just delivered the *Gettysburg Address.*

Cason didn't smile back. He got lost at the 'crossover tube' in the sales pitch, and he didn't care if it had had a vasectomy. He just knew he wanted the truck. "That's nice," he answered flatly. "So . . . what's the final bottom price? I've got another used car lot to check today." He just stared blankly at the man and shifted his eyes away from that beautiful truck.

"The boss says he'll take off another three hundred dollars and give you an extra year on the financing. That's the best he can do."

An hour later, Fast Eddie drove off the lot and went to a nearby Jiffy-Lube outlet where they changed the oil, both engine and transmission checked all fluid levels, tire pressure and whatever else it needed so that he knew everything inside his "pow" engine was ready to go.

Then he took it on the freeway and on some back roads to test it out. "The manuel wasn't kidding," he said out loud. "This baby can do zero to sixty in four point nine seconds." *That would be impressive for a Stealth, or a Corvette ziti!*

The following week, Cason had been re-assigned to the Collins Crystal Cave area and he had the opportunity to walk along with some of the tourists and see the beautiful and unusual crystal formations and other wonders further inside.

He had learned that in Summer or Winter, the inside temperature in all the caves was always around fifty-four degrees and was glad he'd worn his jacket since it was warmer than that outside.

Just before the Thanksgiving holiday, Cason decided he just had to go exploring. He'd heard that some experienced cavers had received permission to explore a new area recently discovered in the Collins Crystal Cave and thought he would follow them inside. The problem was that he didn't tell anybody where he was going, and he made the beginners mistake of going by himself. Even experienced cavers should never go alone, and then only if they tell someone where and when they should return.

Cason walked into the cave behind the four cavers and began to trail along behind them and see what they discovered. That way he figured, he couldn't get lost. He turned on his head lamp and stayed with them for three hours until they passed through a vertical chute where each caver, one at a time, worked his way down the chimney bracing himself on either side.

It was here that he had fallen behind while crawling out of a tight section of the cave that required inching along on his stomach, pulling his back pack behind him and keeping his head turned sideways so he could slide through.

By the time he squeezed past that tight area, they were out of sight, but he could still hear them. Ten minutes later he found himself in the opening to a large cavern, sixty feet long, forty feet wide and easily that high.

The problem started at the far end of the big room where there were three openings that led to other parts of this intricate network of tunnels and caves, underground streams and dead ends. He chose the wrong one and got very lost wandering around through more of the underground maze.

Then he stepped onto a smooth rock that was turned to the side at an angle. With the next step his foot found a wet, muddy spot and he slipped down the long slick boulder into the cave wall where he broke his left leg. He screamed out in pain. The decibel noise level must have been too much for some overhanging, splintered rock and it came down the slope after him, pinning Cason to the cave wall. That rock slide broke his right arm and knocked him unconscious.

Now he really had a problem. No one knew where he had gone and he couldn't get out. The pain brought him back to consciousness sooner than normal. He wished it hadn't as he grunted through clenched teeth.

His helmet light was still working and he looked groggily around the cavern. He knew from the pain that his arm and leg were probably broken or badly sprained. He tried to move a little and sit up on the big rock next to him. But he couldn't get away from where he was wedged in between the rock and the cave wall.

"Oh, my God," he said out loud. "I'm trapped." Cason started to panic and pushed hard to get up. The pain almost made him pass out again. He knew then that he had to get a grip on his emotions.

Breathe deep, lean back and relax. He felt something move behind him and realized it was his back pack. *Now that's positive.* At least this was something he could do. *Get the back pack off and retrieve the supplies inside.*

In a few minutes he had the pack open. He took a sip of water and tore open a power bar and ate. Then he thought about the possibilities. *I'm supposed to show up for my shift tomorrow. That will work in my favor. I'll be missed.*

Chapter 12

By noon time the following day, Cason's supervisor called his mobile home. There was no answer but he left a message anyway. "Hey, Eddie. You were supposed to be at Sand Cave this morning at eight thirty. Are you all right?"

After lunch the super called Karlene Owsley. "Eddie never showed up for his shift today. Have you seen him?"

"No. I can call his house and see if he's okay."

"He wasn't there. I already left a message."

"I'll run by and see if his truck is there."

"Good. Let me know, Karlene."

When she got back to her office the supervisor was just ringing her telephone. "Just got word from park personnel at Crystal Cave. Eddie's black truck is parked there. They thought maybe he showed up there by mistake, but they can't find him."

"Eddie was off yesterday, wasn't he?" Karlene asked.

"Oh, damn! You don't suppose he went caving by himself?"

"He's been talking about it for the last ten days," she offered.

"I'll have the personnel on duty check who went into the cave for an overnight or longer. They can question them when they come out."

Several hours passed. At 3:00 PM, the supervisor's phone rang.

"This is Doug up at Crystal. A group of four just came out. They said a lone guy was trailing them but they figured he just went off on his own after they went down the chute."

"Did the loner ever come out?"

"Nope. And you know we don't get many loners deep cavin'. Hold on a minute." There was a short pause and then Doug came back on the phone. "Sheila was on duty yesterday. She said she talked to Eddie around nine in the morning. He said he was going to follow the four guys so he wouldn't get lost. Said he planned to come out yesterday afternoon."

The supervisor called Karlene and told her. She thought for a few seconds and then responded definitively. "I know who I want to lead the search," she said. "He's one of the best cavers in the area and a member of the National Cave Rescue Commission . . . Floyd Richards from the geology department at UK. I'm calling him now." He was in the middle of a class. She left word for him to call as soon as possible.

"Hey, Karlene," he said when he returned the call. "I haven't seen you in a while, but I don't like the sound of the word, 'emergency,' you left on my recorder." Richards shook his big shaggy head as she explained the problem.

"Well . . . he's been in there for a day and a half, and it'll be morning before I can put a team in the cave. I'll call you back tonight, Karlene, and don't worry. We'll find him and bring him out."

Richards sat there making notes on a pad. He wrote down the names of people and equipment that he would need. Then he glanced outside the window of his office at the grounds around the building. *This will delay getting back to my cave discovery, but that can wait. Saving a human life is the most important thing a person can do.*

He had known Karlene Owsley for a long time and he had seen her often during the times he had been caving around the Mammoth area. So that afternoon and on into the night he made his phone calls and by ten o'clock he had put his group together.

Everyone met at the cave at 7:00 AM. The weather had turned cold, about forty-five degrees at that hour. All the leaves were off the trees and the ground was covered with a light frost that sparkled in the bright morning sunlight.

The park superintendent and some of his staff were on hand along with two deputies from the Hardin County Sheriffs department plus Karlene and her husband. Karlene had tears in her eyes as she spoke.

"Bill and I want to thank you so much, Floyd, for helping my brother. He's new here and he got careless or he wouldn't be in this jam," she said.

Richards gave her an easy smile. "We were all new at this at one time or another, Karlene, and each of us had to learn. Some just have to learn harder than others."

Richards introduced his search team to everyone assembled there. He had two other experienced cavers, friends of his, and two of his senior geology students who had proven ability in cave exploration.

"Eddie Cason is the name of the man we're looking for," Richards said as he glanced around the group. "We'll probably have to break up into three, two man teams as we get deeper inside, especially where tunnels and caves branch off."

"You've only got five members," the super said, looking puzzled.

Richards pointed. "There's one more person coming out of the woods over there with his dog."

Everyone looked and saw a man walking with a big hound. The large dog stopped one more time to pee on a tree and then they joined the group.

"This is Augustus Laffoon, everybody, and that's his dog Ruby, the best pure-bred tracking bloodhound in the county."

Laffoon was a grizzled country man with a heavy growth of facial hair and a mop of it on top of his head which he exposed as he took off his cap to greet people in the proper southern manner that he had been taught as a child. He didn't speak. He just nodded as he took in every person there with careful inspection.

"Gus wouldn't tell you," Richards added, "But his great granddaddy, Ruby Laffoon, was governor of Kentucky back in the early thirties. Out of respect, Gus thought he'd name his best hound after him."

"Never heard of taking a dog caving," the new superintendent questioned.

Laffoon turned away slightly, fired a stream of tobacco juice on the ground, and turned back with a disgusted look on his face. He reached down to pat Ruby as he spoke. "This four year old is one hundred pounds of pure energy," he grumbled. "The dog's not scared of dark or tight places like people can be. If the man's in there, Ruby'll find him."

"A bloodhound is the best trailer, or tracker dog in the world," Richards said, adding credence to Laffoon's statement with some fact.

He explained that once you give a hound the scent like Gus was doing now with socks and underwear from Cason's dirty clothes hamper, you could put fifty people in there and Ruby will only pick out Cason's scent like nobody else was even in those caverns.

Richards said, "This hound follows skin cells that constantly fall away from your body, but they retain the person's odor for a long time."

Everybody was now looking at Ruby as Laffoon patted him. Like all pure breeds, he had a sad looking face with a long nose and jowls and big droopy ears. He was a red and tan, part of the reason Laffoon named him Ruby, and he had loose skin with short hair.

Bloodhounds work best from a PLS, or "place last seen." From that point of reference, even four or five days after the person is missing, a good pure-bred hound can capture that one person's unique scent and take off trailing, with its nose to the ground.

Checking his wristwatch, Richards said, "Everybody set their watches at seven thirty four. If we separate, we'll set time limits to meet up again at certain points. If you get into trouble, use your hand radio phone."

He continued. "Now here's the problem. Cason's been in there for almost forty eight hours. He might be hurt and not moving much, and with the cave at a constant fifty four degrees, the body cools down to hypothermia very soon. So let's find him quickly."

He turned to Karlene. "We may be in there overnight, but we'll try to stay in touch if our communication equipment doesn't get too blocked down there."

In two hours and fifteen minutes Ruby had no doubt where he was going as the search team got to the vertical chute that dropped down some thirty feet. The doleful looking hound started barking as he stood near the steep drop. He kept looking back for Laffoon.

"Hold on, Ruby. Hush boy." Laffoon looked at the other team members as the bright light from his Petzl Tikka LED, or "light emitting diodes" head lamp illuminated their faces. "He's telling us that the trail goes down that chute. But he's also saying he ain't gonna' jump."

Laffoon unraveled some heavy rope that had a wide leather strap on one end which he buckled around Ruby's chest, just under his front legs. "You're going for a ride, Ruby."

Richards turned to his experienced cavers. "You two repel down the shaft. When you're set, we'll lower Ruby down to you."

"Give me a hand, Floyd," Laffoon said. "This dog's gettin' heavier every year."

The two big men lowered sad-faced Ruby down the chute and out of sight until they heard from the first cavers down. When all four were down, Ruby took off again with a series of howls as the team's headlamps lit the way.

At the end of the big cave, they had three choices of openings to follow. Remembering what the four cavers had told the superintendent, Richards sent one expert with one student off in one tunnel, the second team disappeared into another opening, and Richards went with Laffoon and his hound.

In another hour, Ruby scooted on ahead of the two men. "We're gettin' close to him," Laffoon said. "Ruby don't run off like that unless he's hot onto somethin'."

Then they heard the dog just barking like crazy. When they arrived, Ruby was licking the face of Eddie Cason, who was half delirious. He was running a fever and in considerable pain from the two bone breaks.

He had subsisted on some sandwiches, several power bars, and two large water bottles he had in his pack that he rationed out every six hours when he wasn't passed out from the pain or unable to fitfully sleep.

He did have an extra jacket in his backpack that he had managed to get partially on over his sweater. But laying still in that damp air with the cold rock pressed against him, he got chilled quickly.

"Thank God," Cason said weakly. "Hearing that dog bark was the best sound I ever heard."

Richards was talking on his hand held radio to the other two groups. "Retrace your steps and get here as fast as you can." Then he looked at the trapped man.

"Are you Eddie Cason?"

"I am." He said with tears of joy in his eyes.

"We just want to be sure there weren't two of you stuck down here. Now, where do you hurt, Eddie?"

"My right arm and left leg are throbbing like hell," he groaned.

"I've got good pain killer in my pack. It's Demerol. In just a few minutes, you won't feel any pain. Then we'll jack these rocks away from you and get you out."

Laffoon had a thermos of hot soup and forced Cason to drink a lot of it for energy and warmth while Richards administered the shot.

Laffoon was searching for a place to support the jack so it wouldn't slip and they could force the rock away from Cason enough to pull him out. When they saw Cason's head plop back and his body relax, they knew it was time to start.

They slid him out. He was groggy from the Demerol, mostly unconscious but not in pain. The two cavers cut away his left pant leg, pulled and set the leg as well as they could, wrapping tape around the splint. They did the same for his arm. Then they wrapped him in a thermal blanket. By the time the others had arrived with the sked, they all felt he was ready to travel.

The sked was part of the basic rescue system that provides protection for the patient while allowing extraction through the most demanding confined places. It was formed from durable plastic with straps to hold the patient in place, yet it would roll up for storage in a Cordura backpack and weighed only nineteen pounds.

Richards called Karlene and told her that Ruby had located Eddie. Then he described his condition. "Have an ambulance at the cave entrance in about five hours."

Even with six strong men taking turns, it would be a real job carrying a mostly unconscious man out of the depths of that cave.

Chapter 13

It was now into the last week of November. The year end would be very lonely for Floyd Richards. This should have been a happy time for him. His children were off from school for half the week over the Thanksgiving holiday, but Richards did not have his son and daughter sitting around the family dining table with his wife. Now they were getting used to being with Dr. Kal Barakat in his home.

Richards had eaten a Thanksgiving evening dinner with a neighbor's family. The man was also a professor at the University of Kentucky, and his wife knew what had happened between Floyd and Doris, so she had invited him over for the big turkey "extravaganza" as she called it.

"You can't eat alone at your place or in some restaurant, Floyd," she told him. His neighbors had two young girls, about the same age as his kids. The wife studied Richards as his big frame filled a large stuffed chair in their small living room to sip coffee after the traditional dinner.

He sat there quietly contemplating. She recognized the expression on Richards' face. She saw the pain in his eyes as he watched her little girls play "house" under the dining table in the next room. They were both dressing their baby dolls and talking incessantly.

Maybe it would have been better if he had been by himself. I hope I did the right thing, she reasoned.

The cushions in the chair were soft and under stuffed. They kind of folded around him, engulfed him, and he liked it. He needed someone to hug him and hold onto him about now. This big chair would have to do for the moment.

He had been alone now for almost two months and he didn't like it. This was loneliness at its worst. It would be different if he had been in some commercial venture where he traveled a lot. Some corporate structure where he had to be overseas on a special business deal during the holidays. But then he could still call home and talk to his family, tell each one that he loved and missed them, and that he would be home soon.

Now it was three weeks later. The Christmas season in 1998. Richards had his kids for the weekend. He had taken his two small children, six year old Robby, and Karen, his adorable little four year old girl, to the mall to see Santa Claus. He would even buy a gift for his wife.

Maybe letting the kids give Doris her Christmas present from me was just getting even. Trying to make her feel bad, even feel sorry for me.

He was carefully watching the kids standing in line to see Santa. The mall personnel had wisely set up a walkway between a thirty inch high decorated white fence to keep the children corralled so they couldn't wander off and let some sicko grab them. The fence was low enough so the children could see their parents over it. There were little printed signs along the way that read, "This way to the North Pole," and, "Santa's workshop just ahead."

No. That wasn't the reason, he realized. He wanted to give her the gift because he still loved her very much. And he desperately wanted her back!

Richards was pulled out of his reverie by Karen yelling at him. "Daddy! Are you watching? Look at me. I'm sitting on Santa's lap," his little girl said. And then she was very occupied telling Mr. Claus just what she had on her list and it was a long one.

Santa cocked his head at an angle as if he were listening intently, but he would do a Groucho Marx act, popping his large fuzzy white eyebrows up and down, or he would grab his chest with one hand and let his eyes bug out as if he were just asked for a new bright red Ferrari Lamborghini convertible.

The inevitable deep voiced, "Ho, ho, ho would come out of a mouth well hidden behind a white beard and mustache, and the parents loved it.

They were all smiles as it was a time of joy and a time for all believers to give thanks to God and for the Christians to celebrate the birth of Jesus, the Christ child. But as he stood there with the other parents, Floyd Richards could only think of a quote from the famous nineteenth century American author, Mark Twain. "To get the full value of joy, you must have somebody to divide it with."

His son was next on Santa's lap. "And what's your name?" It was the opening line for all the Christmas

Santas. Robby responded. Then he pointed at his dad in response to Santa's next question, "Is your mom or dad here?"

Santa recognized Floyd and gave him a nod and a wink. Richards looked at him closely and then realized who was in the Santa Claus suit. It was the fifty year old roly poly mall manager who was built just like the jolly old elf himself. His son was a sophomore at UK and was currently taking a class from Floyd Richards.

Robby was squirming on Santa's lap, twisting his arms together, and looking down at the floor as he spoke. *That wasn't like him,* Richards thought. Robby was uncomfortable. Richards stared at the two of them seated next to the brightly lit and decorated Christmas tree with the empty, but beautifully wrapped boxes all around the base.

Robby was saying something that was difficult for him to talk about. He was struggling to get the words right and confide in someone about the heavy burden that he carried in his mind and heart.

Ralph, the mall manager, was now listening intently. With a jerk of his head, he glanced up wide-eyed at Richards. There was concern in his face. *No. There was more than that. Ralph looked frightened.* He stared at his son and knew that something was very wrong.

Santa smiled and gave Robby a big hug before the boy slid off his lap. An assistant had come out and stopped the line. She gave everyone numbered tickets to come back in an hour. Santa had to eat lunch, she told them.

Santa motioned to Richards to come with him. Then he told his assistant to look after the children.

"Get them an ice cream cone," he said. "That's all right isn't it, Floyd?"

Richards quickly agreed and walked off with the mall manager. In his office, Ralph tried to smile as they both took a seat. He looked at Richards whom he had known for several years.

"It may be nothing, Floyd. I didn't even know that you and Doris were separated. But Robby is upset. He was very brave and adult to tell me things. I know he must have been thinking about what he was going to say before he sat on my lap."

Richards' face went flat. No expression. He was taking shallow breaths, like he was waiting for a diagnosis from an oncologist, and he didn't want to hear what the doctor had to say.

Ralph continued. "Robby isn't happy. It's probably due to the situation between you and Doris. In his eyes, the family has been torn apart. He didn't say the word, divorce. At his age he probably doesn't know what that means. He just said, 'Mommy and daddy aren't together anymore.' And he had his head down. He wouldn't look at me because he was embarrassed."

Richards spoke up. "But Robby could talk about it if he stared at the floor. That I recognized when he was talking to you."

Ralph told Richards that for Christmas, Robby wanted his Mommy and daddy to be back together again. "That part was tough to hear," he said, "but what came next was the reason I wanted to talk to you privately."

The mall manager had a concerned expression on his face as he spoke. "Robby told me that he didn't like this man, this dentist, with whom they were now living. And he couldn't pronounce his name."

"Barakat," Richards said quickly.

"Yes, that must be it. Then he told me that the man was mean to him, to his sister and to his mommy. And your son said that Barakat told him, 'don't you say a word to anyone, or I'll hurt your mommy. Do you understand, not to anyone!'

"Then what almost broke my heart," Ralph said, "is what he told me next. He said in that little soft voice. 'I thought I could tell Santa because he's not just anyone, he's Santa Claus.'"

The store manager straightened up in his chair. "That's when I knew I had to speak with you," he added.

Richards turned away with tears welling up in his eyes. He had always been a mild, calm person. Now, quick angry thoughts raced through his head. Anger and violence began to build up inside. His head turned back and then down as if to study the floor. *I've got to get rid of these negative thoughts. I need positive ideas.*

Slowly his head came up and Ralph thought Richards had aged ten years in those few seconds. He looked tired and drained, like he had just run a marathon.

"Being mean to a six year old can be many different things," Ralph said. "Dr. Barakat may not have any harm in mind and possibly Robby has been difficult living in his new circumstances. He may be rebelling a bit. I wouldn't jump to any conclusions yet, Floyd."

"You're right, Ralph. It's automatic to respond by thinking of the worst possible things that could happen. I'll just check into it." Richards thanked the mall manager, wished him a merry Christmas, and left to pick up the kids at the ice cream factory.

He checked the children over carefully when they took a bath that night and couldn't find any bruises or marks. Then he saw a feint red circle around Robby's forearm.

"Have you been playing Indian burn with kids in your class, son? You know how someone will grab your arm with both hands close together and twist in opposite directions. It pinches the skin and burns a little," Richards said with a smile.

Robby's eyes got big. "No daddy. It just happened playing in the school yard, I guess."

Richards saw his son was defensive and uncomfortable with his question.

"Well, give me a big hug, it's time to drop you both back at your mom's."

The six year old boy leaped into Richards' arms and gave his dad a much bigger squeeze than he ever had before. And unlike most little boys that age, he didn't jump down right away to run off to some other new adventure.

Softly, his son said, "I love you daddy. A whole bunch."

He answered without emotion in his voice so he wouldn't scare or upset his son. But he did say it lovingly. "Robby. You would tell me if something was bothering you or your mom? You know your dad will always be there for you and can make things right."

His son didn't respond. Richards could tell he was thinking it over. "I would tell you daddy if something was real bad." Then he jumped down and grabbed his coat.

Richards let the subject drop. When he took the kids back to Doris at Barakat's house, the doctor came out of the front door with a congenial smile. "You brought the little ones back looking full of Christmas cheer," he said. Barakat opened his arms as if to welcome the children, but Richards held onto each of their hands.

"I want to speak with Doris, Kal. Ask her to come down to the street."

Richards' tone was flat, void of emotion, with no anger. He didn't want to give Barakat any reason to do anything later, if he was in fact an abuser.

His smile waned. "She doesn't want to see you right now, Floyd. You know . . . under the circumstances and everything that's happened," he answered.

Richards didn't believe him. He knew Doris. And like any loving mother, she would be there to greet her children. *She wasn't mad at me when she left our home. It was her idea and she had always been civil, even pleasant to me in the past.*

He put the children back in the truck; calmly shut the passenger door; turned his back to it; looked straight into Barakat's eyes, and folded his big arms over his chest. Defiantly, he said, "I'll wait."

The dentist watched Richards cross his legs, one foot over the other, and then lean back against the truck door in a gesture that sent a message. He wasn't going to leave until he spoke with Doris.

"I'll see what I can do," Barakat responded coldly, and walked back into the house.

It seemed to take a little longer than necessary for Doris to make an appearance. When she did she walked slowly down to the car with little expression on her face.

"You haven't called me lately, Doris. You know . . . to talk about the kids and what I'll do with them when they're with me. That's not like you."

"I've been very busy lately," was her short response.

Richards studied her carefully. She was avoiding his eyes. "Robby was so upset that he told Santa Claus, you know, Ralph the mall manager, that Barakat was mean and would hurt you if he said anything to anyone. But telling Santa was different for Robby. He was somebody he could trust."

Doris looked like she might cry. But she looked straight ahead at the children, waved and tried to smile at them. "Hi. My sweeties are back."

She leaned past Richards and opened the truck door and the kids spilled out, happy to be with their parents who were both together now, even for just these few short minutes.

Doris didn't acknowledge anything that her husband had said or asked. "Thanks for taking the children, Floyd. I'm sure they had a good time with their dad. Have a nice Christmas."

She turned away, holding each child's little hand and walked back up to the front door. Richards watched her intently. Doris glanced back as she pulled the door open. At that distance, it was difficult to tell, but it seemed to Richards that she had a look of longing in her eyes.

Little did he know the depth of Barakat's possessive behavior that was manifesting itself more each and every day. Doris couldn't say anything to him at the truck. Barakat was listening to every word spoken. She had been wired for sound.

Chapter 14

One month later it was Christmas Eve, and the Owsley family was having their big holiday dinner that night. Eddie Cason was there and so was Floyd Richards. Karlene made sure that he was entertained as much as possible to ease the pain, the burden that he carried in his heart.

Richards appreciated all of their efforts, and even the attempts recently to encourage him to date other women. After all, he would soon be a very eligible single man. A man who would earn his doctorate in science. A man who had a promising future at the University of Kentucky with a full professorship.

But most of all, Richards wanted his family back. They were spending the Christmas season at another man's house and his wife was sharing another man's bed. He was losing sleep and losing weight. He wasn't eating right. Just fast foods and a pick-up sandwich on the run from one event or class to some other activity at the college just to keep his mind busy.

If he didn't still care for her, if he had left her for someone else, there wouldn't be a problem. But all of this was made even worse, compounded by the fact that his family might be in danger by an abusive man who would soon be her husband and then, supposedly, a new father figure to his children.

Richards had gone to visit Cason several times while he was in the hospital recovering from his ordeal in the dark labyrinth of the Collins Crystal Cave system.

The orthopedic staff had to make sure his broken limbs were set properly, and treat him for the infections that had occurred around the bone breaks plus a case of pneumonia that he had contracted as he sat in the cold depths of the caverns.

Richards had also been over to the Owsley home, along with Gus Laffoon, and of course, Ruby, the big blood hound who had contributed greatly by finding Cason soon enough to save him from pneumonia and perhaps a painful, cold death.

It was the third night back from the hospital that Cason felt strong enough to fully enjoy an evening with his sister's family. He had hobbled in on crutches, his leg and his arm still in casts, but with all the enthusiasm that he always maintained for life.

He proudly showed off the signatures people had penned all over his white casts. The surgeons and anesthetists, the nurses and orderlies were first. Then the television crew from WTVQ 36, the local ABC affiliate that picked up on the story. Every human that entered his hospital room was required to sign a cast, either on his arm or leg.

And of course, Gus Laffoon, who enjoyed all the attention his now famous dog, had brought to him. After all, he was a breeder of pure-bred blood hounds and the article in the Lexington Herald-Leader was picked up by the Associated Press and distributed by wire service around the world.

The news had made most of the major newspapers in the country and some papers overseas that were always looking for human interest stories. Ruby was photographed sitting dutifully beside his master, Gus Laffoon, who had his thumbs stuck in his suspenders.

"Ruby barked when he saw his picture in the newspaper," Laffoon boasted.

The dog breeder had more notoriety than he wanted. He couldn't answer all the letters and phone calls wanting to buy his bloodhound puppies.

"The stud fee deposits are pouring in," Laffoon told his breeder friends. "And Ruby sure is happy," he said with a sly smile. "I just hope he don't screw himself to death too soon!"

Now at Christmas dinner, Eddie Cason had a selling job to do with Laffoon. The breeder tried to keep his dogs and bitches on a strict dog food diet and not feed them table scraps. But finally he relented and told Cason he could feed him some people food.

That night the big hound had his plate set on the floor at the dinner table right beside Cason. He would lean down, pat Ruby and ask him if the food was up to his standards. Ruby would wag his long tail which meant just keep bringin' it on.

Richards had been with Cason a number of times before this Christmas dinner. Since they were basically both bachelors, and Cason couldn't drive for a while with the casts on his limbs, Richards had picked him up in his truck and they had gone out to dinner together.

Richards had taken an interest in Cason. He had never met anyone like him before. He had a gift of gab and a certain charm and Richards could see how he excelled at his former profession.

He didn't hold any prejudices about Cason's past either. In fact, he was fascinated by the man's life in crime and his stories about living in prison. If ever there was a case of opposites attract, this budding friendship was the epitome of that statement.

And Cason knew that Richards was basically responsible for him being alive. It was Richards who had put together the rescue team, found him in time, and literally pulled and pushed him out of that cave.

Cason had always been a loner. But Richards, who was established in a community like Lexington, Kentucky, had befriended him, and he wasn't looking for something in return. No pay back was due. Cason didn't owe him. This was a new experience for Fast Eddie. To have a friend with no strings attached.

"When are you going to get out of those casts, Eddie?" Richards had asked.

"The doc says they can take them off towards the end of January. By then they'll have been on for over eight weeks."

"Good. Maybe a couple of weeks after that you'll want to try caving with me. I can take you along with my students and you'll learn to do it the right way," Richards said.

"Kinda like falling off a horse, huh?" Cason answered. "Get back on quick or you'll chicken out."

"Something like that," Richards smiled. "If you're going to take people on tours in those caves, especially the more strenuous ones with some tight squeezes, you need to be comfortable doing it."

Chapter 15

Christmas day in 1998 came on Friday, and New Years Day came on the following Friday. The students at UK weren't required to return to class until Monday, January the fourth, which ended the holiday season.

Floyd Richards had time to kill. *I don't want to go to some new year's party and celebrate. Celebrate what?* He thought. *I've lost my family. Outside of my work, they were everything to me.*

He had tried to see Doris at the dental office on Monday. He wanted to see her and ask her if she and the children were all right. But Barakat's reply came through his embarrassed receptionist who had known Richards for several years.

"I'm sorry, Floyd, but Barakat said only patients are allowed in the office and no socializing." She leaned over towards the sliding glass window and whispered. "Barakat said that you weren't even family any more. What a cruel thing for him to say. You're still the father," she added in disgust. "Barakat's not the same man, Floyd. He's changed."

Richards didn't lose his temper as most men would have hearing that kind of statement. As with most problems, he thought about it and then spoke.

"Well then . . . when can I have an appointment? I need to have my teeth cleaned by my dental hygienist, which is Doris. Tell Barakat not to try and switch me to someone else or this office will experience a definite scene. I can guarantee that everyone in the waiting room will leave!"

The receptionist gave him an appointment in two weeks and told Barakat just as Richards had requested. She also added, "I've known Floyd for three years. He's always been a gentleman. But there was something about the way he looked and how he said it. I wouldn't take it lightly." She turned and walked out of Barakat's private office.

Richards went home to pack for a caving trip by himself. He had the rest of the week. Between the divorce; adjusting for visitation with his kids; mid-term exams to prepare for his students, and the holidays, he had not been able to explore his new discovery. He took enough food, water, and clothing for up to three days, if necessary, under the earth.

Of course it could be just a one room cavern or more likely a small cave system. There were a lot of those that didn't amount to much. But he knew that he was breaking the cardinal rule of spelunking or caving. You don't go by yourself. If you get into trouble there is no one to help you.

The rule is that a threesome is best at a minimum. Two might fall into the same trouble at the same time. Both could fall down a vertical chute. A rock fall could catch two people, or two might slip into a deep, fast flowing stream, lose the light from their head lamps, and drown in total darkness.

Of course he knew all that. But he couldn't risk taking anyone else right now. If this turned out to be a major system, it could be financially very rewarding. Richards didn't want to argue with others about who owned it. He knew partners could have a falling out as each one would have different agendas in their lives and different needs.

But right now, to compound his problem, Richards would be entering a virgin cave, perhaps untouched and unexplored by any human. If so, then every step deeper into the cave would be a step further into the unknown, the unfamiliar.

But for all cavers, Richards included, that was the lure. The excitement of not knowing where it would lead and what sights the caver would find wile probing into the depths of the earth, walking where no other man had ever been before. The discovery of something new and then in time, sharing it with the world. *It just doesn't get any better than that,* Richards thought.

He drove towards Radcliff to park at the same place off state road 31 West. He left a dated note on the car seat in case he didn't come out. It explained where he went and how many days he might be gone. If the worst did happen, others would know how long he had been inside the cave and what supplies and rescue gear they would have to bring.

Richards worked his way through the trees and brush back to the series of sinkholes. The one he would explore was only three hundred yards from the highway. There it was with the big oak tree in it, its branches still hiding the opening into the cavern.

He tied a rope to a nearby tree and repelled down into the hole. He knew that would be an obvious clue as to where he had gone. He tied the other end to a branch near the cave entrance which could lead rescuers right to it and save time.

The leafy shrubs that hid the opening were still in place. No one had been there since he discovered it. He pulled them back to expose the entrance. Richards tied off another line to a big oak branch; turned on his Tikka LED headlamp; crawled into the cave and with his heavy gloves on, repelled his way down the rope until his feet touched the cave floor where he coiled the rope for his return.

He switched on another large hand held torch. Its powerful light swept across the cavern to the opposite wall over sixty feet away. The dust had settled now, he noticed. About forty feet above him the light revealed a dome shaped ceiling.

Let there be more passages ahead, he prayed as he walked over the rocky floor to the other side. Excitement surged through him when he found another opening. A tall vertical passage with smooth tan walls, twenty feet high but only three feet wide, that led somewhere else. As he entered it he found that it went down and continued downward for forty more feet where it opened into another room.

Richards made detailed notes on a small tape recorder as he hiked along, including compass readings every time he turned. Usually that was one man's job as the other team members led the way. Now he had to do all of it by himself. He hoped these notes would lead him back out.

The second room was smaller and he quickly crossed it to find two tunnels on the other side. Now he had to make a choice. *Or do I,* he thought. *Someone else made the choice before and marked it. Another human has been here,* he realized. But how many hundreds of years before? His heart pumped faster.

The light revealed black soot smudges on one tunnel entrance. Quickly he glanced down. The head lamp followed his eyes as he searched the cavern floor for what he knew must be there. His search ended. He saw the tiny blackened pieces of sticks and reeds that had broken off when purposely swiped against the cave wall to mark someone's passage long before.

The passage of Indians or early white settlers. They carried bundles of tightly wrapped reeds smeared in tallow or pitch. Richards knew that this area of the cave, near the surface, was a dead cave area. It was dry and no water dripped or ran down the rock faces. That's why the smudges and remnants of the old torch were still there.

He chose the passage marked by his forebears and moved on ahead. The tunnel was short, and a little low as his big frame had to stoop over to make it through. But it opened into another big, beautiful cavern, lower down than the first ones, with incredible stalactites hanging from the ceiling and the larger stalagmites still growing up from the floor as water dripped from above. Now he was below the water table.

"Good Lord," he said out loud. His voice came back to him as it echoed off the rock walls around him. Then with his arms extended, he yelled. "It's beautiful down here." He now knew he was in a live section of the cave system. It was still growing and changing.

"I'm in a Go-cave," he yelled, as happy as he had been in months. It was a cave that opens up for exploration. His words, "Go-cave, Go-cave, Go-cave," came bouncing back to him as if others were down there with him, voicing and confirming what he now knew to be the truth.

Richards continued on and went down further into the cave making detailed notes for future reference. He saw more signs that others had made it this far also. The ink black soot marks jumped out from the tan walls. He ran into dead ends and areas that pinched-down to the point where he had to put on his knee crawlers, pads for protection, as he inched along on all fours to make forward progress.

He crawled for five full minutes when suddenly the bottom dropped out below him. He looked down a chute for what he estimated to be a vertical drop of thirty feet. It was narrow, so he could work his way down spread-eagled, hands and feet gripping each side.

Then at the bottom he found proof of who had been here first. There was a four inch stump of an old reed torch on the cave floor and next to it a broken arrow made of wood with a stone ground flint tip.

"Indians," he said out loud. *One of them must have fallen down the chute.* Again he spoke out. "But how long ago were you people in here?"

He put the broken arrow in his pack. *I'll give it to the William S. Webb Museum of Anthropology. They'll nail it down.* Founded in 1931, and now in Lafferty Hall, the museum features exhibits tracing human history in Kentucky from 12,500 BC to the present.

The caverns got damper and wetter the deeper he went until he walked through standing water and found a running stream. His altimeter indicated he had dropped 220 feet from ground surface and the compass told him he was moving steadily in an easterly direction.

Excitement had kept his energy level high, but suddenly he felt tired and he checked his watch. He had been at it for twelve hours. It was now 10:00 PM. He decided to camp for the night right there in the bowels of the earth.

After six hours he was up and going again. But he knew he couldn't go as far since he still had to trek all the way back to the entrance. But he could move faster coming back since he didn't need to take notes over ground that he had already covered.

At noon on the third day he was back to the cave opening. His Finnish, Suunto watch indicated that the outside temperature was only fifty-seven degrees. After carefully disguising the cave opening again, he climbed back up the side of the sinkhole, dropped down on the ground face up and let the warmth of the sun cover his body.

Even an experienced caver starts to get claustrophobic after that kind of time underground, especially with no human companions. He relished the feel of the sunshine, the breeze moving over his frame, and the smell of the piney woods in his nose.

He lay there relaxing and let his mind wander. He thought the sinkhole must have covered the entrance to the cave many years ago when the ground collapsed around it. Before that the Indians had used the cave. Near the entrance on the way out he out found remnants of campfires and other Indian articles strewn about.

The cave system stayed hidden until the recent earthquake shook the ground and opened that small hole near the surface. And drawing from his experience, he hadn't come close to finding all of the many different paths he could have chosen while he was below ground in that tremendous, virtually unexplored labyrinth.

Then his mind raced forward with the potential of his discovery. He knew the land east of state road 31 was owned by the federal government since Fort Knox was right there. To the west where he found the cave opening, it might be owned by the state, or by an individual, or a corporation.

He had to find out if it was for sale. Then he could develop further plans. Finally he arose and hiked back to his truck. It was Thursday. He had time tomorrow to check on the owner. If available, he would try to buy the property. Then he could announce his discovery and take others to explore and map the cave system more completely as he developed plans to open it to the public.

Chapter 16

Her name was now Doris Barakat. They were married on Sunday, the third of January, 1999 in the local Islamic center known as, Massid Bilal lbn Rabah, on south Limestone Street.

In her naiveté, she had no idea that Kal Barakat was a Muslim. He had never said anything to her about it in the three years that she had known him or during that third year when they had become intimate with each other. He had told her that he was born in Lebanon but didn't mention anything about religion.

If she had known about it and if he would have agreed not to try and force that religion on her children, then she still would have married him. But that wasn't the only problem she now faced. She was just beginning to find out about this man.

He did tell her that he would raise her children and look after them and he had been doing that. He had not lied to her, but what he didn't tell her was now becoming all too apparent to Doris.

When Doris, Robby, and Karen first moved into Barakat's home everything went fine through the rest of October. And the four of them seemed okay together during the first two weeks or so of November. He enjoyed showing the children his home, their rooms, and even took them down to his office to learn what he did for a living.

It appeared that everything was going along all right as they adjusted to each other. But then his attitude began to change. Slowly at first, Doris realized. Just little things that individually didn't amount to much but the requirements instigated by Barakat started to escalate in December.

The children found themselves forced to stand in the "punishment corner," as the doctor referred to it. They had to face the wall in the corner of the hallway just inside the front door for infractions of the rules in his house.

"It has to be that particular wall every time," Barakat told Doris. "We must instill order and discipline in their lives," he added.

The first infraction during any week beginning on a Monday meant five minutes in the corner. The second mistake meant ten minutes, and the third fifteen, and so on until the week was over and then they could have a clean slate starting again on Monday for the next seven days.

Just before Christmas, which Barakat learned to celebrate himself after his family came to this country; Karen was all excited about Santa Claus. She was more animated and boisterous than usual. Quite normal for a four year old girl. Then she misbehaved and broke one of the rules of the house for the third time that week.

Doris watched as little four year old Karen tried to stand straight up, keep still, and be quiet for a full fifteen minutes. And the punishment time started over if the child spoke, turned, or sat down.

The little girl started to cry and Doris went to her, picked her up, and consoled her as she walked her upstairs to her room and put her to bed. Six year old Robby saw it all from the second floor near his room. Quietly he sat down and peeked through the banister railings that ran along the hallway.

Barakat watched the whole scene with Karen. He saw his authority being thwarted, challenged by the woman whom he would soon marry. The twitching of his right eye started again. That facial tic started the instant stress began to build in his mind. He grew more hostile by the minute.

"Doris," he called out pleasantly enough. "May I talk to you in our bedroom, please?" He didn't want six year old Robby to witness anything.

Doris took ten minutes to settle pretty little blond Karen down. She had cried for a while, then sobbed, and finally dozed off in her mother's arms. Doris put her under the covers, adjusted the thermostat as Karen's bedroom seemed a little cool, and finally went to meet Barakat in their bedroom.

"You certainly took long enough," Barakat snarled as he snapped the lock on the bedroom door behind him.

Doris had never heard him speak to her with such vehemence in his voice. She was startled at first and then remembered what just happened to her daughter.

As any loving mother would, she spoke up. She stood her ground.

"What kind of a man are you?" she asked. "How could you be so cruel to such a little girl? Fifteen minutes is just way too long . . . even ten minutes is too long for a little person like her."

Barakat smiled showing no teeth. There was no warmth in it or in his eyes either. "Five minutes didn't seem to work, but they will learn quickly standing for longer periods in the corner. Both of them will benefit from a little discomfort," he said.

"Well, I don't like it." Doris spoke quickly when she was upset. "Five minutes is enough . . . then for the second offense within a week they can be sent to their rooms for those longer periods." Doris stated.

Slowly he answered. "They will just play in their rooms without caring about what they did. But downstairs in that corner, in a place they don't want to be, that will make them aware of their misdeeds."

Barakat's voice was stronger, harder, but not louder. He enunciated each word more carefully so that she began to sense and then see the anger build in his eyes and face.

"Standing there they will have time to think about each mistake." He ground the words out, pronouncing each syllable as if he were talking to someone with a mental disability.

"In Karen's case she would play with some doll on her bed. That won't teach her anything."

"I don't agree with you, Kal." She said it softly, kindly, not wanting to upset him more than he already was now. But Doris wanted to make her point.

"Well now," Barakat growled. "Let's start with your first offense, Doris."

She stared at him. *It's like something has snapped inside him,* she thought. Never had she seen this expression on his face before. Barakat walked toward her with a flat, emotionless stare. He looked right into her eyes when he stopped in front of her.

Quickly he grabbed her arm, twisted it sharply so that she cried out and was forced to turn around as he bent the arm up behind her back until it hurt even more.

"Ohhh," she groaned. The pain was intense enough that Doris thought she might pass out. "Please stop," she begged.

"I'll stop when you agree not to argue with me!" He barked in her ear. "You know you did that just now!" He added.

Then he pushed her arm up further, forcing her to bend over their bed. "Secondly . . . you'll be punished for interfering with my decision in front of the children. You have tried to usurp my position as the head of this household. Now, just like the children, Doris, you must be punished too. This will remind you to never to do so again."

He drew his fist back and delivered a punch to her kidney. It was a short jab, but he knew from experience just how to do it for maximum pain with the least effort on his part. The agony of the blow made Doris grunt. She dropped on the bed as the force of it knocked the breath out of her lungs.

"Aahhh," she cried out. It felt like a knife blade shoved into her side. The pain was excruciating. When she cried out again, Barakat slapped her hard across the face. "Shut up," he said. "Don't let the children hear you cry."

Kal Barakat straightened up and went into the bathroom. He carefully turned on the water until it was exactly the right temperature and then thoroughly washed his hands with a special soap. He took his time drying them on the clean hand towel hung by the basin. After he had used the towel just once to dry clean hands, he deposited it in the dirty clothes hamper and hung a fresh towel on the rack next to the sink. This precise mannerism was a part of his anal compulsive and possessive mental condition.

He walked back into their bedroom and saw that Doris had slid off the bed. Still in pain, she was laying on her back on the floor. He went over to his closet to get his pajamas. Then he began to undress for bed. He had a big day tomorrow at the office. *People put off minor dental problems during the Christmas holidays,* he thought, *but now he would have a couple of busy weeks.*

Psychiatrists refer to Barakat's problem as *Activation.* It is "extraverted" instability or proneness to develop "extraverted" types of maladjustment under perceived stress. These people are usually struggling all the time and have mental conflicts. They can become sadistic or extra-punitive. His forthcoming marriage plus the two children were the trigger for his *Activation.*

This condition was completely out of the realm of understanding for young Doris. She had only seen him during work at his dental office or during love trysts on the couch in his private office or at his house. She had never spent any real time with this man, yet she thought she loved him.

The next morning, Barakat said, "I'm not usually violent like I was last night, Doris. But all of us have had to adjust which I know you understand. It won't happen again, darling."

"I think we should put off the marriage for a few more months, Kal. I can't take that kind of punishment. I shouldn't have to worry about it happening again either."

"But we've made all the plans already. The mosque has been reserved and guests invited. We will be married as scheduled, darling."

"The children and I need to have some time alone. Maybe just for a week when we can be with each other and talk about our life here with you. You can understand that, can't you?" She asked.

He gave her that flat, dull stare again as the stress pressured his mind. He had to release it. He said, "I'll get Robby and bring him up here to talk about it now. But first I'll do to him what I did to you last night. I'm sure he'll agree that we should marry when I say so." He started for the bedroom door.

Doris gasped! What he had just said was like a blow to her stomach. Then she tried to speak, but could only stutter for a second. "Pl. . . Please . . . Da . . . don't hurt him. I'll do it. I'll marry you as planned." She finally got the words out of her mouth as he was entering the upstairs hallway.

He turned slowly around. "Is that a solemn promise, Doris?" He fixed her with a hard stare.

"Aahh, yes, yes, it is a promise, Kal."

She was afraid for her children now. And afraid to run away from him. Doris didn't know if Floyd would take her back. If not she had no place to go. Her father had died young and her mother had only a small place in Tennessee. Doris didn't have any money saved up for such a contingency.

I'll make it work . . . for the children's sake, I'll do everything he asks. He won't have any reason to get mad again. Maybe he could get some treatment for this problem, she thought.

Doris and the children would now receive the brunt of this man's sick mind. This Jekyll-and-Hyde dentist, Dr. Kalid Barakat, whom she would be forced to marry in just a few days.

Chapter 17

Floyd Richards phoned a friend in Lexington who specialized in commercial real estate. He told him where it was located, and said, "Of course it would depend on the price."

"Price determines almost all real estate transactions, Floyd. If the buyer and seller agree, then it's a done deal. What kind of property is it?"

"It's all raw land, a forested area past Radcliff near Fort Knox," Richards responded.

"How much acreage is involved?"

"I only want ten acres with public access," Richards answered. "See if it's available."

"I'll drive down and park where you told me and look around. I'll find out who owns what along there and let you know."

Then his friend hesitated a moment. "I hope you know exactly what you need it for, Floyd. You can't put a gas station, a fast food restaurant, or much of anything else on that land."

"If I can't do what I want there, then I won't buy it. Just let me know."

Three days later the realtor called back. "There's a timber company that owns over ten thousand acres in there. They don't have it on the market, but the area you want to buy has a number of sinkholes on it. It's unstable land and of no use to them. He told me they don't want to lose any heavy equipment down in one of those holes.

"So I asked him why he wouldn't sell ten of those unusable acres to you for a low price. He called me back after checking higher up on the corporate ladder. He said that they would only sell in one hundred acre lots for twenty-five hundred dollars per acre. This is a one time offer, take it or leave it."

"What's that mean?" Richards asked.

"That means we can't come back with a counter offer. You know . . . we can't negotiate the price."

"That's two hundred and fifty thousand dollars. I can't afford anything like that!" Richards grumped.

"Well, whatever idea you've got, take it to a banker. Worst he can say is no. You've got two weeks to come up with a deposit of fifty thousand dollars. The rest to be paid at closing. Good luck, Floyd." The realtor hung up.

Richards just stared at the phone. *High finance, land deals, banking arrangements. I don't know anything about that,* Richards thought. But he was a good college professor. He knew the academic side of life. Business and all that was Greek to Floyd Richards.

He made an appointment with a commercial loan officer at Bank One of Lexington, a banker acquaintance whom he knew. The man had a son at UK who was a hell of a football player, but not much of a student.

"Hello Floyd Richards," greeted the cheery, hefty, bald banker with his meaty fist extended. Richards shook hands and sat down. They chatted about family and other subjects until the banker could see that Richards was uncomfortable. He didn't know how to start.

The banker made it easy for him. "What can I do for you, Floyd? Do you need a loan for some project?"

He smiled stiffly. "Yes. I want to buy some property, but I don't have any collateral. I know it would be a good money maker."

Richards proceeded to tell the banker everything. Then he said, "Look at these pictures." He had taken a series of photographs as he explored the cave.

The banker looked over the pictures carefully. Then he leaned back in his executive chair and studied Richard's face.

"I'm going to the American Bankers Association meeting in San Francisco next month. I want to see their faces when I tell them we loaned money on a hole in the ground." He leaned back in his chair and laughed.

"You mean you'll do it?" Richards said with a surprised look on his face.

"Since you don't even have enough money to put up the deposit, Floyd, much less the money to start the business, most bankers would say I'm crazy. So what you need here is a venture capital loan. We have a subsidiary corporation up in Louisville that does just that."

He leaned forward, putting his thick arms on the desk. "But you're going to have to share the ownership. I think they'll put up the money because that is cave country. There hasn't been a discovery as big as this since the Crystal Onyx Cave in nineteen sixty. And we know the kind of money some of those cave owners make."

The banker explained that twenty to thirty percent of this new business would be owned by the venture capital group because it still carries some risk and they would be putting up all the money.

"Of course you would have to sign for the loan, Floyd. But the first thing they'll want to do is inspect the cave. You can understand with this kind of investment we have to be as excited as you are about the possibilities. I'll get in touch with them and set it up."

The following week Richards met the venture capital investment banker in Lexington and drove him West on the Blue Grass Parkway to Elizabethtown and then North past Radcliff and off highway into the wooded area where they walked to the cave.

He was agile, in his thirties, and he wanted to see almost everything that Richards had found. They spent ten hours tracing Richard's trail and found some more caverns he hadn't seen yet.

When they came out that evening around eight o'clock the banker stopped at the top of the sinkhole and stuck out his hand. "Mister Richards, you've got a deal." Richards shook hard and thanked him.

As they walked back to the truck the banker asked. "You know why we really like this?" He didn't wait for an answer. He just explained.

"This is better than a gold mine. Here's the reason: No major investment in heavy equipment; no big processing plants; no huge payroll; no union problems; no depletion of the asset, and no cost of reclamation."

Richards said, "All we need is a paved road to a parking lot, a small building with limited food available, rest rooms, a ticket booth, a few guides, and pathways cleared for easy walking through the caverns. The land is the only big start up cost plus advertising."

On the way back the banker asked. "Are you going to quit teaching? Somebody has to make this venture fly."

"I don't think so. I love it too much. But I've got someone in mind to promote this business for me."

A few nights later, Richards had dinner with Cason. Over coffee, Richards asked, "How are you healing up, Eddie?"

"I'm feeling good. The casts have been off now for a month and I've been back at work."

Richards studied him carefully. Then made up his mind. "You've always been a promoter, Eddie. You have a quick mind and ways of making people feel confident in what you tell them."

Richards leaned forward and frowned, making deep furrows across his forehead. "But speaking frankly, what you've been involved in was mostly illegal. I think if you got your teeth into something good, you could run with it." It was more of a question than a statement.

Cason sat back with a puzzled expression. "I know I could. But I haven't found it yet."

"I've got a venture I want to tell you about. If you're interested, there's an opportunity for you to own twenty percent of the business. You work hard at it, produce results over the next twelve months, and you'll own that share with no investment. And you'll get paid more than you're making now from day one, Eddie."

Cason gave him that easy smile. "Tell me about it."

Richards shared his discovery with Eddie and that weekend he took him down to see the cave. Cason was ecstatic. "I'm in, Floyd . . . when do we start?"

The next week Richards signed the loan agreement and the property was purchased from the timber company in late February.

In March, Richards and Cason met with a reporter from the Lexington Herald-Reader and gave him the story. A few days later it was front page news with big headlines announcing the recent discovery and the new company that would develop and promote the "Floyd Richards' Caverns," as it was now referred to in all the media. Even the major television networks picked it up as a national news item.

The morning the article appeared in the Herald-Leader, Richards took the newspaper with him to the head of the geology department so that he would also be informed. He didn't want to offend his boss.

Cason was already putting together a team of experienced cavers and spelunkers to begin further exploration of the cave. Depending on its size, the project could take months. But they had to find out how big a discovery they actually had to advertise it properly in the future.

As a part of the marketing effort, Richards and Cason felt that officials from the Mammoth Cave National Park system and other cave owners in the area should be invited to view the discovery. It wasn't long after that tour before the problems started to develop for the two young entrepreneurs.

Chapter 18

Jay Cohen was jogging by six o'clock in the morning as he did every day of the week, except for Saturdays and Sundays. He took those days off from his law practice and he didn't jog then either. But he did play tennis with non-law partner friends both days for two hours and then came home to be with his wife and their two teenage daughters if they hadn't gone shopping for winter, spring, summer, or fall clothing, which to Jay Cohen seemed to be their total dedication in life.

By seven o'clock on Monday morning, attorney Cohen had returned home to jump into the shower, then dress in one of his rather severe blue, gray, or black Philadelphia lawyer suits, worn with a white shirt, always a conservative tie, plus black, wing tip shoes, never loafers.

He came downstairs to eat his standard healthy type breakfast; fruit juice, a no sugar coated, but shot-from-guns energy packed cereal covered with fresh berries and skim milk. Two cups of black coffee ground from whole beans and the Philadelphia Inquirer newspapers.

Cohen read the local business news first, then the international news followed by the financial section, if time allowed. His family was usually there to converse with and if they asked him a question, he would condescend to answer, albeit, a short one.

His slim, attractive wife glared at him but he couldn't see the acid look through the newspaper that was held up in front of his face. She had talked with him innumerable times over the years about being so self absorbed. Usually, she did it in a kindly manner.

The last time, just one week ago, she had finally had it. She waited until they were upstairs in their bedroom where he began making some amorous suggestions. Then picking the right moment, like an eighteenth century pirate ship sliding along side an unsuspecting English merchant vessel, she gave him the full twenty gun broadside of cannon shot. Timing in life is everything.

"You're only interested in your work, your exercise or those damn national parks. Can't you take an interest in those who try to love you, and yet never receive anything in return?"

She told him that he had no interest in their lives . . . no warmth . . . no nothing! If he showed displeasure with them, at least that would be human contact. That would be an emotion directed towards one of us anyway.

It worked for one week. Now at breakfast the man just sat there reading the morning paper, again totally self absorbed. *I should think about filing for divorce,* she thought. *This is just like living alone anyway. Our two daughters sense his disinterest. They've given up trying to talk to him.*

Unless traffic was horrible or a wreck occurred, Cohen would arrive at his office in downtown Philadelphia at nine o'clock. On the seventeenth floor, where all senior members of the firm had a window view of the city, the brass name plate on the huge twin walnut doors read, *Cohen, Brooks, Belzberg, and Murray, Attorneys at Law.* They needed one Irishman in the group in case a client held some prejudice.

The decor inside was beautifully appointed, with rich, but quiet tones befitting the always conservative nature of their practice. Only corporate law, real estate, wills and estate planning. No criminal or domestic cases or high profile trials taken, in keeping with their well developed public image.

Jay Cohen's one avocation was his interest in the great outdoors and hiking with his wife and other friends who enjoyed the mountains. He was on the Board of Directors of The National Parks Conservation Association, a group of private citizens concerned with keeping the beauty of America as pristine as possible against the encroachment of mankind in any form, whether it was by the government, by business, or due to a housing development.

Then about five years ago, he was asked if his firm would represent the National Park Service in all real estate transactions nationwide, including when land was donated by a wealthy citizen or purchased by the federal government. Cohen was delighted and readily agreed to accept the federal government as a new client. This addition certainly added more prestige to their legal practice.

Their real estate section had handled these acquisitions and any law suits that occasionally occurred. And he was a fierce defender of the National Park System. In a sense the parks did in fact belong to the public who paid taxes and fees to sustain and support these beautiful oases across the United States.

But Cohen, in his zeal, acted instead as if they all belonged to him. It became a personal affront to him if anyone or any corporation attempted to do anything on park land unless it benefited the park system and did not destroy or affect its natural beauty.

Recently he helped stop the public from using snowmobiles in the Grand Teton and the Yellowstone National Parks for several reasons. First, their exhaust was five times more polluting than an automobile, second, it was the worst kind of noise pollution, and third, some irresponsible idiots would illegally chase elk, deer, and other animals which could both scare and exhaust the animals in a time of short food supply and lead to their possible deaths.

So when attorney Cohen saw the memo from the Director of the National Park Service in Washington, D. C. regarding the announcement of a new large cave complex in Kentucky, not far from the Mammoth Cave National Park, he read it with great interest.

He knew that other private cave owners benefited from the reputation of the Mammoth Cave System since it brought customers to their caves also without much advertising on their part.

"They are a bunch of freeloaders," he had called them one time when asked about the privately owned caves. He noticed the footnote on the memo from the Superintendent of the Mammoth Cave National Park.

It is my opinion that the Floyd Richards' caverns start on private land, but go under state highway 31W, and then beneath property which comprises a part of Fort Knox.

Cohen leaned back in his executive chair and studied the footnote again. Then he picked up the phone and called the Director of the National Park Service in Washington, D. C.

"We need a determination made about this footnote on the memo you sent me. If this new cave system is mainly on government property, I want to know it for a fact, not an opinion."

Cohen listened to the reply and then said, "Thank you, I'm glad we agree," and hung up the phone.

Chapter 19

Dr. Kal Barakat lay quietly on his back. His head was slightly elevated on a hard pillow and his eyes were closed as he relaxed on the firm but comfortable couch. The room was acoustically built to be sound proof and the music system had been turned off.

Slowly, he opened his eyes and studied the ornately carved wooden ceiling with its exact squares made of intricately patterned cross beams with all its accompanying ridges, corners, and multiple levels of wood, each one stained in slightly different shades which seemed to open avenues of thought or memory, as was its purpose.

Barakat breathed deeply and then spoke. "The anger and the violence; both have started again, and it's getting worse."

A man's voice said, "The last time you were here Doctor. . ." He hesitated slightly as he checked his notes. ". . . was over two years ago. Then you were dating a woman by the name of Anne Stuart. You told me at that time that you didn't have any indication of possessiveness. The symptoms didn't begin until she moved in with you. Do you remember telling me that?"

Barakat's eyes roamed slowly around the ceiling. "Yes."

The psychiatrist leaned forward. "Then you told me that the problem started to build up as this perceived stress increased in your mind. Is that also correct?"

"Yes, correct." Barakat squeezed out the words. "She was a strong willed woman."

"According to my notes," the psychiatrist continued, "she moved out after two months. She left you a note that she couldn't take your violent mood swings anymore."

The doctor carefully observed Barakat when he made the next statement. He wanted to gauge his reaction.

"When we talked about that, you told me that this anger problem occurred in your first marriage also. That was the reason for her going to court, getting a restraining order, and subsequently the divorce."

Barakat's eyes had squeezed shut as he listened intently to the psychiatrist. When the voice stopped he opened his eyes and continued to lay there quietly and breath deeply as the doctor had instructed him to do on previous appointments. This enabled him to discuss some prior disturbing events without experiencing the accompanying anger that usually occurred simultaneously.

"That's why I came to you then," Barakat blurted. "I knew that something was wrong with me. Emotions that I did not understand nor could I control. I didn't know how."

"You have been married now for over two months to a woman named Doris, who brought two children into the marriage. Tell me about all of them."

Barakat recited in considerable detail how he met Doris, became attracted to her, and pursued a sexual adventure which led to romance and love, as far as he was concerned.

"She has two nice young children." He continued to describe them in positive terms.

The psychiatrist interrupted. "But when all three of them came to live with you in your home, Kal, that's when your compulsive, possessive nature manifested itself, wasn't it?"

The therapist kept pressing. "The children did little annoying things around the house, didn't they Kal? They yelled too loudly . . . ran around too much . . . and spilled food. They were just too messy, weren't they Kal?"

Dr. Barakat was holding his head. He began breathing hard. His eyes were darting around on the ceiling without locking on anything.

The psychiatrist was unrelenting in his questions. He continued to push Dr. Barakat and didn't care about the answers. He was trying to create enough stress to try and force the dentist into an *Activated* state.

"And Doris, she defended them, didn't she? They're just little children she told you . . . they're learning, she said. That you would have to live with their growing up. Isn't that what she kept saying, Kal?"

Barakat held both fists to his forehead. He pressed them viciously into his skull and groaned as the pain built up. He couldn't stop it. His eyes bulged out of his face. "Yes, yes, yes," he hissed like a venomous snake.

"They needed order in their lives. They needed discipline . . . all three of them. They needed my guidance to make them understand their many faults. Only then could they lead a proper life."

The psychiatrist now felt he was on the right track. But he would have to pull it out of Barakat. He knew the dentist had not been totally honest in the description of his relation ship with other women. He hadn't yet revealed the depth of his problem.

"Tell me what upset you recently with Doris?"

"Last month her former husband came to the office to have his teeth cleaned by her. They seemed to be plotting against me in that room. I could hear whispering several times as I went by the opening into the treatment cubicle."

"Why did you think that?" Did you find any proof?"

"I found the new cell phone in the pocket of her white office coat. He had given it to her to call him back and talk about me."

The psychiatrist wanted him to relive that moment, to remember the stress that it caused. "How did that make you feel? What sensations did you experience then, Doctor Barakat?"

"I had been betrayed," he boomed as he rose up on his elbows. "That proved her lack of trust in me. She doesn't know how much I love her!"

"When she did something to annoy you, no matter how small, thoughts of punishment began to simmer, didn't they? Then those thoughts began to control your mind . . . right, Kal? Then the pressure built up to an unbearable level. And finally, like a volcano, you exploded and your mind went past blank, didn't it?"

The psychiatrist didn't wait for any response. He probed harder and pushed deeper into his patient's mind until he could be sure, absolutely positive, about the magnitude, the extent of Barakat's condition.

His voice grew deeper and stronger as he pressed to expose the darkest corners of this malfunctioning brain that lay there before him. The psychiatrist knew he was close. Soon Barakat would slip over the brink of reality and sink into the depths of his illness.

"It actually went *white!* Didn't it, Kal?" The psychiatrist was leaning over the couch, his face just twelve inches away, speaking directly into the side of Barakat's head.

"Your mind went *white.* Inside your head was a white wall and you could see nothing past it. A total white out, worse than a blinding snowstorm, wasn't it?"

Barakat was twisting and turning from side to side on the couch as though he were being subjected to physical torture. He felt like he was extracting his own infected back molar without the benefit of anesthesia. Through his excruciating mental anguish, he cried out.

"They needed to be taught a lesson."

Now the psychiatrist's voice bounced off the walls around the room as his words jammed into Kal Barakat's conscious mind.

"Punishment! That's what they needed . . . right, Kal? To feel it hurt inside as you do. To experience your agony, your torment . . . they must suffer too!"

He told Barakat that the very act of inflicting pain was the release he so desperately sought. Just like sex.

It builds to a climax and it can't stop. The orgasm washes over you . . . and then you have it . . . sweet release.

"Only this is better than sex, isn't it, Kal? When you physically inflict bodily injury it melts away that pressure, that pain, that total whiteness in your head. This was what you needed. The release you needed."

Barakat's eyes opened wide. He stared straight up at the ceiling. He could see it all now like the replay on a video.

"Yes. I had to hurt her. So I beat her body with a ping pong paddle. It produces a stinging pain, but little bruising." An expression of joy appeared on his face.

"Then I watched as my open hand slapped her face . . . back and forth. But even that wasn't enough." Now he smiled in delight. "I had to feel my fist hit her body . . . to hear it smack and pound into her flesh."

He turned over and sprang to his knees, facing the office wall. He swung his arm as if he were hitting someone. His knuckles bit into the wall board, leaving an impression of his fist. He yelled out in pain.

The psychiatrist, a big man, stood up and grabbed Barakat by the shoulders, pulling him back down on the couch before he could strike and injure himself further.

"It's all right, Kal, it's okay. It's over now."

Barakat responded slowly. Finally he sat back and eased himself down to lie prone again on the couch. His chest was heaving as he breathed deeply and sweat poured off his forehead. The blood vessels in his temple pulsed as if he had experienced aerobic exercise.

Once satisfied that his patient would come down from an almost hypnotic spell, the psychiatrist stood up from the straight-back chair next to Barakat and returned across the room to his large desk with the swivel, recliner executive chair. He leaned back in his seat and spoke into his recorder.

"This was a difficult session. I had to be sure of his condition. I couldn't guess or just have an opinion. I had to be absolutely positive about my diagnosis regarding Kal Barakat."

He continued to record that the patient suffers from an acute case of *Activation.* Until I provoked him and took him back to some of his relationships, he would not reveal the punitive, even sadistic nature of his condition. But his case is so severe, that the session didn't even require hypnosis. He reacted violently right here in my office.

He clicked off the recorder and returned to the straight chair. Barakat was breathing almost normally now. The psychiatrist spoke calmly. "You have got to differentiate between possessing things, material things, and your relationship with people who are close to you. Particularly, with your own wife and family."

He turned his chair to look directly into Barakat's eyes. "But when you lose your temper and you mistreat another human being, that's where you cross the line, Doctor Barakat. That's where you lose reality, the point at which the other person, whom you profess to love, begins to suffer from your own mental torment. You torture them, Kal. There is no other way to put it. And none of them want to stay with you."

"Can you give me something to calm me down? A medication that will relieve this acute stress that I feel?"

"Frankly, Doctor Barakat, you need to commit yourself to a month's treatment in a hospital and get away from your family. You desperately need help . . . long term help. If you continue like this you may end up in jail. Someone may call the police. Or her ex-husband will confront you. You've got to do something now, Kal!"

The psychiatrist was as emphatic as he could be, realizing that he could not yet commit him to a sanitarium, nor could he reveal what he had learned in private session to the police or anyone else. This was private, privileged information between a doctor and his patient.

Barakat turned away from the psychiatrist as he rose from the couch and responded bluntly. "I'll give that some thought, Doctor Whiten." He left the office quickly without setting up another appointment with the receptionist.

As he drove away, he thought. *There's no way I can take off that kind of time from my practice. And Doris might get away from me. I couldn't stand that. I'll just write a prescription for some stronger medication for one of my patients. Then I'll pick it up at the pharmacy myself so no one else will know.*

Chapter 20

Floyd Richards was riding a roller coaster. His concern for his ex-wife and the lack of communication between them weighed heavily on him. Before she married Barakat, Doris had been in touch about the children and had wanted to talk about them every week. How they were doing in school; their social development with the other children in class, and the new neighbor kids.

Now, not only did she not telephone him, she didn't even return his calls. The children were strangely quiet about her and about Barakat. They not only didn't talk about him, they acted like he didn't exist.

Two weeks had gone by since he had given her a cellular telephone at Dr. Barakat's office. She seemed so relieved to get the phone and promised to call the next day. Not one phone message had he received. Now he didn't want to call her either for fear that Barakat would hear it and find it. He had to do something but he didn't know how to go about it.

On the business side of his life, everything was coming along beautifully. Eddie Cason had taken off with this new venture, coming up with all kinds of inventive promotions that wouldn't cost too much and the publicity they had received from the news media regarding the discovery had really been a great help.

The new company had to put in several telephone lines to handle the incoming calls regarding requests for information generated from the web site that Cason created.

Questions that included: when would the new cave tours be available to the public? How long was the underground system? How big were the caverns? Were there a lot of crystalline formations? When could professional spelunkers and cavers explore further into its unknown depths and multiple tunnels that they knew from experience must exist?

All this could be handled by recorded messages that were updated bi-weekly with positive answers to keep all the public interested. The land clearing for the road into the site and the parking lot was ahead of schedule. Richards was now a celebrity at the university and had been interviewed by local radio stations, television channels, and the newspaper.

And more students wanted to take his classes, so he was more important to the geology department than ever before. This side of his life was the natural high that kept him going. He had plenty of company on weekends to explore further into the cave on overnight trips which kept his mind off Doris and the children.

Then the letter arrived at his duplex home. It was there waiting for him in his street side mailbox when he came home on a Sunday night after two days in the caverns with some students and friends.

The envelope's paper was thick and textured. The color, a rich, ivory cream with raised, black lettering printed in the top left hand corner that stood out due to the fancy script read:

Cohen, Brooks, Belzberg, and Murray, Attorneys at Law,
17th Floor, Suite 1703-1705
1250 Walnut Street, Philadelphia, PA 19102

The letter inside was no less impressive with the same stylistic print down the side of the stationary. The contents were rather short and to the point. For Floyd Richards, what it said exploded in his brain like an incendiary bomb.

Basically he was told that the Floyd Richards' Caverns, et al, were hereby put on notice that all commercial development of the property must stop until ownership of the cave system could be properly evaluated and established.

It was the opinion of the undersigned that the opening to this new discovery started on private land; proceeded in a westerly direction beneath state highway thirty-one west; continued under United States Government property, and was therefore off limits to private development. The letter was signed:

Jay Cohen
Chief Counsel for
The National Park Service
Washington, D. C.

Richards had been standing up in the kitchen area where he usually opened his mail. As he read, and then slowly re-read the letter, his legs trembled. He had to lean on the dining table as he sank down into one of the four chairs in the dinette area that was part of the kitchen.

Slowly, the letter fell from his fingers onto the floor as he brought both hands to his face. He sank down until his elbows found support on his big knees. Gently he rocked back and forth as he muttered, "No, no, no, no. Please God . . . not this too!"

Chapter 21

On Monday after classes, Richards had a meeting with his partner and showed him the letter which Cason also had to read twice.

"I can't believe these attorneys are for real," Cason stated. "The entrance to the caverns is on our property and they would never have known anything about it if we hadn't disclosed our discovery to the Mammoth Cave personnel."

Cason talked as if he were already a partner, Richards noticed, and he liked that attitude. He would be a good partner addition by the end of the year if there still was a project by then.

He glanced at Richards with a look of disgust. "We'll have to call our venture capital partners, Floyd. They'll want to protect their investment and use one of their corporate attorneys to help us fight these guys."

One week later, Richards, Cason, and an attorney representing Bank One's venture capital group met with Jay Cohen and a legal assistant from his firm, in one of the conference rooms at the Hyatt Hotel in downtown Lexington.

"By now I'm sure that you've had time to review the law," Cohen said, looking around the conference table as he poured cold, bottled water in a glass with no ice.

"Both the state law here in Kentucky and federal law regarding the ownership of real property is similar. Such ownership includes the air rights above the subject property plus any mineral rights that are found under that real property."

He leaned back in the chair, picked a piece of lint from the vest of his three piece suit and using his open hand, smoothed back his slick, jet black hair. Then he sipped the water and glanced around the room while he sized up his opponents.

"Yes, but there are no minerals," Richards said. "There is just a hole in the ground that I found and then it disappears further into the underground caverns."

"Quite right," Cohen came back. "If you found gold under my property, the law states that I am the legal owner. It's also the same with the caves that have a definite commercial value. It is considered an equivalent asset whether it is mineral or not."

The bank's attorney, a short and portly man with thick spiky eyebrows, leaned over to Richards and whispered. "I told you yesterday that the bank had made a major mistake. They did not do their homework before making you that loan. Unfortunately, the federal government has the law on its side. Now we'll have to work on a compromise . . . try to salvage what we can," he concluded with a thin smile.

The portly attorney looked at the Philadelphia lawyer. "Mister Cohen, my clients were unaware of the law, but they do own an important part of this asset which the government needs to purchase."

He leaned forward. "Where the opening to the property is located adds great value to the discovery. It is without question the original entrance, found perhaps thousands of years ago by Indians that lived in the area and those artifacts they've left behind are mostly in those first rooms owned by the Floyd Richards group. It is part and parcel of the whole cave system."

A good argument, Cohen thought. *I'll have to short circuit that position.* "The public will accept our version, if necessary," Cohen retorted with a bored countenance. "They'll be told that a cantankerous land owner didn't want to be part of this project. So we had to improvise with our own entrance to the caverns."

Richards stood up. He leaned over the table and pushed a straightened forefinger in Cohen's face. "This is my discovery, a project which I wanted to share with the public. It's not yours and not the Federal Government's. Or are you going to distort that truth also?"

Cason had never seen Richards so upset. He pulled him aside. "Listen, Floyd . . . that's just what Cohen wants. He wants to get anyone and everyone upset. Play it tighter to the vest, partner."

Their portly attorney sat back casually, trying to defuse the tension as he spoke. "It would be like finding the bejeweled mummy from some ancient society in a sarcophagus, half on your property and half on my clients. To cut the mummy in half would ruin its intrinsic value. Neither half would be worth much."

The meeting continued with sparing back and forth and discussions about who should get what and for how much. Finally, Cohen said, "The Park Service is willing to buy that particular twenty acres of your property that encompasses the cave opening at the same price that you paid per acre plus the cost of construction to date."

"But my client had to buy one hundred acres or the timber company would not have sold any of it," Richards' attorney responded. "Now you only offer to buy the choicest piece of the land for the same price per acre as all the rest. That's not going to happen. It is entirely unfair to my clients."

"What Mister Richards was required to buy is not our concern," Cohen argued. "We don't choose to do so. We don't need it. And you can't continue to merchandise your portion of this discovery if you only own a small percentage of the caverns underground. That would not appeal to the public," Cohen responded.

Richards' attorney sat up in his chair as his wild porcupine eyebrows moved spasmodically up and down.

"If you want the historic opening into the cave along with the rooms and tunnels that lead under the highway, then the Federal Government must purchase the whole one hundred acres based on its new commercial value as established by a real estate appraiser, plus the cost of improvements to date, Mister Cohen."

"Improvements, yes." Cohen read from his legal pad. "We will reimburse your clients for the cost of the road into the caves; the parking lot; building costs to date; the steps and the lighting system down into the caverns and other additions made inside the cave for the convenience of the public. We would need all of that anyway."

Cohen stared at Richards and the bank's attorney with a thoughtful look. "Regarding the property and the commercial value of the cave opening, the Park Service would be willing to pay you one hundred and fifty thousand dollars for everything. That is all it's worth to us."

"But my clients have loans on the total property, Mister Cohen. What you're offering will not cover their obligation to the bank. The National Park Service is going to realize a windfall on a minor investment.

The portly attorney asked Cohen if they could call it a finders fee, a commission, however you might wish to define it, Mister Cohen, but pay the man enough to cover his debts. This marvelous discovery of his will be a valuable addition to Mammoth National Park that thousands of visitors will enjoy for years to come."

Jay Cohen stood up and gathered up his papers. "I've made a most reasonable offer. The Park Service has limited funds for expansion and this is the best I can promise. If you change your minds, let us know."

With that remark, Cohen picked up his soft, suede briefcase from the table and left the conference room with his associate. The meeting was over.

Richards slowly looked over at Cason and his attorney without any expression on his face and began shaking his head from side to side.

Cason said, "That leaves you short, Floyd. You would still owe the bank one hundred thousand dollars."

"But the venture capital group has a vested interest in this project." He stared at the bank's attorney. "They own thirty percent of the partnership, so the bank has to absorb their percentage of the loan themselves. Isn't that right?"

"I'm sorry to tell you this, Floyd. But the bank is not obligated if for some reason you never had clear title to the entire cave system. It's in the small print on the back of the loan agreement. Standard in most all of these venture capital loans, I'm afraid."

The portly attorney stood up pursing his meaty lips. "Well, we haven't agreed to these terms yet, gentlemen." He turned his head to glance at both Richards and Cason. "Let me work on that Philadelphia lawyer a little bit more and see if we can't get them to be more reasonable. Just might get enough to pay the bank in full." He smiled at the two and left the room also.

Richards slumped one elbow on the table and held his head. "It just gets worse and worse, Eddie. Every time I turn around, something else goes wrong. Either with this new venture or my family."

Cason spoke up in his usual positive voice and tried to console his friend about both problems. But it didn't help.

"Hey." Cason said, getting up and patting his friend on the shoulder. "The ship hasn't sunk yet. Let's see what the attorney can arrange. We're all in this thing together."

Chapter 22

The following week of classes at the University of Kentucky would end one day early for spring break. Thursday, March 25th, was the last day of classes for ten days until April 5th, a week from the following Monday.

Then like flocks of birds from across the country, the great migration would occur as they crowd the beaches along the Gulf of Mexico from Louisiana, where they were close to New Orleans for late evening forays, on east to Mississippi and Alabama where both states have beachfront on the water.

Like a plague of locusts, these fun loving youngsters pour across the panhandle of Florida, all the way down to Fort Lauderdale and back up the Atlantic coastline to Daytona Beach to meet and mingle with other college students all intent on drinking beer and judging wet tee shirt contests.

This gives the teachers and professors time to catch up on everything they had stacked up on their desks, plus plan the curriculum for the final semester.

Since the majority of the cave system was under government property and his venture was in a shambles, Richards was caught up in the effort to be just as good a geology professor as his department head expected of him. He wouldn't have his children until next Saturday and Sunday, the first weekend in April, so he stayed busy at the science department.

His phone rang at his office desk in the Geology department. It was the portly lawyer from Bank One who had represented them at the meeting.

"I've been on the phone with Jay Cohen for almost an hour exploring how and why his client should pay off your entire loan. But he was adamant in his position that the National Park Service can't pay any more than what he offered at the meeting.

"He repeated the fact that they could open an entrance to the cave system on government property, if necessary, and felt that you were being difficult."

"I'm being difficult?" Richards exclaimed. "They're going to make money every year when they open those caverns and advertise it in conjunction with Mammoth Caves."

Richards was exasperated. "They're trying to steal my discovery and make money with it."

He told the attorney that he had a promising professorship here at the university and that Bank One screwed this up too. They should have known better about the property ownership. They need to reduce the interest rate by half so he could afford to pay it each quarter. The principle balance would have to wait.

Richards banged his fist on the desk. "And you can tell them they're not much of a partner either. They're not going to lose anything. So they damn sure have to work with me."

"All right, Floyd. I'll try to sell that. I agree that their research, their due diligence about the ownership of the caverns, was totaling lacking. They were eager to make a buck also and I've already told them that as their attorney. I'll get back to you."

An associate at the firm of Cohen, Belzberg, Brooks and Murray buzzed the intercom in Jay Cohen's office. He reached for the telephone as he continued to study the brief that was in front of him on his big walnut executive desk that was polished faithfully once a week.

Large legal firms have a manager who handles everything in or out of the office: The office lease; the purchase or lease of all office equipment from pencil sharpeners to huge copy machines; facsimile phones; desks and chairs; books and file cabinets for the law library; lunchroom equipment; initial interviews with new secretaries and receptionists, and a myriad of other duties.

This allows the members of the firm, the practicing attorneys to have total freedom to do what they do best, practice the art of law.

Cohen punched the intercom button and said, "Yes."

"I've accumulated most of the information I believe you'll need for the Kentucky problem, Mister Cohen. Shall I bring it to your office?"

"Yes. Right away." Cohen hung up the phone.

Chapter 23

"You should take Robby and Karen for Easter weekend, Floyd. Kal is standing right here and encouraged me to call you regarding the children. You can take them to services at our church."

Richards hesitated a moment. *She's warning me that he's there and might be listening on the extension.* "That would be good," he said. "There's an Easter program at the First Methodist Church that includes not only Sunday school for them, but an Easter egg hunt on church property afterwards."

"That sounds wonderful for Robby and Karen. You can pick up the kids Friday afternoon. I'll have extra clothes packed . . . talk to you later," she concluded.

The rest of that week passed quickly for Richards with all the work he had to finish for the next semester. On Friday he arrived at the Barakat house on time and walked up to the house and used the brass knocker to announce his presence.

Doris opened the door. The children's suitcase was on the floor and both of them were ready to spend time with their dad. They rushed into his arms and gave him big hugs. Richards glanced up at Doris and his eyes narrowed.

"Your lip looks puffy, Doris. What happened to you?"

"Oh . . . clumsy me. I tripped over Robby's toy fire engine on the kitchen floor and fell."

Richards was looking over her shoulder. He knew Kal Barakat was just inside. Slight movements on the staircase made him glance up. The dentist was standing there watching and listening to everything.

Richards answered Doris but Barakat was the focus of his hard stare. He glared at him as he said. "If that ever gets worse, you'll need to see a doctor. I'll call the dental office Monday and talk to the other girls."

He turned and took little Karen's hand, grabbed their bag with his other hand and walked down to his truck with Robby right beside him.

Barakat knew what he meant. Richards could call down to his dental clinic and get some information if Doris looked worse. He knew the dentist could not afford to have one of his dental assistants call the police on him, or call Richards for that matter.

"So! I have been warned by your ex-husband," Barakat said as he stepped down the stairs to the first floor. "I'm sure he's already talked to other employees at my office. You've probably arranged for them to spy for you."

He stepped over to Doris as she backed up into the living room. "That's not true, Kal. I haven't said a word to the office girls. I promised if you didn't touch my children, I'd do what you wanted."

Then Doris stood her ground. She stared at him with determination. She spoke softly, which made her statement even more defiant.

"But if you ever do hurt them again, I'll call Floyd to come get them and tell him why. Because then nothing you could do to me after that would make any difference as long as my children were safe, and away from you."

Barakat had never seen her act so bravely. *She has taken a position. A final stand against me,* he realized.

"Well. I won't teach you a lesson again today, Doris. Your ex-husband might learn about it if you got marked up on the outside."

He grabbed her around the waist and pulled her against him. "The children are gone now, Doris. We should take advantage of that and have some fun right here in the living room."

Barakat kissed her and Doris tried to show some interest so he wouldn't hit her in the stomach again. They kissed standing up for a few seconds; then he turned her around; pushed her down and over the back of the big living room couch.

"You stay right there, dear." He spoke with a syrupy sweetness. "I'll be right back." Doris did as ordered, still afraid of him, but willing to endure the sex if he stayed away from Robby and Karen.

The dentist went upstairs. He undressed completely and whistled a tune as he walked back down to the living room. He pushed up Doris' skirt and pulled her pants down to her ankles.

"No one will see any marks on the outside of your body, Doris. And if you relax this will be very enjoyable for you too."

135

He squeezed the tube of KY jelly and smeared it all over his erection. Barakat was excited by the very act of this quasi-rape of his wife. He mounted his wife and screwed her slowly. He wanted to enjoy all of the tingling sensations.

"You're being so gentle, Kal." Doris said, still trying to be a good wife.

"Then this should feel good too, darling," he added with exaggerated kindness.

Since she was bent over the couch, her ass was spread enough for him to just hold his penis with one hand and push down hard on her back with the other. Barakat pressed his erection against her anus and then shoved it in hard before she could relax or react.

"Aaah!" She screamed. "Oh that hurts. No, Kal . . . please stop. Please don't do this," She cried.

"Shut-up and enjoy, dear. The girls in the office won't see where this hurts!"

He continued to sodomize his wife. Doris had never experienced anything like this before. He was pumping it in and out quickly to maximize her suffering before her sphincter muscles could relax, expand, and lubricate her internally.

She groaned. Tears came to her eyes and she gritted her teeth, moaning through the pain.

The visual scene excited him as much as the act itself. He wanted to come quickly. The further swelling of his erection during orgasm would increase her agony.

The kinky sex act was pure ecstasy for Barakat and pure hell for Doris. She held her head with both hands and withstood the unwelcome intrusion into her rectum. It was over soon as the dentist released his ejaculate in waves of sexual relief.

Chapter 24

"Bath time, little ones. You know after school and play you have to get cleaned up." Their father gathered them both into his big arms as he whispered conspiratorially. "Then after you get dressed we'll go out and eat some pizza and then we're off to a Disney movie. The new one they just released."

Of course Richards knew it was a re-release, a movie that Disney made years ago and brought back to the screen every so often for a whole new crop of kids.

"Yes, yes," Karen said, and "okay, okay," Robby chimed in. Since they were now seven and five years old, their Dad told them it would be better if they each bathed in a different bathroom.

"But you'll both sleep in your old bedroom in the bunk beds just like you used to do," Richards said clapping his hands which the kids knew meant get going, and they squealed with delight to be home with their loving father.

Richards went into each bathroom to visually inspect each child closely, but not so that it would alarm them. It also gave him a chance to separate them so they might talk more freely to him about what was going on with Barakat.

He didn't learn much from Karen, who told him that she had to stand in the "punishment corner," every week for some reason, but she didn't cry when she mentioned it.

In Robby's case it was different. Richards had noticed the bruised eye right away. It was dark around the eye like he had taken a punch.

"How did you bang your eye up, Robby?" Richards asked.

His son didn't look up at him as he usually did when his Dad asked him a question. Richards had taught him to always look into the eyes of the person when spoken to and when giving an answer. He told Robby it gave a good solid impression. Looking down or off in the distance made people think you were weak and lacked strength of character.

"At school," Robby answered staring straight ahead.

"How did it happen at school?" His Dad came back.

Still looking away from his Dad, he answered. "I walked into the door. I just didn't see it."

"Well. It doesn't look so bad now. Makes you look like a real boxer, Robby."

Then Robby looked at his Dad with a smile. He knew the scary questions were over and he could act normal. Before, he had to think exactly how to answer his Dad. Just like Barakat had him repeat it over and over until he could do it easily, looking away to concentrate better, the doctor had told him.

"Remember, Robby," Barakat had told him. "Your mommy is going to stay here with me. And you don't want her to get hurt, do you. So you must keep our secret, about what happened to your eye."

Richards made a mental note to check with Robby's teacher on Monday. He would find out if his son was hurt in class or not. He was sure he was not. Richards was sitting on the big chair in the living room of the duplex thinking about his family.

He knew if he went to the police that they would not do anything without proof of abuse. They would just chalk it up as a complainer trying to make trouble in his ex-wife's new marriage. And he couldn't confront Barakat about it or hit him. The dentist would have him arrested for assault and then beat Doris even more, if that's what he was doing.

While the kids were getting dressed, he thought about who he could talk to about this heart wrenching dilemma. No one at UK. He didn't want to make any waves at work and risk a report being put in his file. His neighbors couldn't help. They would be sincere in their concern, but somebody would gossip and then it would be common knowledge.

He thought about it some more. He still couldn't think of someone he could trust who was unconnected to work, family, neighbors, or relatives. Then the phone rang. He picked up the receiver and before he could speak, he heard a "Hey, Floyd. This is your partner calling."

It was the effervescent Eddie Cason calling who always said something before you could say hello. It was his calling card, so to speak. "Always get in the first word," Cason told him. "That's the art of being a salesman."

Richards' problem was solved. Eddie Cason would be perfect. He was not married, so he couldn't say something to his wife. He was basically distant from all others, connected only in their failing venture, and after Richards saved Eddie's life, he never forgot how sincere Cason was laying in that hospital bed when he said to Richards.

"I owe you one, big time, Floyd. I hope I can return the favor in some small way."

Then he beamed that Cason smile that made believers of so many people. "Of course, I hope I don't ever need to save your life. Just help you out somehow." They both laughed.

Richards tried to remember the last time he'd had a good laugh. He couldn't. He asked Cason to meet him for dinner Sunday night after he took his children back to Doris.

Chapter 25

For Floyd Richards, the first week of the final semester after spring break went well until Friday. The phone message had been left on his office recorder. It was from the portly attorney that represented Bank One and Richards at the meeting with Jay Cohen.

"Cohen says he can sweeten the pot with another twenty-five thousand dollars, Floyd, but that would be the final offer," the attorney reported.

"I won't accept that. They stand to make a lot of money over who knows how much time. I'm not asking for a profit you know. I just want my own government to make me whole on the deal. They can afford it and I'm entitled to a discovery fee or commission for all the searching that I did to discover those caves."

"I'll relay that message, Floyd. I'll let you know."

Richards replaced the receiver on the charger. *They should be paying me a profit,* he thought. *Their best offer doesn't even cover my costs. The heck with them. I'll tough it out. Maybe they'll look at the cost of digging a new entrance and realize it would be cheaper to pay me off and have the historical and original entrance.*

Another week went by and the news got much worse. Dr. Foster, the head of the science department, called Richards for a meeting in his office.

"Hello, Floyd. Come on in and sit down."

Richards didn't like the tone of Dr. Foster's voice. It was overly warm. He had known Foster for the past five years and had spoken with him on any number of occasions.

Richards sat down. Dr. Foster was already sitting in his swivel chair with both thumbs hung in his trademark wide suspenders. First he talked about the weather, then UK's championship basketball team and then started on some other trivia.

Richards knew Foster was having trouble getting to the point. He looked very uncomfortable. So Richards broke the barrier. "Why did you want to see me, Doctor Foster?"

"I guess I've been babbling, Floyd. But I don't like what I have to tell you." Foster turned his head and glanced outside through the window. The department head couldn't look at Richards and say it. "We've got no choice but to let you go, Floyd. You know how it is."

Foster turned back. "We've just had a budget review and the administration wants every department head to make some reductions. Personnel cut backs and all that."

Richards didn't get excited, come to his feet, or say anything for fifteen seconds. He took his normal calm approach to every problem and chewed on what he had just heard. He appraised Foster. The elderly gentleman was sixty-nine years old, distinguished looking with a full head of gray hair, and would retire when he reached seventy. He had always been a straight shooter and didn't have a devious bone in his whole body.

The lack of response from Richards was unnerving to Foster. He was glancing away again, scratching his head with his right hand, and avoiding Richards' gaze. *Clearly the man was majorly embarrassed by this situation.*

"Is that the total reason for my dismissal, Doctor Foster? Just six months ago you gave me accolades at a department meeting. In front of everyone in the science department you said that I had been an exemplary young associate professor and would no doubt receive my doctorate before you retired next year. What has happened since then?"

Dr. Foster got to his feet, walked to his office window, and stared out of it for several seconds. He released a deep breath with a sigh. Then he turned back to face Richards and this time stared right into his eyes.

"Nothing to change my opinion about you, Floyd." He returned to his desk and chair, waving his arm at Richards as he sat down. "It was true what I said about cut backs," he grimaced. "But then the administration always asks for that."

Foster put both hands on his desk and leaned toward Richards. "Damn it, Floyd. What I'm going to tell you now is off the record. You didn't hear it from me . . . understand? My retirement might be jeopardized if . . . well, you know how bad things can get when big money enters into the picture."

He continued to hold Richards' eyes. "The fact is that pressure has been brought to bear to get you off the payroll. You're a hot potato, Floyd! It's that damn cave business you got into."

He had gotten it off his chest. Foster relaxed and leaned back in his swivel chair. Now he would help all that he could under the circumstances.

"The President of UK himself told me confidentially that all of our federal funding has been threatened. He said that the powers that control our money went right down the list."

Foster stuck out his right forefinger and tapped it with his left forefinger. "First, UKAT. UK's Assistive Technology Project."

Foster's right middle finger joined his forefinger and both were struck by his left forefinger. "Second, The Graduate Fellowship listings. As you know, Floyd, these grants are so important to our students."

He tapped three fingers when he told Richards that The National Science Foundation could pull its support for the undergraduate education programs, research and awards, etcetera.

Then fourthly, as he tapped four fingers, he emphasized that UK could lose COS, the Community of Science program that provides UK with access to services on the Internet that locate potential collaborators, find funding, and conduct research with other leading universities, government agencies and research and development organizations. Dr. Foster slapped both knees with open palms. "I could go on, Floyd, but I'm sure you get the picture. What it boils down to is when we let you go, all of the funding programs I mentioned stay in place."

145

He looked at Richards sympathetically. "I'm really sorry, Floyd. This is not my doing or UK's president. Someone big has it in for you and they're pulling all the strings."

He rocked back in his chair, relieved to have told Richards the truth.

Richards leaned forward. He put his elbows on his knees, clasped his hands together, and stared out of the window at the other buildings and trees around the campus and contemplated what he had just heard.

"Well I know who is doing the pulling, Doctor Foster. But I better keep that to myself. The less you know then chances are you won't get dragged into this mess either."

Dr. Foster stood up and stuck out his hand. "You've been a darn good professor of geology, Floyd. You can be proud of your record and I'll give you that recommendation in writing if you need it. You shouldn't give up on your career. There are other colleges and universities that need good people like you."

Richards shook the offered hand and thanked Dr. Foster for his forthrightness. "When will my termination be effective?"

"Two weeks was the requirement, Floyd. Enough time to turn over the classes to someone I'll have to choose. You have anyone that you would suggest?"

"Not really. I think you need to juggle your professors as best you can. Thanks for asking though."

Richards turned and left Foster's office. As soon as he closed the door behind him he just stood there staring blankly at the wall across the hallway.

The weak smile he had given Dr. Foster left his face. Dejection and rejection weighed heavily on his mind as his face drained of color. He looked as white as a new, linen bed sheet.

Chapter 26

Richards spent the weekend down in the caverns that he had discovered. He felt at peace there with the knowledge that he had made a major find and he had been credited by the television and the newspapers as having added to the history of the Kentucky cave systems.

He felt pleased with that and enjoyed a sense of accomplishment as he sat in the darkness some two hundred feet below the surface. The light from his lamp made shadows that moved across the cavern walls.

He thanked God for what he still did have; his good sense, his physical health and his love for his family and friends. He said a prayer and then felt that he had unloaded his fears and concerns and that God would help him find a way. In five more minutes he would be sound asleep in the warmth of his sleeping bag and his strong faith. *Life would be all right. He would get through this, too.* Those were his last thoughts as he drifted off.

Monday morning he was back at his office going over the transfer of his duties to another young associate professor. He had made the announcement to some of his students in class and he would talk to the others as the week progressed.

"I'll be looking to take a similar position at another college," he told them, which was as close to the truth as he dared to get. He had thought about taking the whole mess to the newspapers and let them disclose the ugliness of the federal government at work. But he figured most people already new that and it might hurt his chances of a professorship somewhere else. *The federal government has a long arm. And I'm not going to give them a second chance to hurt me somewhere else.*

Later that day he met with the portly attorney in his office in downtown Lexington. The receptionist had brought him a cup of coffee and was asking if there was something else she could get him. Richards was so removed from the dating scene that he did not realize by the way she asked it that he was getting hit on.

He smiled thinly. "No thanks." She left the room as he sat there deep in thought. In a few minutes, the attorney appeared and sat down behind his desk.

"Well, I've heard back from Cohen. He says the extra twenty five thousand dollars that he offered is still the limit. He sent me a contract for you to sign if you're interested."

The attorney pushed the contract over to Richards. "Bank One has agreed to it. A bank officer has signed it where required for their venture capital portion."

"Just like that," Richards barked. He was mad now. "They didn't even offer to talk to me about it. Just sign off without any discussion and leave me with a debt of seventy five thousand dollars that I still owe them."

He sat back from the attorney's desk refusing to pick up or look at the contract. "I think that stinks," Richards said. "That shows a lack of respect for me. We went into this thing together . . . I thought."

The attorney eased back in his chair. He frowned as he glanced at Richards. His huge eyebrows wiggled as he quietly explained. "The bank signed off because the alternative is worse. Cohen put a time clause in the contract. If it isn't signed and returned in ten working days, he'll withdraw the entire offer. The bank wants to recover what they can get now."

Richards didn't respond. He just sat there staring into space.

"They authorized me to give you very good terms on the balance. Interest at the prime rate. That's the rate charged to only the biggest customers . . . and ten years on the pay-out. That's seventy five hundred dollars each year plus the interest, Floyd."

"That would be tough even if I were still employed at the college. I've got a car payment; rent payment at the duplex, and child support to my ex-wife. But thanks to Cohen, I was fired last week. Two more weeks of pay and that's it. How does the bank expect me to even pay that amount?"

"Well that does change the picture, Floyd. I didn't know that Cohen got to you too."

"What does that mean?"

"Bank One has had the Mammoth Cave account for many years, Floyd. They run a lot of money through the bank in the course of a year and the bank was informed that they would lose that account if they didn't sign the agreement drawn up by Jay Cohen."

Richards leaned back in his chair and took a deep breath. "Let me see that contract."

He read it over and saw that they were buying all the rights of ownership to the cave system, but they were not going to use the name, *Floyd Richards' Caverns.*

"Why aren't they going to use my name? I'm selling the rights to it! They own the name. It would be nice to have some recognition. After all, I discovered the caves, didn't I?"

Richards was finally starting to break down. He couldn't handle the cruelty shown by this man Cohen, the Philadelphia attorney. He turned away from the bank's attorney as his eyes welled up with tears. He thought, *this was the final insult.*

"Cohen was concerned that you might file a lawsuit sometime in the future if they used your name. Constantly using *Floyd Richards' Caverns* in advertising might establish some precedent years down the road.

"He emphasized that laws do change with time and handling the problem this way eliminates any possible conflict. He didn't want to get the public interested in this new cave system and then have to change the name at a later date."

"That's a lot of bull," Richards came back. "I don't have the money to even think of taking on the government."

"Well, he is one smart, tough, lawyer. I'll give him that, Floyd."

"But he doesn't have a touch of humanity in his soul. Between you and me, it's just plain dark down there in the center of his heart," Richards said sadly to the bank's attorney. "He's forcing me to sell, because I have nothing left."

"Well for some reason, he said if you signed off today, he'd offer you a job searching the cave system you found. He thought you would be interested in that." The attorney glanced at Richards to see his reaction.

"Why would he do me any favors? He's done everything he could to ruin me."

"They need to know how big the system is, where it goes, how deep, how long, and if some of the smaller tunnels lead to some even more spectacular rooms."

Richards thought about it for a while as he paced around the attorney's office. It would be getting paid to explore further the cave he had discovered. That couldn't be all bad. He would just have to swallow his pride. He needed the job. It would probably take a year or more to find everything. Maybe longer.

"I don't go caving without at least one partner. It's a safety precaution."

"He knows that. He said you could pick anyone you wanted."

"I'll take Eddie Cason. He's in need of a job too and he's becoming a pretty good caver. He seems to have an instinct for it."

"That's fine, Floyd. The two of you have the jobs at an annual salary of twenty thousand dollars plus expenses. Now you'll need to sign off and we can get this business over with for all our sakes."

Richards reluctantly signed and left. The coffee had gone through him and he went to the men's room outside the office near the elevators. There were several men using the urinals so he went in a booth and closed the door to relieve himself.

He was just finishing when he heard the portly attorney's voice. Obviously he wasn't talking to him. The man didn't know he was inside the enclosed toilet.

"I didn't have the heart to repeat what Cohen really said. I couldn't believe it myself."

"What was his comment?" another voice asked.

"It was when he told me to offer Richards a job. He thought that might loosen him up. Make him sign the contract. Not that Richards had any choice after what Cohen did to him. But this is what he said. 'I'll throw him a bone. Every dog needs to eat.'"

Chapter 27

Both Floyd Richards and Eddie Cason were now employees of the National Park Service. They weren't issued uniforms like the other entire park employees wore since they would not be in contact with the public.

They could be getting wet or muddy from exploring the new cave system and until the exploration was more complete and made visitor easy with cleared pathways, lights and possibly rest rooms, park management would not allow the public inside.

Also, the park service wanted to advertise the most interesting features found throughout the caverns such as stalactites; stalagmites; crystalline flowers; underground streams and pools; the rock wall drawings, and artifacts left by American Indians over the last several hundred years or longer.

The two explorers would spend a minimum of three days every week underground. Anymore time down there would be too mentally depressing in the cold darkness of the unknown where a misstep might mean injury or death.

The other two days in the week Richards and Cason would complete detailed reports to include maps and descriptions about the length, width, and height of each room or tunnel, plus what features existed in each one with photographs attached for illustration.

Also the depth of each section of the cave below the earth's surface and the compass direction as the explorers moved from one room through a tunnel or crevice to the next had to be recorded. Eventually, a three dimensional color diorama would be part of the permanent history of this discovery on display for the public.

Every week for a month Richards and Cason would drive down from Lexington to Elizabethtown on the Blue Grass Parkway and exit onto state road thirty-one west that went through Radcliff to Fort Knox, home to the Sixth Armored Division and the Fifteenth Artillery Regiment plus other smaller army units.

Visitors that come there enjoy a walk through history in the General George S. Patton Museum. Patton with his armored tank division was the most feared general that Nazi Germany faced during World War II. Both United States Army and German tanks plus other heavy military equipment are on display.

By the end of June, the second month of exploration, the two cavers had finished mapping some ten miles of the cave system. All of it had been towards the northwest, most of it literally going under land on which the army base was situated.

There were some vertical chutes down to lower levels that included a waterfall into a lake, some small ponds and a stream, but Richards and Cason had marked those passages with white chalk to explore further at a later date.

It was on the way out of the caverns after two days of hard work that Richards walked around a large boulder to relieve himself in a soft plastic container. No food or human waste was allowed to be left in the cave system. While standing there he looked around. His head lamp revealed a four foot by thirty inch high crevice directly behind the huge boulder.

"Hey, Eddie. Come over here. See that little hidden crevice there? We've walked past this boulder every time we came in or out and never saw it."

"Could that be anything? I mean it looks like a dead end," Cason answered.

"Moving ground water does strange things, Eddie. That could open up into another big discovery or it could just go no where."

Richards made a note of it on his recorder. The two friends packed their overnight gear and cooking utensils in the back of Richards' Ford truck and headed home to Lexington to shower off the cave mud and eat a good meal.

"We need to finish exploring every opening we can find on level one before we tackle those vertical chutes down to level two," Richards told Cason on the drive back.

"But we ought to take a look in that crevice," Cason responded.

"Oh yes. We'll find out next week if there's anything there."

Over the next two days they prepared more detailed weekly reports to submit to the Mammoth Cave National Park Superintendent.

Chapter 28

On Monday the two friends worked their way back into the cave a half mile to the crevice that Richards had found the week before. The light from their head lamps revealed the chalk symbol they had marked on the front of the rock.

Cason said, "The opening's at ground level behind this big boulder."

"Easy to miss in the dark," Richards responded.

"It still doesn't look like much," Cason added.

"Big enough for us to squeeze through, Eddie," Richards said as he recorded the exact measurements Cason had just given him.

Richards stripped off his back pack, secured rope around his butt, and wiggled through the opening. He braced himself with his feet against the rock wall and peered down, his head lamp revealing a narrow vertical drop.

"I'm going down, Eddie."

When Richards' feet hit bottom he yelled for Cason to join him. Together again, they found themselves in a vertical tunnel twenty-five feet high, but only forty inches wide. Sometimes they had to turn sideways to get through and it measured sixty-five feet in length.

"Look at this!" Richards exclaimed as they entered a large room.

"Wow," was all Eddie could say as their headlamps continued to play around the big cavern.

"Looks to be about forty feet wide and about that high, but I can't see the end of it," Richards estimated.

They continued exploring and finding more rooms as this section of the cave led them into more new territory. "We'll just go a little further today," Richards said after a sandwich, power bar and water lunch.

"We didn't start in the same direction as everything else we've explored," Eddie said checking his compass. "Since we dropped down from that crevice, we've been swinging around to the northeast. Now it's almost due east."

They continued following what nature had washed out over thousands of years and it led them up instead of straight ahead or further down. After another thirty minutes they were in a fair sized room, walking the perimeter of the cave, chalk marking their progress and recording their findings.

Suddenly Cason exclaimed, "What the heck is this?"

His head lamp revealed an ebony colored lump of rock about the size of a football. Richards picked it up and rubbed his hand over its black shiny surface.

"That's what I thought it was," Richards said. He turned his hand over and showed Eddie the black smudges on his fingers.

"When I got it close to my light, I knew darn well it wasn't limestone, sandstone, or any stone. Look at that, Eddie. It's a hunk of coal!"

"Where the hell did that come from?" Cason exclaimed. "I mean . . . nobody in their right mind would bring coal this far in for a fire."

Their lights reflected off the cave floor and they found a few more pieces of coal. Richards scratched his head and they looked at each other dumbfounded.

"Let's check the walls in here again, Eddie. There must be a coal seam in here where the ground water cut through. We just haven't seen it because it's so black."

Carefully they checked the twenty-five foot high walls around the room and found nothing but limestone rock. Richards went back to where they picked up the lumps of coal.

Nearby there was a large boulder the size of a small truck. He climbed to the top and glanced up, allowing his head to slowly move along the cavern's ceiling. The light played over the rock face. Then he saw it. An opening at the top.

"There's a ledge up high," he exclaimed. "It's about eight feet wide and five feet high. It goes back in a ways."

"Can you get to it?" Cason asked.

"Not from here. I'll have to climb up that vertical face from the floor with some mountain gear."

Richards banged an Alpine piton into a small crack in the limestone wall, snapped on a carabineer, slid the rope through it and repeated the process as he worked his way up to the ledge. Cason was hanging onto the end of the rope in case Richards slipped so he wouldn't drop but a few feet before the highest piton held him against the rock face.

He watched Richards slip over the ledge and disappear. In a few minutes, Richards reappeared at the edge.

"Tie the back packs on the end of this rope and I'll pull them up. You come up next. You won't believe what's up here, Eddie!"

The two friends worked their way back into the ledge for some twenty feet. The coal rubble got thicker as they walked.

"There's coal all over the place up here," Cason exclaimed.

The ledge ended at a rock face, but their lights revealed a pile of coal chunks in different sizes that rose up to another small opening. The limestone rock all around was a muddy gray brown, but the opening was rimmed in solid, jet black coal.

Richards pointed a powerful hand held torch into the hole. Twenty feet across it reflected off an entire wall of coal. He played the light up and down and found that the ceiling was about twelve feet high. Then his torch found something different on the ceiling.

"Look, Eddie! That's a twelve inch wood beam. It's part of the support system for a coal mine. I can't believe it."

"Are we goin' in?" Cason asked.

"Right now," Richards answered.

Chapter 29

Climbing up into the mine they entered a small room about thirty feet deep and twenty feet wide. They paced off the thirty feet and found themselves in a long shaft that ran perpendicular to their entrance room. They stopped and took their bearings playing their head lamps all around them. The light reflected off shiny black walls, ceilings, and floor.

"What's our compass reading, Eddie?"

"We went due south coming out of the entrance room." Cason turned facing a new position. "This tunnel runs east to the left and due west to the right."

Head lamps and torch played around this eerie mine to get some idea of the scope of their discovery. Richards reached into his memory about the mining industry.

Thoughtfully, he said, "Coal mines are laid out in a grid. We appear to be standing in the main shaft of the mine. That room directly opposite our entrance room will be the same size. Thirty deep by twenty wide. Then you'll have a solid wall of coal the same size between each excavated room. That gives the roof support plus the wood beams they put in as they cut the rooms of coal out."

"It's like an old timey ladder," Cason added. "To save wood they made it with one long center board and nailed cross pieces every eighteen inches so your feet stepped on each side of center as you went up."

"Lay that ladder flat on the ground and you've got this coal mine, Eddie."

Richards glanced up looking around the ceiling. He stepped directly underneath a wooden beam and put his torch on it.

"This appears to be old wood. Look closely at it, Eddie. This timber is hand hewn . . . you can tell by the saw cuts."

Quickly, Richards started to walk east looking down at the mine floor, the light playing back and forth to each side, searching for something. He only had to walk ten feet when he found it.

"Look here . . . iron rails. Built close together too. That's for a narrow gauge car. They used them in all the old mines. Coal, gold, or any ore," Richards explained.

Richards' mind was in high gear. He was fascinated by this new discovery. He paused and glanced at Cason with a puzzled look.

"What's your altimeter read?"

Cason pulled it out of his coat pocket and placed it on the mine floor. He used his head lamp to light up the face of it. "I'll be damned." He had a surprised look on his face. "We're only thirty-three feet under ground."

"I thought so," Richards replied. "This has to be an old slope mine, Eddie. Just one level with horizontal shafts. It had to come down from the surface somewhere."

"How the hell do you know so much about coal mines?"

"I was born in Kentucky. A big coal state. I've been in a few of them over the years."

They agreed to split up. Richards went east and Cason west. Each would blow a whistle carried around their neck every five minutes to stay in touch.

"Set your watch," Richards said. "I've got ten minutes after four. I want to hear from you at four fifteen."

Richards told Cason that when he came to a dead end to give him three long toots. He would do the same and then measure the number of paces back to the start point. They left their packs on the mine floor with a little kerosene lantern lit up as a reference point.

They both turned and stepped off in opposite directions. Each of them saw the same repetitive method used to dig the mine. Solid coal walls for twenty feet and then a mined out room twenty feet wide and thirty feet deep. It was exactly the same on each side of the main shaft.

They signaled each other as agreed after they moved away from their start point. It was easy going between the iron tracks and Richards covered one hundred yards in a few minutes when he came to a dead end. He could see that it was still a solid wall of black, shiny, bituminous coal.

This time he sounded his whistle three times but Cason only responded with two. He hadn't yet found

164

the west end of the main shaft. Richards measured the distance back and just as he arrived at the glowing kerosene lamp, he heard three sharp whistles echo through the mine. Cason had finally found the west end.

Richards was munching on a ham and cheese sandwich and drinking Gatorade when Cason got back. "That looks good . . . I'm starving."

Cason brewed up a pot of hot coffee and they ate supper and talked. "It was one hundred and seventy-five yards to my end, Floyd. And it looked like rubble from a cave in. There was some coal in the pile, but mostly it was rock and dirt."

"Humph," Richards sounded. Then he asked. "Did you notice anything else?"

Cason smiled the smile that warmed his whole face. "You're going to think I'm nuts . . . but I swear I heard a humming sound overhead. Like trucks running down a highway."

Richards grinned and chuckled a little. "You're not crazy. We walked under state road thirty one west some time after we entered the cave. You were heading right back that way. I'll bet you walked under that road again," Richards exclaimed.

Then he told Cason what he found at the east end. "Nothing . . . the miners must have just stopped there for whatever reason," Richards contemplated.

Cason said, "At my end the old iron tracks ran right into that pile of rock. And guess what else I found," he said smiling. "About thirty feet short of the end there was an old coal car sitting on the tracks."

He told Richards that it had one inch thick wooden slats on all four sides bound with iron straps. But the bottom of the car was solid iron and so were the wheels. Cason proudly turned his recorder on play.

"There's a metal plate on the side of the car engraved with, *Cambria Iron Company, eighteen fifty two.* He glanced up at Richards. "This is an old Civil War coal mine, Floyd! Can you believe it?"

Richards flashed his torch around. "I'll be darned. This mine is a whole lot older than I thought."

Then he looked at his friend. "Eddie. We're being paid to explore a cave system that I found . . . nothing else. But this coal mine is our new discovery. It's not going in any report."

The two friends were exhausted from the exercise and the excitement of their entire day. They untied their sleeping bags from their back packs and slept in the coal mine for the night.

Chapter 30

The two friends slid out of the opening from the coal mine and onto the ledge that led back to the cave. Cason repelled down to the cave floor first and glanced back up, expecting to see his friend right behind him. Richards was still standing up on the ledge.

"Eddie," he called out. "Put those pieces of coal we found down there in your back pack and I'll hide them up here."

"Cover our tracks." Cason added.

After Richards pulled the back pack up he moved back out of sight. When he appeared again he called down.

"Walk to the opposite side of the cave. You'll be able to see higher and further back into this ledge."

Cason pointed his helmet light and the powerful torch up at the ledge. "Nope . . . can't see a damn thing."

When Richards was satisfied that nothing of what they had discovered could be seen from the cave floor below, he started back down. He paused at each piton and pried it carefully out of the rock. He rubbed dirt in where he had left a mark that would indicate the wall had recently been climbed.

It took them over two hours to measure their way out of the cave. They wanted exact footage and compass readings at every turn so they could estimate from above the ground just where the coal mine might be situated.

They walked back into the woods and up a hill away from the nearby highway where they could get a good view back across the road.

"Best I can tell where we entered the mine from the cave is two thirds the way up that hill across thirty one west. Right over there," Richards said as he pointed in the direction he meant.

He took the Magnacraft 3-7x 20 rifle scope away from his right eye and handed it to Cason. "You take a look."

Cason adjusted the scope to his left eye and studied the field. "The main shaft runs east up the hill where you walked and due west right under this highway where I ended up."

"You know why that field is open and there aren't any trees or bushes on it?" Richards asked him.

Cason raised the scope higher to the crest of the hill. "Son-of-a-bitch," he yelled out. "That's the gold depository sitting on top. The cleared land all around the building is a defensive measure. It gives them a down hill open field of fire against an attack."

"That's right, Eddie, and I'll bet the coal mine runs right up near it or under it. And they can't shoot you underground."

Cason turned his head and glanced at Richards, expecting to see a smile. There wasn't any. Just a hard stare.

On the way back to Lexington the two friends talked more about their discovery and what they still had to do to explore it totally.

Richards had that same hard look on his face that Cason had not seen there until recent weeks. It was a new toughness in his attitude that he noticed underground when Richards remarked that the coal mine was not going to be written down in some report for the park service to ponder. It was their "find," he had emphasized.

Cason thought back as he watched his friend drive. *Floyd started to get that drawn expression after he was fired from the university, no doubt arranged by Jay Cohen. A move that forced him to sell. They took his discovery, didn't pay him enough for it, didn't keep his name on it, and didn't give him credit.*

"We've been kicked around a lot by the government, Floyd. You more than me. I can't blame you for being bitter . . . and that bank shit. They should have eaten some of that loss. They owned thirty percent of the deal."

"If there is any value to the coal mine, Eddie, I want the two of us to capitalize on it. This must remain our secret. The U S Mint might pay us a lot to find out they've got a cellar under their gold vault and they didn't even know about it."

Cason noticed that Floyd didn't laugh at that remark. A couple of months ago they both would have thought it was pretty funny. *There were lines in his face that hadn't been there before,* Cason noticed.

169

Richards said. "We've got some more work to do in that mine. I want to know everything about it. And, Eddie." He turned to look at Cason.

"No one is to know about this. Not your sister or anyone. Agreed?"

Cason grimaced. Even that made his blue eyes crinkle. "Mums the word, partner." And he meant it.

Chapter 31

On Friday, Richards drove over to Barakat's house to pick up the children. The divorce agreement called for him to have the kids every other weekend and he was eager to be with Karen and Robby. He wanted to see if they had changed any in the past two weeks and hear their young voices tell him about school and their special activities.

He parked on the street, walked up the flagstone path to the two story brick house in white trim and knocked on the front door. He hoped to see Doris and just speak to her for a few minutes if Barakat wasn't around. But he was sure that wouldn't happen.

The dentist just worked half a day on Friday and he was always home and he always answered the door when Richards was coming over. He would call for the children to go with their father. Richards never saw her.

He was about to knock on the door again when the door opened and Doris was standing there. Barakat was no where in sight and neither were his children, who were invariably anxious to be with their dad every time he came to pick them up.

They had learned over the past nine months, at a very young age, the difference between a man who had no feeling for them and treated them poorly and one who loved them dearly.

Karen and Robby looked forward to these too infrequent weekends. For them it was way too long a time for their dad to be out of their lives. They missed the constant attention that their dad paid to them. He would ask them questions about their little lives, what they were doing and how they felt about things. Now more than ever they sensed the warm tenderness in how he cared for them and they knew that dad's love was like a rock. It was always there for them. And there was no other father figure around for either one.

Both his daughter and his son reciprocated in turn. Dad got a whole lot of unexpected hugs and kisses. Even from Robby who was at the age that very young men don't kiss their dads. That was sissy stuff. But not for Robby. For him it was now required stuff. He needed to have the tender attachment of putting his arms around his dad's neck and giving him a kiss on the cheek. That was a touch of affection that he had taken for granted before, but now was very necessary and dearly missed.

And neither of them minded the feel of his sometimes scratchy cheek or chin on their tender faces. He wore a certain kind of shaving lotion that they enjoyed when they smelled it again. It was these little routine things that as children they didn't really notice or give much thought to before their lives were changed.

They had experienced his presence every day and although he had shown them the same affection before, it had been taken for granted. But that was just being kids and all little kids were self oriented. But now under difficult circumstances, maturity came faster, and it seemed that age was forced upon them.

"Hello, Doris. I didn't expect to see you!"

She had a flat dull look in her eyes that he noticed right away. All she said was, "Hi, Floyd."

There was no smile, no how are you? No spark in her voice or banter about the children anymore, like there had been when she first hooked up with Barakat.

"The children can't be with you anymore."

When she said it, she wouldn't look up into his eyes. She stared straight ahead at his neck and there was no emotion in her voice. A recorded message from a telephone marketer had more life in it. Richards just stared at her. He couldn't believe what he heard. And he didn't respond.

"Our divorce settlement, Floyd. It required you to make child support payments every month. Otherwise your child visitation privileges would be suspended."

Richards just continued to stare at her. He knew that this was Barakat's idea. Doris was not vindictive or cruel. He had called her at the dental clinic more than three weeks ago and one of the girls there that liked him put him through to his ex-wife.

He told her that the bank payments were tough on him and that until his pay from the park service kicked in, he would miss one or two support payments. He asked her if that would be all right and that he still wanted to see the children, for their sake too.

"I'll be able to pay it again soon and then catch up on the missed payments over the next nine months," he said.

"You know I wouldn't deny you or our children the fun of seeing each other. That would be fine with me, Floyd, but not with him."

Richards noticed that she kept her voice low and soft. *She must be scared to death of that man.* He couldn't conceive of how cruel the dentist really had become. Barakat was obsessed with owning Doris, and his mental condition was getting worse with the drugs that he self administered.

Richards hissed a response. "Didn't you talk to Kal about my problem with the bank? That I would start paying again soon and catch it all up?" His fists were two hard knots.

"I tried to, Floyd." She smiled faintly. "But he beat me," she whispered. "I couldn't take it."

"Step aside, Doris." Richards stormed into the house and yelled. "Come down here you sick bastard! I'm taking my children with me." His temper had finally boiled over.

Barakat leaned over the upstairs banister with a ringing cell phone in his hand. "The children and I are calling the police, Floyd."

Richards saw that he had Robby and Karen beside him with his arm around the girl. The sight of it took the steam out of him just as quickly.

"You're guilty of breaking and entering our house, Floyd. I know you don't want your children to watch you get arrested."

Richards didn't say a word. Frustration was stamped all over his face. His fists were still tightly balled up. He knew that Barakat had literally choreographed everything. He had anticipated how a father would react to being denied the opportunity to be with his own children.

He turned and walked out of their house and down the flagstone steps to his truck. Now he knew why Doris answered the door. He had never been a violent man, but if Barakat had made that statement to him he would have knocked him flat.

Instead Barakat had stayed upstairs, ready to hide behind Richards' children. He knew that Richards would not come up the stairs and attack him with his daughter and son watching. *The man was a bully and a total coward,* he thought.

Richards drove downtown to the First Methodist Church. It was open on Friday afternoon. There was no service but the front doors were unlocked for those who wished to come in and seek solace.

He settled in a pew at the back of the church and let his eyes wander around this House of God. Only two other parishioners were there up near the alter.

He glanced up at the beauty of the arched windows in stained glass. He just sat for a few minutes trying to quiet his mind. He knew that you couldn't pray with angry thoughts. God was only interested in hearing from someone who had love and peace in his or her heart and genuinely needed help.

After a while, Richards slowly pulled down the padded knee support and knelt, putting his hands together in supplication and bowing his head. He began in humble and earnest prayer to ask God's help in his time of distress.

He just couldn't handle everything that was coming down on him now. It was beyond his ability to cope with the pressure. He didn't expect guidance. He wouldn't hear any suggestions from above. But he knew he would find peace in the very act of prayer. He put his problems in the hands of the Lord and hoped for the best. For a devout Christian, this was always a calming experience.

Chapter 32

The two cavers had turned in their weekly exploration report to the National Park Service without any reference to the coal mine. On Monday they returned to the cave system to explore the caverns and the coal mine further.

They now had two projects to investigate that belonged to the federal government. The first one the government knew about and the second one they didn't.

Richards and Cason started with the mine which had been their stopping point during their last trip. This time they brought some electronic equipment with them that needed to be put in place away from any possible prying eyes. They both climbed from the cave floor up to the ledge into the coal mine and walked to the main shaft that ran east and west.

"We'll walk down hill to the rock slide that you found, Eddie. My guess is that's near the entrance to the mine."

They lit a kerosene lamp and placed it between the iron rails in the main shaft to indicate their entrance point and walked west, as their head lamps lit up a mine that had been dark for 135 years.

As they paced it off for a second time, light sparkled off greasy black, glistening walls of coal on either side and then the torch light would jump back into each mined out room they passed that went north on one side and south on the other.

A few minutes later light illuminated the coal car and then the rock slide twenty-five feet beyond it as they continued on to examine the collapsed area.

Richards said, "Look at the last few steps we've taken. It's uphill from where the car sits on the tracks. It must be at the bottom of the slope."

"The car would roll to the lowest point," Cason said. "We must be near the original entrance."

"I'm going back to the furthest point at the face of the coal mine where they stopped digging and call you," Richards said. Each caver had a Radio Shack portable phone in his pocket.

While Richards walked away, Cason set two, three pound iron bars on either side of the shaft where the mine had been closed. Again he could hear the feint humming from trucks running on the highway not far away.

A few minutes later Richards phoned. "The target is in the center of the mine shaft right between the tracks."

"OK, I'm turning it on now," Cason said. He snapped on the little Sonin Electronic Distance Measuring unit and waited. The device sends out narrow beams of sound waves that bounce off solid

178

objects and back again to the hand held receiver. Because it was a long distance, they used a receptor target which greatly enhanced the unit's capability.

To be positive, Cason repeated the process. Built-in custom electronics and a microprocessor convert the elapsed time into distance measurement.

"I've taken the reading twice and it's the same," Cason phoned to Richards. "Eight hundred seventy seven feet from here to the face of the mine at your end."

"Good. If you're finished, come on up here, Eddie. We'll work with the laser."

Cason had convinced Richards that the Laser Scanner should be rented using a fake name and cash. If they were asked for it, a post office box number could be given as an address. So Paul Stewart was created. A name that would become a person with a fleshed out identity, and that person would be given a presence in Lexington in the near future by both men.

They stood at the face of the coal mine where Union Army miners had stopped digging years ago. Slowly, the two explorers walked back along the shaft as they moved slightly down hill. They had covered only fifty feet when the scanner began to indicate a difference in temperature.

"Look at this, Floyd." Cason was carrying the hand-held detector as they continued to walk along the mine shaft. "The thing is starting to register now," Cason added.

"All right. Let's walk it back and forth to either side of the shaft and see what we get," Richards exclaimed.

179

Cason was holding an infrared thermometer used for accurately locating underground precious metals. Ore bodies were indicated by a high temperature as opposed to rock, or tunnels and caves that had air space and produced the lowest temperatures.

The device throws a laser beam that carries a fast traveling infrared heat sensible wave. The digital electronic scanner reads the temperature at any spot it hits, and can quickly report any difference in degrees, so one can pinpoint the exact spot.

Some objects reflect, as well as emit, infrared energy. Shiny or highly polished surfaces tend to reflect energy, whereas dull ones do not. Precious metals are the best heat conductors when located in the earth.

"Hold it upside down over your head, Eddie."

Cason started to laugh as he complied. "I know the inventor of this gadget never thought it would be used to look for gold over your head."

Another thirty feet along the shaft, Cason yelled out. "This damn thing is going crazy! We must be right under the storage vault itself."

"Let me have it, Eddie," Richards answered as he reached out. "I'll take a turn while we find the parameters of the target."

They walked over to one edge of the mine shaft. There the digital display was at its absolute highest intensity. Richards paced carefully to exactly define the length and width of the defined area. A large mass of gold bars will produce the biggest reflecting heat wave.

"This is it!" Richards yelled. "We're right underneath a giant stack of gold bars. Take that spray can and paint a line behind me while I walk it off again," Richards said.

Cason shook the paint can until he heard the mixing balls rattle around inside. He sprayed a line of white paint on the mine floor as Richards carefully stepped off a near perfect rectangle.

The two friends were separated from an incredible fortune in gold by only nine feet of strata made up of three different materials. First a couple feet of coal, then five feet of limestone, and finally two feet of concrete that was the basement floor of the vault in the most famous gold storage depository in the world, known to most people as Fort Knox.

"I can see it, Floyd." Cason said as they finished the outline on the mine floor. He stood inside the painted rectangle with hands on hips, his head turned up as if he could see through the coal black ceiling as he imagined what he could see inside the gold storage vault.

"We saw how they stored it on their web site," Cason added. "A big pile of gold bars stacked like a pallet of bricks in separate small rooms. It's not in crates or on shelves. Beautiful, huh?" Cason had a big grin on his face.

Richards was quiet as they covered the stripe of white paint with a black tarp and then covered that with dirt and coal debris. On the mine face nearby, Richards made a yellow chalk mark. Then he stopped. He stared hard at Cason.

"Wait a minute, Eddie. Don't be thinking what I know you're thinking. I just want to show the personnel at the depository just how dangerous this mine is to the security of the gold. They would be

181

happy to pay us a hell of a big fee for this information. Maybe a million bucks for each of us."

Cason had taken a long pull on a Gatorade bottle. He took it down from his mouth, screwed the cap back on, and turned his head to look at Richards. His head lamp illuminated what he knew to be the face of an honest, kind, and gentle, but very naive man.

"Damn it, Floyd." Cason threw his backpack on the mine floor in total frustration. "You don't ever learn. For the past nine months you've been fucked by our own federal government."

Cason stuck his fist out with the forefinger pointed up in the air. "The first screwing was by their attorney for the park service, the second screw job was by the federal banking system, and the third by federal pressure put on UK."

By now he had three fingers stuck out. He put his hands on his hips. "That cost you your job and then your visitation rights with your kids."

In the light of his head lamp, Richards watched his friend throw his hands up in the air as he continued to vent the anger which he felt Richards should have expressed.

"Jesus Christ, man! When are you gonna see the light? We've got an opportunity here to do something that would make history and make us rich."

Richards smiled resignedly at his friend's outburst. "I don't want to go to jail, Eddie. I mean, how in the hell are we supposed to pull off such a thing? We can't . . . what we can do is collect a great fee for an incredible service."

"Hey!" Eddie yelled. "We're not dealing with private industry here. They would know how to reward us . . . but the fucking government!" Cason waved his hands in the air in desperation.

"They're not going to pay us anything, man. Maybe a grand a piece . . . that's it! The Feds will give us a framed letter of merit, or some such shit, along with a big splash in the newspaper about how two honest saps saved them from a very embarrassing situation. That's all we're going to get, Floyd! Just a fuck you very much speech."

"All right. I'll think about it. We'll discuss it some more at dinner on Friday night."

They exited the mine and hurried out of the cave system where the two friends walked one mile back toward the highway embankment. They followed the highway as Cason held out the Laser Scanner. Soon it started to register a temperature difference again.

"We're near the old mine entrance. Move along this way."

They paced slowly and then retraced their steps back again for a few yards. Cason swung the scanner to the left and then to the right. The digital numbers increased either way he went.

"We are right between those two sets of iron bars I placed at this end of the mine shaft," Cason said. He watched as Richards walked up a mound about twenty feet in front of Cason.

"If we dug right here at an angle, we'd find the opening to the mine about twenty five feet down in there. You'd be looking at that coal car you found." Suddenly Richards stomped off further into the woods searching.

"Hey, Eddie. Here's the property line stake with the red ribbon still tied on it from the survey when I bought the property. Then the park service put in this fence."

"The entrance to the mine is just fifty yards off the property." Cason stated. Then his quick mind started to work on the beginnings of a plan.

"We could add seventy five yards of fence on the timber company's land. Who would know? Think about it, Floyd. And a locked gate with signs around to keep out."

Richards remembered that the timber company didn't use this land and wouldn't even learn about the additional fence for years.

Cason explained to him how they could open the mine entrance just a few days before they pulled the job. Then on the day of the heist, they would drive two trucks down the dirt road and through the woods to the mine entrance.

"We'd need a small tractor to pull the coal car along the rails to where we'll cut into the vault," Cason continued. "We take a few shuttle car loads and we're out of here. Two miles later we're on the main highway driving to easy times, baby!" Cason was so excited; he was lit up like a big happy face on a neon sign.

But Richards knew better. *There's a whole lot he hasn't considered yet. The extreme weight of the gold would collapse the ancient coal car. And it would take a lot more men and planning to pull off such a spectacular robbery.*

"Let's both think about it for a while, Eddie. Then later this week, we'll get together."

Chapter 33

Fast Eddie Cason was a sprinter, out of the blocks quick, trying to leave the opponents behind. He was on go, ready to get started planning an incredible heist. He couldn't wait to meet with Richards, so during the week he made notes about all the things needed to pull this one off. Then he telephoned Richards about getting together sooner.

Richards was a plodder, more turtle than rabbit, and he liked to think things through, chew on each and every thought that developed.

"So in the meantime, Eddie, between now and Friday, we continue to explore the cave just like we're paid to do. We don't talk about this again until we meet for dinner at my place."

He placed the phone back on its cradle and looked at it. *Cason was crazy. To even think they could pull it off, much less get away with it, was mission impossible.*

He walked over to his favorite big vinyl arm chair, sat down and ran fingers through his mop of brown hair that needed to be cut. Without Doris living with him and not working at the university, he had let himself go a little bohemian.

He leaned back and his feet kicked up on the little foot pad that popped out from under the recliner. *Why am I even thinking about it?* He anguished. *I don't steal from people. I'm not a criminal. And I don't want to go to jail.*

Richards decided that he would end it on Friday night and tell Cason that he wasn't capable of becoming a thief.

Then everything went wrong for Richards during the rest of the week. On Thursday he was in the office of the Superintendent of the Mammoth Cave National Park, who told him that the park system was one of many on the list of recent congressional budgetary cuts, and as a result, he and Cason would be laid off in thirty days.

"When we get the attraction open and get some income from these caverns, then you both can finish the exploration. Of course that won't happen for nine months or more."

"How can we wait until then?" Richards questioned. "We both need to bring in a pay check."

The Super raised his arms with palms up and a hopeless look on his face. "That I can't answer, Floyd. I take orders too, you know."

That night Richards looked through the cabinets in the kitchen. He wasn't a drinker, but right now he needed a good glass of whiskey. Somewhere "they" had a bottle of *Wild Turkey,* good Kentucky straight bourbon.

He still didn't think in terms of something "he" had in the duplex. In his mind it was always "us or ours." *The kids and his wife would always be a part of his life.*

Even now, in his mind, Richards had just thought, *wife,* not ex-wife. He loved them all, although he had come to realize over the past few months that he was very upset with Doris and what she had done to him. *Forgiveness would be tough.*

He poured the bourbon over ice in a tall glass, added just a touch of tap water and sat down at the small kitchen table by the door of the duplex. Richards held the glass up to the light and rattled the ice around in a swirling motion. Then he took a big swallow.

Even cold, the whiskey burned going down. He gritted his teeth.

Quickly, he felt the heat in his stomach. It felt good. Richards took another swallow and it seemed to warm up his whole being. He sat there getting relaxed and letting his mind wander. He began to revisit his situation.

He realized that for the foreseeable future he would not be able to visit with his son and daughter. Just when he thought he could continue with the child support payments, the federal government gave him thirty days notice.

Originally they had promised that the exploration would continue until the majority of the cave system had been discovered and mapped. Richards had counted on some longevity, hoping that they would eventually employ him as manager. He would hire the personnel: ticket sellers; tour guides; restaurant workers, and others to service the visiting public.

He had payments to make plus the bank loan on the cave property. And soon he would have no job. The officers at that federally insured bank should have known better. They were so eager to get a piece of the action and make the loan that none of them asked him what direction the cave went underground. He darn well knew where it went but he didn't realize the significance of that fact. Richards' mood swung toward depression.

It just wasn't fair. They owned thirty percent of the business. So they should have been obligated to pay off thirty percent of the loan.

He thought about telling the Officer in Charge that they had a severe problem with security at the gold depository, but unless they were willing to pay a decent price for the information, he would not divulge it.

No, that wouldn't work. The federal government doesn't do business that way. And their idea of a nice fee would be just what Eddie said. Two thousand bucks with an autographed picture of the two of them standing next to the Secretary of the Treasury. Big deal, That's not even worth thinking about.

He slipped off to sleep for an hour. He had wild dreams. Thoughts seemed to move in fast forward. The *Wild Turkey* put wings on his imagination. All kinds of ideas swirled around in his head. Suddenly he woke up with a start.

Richards went over to the kitchen table, found a legal pad and began to put his thoughts on paper. After another hour he actually smiled.

He stood up. He was a little wobbly on his feet. He steered himself to the bedroom and sat on the bed. The last thing he remembered thinking about was life in general.

Be true to yourself. But sometimes you need to take risks. Life is short and opportunities don't come very often, if ever.

He felt totally relaxed. He keeled over on the bed fully dressed and went back to sleep.

Chapter 34

On Friday morning Floyd Richards woke up with a slight headache. He also woke up with a new determination, a new direction in his life. He had a plan. And the plan had an ending he liked. It would be a long shot, but at this juncture in his life he decided he must take it.

He had been kicked around enough and now he would fight back. He would try to make the federal government and the banking system pay for taking advantage of him.

Cason arrived early that night. It wasn't even six o'clock yet but he was anxious to talk to Richards. The two friends shook hands, cracked a couple of Coors Light beers and started to talk things over.

"I'm more convinced than ever that we can pull this job off and get away." Cason had a very serious look on his face. It wasn't the usual big toothy smile. He was all business.

Richards cut him off. "Eddie. I don't agree with you. Your experience was white collar crime. Pulling cons on people and duping them out of their money, which they gave you freely. But this is different. This would be a big time, major robbery."

Richards got up and opened the refrigerator door. "You like steaks, don't you, Eddie? We'll cook two big sirloins on the grill out back. I've got the charcoal burning down to a nice glow of coals."

"Fuck the steaks, Floyd!" Cason jumped up. "I'm leaving here if you won't at least listen to what I've got to say. And if you're not interested, I need to find someone who knows a good plan when they hear it."

Richards turned around and grinned a little. "You're exactly right, Eddie . . . you do need to find someone else. But I am interested. And we do have a lot to talk about."

He sat down with Cason again at the kitchen table. Richards leaned on his elbows and stared at Cason carefully.

"We need to turn this problem over to the experts. Make a pact with the Devil, Eddie. We tell them what to buy and they bring all their expertise to make it happen. We kind of sit on the sidelines and direct them. And we just take a commission, so to speak."

"What experts? What Devil?" Cason was still mad. "What the hell are you talking about?"

"When you were in prison did you meet or know anyone connected to organized crime?"

Cason's mouth dropped open. "Jesus Christ, man. Are you crazy? If we get mixed up with them we could get dead!"

"It's the only way, Eddie. They have the background, the experience, and the men who could pull it off. But we have the knowledge . . . we know

Kenneth S. Murray

the caves, the mine, and we can put them right on the gold. We have to convince them that it would work."

"You have no idea what you would be getting into, Floyd. This could be so big they wouldn't think of sharing it with us. Outside the family, there is no loyalty and no thought of what's fair. They'd kill you for twenty five thousand bucks. In this deal, you're talking about a billion."

"But Eddie. We don't insist on being an equal partner to split the take fifty-fifty. We ask them for a finder's fee, so to speak. A pittance compared to the fortune they can make in one night. That way they won't get greedy or want to kill us."

Cason looked outside the kitchen window thinking about what Richards had said. "Well. If any group could pull this score off, they would be the ones." He glanced back at Richards. "But I'm still scared of them."

"I am too. But I want to hear what you have in mind. Then I'll tell you my plans. If by the end of the night we can't agree, then you're free to get someone else and I'm out of it."

The two friends talked until midnight. During that time some important facts came out. Cason told Richards he knew a guy from prison. He was an accountant for the mob in Chicago.

"They called him, 'Four Eyes.' That's cause he always kept two sets of books for the businesses they ran. One for the boss and one for the Internal Revenue Service.

"But they got caught and 'Four Eyes,' took the rap for the mob boss. Testified that it was all his idea. He was doing four years and got out when I did. He took a

192

liking to me. Said to look him up if I ever got to the Windy City."

"You're going to find him. You tell him that this job is so big and so sensitive that you'll only talk to the mob boss himself. Convince him, Eddie. This accountant and most importantly, the big boss. You can pitch a sale. That's what you're best at."

Richards watched Cason start to sweat. He took the table napkin and wiped his forehead and face.

"Listen, Eddie. If you can't get them to do it. Then the deal is off. They won't kill you if they say no. If they say yes, you'll be in Switzerland before the deal goes down . . . counting our money!"

"How's that going to happen?" Cason asked. He eased back in his chair as some color came back into his face.

"Even if they like the idea, they won't agree to it until the boss sends some guys down here to carefully check everything out. Then if they want to make the score, they have to pay us some deposit money. Five million dollars Eddie, in advance, deposited in a numbered account in Switzerland to which only you and I have access."

Cason frowned. "So I let you know when the money is there and that we can get to it. Then what happens back here?"

"At that point your partner, Paul Stewart, who's sitting right here in front of you will help them with the details and facts about the area. I'll even be in the mine when it happens. They will insist on that."

"Then you're taking all the risk. If something goes wrong, they're going to hit you!"

Richards actually smiled. "I know that. But my guarantee is you, Eddie. You're going to help me become Paul Stewart. Floyd Richards won't be mentioned. You've got to promise me that, my life will depend on it."

"Remember . . . I said I owed you when you saved me from freezing to death in that cave."

"And one more thing." Richards face got deadly serious. "If it goes bad and I don't live through it. I want your promise that you'll put half the money from the Swiss account into a trust for my children."

"Two and a half million bucks for me," Cason sparkled. "Giving your family the other half would be the least I could do. And something else, Floyd. I'll personally be there for them when they need me. I'm already good old Uncle Eddie to Karlene's kids."

Cason stuck out his hand to shake on the deal. He meant it. And Richards could tell by his expression that even with that kind of money, he could trust Eddie Cason.

Chapter 35

The following week the two friends worked every day and refined their plans every night for five nights. Finally they decided that everything they could think of had been covered, revised, or agreed upon. It was time for Cason to go to Chicago. Richards had already been busy with his disguise. Paul Stewart had been growing a beard and a mustache for two weeks.

It was a quick flight from Lexington to O'Hare. The non-stop on United Airlines left at 11:05 AM and arrived at 12:20 PM. He was down in Chicago's Little Italy an hour later looking for a particular restaurant to have lunch.

Cason entered and found that the man he had spent four years with in prison had made a reservation for them. *So far, so good,* he thought. The Italian waiter with slick black hair, dressed in tux pants, white shirt, and black bow tie, showed him to a corner table with a window view to the street.

He ordered a draft of beer they had on tap. He took a long sip, leaned back on the padded bench seat, and looked around. Small tables with white linen surrounded by black chairs occupied the center of the restaurant. He sat in a row of bench seat dining tables along the sidewalk windows.

On the opposite side of the room, fifteen chrome bar stools with black padded seats lined up along a dark wooden bar, liquor bottles standing in rows in front of the mirrored back wall.

Nothing different . . . just your typical Italian restaurant that could be in New York or any big city. He glanced outside and saw the waiter who had seated him talking to a short portly man on the corner across the street who was staring back at Cason.

He wore a long sleeved shirt and tie, light slacks, had sunglasses on, and wore a straw hat to protect his balding head from the August sun. Cason looked at him carefully and through spaces between vehicles, he recognized his old prison mate.

Traffic stopped at the red light. They both walked across the street and "Four Eyes" came back to the table where Cason was sitting and joined him.

"Can't be too careful in our business, Eddie," he said with a smile and stuck his hand out.

Cason shook it and answered, "That's why you put me in a window seat."

They both ordered lunch, Cason another beer, the accountant a diet coke. When the waiter walked away, they continued the conversation.

"I never thought I'd hear from you again, Eddie. You know how it is inside. Come see me sometime. We all say that, but usually nobody does."

"As I said on the phone, I've got something very big. Can't handle it ourselves. It will take some people with money and connections. That's why I thought about you."

"What's it about, Eddie?"

Cason leaned over on the table. "The less you know the better off you'll be. This would be a federal offense if we're caught. And it would mean a lot of time inside." He said it very carefully. Four Eyes knew he didn't want to go back to jail again, ever.

"I don't like going to the man without good reason. He doesn't like wasting his time on junk."

"Can Mr. Ochopinto have his 'consigliore' there?"

The accountant leaned back in his seat and stared at Cason. "If this thing is bullshit, I'm going to be in trouble and you'll get thrown out on your ass."

"I did you a couple of favors inside. It saved you a lot of grief. You owe me," Cason replied with a hard look.

"I'll do my best," the accountant said with a big sigh. "Where are you staying? I'll give you a call tomorrow."

Cason told him and their food arrived. The conversation lightened immediately and they talked about old times and guys they knew in prison.

True to his word, Four Eyes called the next day at 2:30 PM. Cason watched the news; old movies on television; had room service deliver both breakfast and lunch, making sure he would not miss the accountant's telephone call.

"The boss told me that this better be good. So your plan gotta' have a big pay off, Eddie. Not some little corner bank job or jewelry store. That stuff's for the druggies."

"Don't worry. He might even thank me when I'm done explaining this one. Thanks for setting up the meet."

He told Cason where to find Louis "Nine Ball" Ochopinto. "And he told me you had better be there at six tonight or don't bother to show up."

Cason knew from his time spent in prison that Ochopinto had gotten the moniker, Nine Ball, when he was making his bones with the mob. He was trying to collect a loan shark debt from a guy who owned a pool hall.

The debtor wasn't too cooperative, so Ochopinto picked a ball off the pool table and smashed him in the head with it . . . about ten times. The guy was dead after the sixth or seventh smack. It was the white and yellow nine ball. Now that he was the Mafia Don in Chicago, nobody ever used that name around Ochopinto.

Chapter 36

Cason drove the rental car to the fashionable North Shore, the heart of Chicago's "Magnificent Mile," that included shops, theaters, apartments, and villas. It was a ten story apartment building and the Mafia boss had the top floor so his men could get out on the roof and look around or Nine Ball, with his wife, could go sun bathing and not be disturbed.

He was stopped inside the front door by a smartly uniformed older bellman who made a phone call. The bellman said, "Take the elevator to ten. You'll be met there."

There was a big unfriendly looking guy waiting when the elevator doors opened on ten to disclose soft pastel colors on the walls and a matching thick carpet.

"Come on over here and stand still." He said. Another guy appeared and watched while 'Unfriendly' patted Cason down. "This way," he said and walked him over to knock on solid oak double doors with brass fittings.

Another tough looking character opened the doors and 'Unfriendly' said, "He's clean . . . no gun, no wire," and walked away.

The second tough guy looked at his watch and said, "Okay. Have a seat." He pointed at a cluster of chairs around a medium sized cocktail table. Cason sat and looked around. His watch read 5:50 PM. He figured that was acceptable.

Then second tough guy got a message. He was wired to a hearing aid device like the Secret Service uses to protect the President of the United States. He looked over at Cason and motioned for him to come with him.

Second tough guy opened another door and Cason walked into a grand looking combination of a living room, library, and an office. Just inside the door, there was a large desk that housed a computer with a monitor and printer.

A huge entertainment center had been installed in the middle of the room, surrounded by several comfortable lounge chairs for viewing. Bookshelves were interspersed around the perimeter of the room with art items and many books.

Cason looked around carefully, taking everything into his memory bank. *This is not what I expected.*

At the far end, Louis Ochopinto was seated in a black leather executive swivel chair behind his black leather topped wooden desk. He was a fairly big man in his late fifties with graying black hair, black eyes, and was dressed in navy blue slacks with a cream colored, long sleeved shirt.

To his right sat a slim, older man, balding with a pencil thin mustache, who wore a three piece grey suit, white shirt, and black tie. Cason figured he was the consigliore. Two other men were also in the room. Capos or captains, high up in the ranks of the Chicago Mafia.

All of them just stared at Cason and said nothing. Cason continued to approach the men and broke the ice. "Good evening. I appreciate you seeing me, Mister Ochopinto."

"Sit down," the don said. He pointed to a chair right in front of his big desk. Cason stepped over and sat down gingerly, like he was testing a bed of nails. He started to get very nervous. Small beads of perspiration broke out on his forehead. He wondered if he could sound both confident and convincing.

"Want something to drink?" Ochopinto asked.

"Well . . . ahh, yes. My mouth's a little dry. I'll have a Coke, thanks." Finding no nails, he eased himself back in the chair. The Don made the slightest head movement and one of the capos fixed the soft drink from a bar that made a half circle out from the wall into the big room.

Ochopinto fixed him with a stare. "You're Fast Eddie Cason. My chief accountant says you have something big, and we can trust you." Then his voice hardened. "But . . . why the fuck is a small time con like you askin' to have my attorney here?"

That remark came out so quick and harsh that Cason got flustered. He glanced back and forth between the consigliore and Ochopinto. Then he said the first thing that popped into his mind trying to smooth things over.

"Well, Mister Ochopinto, I'm not going to sue you."

For a few seconds nobody said anything. Then one of the capos slapped his own forehead with a grunt, dragged his hand down his face and muttered, "No shit."

The don was tilted back in the big chair with his hands resting over his belly. With that response his head arched back, his mouth opened, and he broke out in a big horse laugh. Then everybody laughed with him including nervous Eddie Cason.

"Well. That's a big relief to me you ass hole. Now why the hell are you here?"

Cason decided to drop the bomb on them right away. He had already screwed up at the start.

"I can tell you how to pull off the mother of all heists. Your men probably won't even need to fire a gun. You can steal all the gold from Fort Knox you want and get away with it!"

The Mafia boss folded his arms over his chest as his eyes darted first to his attorney then to his men and back again at Cason.

"You really are a fucking dumb ass. Why the hell did Four Eyes send you in here with this bullshit?"

"I wouldn't tell him about it." Cason sat forward in his chair. "This is so incredible the fewer people that know about it, the better for you."

The Don started to yell at Cason but the consigliore put his hand up. An action that revealed his strong relationship with the Chicago Mafia boss.

"Wait, Louis . . . let me ask him something." He looked at Cason. "Why did you want me here?"

"Because, when he hears how it could be done, I want you to tell him the downside. What would happen afterwards. If he still wants to go ahead after he gets your opinion, then I'm off the hook. He can't blame me."

"Very original thinking, Mister Cason." He turned back to Ochopinto. "Why don't you hear him out, Louis? You can always throw him out." He grinned.

"Bring the kid a real drink. I think he needs it," Ochopinto said. "Breaking into Fort fucking Knox. This guy's crazy . . . but all right, let's hear it."

"You're not going to break into the building, Mister Ochopinto. No way. You can drop the gold out below the vault floor into an old coal mine that runs right underneath the depository."

Cason tells them about his time spent in Kentucky and working for the park service in the caves. He then weaves a little protective fiction into his history. He describes his friendship with Paul Stewart, a forestry professor, who likes to treasure hunt with a metal detector.

"I was out with him one day and his detector went off pretty good. We were below the road embankment and back in the woods. But, right across the highway up the hill we could see the gold depository, which is next to the Fort Knox army base."

"Wait a minute!" the boss interrupted. "I thought Fort Knox was known for the gold."

"Most people think that, but they have nothing to do with each other. They're just physical neighbors, so to speak," Cason answered.

"We started digging, maybe ten feet down and the metal detector went off even more. Ten feet further, through broken rock and dirt, it opened into an old coal mine where we found the iron shuttle tracks."

Cason went on to explain the mine and almost all the details, leaving out the fact that they had originally entered the mine from a system of caves.

"I can put you closer to that gold than anyone has ever been. They allow no visitors." Fast Eddie was selling now. He was on a roll. He had their attention.

"In the coal mine the gold will be just nine feet above the ceiling. You'll have to cut through two feet of soft coal, five feet of limestone, and two feet of the vault floor, which is concrete."

"But how can you immobilize all the alarm systems that I've heard are so sophisticated?" The consigliore asked.

"Yeah," Ochopinto added. "I've said that about other jobs. It would be like robbing Fort Knox. You can't do it."

"That's the beauty of it," Cason added. "You want the alarms to go off. And you need to make sure they do."

Cason told them there are four guard boxes located at each corner of the building, and the yard perimeter is surrounded by steel fencing with sentry boxes located at each side of entrance gate. Each box has one guard.

"You don't want to kill anybody, but you want to do something that will set off every damn alarm they've got whether it's sound, motion or light. A really big diversion will get their attention."

"Shit. This is gettin' worse," Ochopinto remarked.

Undeterred, Cason kept describing the action required and the reason for it. When he finished, some five minutes later, the Mafia boss had a small, but definite gleam in his eye.

"It sounds too easy," he said. He glanced over at one of his Capos. "Whatta' you think?"

"Who guards the building?" one capo asked.

"The depository has a Captain of the Guard and an Officer in Charge. The guard force is made up of men selected from various government agencies, or recruited from Civil Service registers."

"Amateurs! You gotta' be kidding." The capo responded. "I thought they'd have the fucking Green Berets there," he said.

"It's not a military installation," Cason reminded them again. "Like the U S Mint, this is part of the Treasury Department." Cason answered.

"I'll need to take two of our best men down there to check everything out. Then, if it's what Fast Eddie says, we do it." The second Capo said.

"How much gold is in that vault, Eddie?" The Mafia Don asked.

"It never varies much. One hundred forty seven million ounces. If you figure it at three hundred fifteen dollars an ounce, current London quote for gold, that comes to over forty six billion dollars."

There were loud whistles, hoots and hollers of incredulity. "But wait," Cason adds. "We think there are many stacks in different cubicles side by side inside the vault. We just found several of them. The coal mine shaft isn't as wide as the whole building."

"Several stacks will do just fine, Eddie. Like one or two billion!" Ochopinto said.

"I can't believe you're really considering this, Louis," his consigliore broke in. "Do you realize the enormity of this score, if you pull it off?"

"You've never given me bad advice . . . tell me what you think."

"The fall out, Louis. This will hit our country like a nuclear bomb." The attorney stood up and paced the room, hitting the idea from every direction.

"This is not just another bank. This is the most famous gold depository in the world, for Christ's sake. The notoriety, Louis . . . the heat. None of you can imagine how hot this one will get." The consigliore paused to drink cold water.

"The feds will never stop looking for who did it. The press will call it an attack on America. Damn this idea to Hell. You might as well steal the Statue of Liberty!"

The consigliore stopped pacing at a book shelf, pulled down an encyclopedia and turned toward the Mafia boss. Very formally, he continued.

"I implore you to reconsider, Don Ochopinto. This would be the worst decision you could ever make. It's like slapping the face of the government. Since the place was built it's been considered invincible, invulnerable. A symbol of power revered and respected by nations around the world."

He pointed his finger at Cason. "Do you know during World War Two the vault held the British Crown Jewels?" He didn't wait for an answer, but continued to read.

"At other times; the Magna Carta; the Constitution of the United States; the Declaration of Independence; Lincoln's Gettysburg Address, and other important documents."

"Yes, sir. We've done our homework," Cason answered, not at all intimidated.

"It's one of the few bastions of strength left in the free world," the exasperated lawyer continued. "It would break the faith of the American people in our government. They'll hound you for the rest of your life, Louis. Somebody will break. They'll talk." He snapped the book closed and replaced it on the shelf.

The consigliore didn't sit back down again. "That's all I've got to say on the matter." He looked at Ochopinto. "I don't want to hear the other side of this, Louis. If you don't need me anymore, I'll leave."

The Don nodded and said, "Yes, old friend. You're a patriot, counselor. I thank you for your advice . . . have a good night." The consigliore picked up his leather briefcase and walked to the door.

After the door shut, one of the capos glanced at his boss and nodded at Cason. Ochopinto said, "Anything else you want to add?"

"No, sir. I've described the whole deal. Except our take."

"Whatta' you asking?"

Cason looked from one to the other as he spoke. He wanted to see if he could catch any bad reaction.

"After you study the plan with my partner, Paul Stewart, and you decide it's a go . . . then you wire transfer five million dollars to a Swiss bank account. I'll be over there waiting for it. Call it a finders fee . . . we get it no matter what."

So far neither capo nor the don showed any emotion. "Then when you get the gold, our take is fifty million, right there in the mine. Stewart will be with you during the score, so our neck is on the line too. Besides, you'll need him for technical assistance the whole time anyway."

The three men glanced at each other. "Fifty five million!" Don Ochopinto questioned. "If we take one or two billion out of Fort Knox, you'd still be happy with that?"

"A small percentage. Yes, sir. That's why we're not asking for much. If we did, you might think we were pigs . . . and pigs get slaughtered."

One capo allowed just the slightest bit of amusement to appear on his face.

Then Cason added. "If you decide to do the job, there would be one personal favor I'd ask of you while you're down there. It's not a big deal."

The Mafia boss finalized it. "We'll get in touch. Have your partner available."

"Yes, sir. I'll wait for your call."

There was no handshake. Cason was escorted out to the big double doors. After he left, one capo said. "Maybe it's time for a wake up call for the feds. Might tighten up their security after we hit 'em."

"Everything our consigliore said is true. It'll be a fucking man hunt like we've never imagined." Don Ochopinto said.

"You'll be the most famous of all the dons," the other capo said. "Inside the family, rumors move around. You'll make Dapper Don Gotti look like small potatoes. Nobody ever pulled off such a spectacular score. And you'll be in Europe, Louis, with plenty of witnesses. In the Cosa Nostra, they will pay you great respect."

Don Louis Ochopinto was thinking. *I've never had the respect I deserve. Some other don from New York or New Orleans is always the smartest or the best.*

They always get great respect at the council of bosses. Maybe I could change that.

In his mind, he could see some of the other top bosses kissing his ring finger in admiration, or bowing their heads slightly in recognition of his greatness in the near future. The don was starting to embark on an ego trip.

Chapter 37

Eddie Cason returned to Kentucky. A week went by and they heard nothing from Chicago. They were still employed to explore the cave system, but they also dug out the opening to the coal mine exactly where the Laser Scanner metal detector indicated it would be.

They leveled out the excavated boulders, rocks and dirt to form a driveway twenty five feet long that went down the hill and led underground into the old slope mine.

The old iron rails for the coal car came partially up the new driveway. It was a place where trucks could back up and load the gold.

While Cason was in Chicago, Richards went to see a friend who worked in the administrative office for the Department of Sciences at the University of Kentucky. He had known her for some time and she knew the federal government had put pressure on the science department to dismiss him. She was quite sympathetic.

"I just need to use your computer to get some information about other professors who might help me secure a position at another college. I'll be done before you get back from lunch."

Richards reviewed the software program under academic staff where professors were listed, including their qualifications and achievements. He opened the 'create new' file; inserted the name Paul Stewart, professor of forestry within the College of Agriculture and filled in the blanks with all of his newly created background, address, and other credentials. It now read that Stewart's date of employment at UK began in 1997.

Richards had been working on his new appearance too. The full beard and mustache were growing out nicely and the day after he visited his friend in administration, he had shaved his head. Also contacts changed his eye color from brown to bright blue.

He had moved into a mobile home under the name of Paul Stewart, but not in the park where Eddie Cason lived. He canceled his post office box number they had used as an address when they rented the Laser Scanner. Now he had a street side mail box like his new neighbors.

Richards went to a local dry cleaner and had them put the name Stewart on a tape strip inside the waist band on several of his dress pants. "I've been losing some pants . . . maybe that will help," he had told the manager.

He left magazines and other junk mail addressed to Paul Stewart around inside the mobile home, along with a recent bank statement he had opened under his new identity. Eddie Cason's prior life helped also. He knew a guy from prison who had done time for forgery. He had forged all kinds of documents, and one time before his release he told Cason, if you ever need some great looking ID, call this number. Cason called him and found that the guy was back in business.

"Just so happens I've come into possession of some blank social security cards plus some stolen blank drivers licenses from Tennessee. Send me a picture of your friend, his name and address, and I'll fix him up."

Richards applied for a new Kentucky license plate for a vehicle he had just bought. He showed the clerk the title for a 1995 Ford truck he just purchased. What he didn't mention was the fact that the newly purchased truck had been totaled in a wreck just a few weeks ago. The dealer also owned a junk yard.

He would put the new plate on his Ford truck if their new acquaintances from Chicago were in town. If they checked at the license bureau, they would be told that the license plate belonged to Paul Stewart at his new address.

Another week had gone by and still no word from Chicago. The two friends had just one more week of employment and they would be laid off indefinitely. Richards had been using his money to rent the mobile home or buy things needed if the Chicago contact developed as they hoped.

He had not been able to pay his child support and he stopped paying the bank also. He told the bankers that he was going to be laid off soon and they would have to wait until he got further employment. He had no assets for them to attach, which they already knew.

What the two friends didn't know was that over the past two weeks, Louis 'Nine Ball' Ochopinto had meetings almost every day with his top capos and his consigliore.

There had been all kinds of arguing and talk about the coal mine caper, as it came to be known within the tightly knit group.

Finally, the head of the Chicago Mafia decided they would look into it, and his attorney got him to agree to be in Europe, if and when the heist went down.

But first they had to check out this Eddie Cason and his professor friend, Paul Stewart, very carefully. The whole deal had to look and smell perfect. There couldn't be any hint of something that didn't seem right, or they would call off the score.

Ochopinto picked three of his best men. One capo and two soldiers who were smart and tough. It would be their job to report everything to the Mafia Don so he could make a final decision.

"You make one freakin' mistake on this deal and you know what'll happen." Nine Ball told his men.

The capo called Cason on the following Monday, which was already into September.

"Is this Eddie Cason?" He asked when Cason picked up the telephone.

"Yeah. This is Cason," he replied, knowing who this might be.

"This is Tomaso Grimaldi from Chicago. You were up here couple weeks ago."

"Yes, sir. I remember meeting you at Mister Ochopinto's apartment."

"Well. We're going to get a lot better acquainted very soon. So you can call me, Tommy. Okay?"

Grimaldi didn't wait for an answer. He just kept on talking. "We're coming down this weekend on Friday. We'll rent a car at the Louisville airport and drive down. That way we'll know if somebody is following or not. Gimme the name of a decent motel on the west side of town. We'll call you on Saturday morning. Okay?"

Cason agreed and called Stewart immediately. He would not use the name Floyd Richards again for some time. He could not afford to make that mistake with Ochopinto's people around. That would be a fast ticket to a dirt bed.

"Hey, Paul. Just got a call from Chicago. They're coming down on Friday. Said they'll call me on Saturday. I gotta' feeling they will do some checking up on both of us between now and then. These guys like to check things out ahead of time when you least expect it."

Chapter 38

Tomaso "Tommy" Grimaldi and his men flew to Louisville, rented two cars and drove down to the motel recommended by Cason. They arrived Wednesday morning, two days early.

After they checked into three rooms, they went to a local restaurant, ordered lunch and looked through a local telephone book. Grimaldi made a list on three different pages of an eight by eleven lined pad and handed one to each man and kept one himself.

"I'm going to check out this guy, Paul Stewart. You check on Eddie Cason," he said to one man.

He looked at his other soldier. "You take one car and get in their mobile homes early this afternoon. Check 'em out real good. Cason said he still has a week to work for the Park Service and the professor ought to be at the college."

"Damn this is lousy Italian food." One man said.

"That motel ain't no prize either." Said the other.

"Whadda you expect? You're in the sticks, not in Chicago." Grimaldi answered.

Later in his room Grimaldi started making telephone calls. He called the College of Agriculture and asked for the Department of Forestry.

"Is Paul Stewart there today?"

The young sounding operator responded. "Wait a minute." It took all of that.

"He must not be teaching today," she came back.

"Do you know him?"

"No. Never met him."

"You're the operator there and you never saw him?" Grimaldi questioned.

"I'm a student, but not in forestry. I just work here on the switchboard two afternoons a week. I did check the computer listing of professors in that department and he has been there since nineteen ninety seven." Grimaldi hung up the telephone. He made a few other calls and waited for his men to report.

"Both mobile homes check out okay." Grimaldi's break-in artist reported. "Stewart's does look like he just moved in. Found out who owned it and she said the professor just rented it a few weeks ago. Still short of furniture and stuff. Guess he's single . . . just pictures of his parents. Lots of mail, even a bank statement out on the table."

The other soldier had nothing alarming to say about Cason. "He did work at Mammoth Caves and now he's on assignment exploring a new cave system, they told me. He's been working for the park system since he got here from prison."

That night the Mafia soldiers got a good look at both men when they arrived, each at their own homes. They took pictures of their cars to include the license plates to check on later. The next day, Grimaldi and one soldier followed Paul Stewart as he went to the College of Agriculture and parked his car. They watched as he walked to the building and disappeared inside with a briefcase in one hand and a couple of books in the other.

"He had tree books and magazines about growing shit lying around in his mobile. Man, they looked fucking boring," the break-in artist offered.

They drove over to Stewart's truck. The two men got out of their rental car and walked around the vehicle, inspecting it carefully. "Break-in" slid a thin flat tool out of his shirt, slipped it down between the driver's window and the door frame, pulled up slightly, and the door lock was compromised. He glanced around and seeing no one he quickly jumped inside the truck and searched it.

Grimaldi suddenly leaned over and peered studiously at the lower left section of the front windshield. He got back in the rental car on the passenger side and waited for his soldier to finish. When he climbed into the driver's seat, Grimaldi signaled him to exit the parking lot.

"What did you see?" Break-in asked.

"I thought I'd found something, but it was just a UK parking sticker for teachers and staff people to take the best spots. Anything in the truck?"

"He must be a real neat-nik. Just a bottle of water in the cup holder, no trash, no food wrappers, nothin' but a few more of those fuckin' tree books. The truck's registration with his name on it is in the glove box. That's it."

By Friday afternoon the Chicago Mafia had checked everything they could think of and found nothing. Grimaldi decided to call Cason and set up the trip into the coal mine.

Early on Saturday morning Grimaldi and his men picked Cason up from his mobile home and drove down the Blue Grass Parkway to Elizabethtown and then up state road 31 west. They were going to be tourists and visit Fort Knox and look around the army base. Then they would go next door and get acquainted with their target.

From the highway, they exited to the right on Bullion Boulevard, which turned into Gold Vault Road, that led up to the top of the hill and the parking lot at the United States Treasury's Bullion Depository.

Grimaldi and his men had cameras and they clicked away. They took pictures of the structure itself, the guard towers located at each corner of the building which were about seventy-five feet away from the steel fence, and the guard sentry boxes just inside the fence gates. That was as close as any visitor could get.

In mid September it was still warm and there were other tourists milling around in shorts, multi-colored shirts, flip flops, or sneakers with cameras in hand or hanging around their necks.

Grimaldi, wearing tan khaki pants and a short sleeved shirt, had covered his head with a snap brim straw hat and his face with very dark sunglasses. He walked casually over to stand close to Cason.

Quietly he said. "Point to the location of the coal mine."

Cason raised his arm with a forefinger extended. "Straight down the hill and across the highway. It's about three hundred fifty yards from here to the mine entrance."

Grimaldi took a few more pictures with a telescopic lens. "Okay, Eddie, now show us the mine."

Cason directed them back onto the highway, then off again at another exit where they weaved on a two lane road back into the woods onto a gravel road and then a dirt road deeper into the oaks and pines and down to the coal mine entrance.

"Who owns this property?" Grimaldi asked.

"It's owned by a timber company. They never use it and we fenced it in to look like it was part of the new cave development by the Park Service."

As they got close they found the area fenced with four strands of barbed wire and a padlocked gate. Cason got out and, using his key, removed the lock, pulled the gate open to allow the cars to enter, and then locked it again.

"We felt like we should keep people out of here as much as possible. They allow hunting back in these woods, but we fenced and posted no hunting signs for fifty yards on either side of the mine entrance."

Paul Stewart was standing there beside his truck when they arrived. Cason made the introductions to the Mafia men. Stewart looked the part of a big outdoorsman. Grimaldi checked out the bald head, the full beard and mustache, and the woodsy clothes.

He also noticed that Stewart had a very strong grip when he shook hands and his voice was gruff or guttural, he thought. Grimaldi studied the man's face and he didn't see anything different or unusual. *He is almost featureless,* he thought.

The nose, chin, mouth, ears, and forehead. It all fit together okay, but nothing distinctive except those bright blue eyes. I guess that's it.

219

Stewart knew he was being carefully checked over. He had been working on a change in both his voice pattern and speech for the past ten days and had used it every time he spoke to anyone all day long.

Since he no longer worked at the university or in the cave system, he purposely stayed away from any of those acquaintances or friends. When he became Paul Stewart, he had to include his new address and telephone number in the Forestry Department files, so he carefully monitored any calls left on his recorder.

He decided against an unlisted telephone number. A college professor has a lot of contact with students and his peers. That would look suspicious to the Mafia. He also didn't have to worry about his former neighbors. He avoided them until he rented the mobile home in the park which was a considerable distance away. His ex-wife had not been allowed to call him for three months and he had lost visitation rights with his children over ten weeks ago.

All of these circumstances, all of the bad luck that had plagued Floyd Richards has certainly been perfect for me, Paul Stewart thought. *Richards had basically vanished from his former habitat, and I have emerged like a butterfly from a cocoon.*

Stewart showed the three Chicago mobsters the entrance to the mine. He instructed Grimaldi on how to use the Laser Scanner. Grimaldi saw how it picked up on the ore car's iron rails. Then Grimaldi used it on their gold rings and one heavy gold chain that one henchman wore around his neck. The digital read-out jumped even higher.

Then they walked into Stewart's world, where he had the upper hand. None of these dangerous men had ever been in a mine or a cave. Stewart showed them how to use their hard hats with the head lamps and explained almost everything as they walked up the slope along the main shaft toward the depository. However, there were a few facts he intentionally left out.

"We don't have any money, Mister Grimaldi." Stewart said honestly. "You'll have to buy all the equipment needed for the job."

"Call me Tommy. And what stuff are we talkin' about?" Grimaldi questioned as they continued to walk.

"We've figured it every way possible. But we always come back to the need for speed after we drop the gold. All of us must be out of the area well before dawn. That requires the purchase of five, twenty-five ton dump trucks and an ore hauler like they use in deep rock mines, plus one heavy duty truck to get it down here. A forty foot flat bed that can haul over forty tons."

"Jesus Christ, man! That sounds expensive."

"About one million three hundred thousand. And that's buying the big stuff used. The specific Toro hauler we need to fit in the mine will be half the total expense."

"Shit. I wasn't countin' on it taken that kind of money to do the heist." Grimaldi was not happy. He stopped and turned to Stewart. He stuck his finger in Stewart's chest and held it there.

"Listen good. If that gold's there like you say . . . and if we can drop it down quickly into this fuckin' mine, you're off the hook. Okay."

Grimaldi poked his finger several times into Stewart's big chest for additional emphasis and his face got ugly as he spoke.

"But after putting up five mill in advance plus all this expense and no gold shows up, you'll be comin' out of this mine feet first dead, if they ever do find you. You got that?"

Stewart had expected him to get tough sooner than later. He looked at Grimaldi without a blink when he answered. "I would expect that if I don't deliver."

"Good." The Mafia boss nodded his head. "Just so you know your ass is on the line. Okay?" He turned and started walking again.

When they arrived at the chalk mark on the wall up near the mine face, Cason and Stewart pulled back the tarp and showed them the white paint marks on the floor. Grimaldi turned on the scanner and it went crazy. "I guess you know your stuff, Professor." Then he asked Stewart. "How many billion did you say was in this vault?"

"More here than any other depository. Forty six billion."

"I'll just take ten percent." In the light from Stewarts' head lamp, the Mafia boss had a definite gleam in his eyes. "Four billion will be just fine," he added.

"One billion," Stewart responded. "We don't have enough time or equipment for more."

"What the hell you talkin' about?" Grimaldi growled.

"I'm talking about weight, Tommy. One billion in gold is almost eight thousand five hundred bars. That weighs over one hundred and sixteen tons. Five trucks at twenty five tons each. That's it."

"We're gonna pull off the world's biggest heist and take almost nothin'. Crap. That's like havin' a hundred broads in a harem and only fuckin' one of them!"

Stewart came right back. "Four billion would take twenty trucks and four times as long. There's no room in this shaft for more than one hauler. They're built to work in huge, deep hard rock mines. We have to be out of here before dawn . . . too risky, Tommy. Too many trucks to be pulling in and out of here."

"Too bad it ain't in fuckin' diamonds." Grimaldi turned away in disgust. He knew Stewart was right. He hadn't figured on such extreme weight.

They returned to Grimaldi's motel rooms and discussed the score in great detail. Stewart handed Grimaldi a list. He wanted to make sure that they would want him in the mine. He would be the point man. Eddie Cason kept quiet, which for him wasn't easy.

"We'll need the following equipment." Stewart went down the page, item by item. They spent two more hours going over the long list.

Finally Grimaldi said, "You gotta come to Chicago . . . oversee buying this technical stuff. Okay."

"We can't take that chance." Stewart responded. He stared hard right into Grimaldi's eyes. "After a robbery like this the investigation will be relentless."

Stewart explained that the Mint Police; FBI; local police; highway patrol, and the sheriff's department will be looking at everyone around here.

"I can't leave. I've got to keep my position with the Forestry Department . . . keep everything the same. No changes."

Stewart had steeled himself to speak to the Mafia men as a formidable person. He couldn't appear to be a weakling. He had to appear strong willed and tough. *After all,* he thought, *I've lost everything that ever meant anything to me. So why be scared. I'll give it all I've got.*

Grimaldi reluctantly agreed. He knew that they should do nothing different, nothing suspicious to draw attention to any of them in what would become the mother of all major manhunts.

"We'll tell Ochopinto what we've seen here and what we think. Then it's up to him. We'll get back to you. But if he says to make the score, then its gotta be soon. Too many things could screw up. Okay."

Cason and Stewart left the motel at midnight totally exhausted. They had been grilled plenty. On Sunday, Cason hung around the motel in his Syclone with a pair of binoculars. He took pictures of them when they left at seven in the morning.

Using the camera's telephoto lens, he photographed both of the license plates, and of course the make, model, and color of the two cars.

He followed their cars down the highway, watched them turn off toward Louisville and stopped the surveillance. He called Stewart. They had a lot to talk about.

Chapter 39

Just five days later, on Friday, Tomaso Grimaldi called. "Don Ochopinto is satisfied that you guys and the project is legit. "When can we start?"

Cason noticed during his telephone conversations with Grimaldi, that he never said anything that could be considered illegal or incriminating. The Mafia was always worried about the FBI tapping their lines.

"I'll fly to Switzerland over the weekend. On Monday, I'll call you with the information you need. Once the money is deposited, you can call Stewart. I'm staying in Europe."

Grimaldi grumbled about advance payment for a job not yet pulled off, but thought again about how cheap it was compared to the billion dollars they would take from the vault.

Cason didn't give an inch. He and Stewart had talked about the fact that the five million might be all they would get and that Stewart would need to watch his back in that mine at every moment.

"It will take until Tuesday or Wednesday before we can send the wire transfer. Where can we reach you, Eddie?"

"I'll call you back on Tuesday at two in the afternoon, your time, and if necessary, again on Wednesday, same time. Don't worry, I'll stay in touch." Cason hung up the telephone. He wasn't about to give him an address in Switzerland.

He called Stewart and they met that night. They spent the next several hours going over every possible idea or problem that might happen during the job. Finally they were done.

Cason said, "I've got a flight Sunday out of Lexington to Chicago. Then American Airlines over to Zurich. The bank I plan to use is Bank Leu Limited in Bern, about sixty miles away. They have numbered accounts. I won't know where I'm staying until I get there. I'll find some out of the way roadside inn between Zurich and Bern. Then I'll contact you."

The two men stood up and shook hands. Then Stewart hugged Cason. He slapped him on the back several times. "I'm going to miss you. You're my best friend."

The action and the statement took Cason by surprise. His eyes showed it as much as his mouth when it dropped open. He'd never had another man say that to him before. Then it dawned on him. *He'd never had a real friend before.*

He looked at Stewart. "You take care of yourself, Paul."

He had trouble saying the words. Some emotion crept into his voice. He had to squeeze the next sentence out.

"I want to see you when I come back."

Then Cason gave him that million dollar smile, with dimples, teeth, blue eyes and all.

Chapter 40

Cason arrived in Zurich without a problem. It was Monday. He rented a car and drove until he found a small inn about twenty miles outside of town. He checked in and then called Bank Leu, Limited, in Bern. Due to the six hour time difference, the bank had already closed.

The following morning he was up early and drove to Bern in order to be there when the bank opened. He met with one of the numbered account managers and told him that he, the account manager, would receive a money transfer from a Chicago bank today or on Wednesday.

"The funds should be deposited in an account, accessible by only two people." Cason instructed. He gave the manager his name and that of Floyd Richards, along with the required identifying information needed by the bank.

He returned to the inn, had a leisurely lunch while he waited until it was 2:00 PM, Chicago time. He told Grimaldi the name of both the bank and the manager.

Grimaldi said, "We'll send it tomorrow, okay." and hung up the telephone.

Early Wednesday morning, Chicago time, Cason was so nervous he had trouble dialing the telephone. When he got through, Grimaldi was slow to pick up and answer. But for Eddie Cason, he said three beautiful words. "Check your bank."

Cason checked out of the inn and immediately drove to the bank. It was late in the day, but the bank was still open. The numbered account manager smiled as Cason shook his hand.

He said, "The money arrived as you said. Five million American dollars has been deposited to this account number." He handed Cason a plastic card with just a number on it in raised lettering. No bank name. Cason checked the amount, questioned the manager about how much interest the money would earn, then thanked him and left.

He drove further west from Bern and checked into another small roadside inn. He knew the phone calls he placed to Chicago yesterday and this morning could be traced back to that first inn.

Cason found a cyber cafe and sent an email to Peter Stryker, Stewart's new, recently opened email account. The first thing he gave Stryker was the numbered bank account, which was put into a code they had worked out earlier.

Stewart had been checking his new email address since Monday night, hoping to receive some news. It wasn't until early Wednesday evening when Stewart drove to the Lexington public library that he found a message waiting. As a public service, the library had

229

several computers where one could access the Internet for twenty minutes free of charge.

When Stryker logged onto his Hot Mail account he read with great relief the email from Elonzo Cassidy, alias Eddie Cason, that gave him the anxiously awaited news. He sent a responding email to Cassidy.

Information received and understood. Peter Stryker.

They both used computers other than their own since hard drives can be searched for email information which people thought they had deleted. But experts can retrieve almost anything, including supposedly deleted emails. The two friends also planned to cancel their new email accounts as soon as the job was finished.

Stewart already knew the name of the bank and it didn't make any difference about where Cason was staying. He wouldn't be there after the score went down. They didn't dare phone each other. Overseas calls were too easy to trace.

On Thursday morning Cason turned in his Avis rental car and immediately took a cab to the nearest Budget Rent-a-Car office where he rented a different vehicle. Inns and hotels requested automobile information when checking in and he was not going to leave that trail.

During the day he finished checking on other possible places to stay that afforded a good escape route, both from the inn or hotel, plus multiple choices of roadways that could confuse someone in case they came looking for him.

By mid-afternoon, he was enjoying a typical Swiss meal at a roadside cafe that offered outside tables. He purposely sat inside away from a window where he sipped on a dark beer and people watched. At this point, he had nothing much left to do. He had fulfilled his end of the plan which he knew was nothing compared to what his friend would face back in Kentucky.

Now for me it's the worst part, he thought. *I've got to sit around and wait for Stryker, alias Stewart, alias Richards, to contact me.* He cracked a Cason smile when he thought about all the subterfuge.

He knew that once the Mafia came back to Lexington, Stewart might have trouble ditching them and getting to a library computer, because they both were sure that one of the Chicago gangsters would stay with Stewart at his mobile home the whole time to keep an eye on him for the duration of the job. But Cason would religiously check his emails every day for any clue as to what was happening.

Grimaldi called Stewart on Thursday morning. "Your commission has been sent as agreed. Okay."

"You can find the used trucks and hauler on the Internet," Stewart instructed. "Some equipment might be in Canada and have to be driven down."

"Then we'll need another ten days to two weeks to get all the gear. Okay. I'll call you when we're ready to come down. Here's a number where I can be reached if something comes up. Any questions?"

"No," Stewart replied. "I'll wait for your call." Grimaldi hung up.

Stewart went to the library that night and sent an email to Cassidy from Stryker about the developments to date and the expected arrival of the material from Chicago. Then he added.

I've got a lot of work to do at the job site as we had

discussed. I will update you every day. I am short on

money Stryker.

On Friday, Cason withdrew some funds from the bank and drove seventy-five miles southwest past the quaint town of Lausanne on Lake Geneva to the city of Geneva near the French border.

He sent a two-day priority Federal Express envelope to Stewart at his mobile home that contained five thousand dollars in United States currency. Stewart did not deposit it in a bank. They had discussed the need for money to live on before Cason left for Switzerland.

Cason drove back to the inn and got a little drunk. He would have to wait for the Mafia to collect all the equipment and get it down to Lexington. Until then he could communicate with Stryker via email.

Once they arrived he would be out of touch. It would take time to set it all up, check everything over innumerable times, pull the score, and then escape. He only hoped that he would actually get a final email from Peter Stryker after the job. He still didn't trust the Mafia.

Chapter 41

Doctor Kal Barakat sat in his office chair with the door closed. His elbows were resting on the desk and his fingers were pressed hard against his temples. The pounding was incredible now. It was almost like a migraine headache.

He had to go back to his patient soon. She was sitting in a dental chair waiting for him. Earlier he had started to drill her tooth to clean out the decay and prepare it for a filling. The patient screamed out in pain.

His dental technician quickly leaned over and whispered. "You hit the wrong tooth, doctor, it's the one next to it that you numbed for the filling."

"Oh, I'm so sorry," Barakat said. "The Novocain hasn't had time enough to work yet. You just rest for a few more minutes."

He turned to his dental technician. "I'll be in my office."

The technician watched him leave the cubicle with a worried expression on her face. *He is just not himself lately. He would never have made that mistake a month ago,* she thought.

Barakat worked the tips of his fingers in a circular motion into his temples. It seemed to ease the throbbing. He thought about taking some more drugs, but he had already made two mistakes today.

I wish Doris were here, he thought. *She gives a good massage on my neck and head. Right now it would really help.* He sat very still with his eyes closed to shut out all of the light in the room.

Doris had not been working at the dental office for the past six weeks. Her face showed too many signs of abuse. Barakat had grown tired of just hitting her body. On high doses of illegal drugs and losing even more control of his *Activated* mind, he began to hit her in the face. He enjoyed watching the skin around her eye darken during subsequent days.

He also liked to see her lip swell up over night. He had learned by practice just how hard to smack her mouth with an open hand so the lip wouldn't split open and bleed too much. He thought it would be a constant reminder to her when she looked in the mirror that she should never question his authority.

It was six weeks ago that Barakat came home earlier than usual on a Friday afternoon. He hoped to catch his wife doing something that he didn't like. Doris had packed some clothes for herself and the kids and left in her car. It was by chance that he saw her car swing around the corner of the street and head west.

He lost her car in the afternoon traffic at a red light. An hour later he hadn't had any luck finding her so he went home. By six o'clock they still hadn't returned. He suddenly thought of going to her former home. By the time he got there it was getting dark and he put on his headlights.

He parked across the street from Floyd Richards' duplex. Searching through the trees and bushes, he saw Doris' car. He quickly looked around for Richards' truck. It was not there.

She must have just arrived, he realized. Doris and the kids were just getting out of her car. She took the children up the outside stairs. She paused to riffle through her purse and find a key. Barakat watched Doris, Robby, and Karen disappear inside the duplex and shut the door.

He contemplated what action to take as he sat in his car. He knew that she had threatened to leave him if he ever hit her children. At the time that Barakat started to use drugs he also began to inflict corporal punishment on Robby for either imagined or minor infractions that a child his age could not avoid doing or saying.

He was just a seven year old boy. Little children learn by repeated and kindly instruction over time. Abuse never taught them anything but fear.

Doris turned on the lights in every room as they looked around. Barakat could follow their progress from one room to another. Then she searched their old bedroom and found that most of Richards' clothes were missing.

His bathroom items were gone too. No toothbrush or paste, no shaving gear, deodorant or other items. *Strange,* Doris thought. *His favorite comb and brush were still there.* When they found his duffel bag and the one suitcase he owned were missing, she began to lose it.

"Look around for a note from daddy," she sobbed to the kids. "He must have left something to tell us where he's gone." But Doris knew that was unlikely. He had been totally cut off from her and his children by Barakat and their divorce decree. *So why would he leave us a note.*

Now it was totally dark as night descended quickly. The door opened silently as Barakat entered the duplex. In the kitchen he searched carefully and found what he was looking for. It was next to the refrigerator. The small metal door to the electric panel with all the breaker switches just inside.

Doris had lost most of her physical strength and mental resolve over the past several months. She had never been exposed to anything like this before. She had heard of abusive people but could not believe that this was happening to her and her beautiful, loving children.

Every day she spent married to this man continued to drain her energy. She tried hard to please him, hoping to turn his displeasure into happiness and warmth. But almost nothing she did was right in his eyes.

Now she spent her time worrying about how to keep him away from the children. His threat to hurt Robby or little Karen had done exactly what Barakat had hoped. It was this threat that kept her from leaving or going to the police.

Doris had no idea how to deal with a sickness that was so progressive. She didn't know that the man needed to be in a mental hospital or under constant professional psychiatric care.

After looking in every room, Doris sat down on a bed and began to cry. Brave Robby knew how unhappy she had been, and even Karen sensed that much was wrong with this doctor they lived with in almost daily fear.

Robby circled his arms around his mother's neck, placed his head on her shoulder, and patted her on the back. This young son was trying to console his mother whom he loved so very much. He was trying to be a man far ahead of his years.

Suddenly the kitchen lights went out. Then the hallway lights went dark. Fifteen seconds went by and the lights in the room next to them were turned off. There was another fifteen second lapse. The lights in the room where they were sitting, holding onto each other, flickered on and off, several times. Off, on, off, on went the lights. Then the lights stayed off.

Darkness and the unexpected always instilled fear. Barakat slowly pulled one switch after another throughout the duplex. He had read the diagram and figured out which room the three of them were in.

His feet slapped loudly in slow, short practiced steps, as he made his way back to where his wife and her children now cowered in darkness and fear. He felt pleasure as he approached them. He wanted them to hear him coming and to dread the touch of his hands.

The power he exercised over them was like an aphrodisiac. In his sick mind it approached the same intense feeling that an orgasm gave to a normal male.

The beating he meted out to each of them, including five year old Karen, was measured in exacting doses of pain that each could endure without permanent scarring or the need of hospitalization.

Barakat enjoyed hearing their voices cry out to stop. "I'll be good. Please don't hit me again," Karen sobbed. But the man didn't stop until he was finished.

Afterwards he forced them to return home in his car. He told Doris that her car would stay there until he was satisfied that she could become totally obedient to his direction about everything.

Doris took her children to Robby's room and locked the door. In the bathroom she washed away their tears and put a soothing lotion where Karen's tiny bare bottom had been deeply reddened by repeated spanking.

In Robby's case, he had received quick short punches on each side of his head above the ears. Barakat figured the boy's hair would cover up any bruises or skin cuts.

"My head hurts bad, Mommy," her son said. In a small voice, he asked. "May I have some Advil or something to make it go away?"

Doris finally broke down. She had realized her worst nightmare. Her children would now be subjected to daily or weekly pain and torture as this insane man continued to hold power over them all.

She cuddled her daughter and son together in one bed and the children sobbed themselves to sleep. Their mother was now completely dominated by this monster and felt she could never do anything to fight back or resist the abuse of her body. She only lived to try and protect her children from him.

She knew that he had to let them go to school. They would be missed and the authorities would investigate their absence. Maybe help would come to them from the school system.

Doris stared out of the window into the night sky. She waited until she heard their steady, rhythmic breathing. Quietly she pulled herself up from the sleeping children and covered them up.

She stepped silently across to the bathroom. Closing the door first so she wouldn't wake them, she turned on the light, walked to the sink and with dread in her heart, looked into the mirror.

"Aaahh!" She cried out into the night. She stepped backwards. Eyes stared back at her from the beaten face of a woman she almost didn't recognize. A face that just suffered two black eyes, upper and lower lips both split, and a bloody nose. The dried blood had caked under her nose and all around her mouth, like the red paint on the face of a circus clown.

Doris filled the sink with warm water. Gently she washed her face and slowly the coagulated blood dripped off into a reddening pool of water. The cleansing renewed some bleeding, but after a cold washcloth compress was applied, the blood letting finally stopped.

A twenty-nine year old woman no longer looked back at her from the mirror's glass skin. The young face was now pulpy and spreading out like a boxer's from the continued abuse. The eyes, sunken and dark with fear. They held no spark of life.

Mrs. Kaled Barakat snapped off the light. Dear God, how she hated that name. Her husband was gradually taking away her youth and beauty. The two things a woman holds dear were now shortened, taken from her in a marriage that hadn't even seen its first anniversary.

Doris crossed the room and raised the window. The cool night air washed across her broken face and eased the pain. She looked down two stories to the patio made of thick slate. Without thinking why, she leaned out further.

How easy this would be. I can end it now, she thought. *Just let my weight go forward. Make sure I hit head first. It will be quick. Yes, it will free my children. Kal won't want them any more. He'll give them back to Floyd.*

Doris suddenly felt relaxed, almost at ease with herself. The tension seemed to drain from her body. This mother had found a solution. She would make this sacrifice to save her two small children. And her torment would end too. She would be in the hands of her God, her salvation. She was teetering up on her tiptoes, squeezing out the last moments of life before she let herself go.

A night bird sounded. A whippoorwill with its loud, repeated call suggestive of its name. The nocturnal feathered creature startled Doris. She looked up into the night sky and glimpsed its total beauty. A full moon shone down on her and a million glorious stars shimmered and shined. Tonight there were no dark clouds in the heavens.

And now there were none in her heart. This moment changed her life. She realized she couldn't trust Kal after she was gone. Suppose he fought to keep the children and abused them further.

Slowly, she slid to her knees on the carpeted floor. She put her palms together in supplication and placed her hands on the window sill. Instead of bowing, she raised her head up high to scan the heavens.

This was the turning point for Doris. She felt a new strength building inside. Then with her eyes wide open as if she were looking at the Deity himself, she spoke.

"You sent a messenger to me. Thank you God. Forgive me my thoughts of taking my own life."

Now Doris bowed her head and quietly repeated The Lord's Prayer. "Our Father who art in heaven, Hallowed be thy name. . . ."

Chapter 42

In the second week of October, Richards, now known as Paul Stewart, supposedly a teacher in The Department of Forestry, was in the coal mine where he had been going over every detail of the plan. He could envision the equipment that would be here soon and how it should be used as he walked along the main shaft.

The straps of a heavy backpack bit into his meaty shoulders as he trudged along the steadily rising incline. He arrived at the mined out room that led to the cave system and walked over to the coal dust covered tarp that helped to hide this secret entrance.

He worked the pack off and set it down while he opened up the tarp. Climbing down onto the cave ledge, he hid the black pack among some coal chunks. It looked like one.

The backpack was loaded with survival gear: Two heavy duty flashlights; a food supply for three days; a cell phone, and dry clothes. The heavier stuff, a small sterno stove, and a gallon of bottled water were put in a black Hefty bag under some other coal pieces.

Back in the mine, he secured the black tarp and stacked coal up in front of it, like a small mound had been left there by the original cutting crew during the War Between the States. One item he carefully wrapped in a piece of oilskin, and hid it among the coal pieces just in front of the opening to the cave.

Stewart continued up to the mine face where he sat down on a crate just under the vault floor of the gold depository. As he looked down his head lamp illuminated notes written on a pad that he had meticulously developed over the past two weeks. He studied them carefully, checking off each item he had completed.

He turned off his head lamp, leaned back against a solid wall of coal and stared straight ahead into the blackness, letting his mind wander around in his memory bank. He thought about the last words Eddie Cason had said to him before he left for Switzerland.

"No matter what they say, you can't trust the Mafia. I'd bet money they'll pull off the heist, but usually they have a twist in the plan. Something you won't expect . . . so be careful."

Well. We'll have them in our mine, Eddie. He thought to himself. *They'll be in our element. Down here where we know the place and they don't. Underground where we're comfortable and they won't like it.*

Those were comforting thoughts, the plus side of the ledger, the assets. Then there was the negative side. The liabilities he had to worry about. He knew they would have him outnumbered ten to one. They knew how to use guns and he didn't. Worst of all, Eddie might be right. They could have an ending for this play all worked out that he didn't know about.

So he had to take charge when the men from Chicago showed up. They would be expecting him to know where the equipment they had brought would be used and just how this whole job was to go down. That included the timing of everything from above ground at the front of the depository to down underneath it in the coal mine.

Stewart was the point man. If he sounded weak or unsure of himself, Grimaldi would call the whole thing off. *But he would pump three bullets into my chest before he left,* he grimaced to himself.

He knew that he couldn't use terms like; "I think"; "I'm almost sure"; "might work, or "probably." That would guarantee his ticket getting punched. So Paul Stewart walked the mine shaft again, talking out loud to imaginary men and telling them in very positive terms just how he wanted everything done. He was the boss. And he was going to act like one. *Again, I've got nothing more to lose.*

When he returned to his mobile home he had a telephone message waiting. The gruff voice said. "Grimaldi . . . call me, okay."

Stewart quickly called back. All the vehicles are packed and ready, Grimaldi told him. "Where do you want them?"

"At the entrance where we met the last time," Stewart replied. "When can I expect delivery?"

"Friday at noon."

"Good. I'll be there."

Stewart immediately hung up the phone. He hoped Grimaldi noticed that. *It meant I'm done, I'm through talking to you, so the conversion is over.* Stewart grinned. He had already begun to take charge.

He also spoke in general or generic terms, avoiding the use of any specifics regarding anything. If federal agents were listening through a telephone tap at the Chicago end, it wouldn't mean much.

It was only Wednesday. Now the anticipation would begin to build. On Friday at noon he would be forced to play the biggest charade of his life. For the Mafia, this would be the biggest score ever attempted by any crime organization. Everyone would be on edge.

By then, there would be no way to back out for Paul Stewart. At midnight on Sunday when it started to go down and the action cranked up, nerves would really be pulled tight. Mistakes could happen and then Lady Luck would leave.

In the early hours of Monday morning, it would be over. Stewart only hoped he would still be alive.

Chapter 43

That same Wednesday afternoon while their father was in the coal mine, Robby and Karen had been summoned to the principal's office at The Picadome Elementary School in Lexington, Kentucky.

Their teachers had walked them to the office and had them sit outside for a few minutes. Both teachers went inside and closed the door. The principal was a tall, stern woman who spoke with authority. She introduced the teachers to the large black woman from the Children and Family Services Office.

"I teach second grade . . . that's Robby's class," Lena said. She pointed at the other teacher. "Robin teaches kindergarten. Karen's in her class. We were talking at lunch last week and I mentioned that I thought I had an abused boy in my class."

Robin spoke right up. "Yes. I was just going to tell her the same thing about Karen, a girl in my class. That's when we found out they both had the same last name, Richards."

"When I asked Robby, he said. 'Yes, Karen's my little sister.'" That's when I knew we had to do something. They both have bruises and red marks on their faces and legs. God knows what's under their clothes!" Lena exclaimed.

"So we took some Polaroid snap shots of them . . . close ups. We told them it was for fun and games, so they didn't mind." Robin handed the pictures over.

The woman from Family Services studied the pictures closely. She didn't say anything as she looked through all twelve of them. Six taken of each child.

"I need to keep these for my report. Let's talk to the children now," she said.

The teachers brought Karen and Robby in and had them sit together on a sofa. The older women sat near them in chairs while the younger teachers sat cross-legged on the floor in front. That way the children wouldn't be looking up at big people in every case. There would be someone they had confidence in sitting below them.

Karen and Robby would only stare at the floor, even when they answered general questions about school, their studies, their friends in class, or games in which they participated out on the playground.

"This is not normal," the black lady would comment later.

Then even subtle comments or questions about the bruises would always bring the same reaction. The kids would stop moving. Literally they would freeze up; look at their hands, which would invariably be in their lap, and always both had the same answer.

"I hurt myself." Karen would offer.

"I fell down," or "I hit my head," Robby would say to every query. After the interview the children took their teachers by the hand as they walked back to class.

"See that?" The Picadome Principal pointed. "Usually, the teachers have to reach out for their hands. And most seven year old boys don't take their teacher's hand. But Robby is desperate for a gentle touch. In this case, I'd guess a loving hand instead of a fist." She spit the last words out as if she had a bad taste in her mouth.

"Anyone else I could talk to . . . further proof someone might have?" The Family Services woman asked.

"You don't need any further proof." The principal barked. "You saw the bruises and how they acted. They've been beaten, for God's sake."

"Don't yell at me." The big black woman responded in a huff. "I always ask for additional comments. I need whatever I can get for my report. We have certain requirements and facts that must be taken into consideration before we go to a home and confront the parents."

The principal's eyes hardened towards the other woman. "Are you going to wait until one child is dead before you do something?"

"If we go there and talk to the parents and can't take the children for some reason, the abuse could get even worse."

The principal turned back to sit at her desk. Then she glanced up at the Family Services Administrator. "I'm not mad at you, understand. It's what is happening to those children that has me so upset."

"I see it all the time," the black woman said. "This may be your first experience, but I've got to approach each case without emotion, or I'll make a mistake."

The principal leaned back in her chair and breathed a big sigh. "I just hope you do something before it's too late."

"Maybe we can get over there sooner," the woman answered reviewing her file. Her notes indicated that they had a call from a woman with the same home phone number and address listed for the children."

"She wouldn't give her name but we have caller I D. We always get the phone number and can cross reference the address. She said she was afraid for her children. That all of them were being beaten. But then she hung up. Her voice sounded desperate."

Chapter 44

Before noon on Friday, Stewart waited at the fence gate in the woods. He appeared ten years older than his age. He had grayed areas of his now four inch long beard and thick mustache before he had first met these Chicago mobsters.

He made sure the gray was put back exactly where it was on that first meeting. He had Cason take a close-up Polaroid picture of his face which he used to check his appearance and do his touch-up.

He kept his head shaved. The bald look added a few years. He was dressed in overalls like a country farmer with high laced boots. The youthful look of his bright blue eyes was an attention getter. People would remember that contrast.

His watch indicated they were ten minutes late. He had walked the perimeter of the property, noting that the fence had not been tampered with and that the gate lock was still in place and worked. He had oiled it just a week ago. Nothing seemed out of order. His posted signs to keep off the property were still up. No one had been hunting in the area where they could have stumbled onto the mine entrance.

Stewart had paid particular attention to the cave development three hundred yards away. Over the first three weeks of October, he had noticed considerable activity down there. Trucks had been coming in to deliver lumber and unload a tractor to excavate the entrance for easier access by the public. That was good. That made a lot of noise too.

Now near Friday noon, all the workmen had left. The fact that they were mostly working below ground level, down in the cave made the mine area invisible. Even when he stood where the cave parking lot would be built, he could not see more than two hundred feet through the thick brush, pine, and oak trees.

As he walked back along the fence line, he heard the rumble of trucks coming down the hill on the dirt road and then winding their way through the big trees and rolling over saplings and brush.

Then he saw them. First came the two lead cars and the small unmarked cargo truck followed by five giant dump trucks, repainted in five different colors. Behind that, came the forty foot long flat bed carrying the huge rubber tired ore hauler with the big scoop bucket on the front.

Even through the woods thinned out into a rough path earlier by Stewart who had anticipated the problem, it was a tight squeeze. Their driver was experienced.

He met them at the fence gate. Grimaldi, in the back seat of the lead car, opened the car window, stuck his head out slightly, and scrutinized Stewart. There was no expression on his face. No wave; no smile; no greeting. Just a stare that stated he was here. It meant let's get down to business.

Stewart swung open the gate and carefully inspected the trucks as they passed through. Each one was an EAST quad-axle dump trailer. Four axles with double wheels on each side. Sixteen tires, plus the cab. Last in line was the flat bed with the big rock hauler chained down tight. *So far they brought the right equipment.*

Each truck had a license plate from a different state. Stewart was sure they had been altered in a Chicago garage. They were stark looking. There was one name painted on each side of the cab. *Morris Hauling, Inc.*, with an address that wouldn't lead to anyplace. No doubt mechanics had also removed all identifying serial numbers from the engines and the truck bodies.

No one noticed that Paul Stewart seemed to be talking to himself. He had a little voice activated microphone hidden in his coat collar. The recorder was in his pocket. Descriptions, license numbers, anything that could be used later was recorded.

He walked down to the mine entrance where the caravan had stopped. Grimaldi was instructing a bunch of tough looking men who were milling around the trucks unloading equipment.

"Hey Tommy," Stewart yelled over the engine noise. "First thing we do is unload that rock hauler and get it in the mine out of sight. Then drive that flat bed out of here."

Grimaldi glanced sideways at him for a moment. He was used to giving the orders, but he was smart enough to know that Stewart had it figured right.

"Do what the man says, okay." The Mafia Capo hollered.

Then two small tractors were driven down a ramp from one of the big dump trucks. Out of another truck came a gas powered generator that would create the electricity needed for the drills, power saws, lights and other equipment.

Stewart directed the placement of everything, including a trial run with the big ore hauler up and back down the main shaft. He put the action on a stop watch.

"We can't cover the gold in each truck with a layer of coal," he said to Grimaldi. "It'll take too damn long. Just get some black, heavy duty plastic to cover the shipment. Then your driver can run the power tarp down over that."

Stewart was everywhere pointing out needs and requirements, shouting instructions to set the material exactly where it could be used the quickest with the least effort. They had gotten everything in place and arranged in four hours.

"That's it for the night," Stewart said. "Let's meet back here tomorrow at nine in the morning. We've got a lot of work to do."

Grimaldi agreed and called two of his men by name. "You guys stay here tonight on guard. Radcliff is about four miles east on highway 31. You can take the cargo truck in there to get food. The big trailers stay here until the job's over."

"Cover the mine entrance tonight with that black tarp," Stewart added. "We'll leave it there when we work tomorrow and during the job. It'll cut down on the noise and no one will see any lights from outside at night."

"We'll take care of it." One of the guards said.

Stewart knew then that he was slowly being accepted by Grimaldi's men. That was important.

"Suppose we catch somebody snooping around?" One guard said looking at his boss.

"They won't get past the locked gate," Grimaldi answered. "But check 'em out easy. No rough stuff. Call me on the cell phone if you think it's serious. Probably just kids making out."

This time the Mafia troops all left for a local motel back twenty-five miles in Elizabethtown. Radcliff was too close and too small a town. Word got around quick about strangers, Stewart had told them.

Stewart went back to Lexington with his appointed roommate in his truck. Grimaldi agreed it would be best in case there were some telephone messages or mail that needed immediate attention. They didn't want anyone snooping around looking for him.

He was going to have a Mafia guard with him around the clock until the job was finished. That was not unexpected. But he would have to hide the tape recorder someplace. It had been on part of the time, dutifully recording names and whatever might be important later.

Paul Stewart just felt better having some evidence available. Some information about what happened, especially if the voices and information might save his life.

Chapter 45

On that same Friday after school, Doris, son Robby, and daughter Karen were having a picnic in their back yard under a big maple tree.

The leaves were turning the brilliant colors of fall; yellow, orange, gold, and red. Many were already starting to drop in varying ways depending on their shape. Some spiraled down rather quickly, others would slide back and forth slowly as they descended, while others would catch a sudden breeze or a swirling wind, and go off one way and come back another.

"Those are the hardest to catch," Robby said. He still had the enthusiasm of youth as did Karen. It had not been beaten out of them yet.

They did not understand cruelty, Doris thought as she watched her children run about the yard. *The inhumane treatment that they sometimes suffered at the hands of this horrible man.*

They were playing a game about who could catch the most leaves while they were falling. You could not pick them up after they hit the ground. Doris pretended to count the leaves each caught and declare a winner during each three minute game.

"You're ahead this time, Karen," she would say. "Robby has won three times and Karen twice. That's the official count." Of course she was just making it all up the way mothers have done for centuries.

Doris had wanted to take them to the park where there were playground activities for children such as swings; slides; forts; tents, and a small rock mountain for the kids to climb. Picnic tables and bathroom facilities were available too.

But Dr. Barakat would not allow it. He didn't tell her, but he was afraid that she might keep going somewhere in her car that she was again allowed to keep at the house.

Since last week, he was even more sullen and moody. He had made more mistakes at his dental practice. Two patients had complained to him and walked out. One nurse came to him on Friday and quit.

She said, "You don't look well, Doctor. Not for the past month or so. You sweat easily. You've gotten edgy and short tempered with everyone. I can't work under these conditions. For your own sake you should get a physical." And with that she left.

Doris knew he was on drugs but she was still under his dominating influence. She had become so afraid of what he would do to her or the children that she was close to having a nervous breakdown herself.

As much as she wanted to take the children and escape, she really had no where to go. She had no money of her own and he had taken away her credit cards. Every week he gave her a little cash to buy groceries and drug store items.

Her father had died and her mother was frail and lived in Tennessee. If she did try to go there it would be an obvious place for Kal to check. She was petrified that he would find them and beat them beyond endurance. Maybe even beat her mother.

She didn't want her children crippled by this sick man. And Doris still clung to her new found strength and growing will to survive if only for Karen and Robby.

She had thought about going to the police, but if they returned her to the house and simply thought that talking to Barakat and threatening him with jail would change him, she knew better. That approach would result in a major whipping. Doris was trapped in the abused wife syndrome in which many women find themselves.

So today she made the best of things with the children in the yard. She went inside to get some more ice and soft drinks for the children when she saw a van drive up and stop at the curb. The door bell rang and Barakat, who was always home early Friday, went to the front door.

At first he thought it was some sales people and he was going to run them off, but they showed him some identification and requested to come inside. They were from The Children and Family Services Office in Lexington.

Barakat looked at the large black woman and the two young, but very big men with her. One black, the other white. Both looked like they might have played football in the recent past. He was not going to intimidate them.

"Is your wife home? We want to talk with both of you," the woman asked as she advanced toward Barakat who stood still in the doorway. He didn't move and both men moved in behind their supervisor.

"What right do you have to come into my house?" Dr. Barakat inquired.

"This order from Judge Wilkerson at the county court allows us to interview you and possibly take your children for their own welfare. This is your copy."

He took the court order and quickly scanned it. Then he reluctantly backed up. Doris had come over to see what was happening. But she stayed back, behind her husband.

"Who are these people, Kal?" Doris asked.

"Right . . . as if you don't know. You probably called them." He answered with a vicious tone in his voice.

The woman from Family Services quickly intervened. "No, she did not. Now where can we talk?"

Doris stepped backwards while Barakat showed them into the living room where they all sat down. One good look at how Doris cowered after Barakat's remark and the black woman knew that his wife was also being abused. She noticed that his wife's heavy make-up didn't quite cover the bruises on her face either.

"We are here because the principal at school and your children's teachers noticed that both Karen and Robby show signs of abuse."

She put her fists on both her ample hips as she continued. "And as a trained observer, I know the children suffer from what we call the beaten child's syndrome. So we know this has been going on for some months. Can you explain this, Doctor?"

Barakat looked directly at Doris. "I've told you to stop disciplining the children so severely, Doris. Now look what has happened!"

Doris was caught off guard. Her mouth dropped open in total surprise at Barakat's response. He had trapped her. If she denied it and blamed him, she knew that there would be hell to pay. A beating like she had never taken before.

Doris struggled with what to say as she unconsciously twisted the sweater in her lap. She looked around at the faces that were staring at her.

All except the supervisor from Family Services. She was carefully studying Dr. Barakat. She saw his eyes narrow and harden. She watched his jaw bone jut out in his cheek as he ground his teeth together. She didn't believe for two seconds that Mrs. Barakat was the guilty party.

"Well. . . I. . . ahh. I'll try to do better." The words stumbled out of her mouth. She was looking away from her husband and directly at the supervisor with a look of desperate hope in her eyes.

"Mrs. Barakat." The supervisor had a wonderful softness in her voice and a kind expression on her face.

"It is obvious to me that you have been beaten also. You could not have done that to yourself. Who did this to you?"

Doris continued to twist the sweater around and around, as if she were squeezing water out of a washrag. Again she glanced at the strangers, but did not dare look at Barakat.

"No. I. . . ahh. . . fall a lot. I have a bad leg that collapses on me from time to time."

The supervisor saw the terrified look on Mrs. Barakat's face.

"Well I have no choice," she said looking from Dr. Barakat and back to his wife. "We must take the children today to the county hospital for a physical and then put them in a temporary home where they can receive some special care."

The supervisor looked directly at Doris. "If you change your mind and wish to talk to me some more, Mrs. Barakat, please call me at my office." She handed Doris a card.

Doris went out into the back yard and spoke with her daughter and son. She could barely hold back the tears.

"Well, you two are off on a big adventure. Let's go upstairs and pack your clothes. You both have to help. You'll be going with some friends who will take good care of you and Mommy will be coming to see you soon and bring you back home."

Chapter 46

Dr. Barakat watched as Doris walked Karen and Robby down to the Family Services van under the watchful eyes of the supervisor and her two assistants. She helped her children climb into the back seat and buckled the seat belts around their waists amid more questions and protests from both of them. Tears were running down their faces and they groped at their mother for a few more hugs.

Doris couldn't hold back the tears either and all three of them held onto each other in a final embrace filled with words of love, hope, kisses, and promises of better times to come. Then this loving mother had to disengage herself from those young arms, close the door and watch the van move off down the street.

She waved at the van since she couldn't see her children inside and blew kisses with her hand from her mouth, throwing them up into the air. The children had seen her do that hundreds of times when she took them to the school bus stop and waited for the bus to pull away or other places where she had to drive and drop them off for part of the day.

It was a simple act, a demonstration of love that didn't mean much to the kids until today when they looked out of the rear van window and saw their loving mother with tears in her eyes throw the kisses. It warmed them both inside.

Karen reached up with her arm and pretended to grab the kisses in her hand as she had done so many times in the past. Sweetly, she placed a tiny hand on her mouth to seal mommy's kiss on her lips.

They never once hugged, kissed, or said goodbye to Dr. Kal Barakat. He didn't exist in their minds. The only way they could deal with his punishment, whenever it came, was to block it out of their memories. Both the pain and the man himself.

Barakat just stood in the doorway. He was emotionless about the children. He never did love them, but he definitely would miss them. They were a part of his pattern of fear in the domination of his wife.

Now he didn't have his favorite threat to hang over his wife's head. Even though he did abuse the children almost weekly, the suggestion that he might do it much more often was a powerful tool that would both frighten and control Doris. He enjoyed seeing her cringe with just the thought of his smacking the kids around.

This problem with Family Services started the pressure inside his head again. A pressure that would build up into pain. His second concern was that this domestic incident would be public information, and might be printed in the Lexington Herald Reader.

He looked at his wife's face. She was struggling with this new and horrible reality as she trudged up the path to the front door. Totally dejected, she walked with her head down. Doris was lost in the distress of losing her children.

It was all due to her bastard of a husband. Kal accused her of beating the children in front of those people.

Now she couldn't be with them or get them back. She had confirmed his lie and confined herself to a life of continued misery, alone and unloved by this sick person. It was over for her, she had nothing left. Finally she arrived at the front door.

She never looked up. She just pushed past Barakat into the house. He quickly followed. "You've put us in this mess, Doris. You must have called them."

She stopped in her tracks. Barakat almost bumped into her as she spun around. There was anger, a rage in her face he had never seen before. Doris was like a mother lioness defending her young.

All the months of abuse had suddenly welled up inside her. Finally she had snapped. Something in her psyche told her. *You've had enough. Now fight back.* Her face was twisted up in hate as she spoke.

"You lying, rotten bastard," she screamed into his face. "I've got nothing to live for now."

With that Doris reached up with both hands. Her fingers were curved into claws. One of the few joys that Barakat had allowed her was to have her fingernails manicured every two weeks. She liked them long and pointy.

Doris raked her fingers down his face as she shrieked out loud like a cat in the night. She had

263

temporarily lost all her self-control. At this moment, she did not fear Barakat. She tried to sink her fingers deep into his cheeks as she pushed her talon-like nails into his flesh and pulled down hard. Then she turned and ran for the kitchen.

Dr. Kal Barakat just stood there for a moment. He was stunned. This had never happened to him before. Then the pain set in and he felt the blood oozing out of his face. It began to drip on his shirt.

"Bitch," he yelled, and went after her. Bursting into the kitchen, he found her standing over the double sink. Her hands were in the basin, her head hung down. She wasn't trying to run or hide. She just stood there. *Submissive again, as usual.*

"You'll get it for this." He unbuckled his belt with the large metal buckle, slipped it off his waist and held onto the leather end. "I'm going to whip you until your shirt shreds off your back," he barked.

He walked over behind Doris and pulled his arm back. She still hadn't moved. Barakat was used to that. She had always been passive, quietly submitting to his abuse. That fact was what Doris now relied on. She would give him a big surprise.

She had been watching him in the window at the back of the kitchen sink that looked out onto the garden with the slate stepping stones. But with the lights on, she could see his reflection in the glass panes in front of her. She waited until just the right moment, and as his arm was raised high, she spun around to her left.

Both hands came out of the sink. Her left hand was empty. But her right hand was gripped around the handle of a large carving knife with a blade some ten inches long.

Without stopping her spin, the knife lashed out at his nail raked face like the strike of a rattle snake. She struck him with a sweep across his left cheek that opened up his flesh in a long cut from his ear down to the corner of his mouth. There was no resistance at his mouth. No cheek bone or teeth to stop the cutting edge since his mouth had opened in a gasp at the first glimpse of the flashing blade held in her hand. Now his mouth was enlarged considerably.

For the second time in sixty seconds he screamed out in pain as Doris ran upstairs and locked herself in their bedroom. She kept the knife with her.

Barakat was a true sadist whose sexual perversion derives pleasure from inflicting pain on a love object. He was definitely not the opposite of that affliction, a masochist, who enjoys being abused and dominated.

The man was so enraged that he paid no attention to his bleeding face. He ran upstairs to find the door locked. Repeatedly, he smashed his fist on the door yelling for her to let him inside.

He needed a release from his tension. He needed to exorcise his demons. He thought his brain might explode. He had to inflict major pain. The last time he beat her the sensations in his groin were wild with sexual excitement. This time he thought he might even achieve an orgasm. The intensity of his sadistic impulse was *Activated* to an all time high.

"I've got two knives now." The screaming voice came from the other side of the door. "I hate you, you bastard! You've have taken everything away from me. If you come in here I'll kill you."

265

Barakat heard the big knife strike the opposite side of the door. She kept on striking it as if she could stab him through an invisible hole she had yet to find. Barakat backed off and stood there for a moment thinking.

In his best, snide voice, he said, "I'll see you a little later tonight . . . we'll have a party. Just the two of us, sweetheart."

Then, even through his pain, with the blood sliding down his face onto the floor, he actually snickered as he walked away.

Barakat went back into the kitchen and found a zip lock freezer bag. He filled it with ice, wrapped it in a thin, clean hand towel, and pressed it against the cut on his left cheek. He went into the garage, cut the telephone lines, then raised the hood on her car and disabled the engine. He got into his own car, pressed the garage door opener, backed out, and drove to his office.

At 7:30 PM on a Friday night no one else should be there. He parked and stood by his car for a moment checking to see if anyone was around. It was getting dark at that hour and nothing moved.

He quickly crossed the parking lot and using his key, unlocked the front door to the lobby, went to the elevator and up to his floor. Letting himself inside, he went straight to the drug cabinet.

He took some amphetamines and waited a few minutes while the effect of the drug swept over him. It removed the pain he felt inside his head as the pressure seemed to slip away, replaced with a feeling of enhanced well-being, a kind of euphoria with increased energy. The drug was a potent stimulus.

In his office bathroom mirror he studied his face carefully. He then injected his cheek along the knife cut in several places with Novocain to completely deaden the pain. He let that work into his system until his cheek was numb.

With medical detachment, Barakat watched as he sewed up his own face. The uppers he had taken earlier made him giggle. *It was like putting sutures in a cadaver,* he thought. *The body was beyond feeling.*

Now he was ready. He salivated at the thought of how he would punish that traitorous bitch. It would be a torture unlike anything she could imagine. Then he might kill her and get rid of the body.

He was slowly losing his dental practice. He realized that much and knew that his psychiatrist was probably right. He needed professional help for his problem. But not now. Now he had to repay a debt. A debt of pain.

He knew she was waiting for his return. Angry or not, defiant or not, she was still deep down inside, afraid of him. Time would allow that anxiety to build. Nervous tension would mount. She would hear sounds inside the house that would make her jump. Alone inside, filled with fear and a fertile imagination, an empty house could be its own horror movie.

He decided to fix himself a cup of Moroccan tea with lots of sugar and a big cut of lemon. *Let her wait longer, until her nerves are frayed from the anticipation, stretched tight like the string section of a philharmonic orchestra. Tonight they would make beautiful music together.*

Chapter 47

Dr. Barakat stepped out of the building slowly, holding still another cup of hot tea laced with lemon. He wanted the jolt from the additional caffeine and extra sugar. He took another sip as he surveyed the parking lot. No one in sight at nine in the evening.

He walked carefully over to his Buick, opened the door, slid in and popped open the drink holder. He drew in another big slug of the brew as he set the cup in place. The drugs were working nicely. He didn't feel a thing from the hot liquid on the inside of his sutured up mouth and cheek.

The dentist turned on the radio and tuned in the public broadcasting station. "Aahh . . . beautiful," he said out loud. "One of my favorite operas."

The station was playing, *Madame Butterfly,* by Giacomo Puccini. He sang along with it as he leisurely drove back to his house.

Doris had listened at the bedroom door after he had yelled at her. She heard him go down the steps. Quickly, she opened the door and ran over to the wooden banister and leaned over. She could tell he was in the kitchen doing something. Then she heard the door to the garage open and close.

Doris jumped back inside the bedroom, locked the door again, hurried to a window and opened it wide. Several minutes went by. She realized that he must be doing something else in there to take so long.

Then she heard the garage door rise up and watched Barakat as he backed his Buick out of the garage and drive off. She waited until the car was out of sight.

Unlocking the bedroom door again, she fled downstairs and found her purse which was in the living room. Grabbing her keys, she rushed to the car. Time and time again she tried to start it, but the realization crawled over her that her husband had disabled the ignition system.

She rushed back in the house and tried the telephone. She would call her friend, the nurse at his office who had told him off and then quit. She would come pick her up. The phone was dead. No dial tone. She tried two other phones and then knew that he had disconnected the whole system.

A healthy fear of him had returned, but she was determined to fight back. Doris thought about going to a neighbor, but she really didn't know them at all except to say hello. None of them had young children. They didn't mix socially. She could imagine that they did not want to get involved.

269

It was dark outside now. *Where would I walk to ask for help?* It was several miles to a strip mall or an all night convenience store. *He might return, see me in his car's headlights and then what could I do?* She swore to herself. *I'm not going to take another beating.*

Doris went into the garage and found a hatchet and a hammer. Back in the kitchen, she took two more big knives, and an extension cord she found in the junk drawer. She also took a large glass pitcher back upstairs with her.

She came back down to the kitchen, made a sandwich and some hot tea with milk, and took a bag of pretzels and some other snacks with her upstairs. *It might be a long night,* she thought.

In the master bathroom, she filled the pitcher with water three times. Each time she went to the open bedroom door, she poured the water on the carpet across the entire threshold, out into the hallway for two feet, and then back two feet into the bedroom. She got down on her knees and sank both hands into the carpet in several places to make sure it was sopping wet.

Doris cut the female end off the extension cord, then split that end, separating the two insulated wires. Methodically, she stripped the insulation off the wires for six inches, and un-twined each wire so the copper threads were flayed out in a fan shape.

Using a kitchen knife, she slit open the carpet just inside the door near the hinge and felt underneath. It was very watery. She slid the two flayed wires under the cut carpet and pressed them down. Doris laid the male end of the extension cord near the closest electrical outlet. *This he will not expect,* she hoped.

Among her bath items, she found a jar of colorless skin moisturizer. Doris returned to the bedroom door and slathered the outside door knob with it. Again she locked the door.

She positioned other items in strategic places where she might get thrown or run to during the coming fight. An extra knife under the pillow. The hatchet in the bathroom.

Then she sat down and ate her sandwich and drank her tea with the bedroom door and windows wide open so she could hear him return.

Barakat drove the Buick up the driveway and stopped. He pushed the garage door opener, waited for it to rise up, and pulled into the garage.

Doris leaned out of the window on the second floor as she thought she'd heard the garage door rumble up. She saw his car's tail lights disappear inside.

Barakat searched through the garage and found two oversized, hollow, red plastic baseball bats. He had actually played ball with Robby and some friends in earlier and much happier times.

This won't break any bones, but it will sting and bruise nicely, he decided. He grabbed the big, long handled axe with a blade on one side and the blunt hammer on the other.

He opened the door from the garage into the kitchen and went inside. Quietly he slipped up the stairs and laid all the items down by the banister near the bedroom door.

Back downstairs again he searched for the proper classical music for this occasion. He put in a compact disk, pressed the skip button until it came to the Fourth Movement of Beethoven's Symphony number Nine in

D Minor for Solo Voices, Orchestra and Chorus, and punched in the repeat mode.

Barakat turned up the Surround Sound speakers and out came the Presto - Allegro, the rapid tempo and robust full orchestra that would build to a crescendo at the finale. The speakers were at the point where they almost rattled and vibrated. *That should cover her screams rather well,* he thought.

Doris knew from that sound he was still downstairs. She quickly opened the door and looked out. She saw the axe and the bats. It made her shudder violently. Then she saw him come to the steps. She locked the door quietly so he would not know she had been watching. Inside the bedroom she plugged in the extension cord to the 110 volt outlet.

Barakat decided an easy, kind approach might make her open the door. He knocked softly.

"We need to talk this out, Doris. Please open the door. . . I won't hurt you."

"I guess that axe and those bats are for someone else, Kal. But I'm in here alone . . . you lying, sicko drug addict."

Like a slap in the face, the remarks had the effect she wanted. His fuse was short and in a maddened reflex action, he automatically grabbed the doorknob hard and tried to twist it. This completed the circuit and the jolt of electricity knocked him back against the banister which almost gave way against his flying weight. He was out for a minute, but Doris couldn't know that.

Barakat rolled over and looked around. He suddenly realized what she had done. He wasn't used to someone fighting back and hurting him. This enraged him further. He got up slowly and picked up the axe and began chopping at the door being careful to stay away from any metal. It took him a whole lot more swings with the heavy tool to break down the door and he was tiring when it finally splintered and popped open.

The hallway was brightly lit, but Doris had turned off all the lights inside the bedroom. He should have waited a few seconds for his eyes to adjust, but he was anxious to hurt her, so he reached around the door frame groping for the light switch.

His wife had anticipated that also and she was standing there next to the switch with her back against the wall in a navy blue jumpsuit, her feet in thick soled sneakers. Wearing thick rubberized work gloves, she reached out with the extension cord she had removed from under the carpet and jammed the wires into his groping hand.

Chapter 48

Again Barakat was standing on the water soaked carpet in the threshold of the door. For a second time, the jolt pounded him and threw him backwards onto the hallway floor. She came out with him trying to keep the wires pressed against his bare skin. But the cord was pulled out of her hand as she reached its full extension.

Doris grabbed a bat and hit him in the face as he struggled to get up and shake off the effect of the electric shock. Since the bat was very light, it didn't knock him down and she ran back into the darkened bedroom to find her hatchet.

The bat had struck his sutured face, and Barakat jumped up screaming in pain. The broken bedroom door was wide open and he slapped on the light switch and kept coming after her. His wife was on the opposite side of the queen sized bed with the hatchet raised high for maximum effect.

The dentist charged around the bed swinging a red plastic bat in each hand. She chopped at him. But the bats were longer, and one caught her wrist making her let go of the hatchet. Doris turned, reached under the pillow and her hand came out with the big butcher knife she had used earlier to such good effect.

But Barakat was pounding at her head and caught her with several stinging blows which forced her to her knees. He quickly kicked at her face and her head snapped back into the wooden night stand beside the bed and knocked her momentarily unconscious. She slumped over on the floor in a crumpled heap.

He had never expected her to fight back like this but realized as he stood there trying to catch his breath that she was fighting for her life and the loss of her children. He had badly underestimated her determined resolve.

But now Barakat had her. He dragged her up and flopped her down on the bed and stripped her naked. He brought in some clothesline from the hallway and tied her wrists to the top of the four poster bed frame and roped her ankles to the bottom. Now she was flat on her back, spread-eagled and helpless.

Barakat felt for a pulse in her neck and the beat was strong. He checked the back of her head and the skin was barely broken. No serious damage yet. He didn't want it to be over that quickly.

Still doped up on amphetamines he went off to find some more pain pills in the master bathroom. Stepping back into the bedroom, he spotted the electric extension cord over in the corner near the door. *Oh, yes. Two can play that game,* he muttered.

He grabbed the cord and plugged it in near the bed. He used the water pitcher and poured a generous amount on her face. Doris woke up coughing. Barakat just stood there enjoying the thoughts of a voyeur.

Just thinking about a plan to torture his own wife was sexually exciting and he felt his crotch swelling. She was a wife whom he had never really cared for once they were married anyway.

Doris was just someone to keep alive so he could continue his humiliation and domination over her. He would have to break this new will of hers and return the woman to her former mental state. The familiar subdued and frightened condition that he so enjoyed.

Barakat's love of classical music interrupted his sick thoughts. Beethoven's Fourth Movement was reaching that climatic finale with the choral of one hundred male and female voices.

One of his favorite sounds was that of the booming kettle drums. He could visualize the musician's hands as they flew back and forth with the ball shaped drum sticks bouncing off its hollow skin to create that deep, reverberating echo.

As if he could contribute to the beautiful music, he picked up both hollow bats and began to pound on his wife's body in short quick strokes, mimicking the musician.

First he worked on her thighs, then moved higher up, like the drummer with several kettles to pound, he beat on her pubic area. Then to the soft belly and finally to her large, voluptuous breasts. Now the stinging pain was incredible and it produced the loudest screams from his wife.

Barakat's head was tilted back and his eyes were closed as his hands flew across her body, moving up and down the length of her torso, from her face down to her feet. He imagined himself producing the deep resounding sounds of the kettle drums, and he relished the tortured cries uttered from the mouth of his once beautiful wife.

But this would not make her pass out. The plastic bats were not like wood which could knock her out quickly and produce deep and ugly bruising over her body. She would be awake the entire time. He would not let her enjoy the peace, the freedom from pain that unconsciousness or death would bring. Not yet anyway.

The front of her body was a deep shade of pink, some places were even red as the blood flowed near the surface of her skin to try and repair the damage to the tissue. Her nose and split lips were now bleeding. *Oh God, how I love it,* he thought. *My mind is free, clear of pressure and pain.*

Then the crescendo of the finale ended. The repeat button had automatically returned to the softer beginning of the Fourth Movement. "Now for a change of pace," he announced out loud to his imaginary audience.

Doris was sobbing in great bursts of relief. The agony had temporarily ended. Barakat was sweating profusely and the perspiration ran off his face. He sat down to rest for a few minutes and drank some cold water. He closed his eyes to block out anything that might intrude on his joy that the classical music continued to produce in his mind.

But the musical conductor will be calling on me soon again, he thought as his eyes popped open. *I must get back to my kettle drums.* He stood up and walked back over to Doris. His eyes roamed over her young, supple body lying there, spread eagle naked on the bed.

"You do have a lovely body, Doris. I hope I won't change it too much. Who knows? I might even fuck you first."

His sick laughter bounced around the room. He reached down and picked up the extension cord and waved it in front of Doris's face. "See what I have for you."

Then he raised his other arm to show her the red hollow bat he held in his fist.

"Now we'll make some more music together, Sweetheart."

With that he jabbed the flayed metal end of the extension cord into the large, dark aureole of her right breast and snapped the bat down on her left breast in a quick wrist movement.

She screamed out loud again in a long wailing cry. The short touch was enough. He pulled back both arms as he sensed her exquisite pain down into his own testicles. He waited thirty seconds and switched his direction of attack.

Now the electricity jolted into her vagina as he smacked the bat down on her right breast. Her screams echoed out into the night. After three seconds, he pulled back again. He didn't want her to pass out.

Suddenly he heard the doorbell ring. Not once but a number of times. It was incessant as someone punched at the button repeatedly. He realized he must not have heard the chime the first time it rang. He glanced at the bedside clock. It was almost eleven o'clock at night.

Who the hell could it be at this hour, he thought. He realized that the lights were on all over the house and the music was really loud. *It could be a neighbor. If I don't answer it they might call the police.*

"Damn it." He said out loud. As he walked out of the bedroom he turned off the lights. He started down the stairs, pausing to turn off the upper hall lights too since the broken bedroom door might be visible from the front entrance.

On the first floor he turned down the music before going to the door. He was still bothered over who was there. He thought, *it might be those trouble makers from Family Services again.*

Bang, bang, bang, a fist knocked loudly on the door. "Okay, okay, I'm coming," he yelled. Whoever was there began to run out of patience.

Chapter 49

Dr. Kal Barakat went to the front door. In his drugged state, he didn't realize how really terrible he must have looked. The bandage had been pulled half off his sutured face. It was just hanging there, and the cut was bleeding again. His clothes were disheveled, his hair a mess, and he was sweating profusely. He also absent mindedly still clung to one red plastic baseball bat.

When he pulled open the door he found two men standing there. It was cold out that night and they were dressed in dark casual slacks and turtle neck shirts. One was big and the other slim. They looked to be in their early forties. He stared back and forth from one to the other.

After glancing at each other with a knowing look, the big man said. "Are you Doctor Kal Barakat?"

"Yes. But it's late and we're trying to turn in for the night. Who the devil are you?"

The man that spoke pulled a thin leather folder out of his pocket and flipped it open. An official brass colored badge was affixed inside.

"We're from the sheriff's department." He snapped the folder closed as he spoke. "Your wife must be upstairs." It was more of a statement than a question.

"We're going to bed if you don't mind." Barakat snarled.

"With that bat in your hand you must be playing baseball with the kids." The slimmer man said.

"If you're from the sheriff's department you should know that the children aren't here." Barakat had raised the tone of his voice. "Now leave . . . quit bothering people in the middle of ——."

He never finished the sentence. The big man punched him across the nose with a quick, hard left jab. Barakat sailed backwards into the house and landed on the floor. He heard and felt his nose break. Blood was spurting out of both nostrils and the pain was incredible.

"Check upstairs," Big Guy said as he stepped across the threshold and into the room. He pulled on a pair of leather driving gloves. Ten years ago he had been a good middle weight boxer. He knew just how hard to hit someone without putting them out for the count.

The slimmer one took the stairs two at a time. He was pulling on unlined leather driving gloves also as he climbed. Neither one intended to leave any fingerprints. He went to the room with the broken door and carefully reached around the door jamb for the light switch.

281

He snapped it on keeping the bulk of his body outside the room. His eyes went to the bed where he saw Doris naked, spread-eagled, and tied up. He could tell she had taken a rough beating.

"Hey lady!" He said as he entered. "Are you all right?" She barely moved her head and groaned.

He went to the bath room, wet a towel with cold water, and put it over her forehead covering her eyes. His action was not a humanitarian gesture. If she did wake up, he didn't want her to see his face.

He checked the ropes to be sure she hadn't gotten them loose, picked up the phone, found no dial tone, and turned off the lights. As he got back downstairs, the big guy was watching Barakat get up on his feet. He was groaning and cursing, talking about getting a lawyer and suing the sheriffs department.

"The Doc tied her naked to the bed . . . then he whacked her good." He informed Big Guy. "And guess what? He's got a fucking extension cord plugged in and the wires trimmed back to juice her." Plus he had this axe." He lifted the tool up into the air with one hand.

Big Guy glanced at it. He looked back at Barakat. "We were told you're a real sick prick."

Slim Man with the axe held high let it come down hard on Barakat's right foot. His aim was good. The blade didn't cut all the way through the shoe. It hit along the joint line of the foot and the toes. The blow broke all five toes.

The dentist dropped to the floor screaming in pain. He was going to pass out. Big Guy leaned over and held smelling salts under his nose. Barakat reacted quickly by pulling back his head. He was still awake.

"Wonder why they call that crap smelling salts?" Slim Man asked thoughtfully. "It smells like horse piss to me."

"Beats me," Big Guy said as he kept pushing it under the dentist's nose.

A pharmacist could have told them it is a colorless-to-white crystalline solid made of ammonium carbonate. In water solution it is known as, *spirits of ammonia,* used to revive athletes when they have been knocked silly.

It works because the fumes irritate the membranes of the nose and lungs, which triggers a reflex causing the muscles that control breathing to work faster.

The slim one held Barakat up from behind and his big friend stood in front and threw several hard punches. His glove covered left fist pounded hard into the dentist's lower right rib cage. He repeated the action when his right fist was delivered to the lower left rib cage. Several ribs were broken on each side of his body.

Slim Man let him sink to his knees as Barakat held his sides, groaning in agony. Slim leaned over and yelled into his ear. "You oughta' appreciate this, Doc. I mean it's a beautiful hurtin', ain't it?"

The two men were giving a first class lesson in how to really inflict exquisite pain to another human. Although Big Guy delivered the punches, Slim had the look of cruelty in his eyes. Like Barakat, he too was a sadist. And he really enjoyed it.

The smelling salts were applied again. The men were very professional. They didn't want to knock him out, so the next punches the dentist received were short jabs to the mouth and nose.

The series of blows split both his upper and lower lips as they were crushed against his teeth, and as a bonus, loosened a few teeth. His broken nose bled badly and stayed bent over to one side.

The session went on for another thirty-five minutes. By the time they were finished, Doctor Kal Barakat lay immobile on the living room carpet. His body was severely battered and broken.

Using the flat, blunt end of the axe, they had smashed all his fingers and thumbs, broke both elbows and both his kneecaps. Plus they didn't forget to take care of his other foot.

They left the lights on just as they found them when they arrived. A few miles away, their car stopped at a convenience store and Slim got out to use a pay telephone. He called 911 and told them he was a neighbor and gave Barakat's address.

"Screams keep coming from the Barakat house. I think someone was murdered," Slim said in a low voice and hung up before giving any more information. The two drove off into the night.

If Barakat had been allowed to look carefully at the sheriff's badge, he would have seen that around the top edge in smaller letters it read, *Cook County Sheriffs Department.*

He could have figured out that these men were from Chicago. He didn't know they illegally possessed a real badge from up in Illinois.

"I don't get it." Slim said. "I mean . . . we did it like the boss said. But why the hell would Fast Eddie Cason want this as the favor?"

"Beats me," Big Guy answered.

They drove back to the motel on the outskirts of Elizabethtown where they reported to Grimaldi.

Chapter 50

Saturday morning, Paul Stewart, Grimaldi, and his men were back at the coal mine. His guard reported that nothing had happened all night. At fifty-seven degrees, the temperature on this cool autumn day was about the same in the mine.

Stewart addressed all of the men. "We need to do this several times. Each one of us has to know exactly what to do and when to do it. The whole operation depends on coordination with the men at the depository who'll be making the diversion."

Grimaldi instructed two of his men. "Take a radio with you in the small truck up to the depository. Call us when you get there." The two men left.

The others filed into the mine and turned on their head lamps. The driver of the flat bed truck was now behind the steering wheel in the side cab of the ore hauler. He had left the flat bed fifty miles away at a Blue Grass Parkway rest stop where there was a constant flow of truckers in and out. The job would be done long before the truck would be noticed as abandoned.

Stewart was instructing the man. "Practice driving the hauler up to the mine face and back again several times. The turn around will be the tricky part. We need to find the biggest mined-out area off the main tunnel to back in and out again quickly.

Then we'll see how long it takes to load coal into your bucket using the two small tractors. We'll time it with my stop watch."

He noticed that Grimaldi stood back listening. He was like Stewart's shadow, always present. They walked towards the mine face where they stopped under the vault at the spot marked with a rectangle of white paint sprayed on the black coal ceiling of the mine. The rock hauler was already there.

"How much noise did we make?" Grimaldi spoke into his radio to a guard left outside the mine entrance.

"I'm standing fifty feet away. I could hear the tractor a little for the first two minutes. Then it died away quickly."

Grimaldi glanced at Stewart. "Just after midnight Sunday, nobody will be around to hear it."

A voice came over Grimaldi's radio. "We're up at the depository."

"Set your privacy code on number thirty seven, okay. Then come back on that channel." Grimaldi responded.

They were using Kenwood Protalk VHF 1-Channel hand held two-way radios. The radios conformed to military specifications including a five mile range and thirty-eight programmable privacy codes.

Although the depository was less than four hundred yards away, they wanted quality radios with strength enough to send and receive inside the mine shaft.

"Do you hear me?" The question came from his man at the depository sitting in the truck.

"You're coming in good." Grimaldi responded. "What's going on up there?"

"About twenty five cars and trucks parked . . . more coming in and out. The tourists are milling around the fence taking pictures of the sentry boxes on each side of the entrance gate and the depository inside."

"What's Vinnie doing?" Grimaldi asked.

"Looks like a tourist. He's walkin' around with that fish shirt hanging outa' his shorts taking pictures with the Polaroid like you wanted. Gotta' picture of the rifle one guard is holding."

"Finish with the pictures and come back, okay. You don't want to be seen hanging around too long. I'll let you know when to go back up."

Stewart asked Grimaldi, "Who has used a compressed air, hand held power circular saw? It's got to be someone strong who can hold it over his head and cut when he's up on the scaffolding."

"Hey, Frankie . . . Bruno. Come here," Grimaldi yelled.

Since the main shaft in the coal seam was cut twelve feet high they had to build a sturdy scaffold made of metal pipe and two by ten inch pine boards right under the paint line that delineated the area to be cut out. The rig had to withstand heavy material dropping from above along with four men and equipment working on it.

Stewart explained that today, they were going to pull out seven feet of coal and rock plus cut one foot up into the concrete vault floor. Then tomorrow night cut into the last foot, drop the gold, and use the time for loading the trucks. He placed four high wattage lamps on the mine floor around the perimeter of the scaffold.

"We'll need the extra light. It's going to get real dusty and gritty in here soon, and you're going to be cutting directly over your heads."

He handed several of the men full face respirators that included a shield which also covered the eyes.

"The mask contains valves to control air movement through the device. Replaceable cartridges contain activated carbon that filters the incoming air," he added.

He helped the men put the dust masks on correctly. "Everybody else has to wear a smaller dust mask too." Stewart added.

He aimed a small pin point flashlight at a spot on the ten by twenty foot rectangle outlined in white paint. "Start the cut there, Frankie. We'll take the coal down first."

The two big men took turns as they worked their way around the rectangle. During the cut, a lot of the coal pieces just dropped onto the scaffold or on the mine floor. The rest was knocked or pried down with crow bars.

"Let's get this coal away from the scaffold. The small tractors can shovel it into the big hauler to clean the area for the next job." Stewart dove right in to help the men.

He told the driver. "Haul the coal down near the entrance and dump it in a mined out room. Practice turning that hauler around until it's easy for you." The Toro had a big set of bright lights on the front and back ends.

Grimaldi turned to the two men who had been up at the depository. "You guys take a car up there this time. Call me when you get there, okay."

They had finished quickly with the two feet of coal and began to cut into the next layer of material. Although limestone is a sedimentary rock, not hard like granite, they still had to cut through five feet of it.

They had several power saws and a lot of extra blades. Part way into the cut, Stewart waved for them to stop. "See if everything is all right outside." He told Grimaldi.

"How much noise can you hear out there?" He asked the guard.

"Can't hear a thing."

"Those baffle tarps you hung across the main shaft helped." Grimaldi said.

A few minutes later, Grimaldi received a call from the men at the depository. He told them if any alarms go off, or the guards start acting funny, or official cars come out or in to the depository area, call immediately.

It was tough work. They couldn't use any blasting material. An explosion so close to the vault area might set off a motion or shock alarm. Fortunately, the rock was layered and somewhat shaley, so it could be knocked down or pried loose with a tri-pod mounted heavy duty drill with a diamond rock bit to coax it free.

The big Toro hauler pushed into the broken limestone rock picking up most of it. The small tractors tossed the balance of the debris into its big bucket. The machine backed up, turned around and headed down to the entrance. The driver was getting the hang of it. He was saving precious time on each trip down and back up the long main shaft.

"Now we've reached the sensitive part of the cut," Stewart remarked. He looked at Bruno and Frankie. Grimaldi was watching and listening.

"I've done the engineering calculations estimating twice what I think the gold would weigh," he continued. "We can cut through one foot of concrete all the way around this section of the vault floor. It will still hold it up with no problem. Part of the last twelve inches will be cut shortly after midnight tomorrow."

Again, Grimaldi talked with the men at the depository, telling them to be extra observant for the next thirty-five minutes. Everything went as planned. But they did not drop any of the cut concrete. It would have stressed the remaining section since it was so hard and not layered. It was like one solid two foot piece of igneous rock.

It was late in the afternoon when they all finally left the mine except for one guard. They agreed to return again at 11:00 AM Sunday for a final check and to review the timing of everything that would happen during the heist.

Chapter 51

Just past midnight on Saturday morning after Slim Man called 911, the Lexington police arrived at Barakat's house. One squad car with two uniformed policemen. They walked up to the front door and looked around for the neighbor who had called. There wasn't anyone in the area at this late hour.

One policeman rang the door bell several times. No answer. Then he rang it five more times. Finally he used the brass knocker and banged it loudly on the wooden door. Still no answer. They tried the doorknob and found it turned easily. It was unlocked.

With a quick look at each other for confirmation of action, they both pulled their service revolvers and entered slowly. One uniform called out in a loud voice.

"This is the police. Is anyone home?" There was a faint, distant answer.

A few steps further, past the vestibule and into the living room, they found Dr. Kal Barakat lying on the floor. There was a fair amount of blood on and around his body. From his obvious condition, he appeared to be dead. One policeman felt for a pulse and discovered that he was still alive. The other uniform glanced around nervously.

Again he called out. "Is anyone here?"

A definitive answer came from upstairs. It was a woman's voice, anxious and weak. "I'm upstairs . . . help me please!"

They ran up the steps and stopped at the broken door with their pistols ready.

"Is someone in there with you?" A uniform asked.

"No. I'm tied up. The light switch is just inside the door." Doris answered.

For the third time that night, a hand reached around the door frame for the light switch. The policemen eased in slowly, eyes taking in everything rapidly. When they saw Doris, bloodied and tied up spread-eagle naked on the bed, one lowered his pistol and exclaimed, "Oh . . . Mother of God."

The more senior uniform snapped his fingers at him and pointed at the bathroom. The other policeman quickly checked inside, pistol ready. Then he left to check all the other rooms in the house. The more seasoned officer found a blanket and covered Doris. Then he untied her.

Satisfied that no one else was in the house, senior uniform used his belt carried squawky phone to call for an ambulance. Both Doris and her unconscious husband were taken to the Central Baptist Hospital. The next day she was visited by a detective to get her story.

Doris told him about the fight that she had with her husband and all the brutality that he had inflicted on her and her children even before they were married last year. Then she related what happened as much as she could remember after she was tied up on the bed and tortured.

"Later, a man came into our bedroom when I was semi-conscious and put a wet towel over my face, checked that I was still tied up, turned out the lights, and went back downstairs. I laid there terrified for an hour while I heard them beat Kal. I thought they would come up and do the same to me."

That wasn't quite true. She didn't tell the detective, but she sensed that she would not be hurt. It was an intuitive feeling that she couldn't even explain to herself, but she knew it to be true. Doris told the detective that she had no idea who they were or why they beat her husband.

"You're a lucky lady they arrived when they did." The detective answered. "Your husband had you tied up for a real sick, painful trip . . . electricity and all." After a few more questions, Doris tired, and he left her hospital room.

Doris didn't tell him that she could visualize every blow Kal received as she lay there tied up and in pain, but very much awake. As his beating continued, she could determine from the sound when he was punched with a fist in the face or body, and relished the solid pound of the axe as it smashed down on his legs or hands or feet.

His screams and cries were like a poultice to her damaged body. It was almost as if her pain diminished as his increased with the precise delivery of each and every calculated stroke of punishment he received.

After it was over and they left she didn't feel guilty. She didn't pray to God to forgive her for enjoying such evil sounds and thoughts. She was only human.

The black lady from the Children and Family Services Office in Lexington came to the hospital the following morning. "I'm glad to hear you'll be released soon," she told Doris. "And I think I can persuade the judge to return your children to you once you're back home."

"But why, how would you ——."

The black lady interrupted her. "I knew when we were at your house that you didn't hurt those children. I've interviewed enough people over the years to spot the bad ones. In his case it wasn't hard. I could tell you were frightened of your husband and since then Karen and Robby told us the truth about him."

By the end of the week, Doris was healing well and strong enough to be released. She was driven home where she tried to put things back in order. Mainly to clean up the blood and repair the damage after the police had tried to take fingerprints around the house without success.

She met with an attorney to file for a divorce. The legal counsel was provided by the kind lady from the Children and Family Services Office. Due to new information, the judge rescinded the order to take her children and Doris picked up Robby and Karen the following week. The reunion was a joyous occasion for all of them, filled with hugs, kisses, ice cream and cake.

They had a party at their house that night to celebrate both the joy of being reunited and the guaranteed absence of Kal Barakat forever. For the first time in a year they could again enjoy peace and happiness in their daily lives.

But Doris knew she had a big job on her hands. She would have to get into their minds, and bring her children back from worry, constant fear, and perhaps despair. They would have a lot of talks and love and togetherness over the years ahead.

Doris wasn't worried about any retribution from her soon to be ex-husband. Not only did she have excellent grounds for divorce and a claim to some property including the house, but the dentist would be in intensive care for six weeks.

Barakat had been in surgery with four orthopedic surgeons, four surgical nurses, and two anesthetists taking shifts for twelve hours. He had so many broken bones and multiple fractures that bled internally; he almost died from the infections that festered throughout his body. The doctors had him on massive doses of antibiotics to try and keep him alive.

It would take one year to get back some use in his arms, hands, knees, and feet. And he would not enjoy a one hundred percent recovery in any area. Not even close.

Every night that he gingerly crawled into bed he would think about the next day's rehabilitation with dread. Each session would be painful. It would be a slow process just to learn how to walk. And he would always do that with a limp.

He could never practice dentistry again. His fingers would never be nimble enough. Several of them wouldn't bend but half way. His practice was sold at a big discount.

When he was well enough to travel, his parents took him back to Pennsylvania to recuperate with them. He would never forget that night with Doris when he heard the ominous knock at the front door.

Every morning he arose with something that hurt. A constant ache in one or more fingers, an elbow, a kneecap, or someplace that would remind him of that fateful evening for the rest of his life.

In just a few years, early for his age, arthritis would creep into his broken joints and set up a pain shop. With each move of some limb, pain would be his constant companion. A permanent part of his existence until the day he died.

Chapter 52

Paul Stewart was up early Sunday morning. He was nervous. He couldn't sit still. He wasn't used to feeling this way. He walked outside to look around. His constant companion, one of Grimaldi's men, stayed inside having a cup of coffee.

Stewart glanced around the yard and wandered down to the street casually as he did every day even before this Mafia henchman started living with him. He was actually looking for anything suspicious in the way of cars or people in the neighborhood.

He peeked in the mail box nailed to a post beside his dirt driveway as if he had expected to find something. This gave him a chance to peer towards the back of the rental mobile home to see if anything different was happening with his neighbors.

There was nothing. He almost started with newspaper delivery so he could pick it up every morning and pretend to read it as he walked back up to the mobile home doing his surveillance. He decided against it. That would entail setting up an identity with a company that was involved with digging up the news.

When he walked inside, the henchman was watching the television. "Anything going on, Frankie?" Stewart asked.

Stewart couldn't remember Frankie's last name. He thought it started with the letter, *S,* had five syllables, lots of vowels and ended with the letter, *i.* It would sound and look good on a menu in an Italian restaurant.

"Just the local stuff. You know, the who shot who shit. There was one good one. The cops found a guy beat to hell downstairs, and his wife beat up and tied to the bed upstairs. Now you gotta' ask yourself." Frankie said with a grin. "How did that happen?"

"Then churches!" He continued before Stewart could ask him if he got their names. "Jesus Christ. I never seen anything like it. Every channel is somebody praying or singing." Frankie turned his hands palms out. "I wanna get the sports. Don't you have cable?"

"That is basic cable. Just twelve channels. You'll get the football games on the major networks this afternoon."

He caught himself before he asked the names of the people found beaten by the police. Stewart didn't want to make a mistake and say he knew them because everything he said went back to Grimaldi. One thing this man did have was a good memory.

Big Frankie got up. "Let's go down to Hardies for breakfast and a newspaper. I gotta' check the spread on some of the games."

At eleven o'clock in the morning, Stewart and his Mafia companion were back at the coal mine. Grimaldi came ten minutes later with one man. They had agreed that too many people showing up all the time might get someone's attention.

The guard reported no activity except some dove hunters banging away with shotguns off in a distant field early that morning. The two men walked the length of the mine going over every detail again. Stewart stopped under the vault area. His helmet light shone on Grimaldi's face.

"Midnight," Stewart said. "That's when it starts."

"Back here at ten tonight, okay." Grimaldi said. "No sense havin' the boys sitting around getting nervous for too long."

Back at the mobile home, Stewart made the Chicago tough guy take a long jog and walk that lasted for two hours. He complained the whole way, but Stewart told him that exercise was a good way to get rid of nervous tension.

"Let's get back and watch the pre-game show," Frankie gasped.

Stewart couldn't sit still. Finally he said, "How the hell can you sit there smoking cigarettes, drinking beer, and be so interested in a game with what's going to go down tonight?"

Frankie glanced up at Stewart with a quirky expression. "Look professor . . . in our business it's part of the job. Over the years, I taught myself how to relax before we're going to pull off a big one, or even whack somebody. You can't think about gettin' caught. That's bad vibes!"

Stewart shuddered inside. He hoped that Frankie didn't notice. Again he thought how alien these people were compared to the general society. The man talked about murder like it was just part of a day's work. Then Stewart realized that his mortality could be on the line tonight. *It would just be part of one night's work.*

"I'm going to take a nap," Stewart told him. He went into one of the two bedrooms, closed the door, laid down, and stared at the ceiling fan turning ever so slowly.

He thought about the past two days, when at different times, he had shared a laugh with some of them, talked politics over lunch sitting in the mine, worked at cutting up into the ceiling through the stone and eventually into the bottom of the depository itself.

When Grimaldi saw the bottom of the vault's concrete floor appear and watched the cement powder fly away as the saw cut into it, he spoke with half a smile, half grimace. "Until now I wasn't sure about this job, Stewart. I guess you know your stuff."

Stewart understood he wasn't really getting to know these men. Before Cason left for Switzerland, Eddie told him, "When you're with them, Paul . . . never forget! These guys can do two things at once . . . smile and shoot you at the same time."

He closed his eyes but sleep wouldn't come. As a college professor he never had this problem. *That seemed a long time ago.*

His eyes blinked open and the fan was still there, turning and turning. He felt like Dorothy from *The Wizard of Oz,* tossed by a tornado from a comfortable place she knew in Kansas; to a world of make believe in her dreams. *Only this was real.*

He decided to review the ten men in his mind. There was the boss, Grimaldi. Then five men who in the early hours of the coming morning, would drive away in the giant dump trucks loaded with government gold.

That left four. Two he learned were expert at electrical and mechanical problems. *The two others, more expert in other areas,* he guessed. One was a big guy who had the pummeled face and gnarled hands of a fighter. Stewart was bigger, but up against a professional like him, he wouldn't have a chance.

That left the slim man who seemed to be Big Guy's friend. When he had a chance, Slim One took out a revolver and carefully cleaned it. Almost lovingly, he would take out the bullets, wiped them off, or put a drop of oil on the cylinder, and flip it back into the frame with a chilling, metallic snap. He was like a CIA assassin, a paid killer, always checking his deadly equipment.

He gave Stewart the creeps. There was just something about him. *There was cruelness in his eyes. A blank stare with death hidden behind it.* He would need to watch those two, plus their boss, Grimaldi, who gave the orders.

Finally, around seven o'clock, they decided to go out and get a pizza and bring it back to the trailer. They could not have it delivered, Stewart told Frankie. "You go inside and pick it up. I might be recognized by someone and I don't want to answer questions."

It was a plausible reason for Frankie. The real concern for Stewart was that someone who knew him as Richards could say, "Hi, Floyd . . . what's with the bald look?" Then it would be all over.

As agreed, they drove back to the mine at ten o'clock and all the participants were there. The final timing of the action and each individual's responsibility was reviewed again by both Stewart and Grimaldi.

Then they all sat down around the vault area. Stewart noticed everything. The Chicago men brought two cooler chests, one filled with sandwiches, the other with soft drinks, and a big commercial thermos of coffee. They knew it would be a long night.

After eating, he watched as several men smoked cigarettes or big cigars with a side of coffee. Sitting around on the mine floor, waiting for midnight to come, was very tedious. Talk was short. Nerves were pulling muscles so tight they could hum a tune.

This wasn't just another job like Frankie said earlier today. This would be the biggest heist since man put stuff in a box. And all of them knew it.

Chapter 53

At 11: 30 Sunday night it was time to make history. They were standing just outside the mine entrance. Stewart pulled off his baseball cap and a forty-four degree breeze blew over his bald head. The night was clear of clouds and it had cooled down fast He glanced up and saw half a moon. All the stars seemed intensely visible.

Two men stood beside the small unmarked cargo truck listening to Grimaldi. "You drive. Don't get out of the cab." He turned to the other man. "You stay in the truck for the whole trip. When you're done, get back fast."

Then with his forefinger pointed at the driver. "If for some unlucky reason the cops are on your tail, don't lead 'em back here. I'll shoot you first. Okay?"

"Yeah, boss. We'll be out of town and gone."

They both climbed into the truck and left. The rest of the men walked back to the vault area in the coal mine to wait for the signal. Grimaldi stayed near the entrance but up higher on the hill so he could see the depository.

Fifteen minutes later, Grimaldi's Kenwood two-way radio beeped. The Mafia Capo listened.

"There's a change of guard for the midnight shift. We're gonna circle around and come back in ten minutes."

Grimaldi called Big Guy in the mine. "It's going down tonight. Nobody else is up there. Get ready."

Each minute dragged like 120 seconds. Finally the driver called again. "Just one guard in each sentry box. I'm passing the parking area . . . backing up to the cement stops in front of the gates. You'll see it in fifteen seconds." He left the engine running.

The man in the truck body unlatched the heavy rear doors from inside and swung them open about two feet. They had been lined with bullet proof metal sheets and so had the sides of this particular truck all the way up to the back of the cab.

He leaned over and picked up the wicked looking M136. A lightweight self-contained anti-armor weapon consisting of a free flight, fin stabilized cartridge packed in an expandable launcher.

He aimed at the center of the iron fence gate just thirty feet away and pulled the trigger. It fired an 84 millimeter HEAT, a high explosive anti-tank rocket capable of penetrating and destroying light weight armored vehicles. The missile exploded with a huge ball of orange fire. The gate blew wide apart.

The experienced Sicilian never bothered to look at what the guards were doing. He guessed they were young, inexperienced, civil service employees who were either knocked flat on the ground or got there by choice.

The shooter loaded the launcher with another rocket. Quickly it was back on his shoulder. He took careful aim at the front doors of the Bullion Depository, an estimated seventy-five feet away.

The missile ruptured the heavy doors and barely broke them open. Just what they wanted. No casualties, but the explosion had the desired effect. It set off every alarm inside and outside the building.

The truck driver had been watching each sentry box in his two, extra large, rear view mirrors, installed specifically for this purpose. After stopping, he used a dashboard mounted switch to electrically move each mirror from his driver's seat to select a perfect view without arousing suspicion from anyone outside.

At the back of the truck, mounted at the top of each corner of the truck body were twin, high intensity flood lights aimed at the guard houses. The measurements had been taken when the Mafia soldiers visited the parking area the first time.

The instant the shooter fired the first rocket, the driver turned on the lights using another dashboard switch. He watched the guards after the initial strike. One suspicious guard had stepped out of his sentry box as the truck's rear doors opened. He was knocked down by the explosion sustaining a few cuts from flying debris.

The other guard dove for the ground. He tried to get up just as the glaring bright lights blinded him. Expecting to receive more incoming enemy fire, he again dropped to the ground. A few seconds later, the second rocket hit the depository doors. Both guards stayed down.

The instant the second rocket exploded, the truck roared off down Gold Vault Road and onto Bullion Boulevard, making a right turn onto State Road thirty-one going west. He immediately crossed over the grass median strip and made a U-turn getting to the exit that would quickly lead to a country road, then to the gravel road, and onto the dirt trail leading back down into the woods.

A guard was waiting at the fence line with the gate open for the truck to pull in and drive back to the mine entrance. The truck was back ten minutes after the attack. Right after the second rocket exploded, Grimaldi spoke into his radio to the big guy inside the mine. "Hit the vault now, okay!"

He was standing up in the woods, high enough to use binoculars trained on the depository building. He had been watching as the diversion took place, while all the other men were waiting and ready, down under the vault floor.

For the next thirty minutes, with occasional radio calls inside the mine to determine progress, Grimaldi watched in total fascination. The alarms were in full howl, blaring outside the depository across the grassy hilltop and the surrounding woodlands.

Within a few minutes, two jeeps appeared with search lights glaring from top mounted fixtures. Figures jumped out and ran toward the shattered fence gate. They spoke with a sentry. Almost immediately they were back in the jeeps laying rubber as they tore down to the highway. The Mafia boss had watched his truck loop around and get off the highway before the depository guard force jeeps left the hilltop.

The second procession of official cars came from the Fort Knox Military Police. Then a few minutes later cars from the Hardin County Sheriffs Department and the Radcliff Police Department arrived with sirens screaming or whooping. The personnel from each organization had to wait outside the depository.

The third entourage of vehicles included military and civilian ambulances along with both army and local fire department trucks with all of their noise makers whooping and screeching in the middle of the night. Those people were also kept outside the building. Then a patrol car from the Kentucky State Highway Police showed up. He joined all the other frustrated law enforcement people who were forced to stand around in the cold of night.

In another twenty minutes, two helicopters were zipping around overhead with harsh spot lights roaming over the ground. Agents of the Federal Bureau of Investigation from the Louisville district were on their way to the Fort Knox area.

Grimaldi knew that they would not be allowed inside the depository building either. Stewart had explained that no visitors, no matter who they were, could ever get into the United States Treasury's Bullion Depository. That was official policy.

Inside the lobby entrance are the offices of the Officer in Charge and the Captain of the Guard. They were recent arrivals at that time of night also and were trying to assess the damage.

They stared at both the shattered iron fence gate and the depository's broken front double doors that now stood ajar, one hanging at an angle from a giant broken hinge. This unprecedented event was way beyond their scope of office.

Various protection agencies from the local area, the state, the United States Army, and soon, agents from the federal government's own FBI would be clamoring to be allowed access inside the building to begin multiple investigations. Of course the press would be right behind them.

The Officer-in-Charge placed a telephone call to the headquarters of the United States Mint Police in Washington, D. C. He glanced at his Captain of the Guard as he drummed his fingers on the desk. "Whoever is on duty had better damn well wake up the boss."

The security of the gold was another entirely different problem. Since nobody had actually gained entry into the depository the Mint Police were not yet concerned with a theft. But it would be standard U. S. Mint procedure to view the gold in the vault and take an inventory.

That's where their second major problem started. Not even the Officer-in-Charge or the Captain of the Guard could open the twenty ton vault door in the basement. No one person was entrusted with the combination. Various members of the depository staff must dial separate combinations known only to them. They would all have to be brought here immediately.

But Lady Luck had dealt the government two bum cards. One badly needed staff member was still on vacation overseas and not due to return to duty until Wednesday.

Worse yet, her back-up was recovering from an emergency acute appendicitis operation performed on Saturday and not due out of the hospital until Tuesday.

Now for the capper. Even if they could be contacted by telephone, email, facsimile, or carrier pidgeon, neither one could divulge the necessary part of the combination that each possessed. Secrecy required that each portion of the number can only be dialed at the vault by each possessor.

Paul Stewart had already discussed the fact with Grimaldi that it took several Mint employees to open the vault and they would not be on duty at night. The robbers did not know about the coming delay to open the vault and it would play beautifully into their plans.

Grimaldi continued to have a ringside seat for the melee that was just beginning to develop. Through expensive, high powered binoculars, he watched as local television trucks and news crews started to arrive on the scene.

What a beautiful fucking mess this is, he thought. *All hell has broken loose and they don't even know the half of it yet.*

A broad smile appeared under the field glasses as his eyes blinked open wide in almost disbelief. Even though he knew it to be true, it was hard for his mind to comprehend that this was actually happening.

Tomaso Grimaldi was the only previously informed witness to an incredible historical event that even he couldn't fully appreciate yet.

Chapter 54

The truck driver had called Grimaldi as soon as the shooter fired the second rocket. It wasn't necessary. When the Mafia boss saw the ball of flames burst against the depository's huge front doors he called his men inside the mine on a different radio frequency.

It was 12:02 Monday morning when they received Grimaldi's call. Bruno and Frankie were standing on the scaffold, ready with diamond saw blades to cut through the last twelve inches of concrete. They worked on opposite sides of the rectangle. Four inches up they ran into an unexpected problem. Hoop bands of steel had been encased in the floor when the concrete was poured.

"Gimme the torch," Bruno yelled. The acetylene torch was handed up to him. It had a twenty foot long hose that connected to the gas and oxygen tanks. It took a few seconds for him to adjust the flame with the right combination of gases to produce the six thousand degree heat. Then fifteen minutes of precious time was lost to cut through the steel hoops all the way around the ten by twenty foot rectangle.

But just as they continued with the saws, a cracking sound made them jump down off the scaffold. The basement floor had started to give way. No one wanted tons of gold to crush them in an instant. But the floor held for the moment.

Another member of the Chicago team stepped forward and without a word spoken, climbed onto the scaffold and began to work some plastic explosive inside the saw cut for twelve feet along each long side of the rectangle. Then he inserted two wires into each section of the soft material and stepped down and away from the expected drop area.

He didn't have to say anything. Everyone there knew what came next and they got out of range. "Fire in the hole," he yelled as he set off the charge electrically. It produced a pretty good bang, like a two-inch salute would make during a Fourth of July fireworks show.

Then with a crashing boom, like a small avalanche, the whole two hundred square foot section of the vault basement dropped to the floor of the coal mine and crunched the scaffolding flat on the way down.

It was far better than pennies from heaven. Thousands of gold bars showered down. The air was filled with concrete dust and debris, but the shimmering yellow of the ingots flashed its color through it all. It took a full ninety seconds before it settled and began to clear.

As Stewart had explained to Grimaldi the bars were not individually wrapped, they were not in wooden boxes, not on shelves, and not in cabinets.

That would have required climbing up into the vault and handing the heavy bars down two at a time.

Fortunately for them, the ingots were packed tightly together, like a pallet of red bricks but without the straps around it. And they were stacked up higher than your head in one concentrated mass in different rooms in the vault. So several giant piles of gold bars just dropped right into their waiting hands.

It was the veritable pot of gold at the end of the rainbow that now revealed itself to the men standing around it. The gold ingots sparkled and gleamed from the intense, bright light the miners' helmet lamps created as the men surveyed the fortune that now lay at their feet.

"Jesus Chri ——." one man started to say. He was cut off by the sound of alarms that came from up inside the vault.

Stewart had the presence of mind to grab an aluminum adjustable ladder, run it up against the broken edge of the vault floor, climb up and peek slowly over the top. Other than depository employees, he was the first visitor, in a sense, that had ever looked inside the gold chamber at Fort Knox, except for two former Presidents of the United States, Roosevelt and Truman.

He disappeared over the top for twenty seconds. Stepping back down to the mine floor, he saw Grimaldi standing there out of breath. The Capo had hurried along the shaft from outside. He wanted to witness this historic event in the annals of major crime.

They all stood around Stewart. He told them that in the vault there are several corridors with rows of tiny rooms on each side. Each room has a door that opens

313

into its own storage area. But the twenty ton main vault door was closed and the red laser beams just inside the door had not yet been disturbed.

He said. "The depository staff has to disarm the beams before they open the vault door, and with all the other confusion, it will take them until dawn before that happens.

The best news is that the gold we dropped out of several rooms can't be seen when they do open the big vault door anyway. They'll have to walk around the end of one corridor."

Stewart suggested further that the movement of the gold activated a motion alarm, and the noise it made when it dropped set off a sound alarm inside the gold storage area. No one upstairs in the building, or for that matter, standing just outside the basement vault door could hear the alarms inside the vault anyway.

But up on the first floor in the security office the blinking red lights on the monitor board plus the buzzing sound would have alerted the men on duty, under normal conditions, that there was a problem in the gold vault itself. But conditions were definitely not normal.

Usually, at that time of night there was a limited guard detail on shift and no other employees. By now, however, the Captain of the Guard brought in additional men to either help outside the front of the building to keep all the other law enforcement personnel from entering the depository, or inside the office of the Officer-in-Charge, receiving multiple orders.

"Turn off the audible on those damn alarms," the Officer-in-Charge ordered. "I can't hear myself think, much less speak."

A staff employee left and got the sound off on all systems except the outside alarms, which helped to further annoy the news reporters and the police. Another employee was reporting to the Officer-in-Charge.

"I didn't notice it before, but the monitor now indicates that two alarm systems inside the vault have been activated."

"Do you think they have been on since the attack or just came on now?" The captain asked.

"I don't know, sir. The blast at the front door could have shaken the basement enough to kick them off immediately . . . or it's a delayed reaction."

"I already knew that." The captain looked disgusted.

The gigantic Toro LHD, model 0010, made in Finland and recently bought used in Canada, sat just short of the drop area. Built to unusual specifications, the ore hauler was used in deep underground mines. Its height at nine feet and width at nine feet, eight inches, were purposely small to fit into tight places. But its length was thirty-six feet, five inches and it weighed in at a hefty 84,000 pounds.

On the front was a giant scoop, an eleven yard bucket, capable of lifting 35,500 pounds or seventeen and one half tons at a time. The driver revved up the 350 horse power Detroit diesel in-line six cylinder engine, and like some prehistoric cave dwelling behemoth it lumbered slowly forward.

Carefully the driver dropped the bucket down to the mine floor and pushed far into the pile of gold, then turned the scoop up, which allowed the bars to slide down to the bottom.

Like mosquitoes in comparison, the two small tractors scooted in and out from each side with shovel scoops, adding to the load as they dumped their gold into the Toro's huge maw.

"Come on." Grimaldi yelled over the noise of the tractors and the din of the alarms above them. "Pick up some bars and load 'em." With that Grimaldi picked up a bar in each hand and dropped them in the big scoop. The others followed suit including Stewart.

Time was not on their side. Now it was working against them. And this was not quick or easy work. The bars, somewhat smaller than a building brick, are formed to exact specifications; 7 x 3-5/8 x 1-3/4 inches. The fine gold bars contain 400 troy ounces refined to a purity requirement of 999.9 parts per thousand and the avoirdupois weight of each bar is 27-1/2 pounds.

Once loaded, the Toro backed into one of the mined out areas that ran perpendicular to the main tunnel and turned around. The drive speeds were 3.7 miles per hour in first gear up to 16.2 mph in fourth gear, if terrain and load allowed for it.

Stewart had a stop watch and he was timing the loading of the gold into the Toro's bucket, and the time to turn it around. Then he jogged to keep up with the big hauler down to the mine entrance. Outside in the area cleared for loading, the behemoth pulled up beside a twenty-five ton dump truck.

Stewart continued to separately time each operation, so he could help the driver improve performance. Bucket motion times were standard on this hauler: Raise time, 8.3 seconds; tipping time, 2.0 seconds; and lowering time, 4.3 seconds. Stewart followed the hauler back up the main shaft which completed one trip. He looked at his stop watch, made some more notes, and looked up at Grimaldi.

"Twenty-five minutes to complete one round trip. It'll take six more trips to take out over a billion in gold. That's another two and a half . . . maybe three hours."

"Worst case we're out by four," Grimaldi answered.

They continued to move and work fast knowing that in just a few hours armed guards might be looking down from the vault into the mine. The Toro went back for another scoop full to top off the first trailer.

Then the driver slid a power tarp down over the load and the truck rolled out of the woods and weaved its way back to state road 31 west where it would lead to Louisville, roar into Indiana, and then north towards Chicago.

While the Toro took another load down to the second truck, Stewart had the driver of one small tractor pick up some gold bars and move them to a specific area. This was their payment as agreed on with the Chicago Mafia.

The tractor dropped the gold bars right in front of the hole where he and Eddie Cason had entered the

317

coal mine from the cave below. Even with the light on the front of the tractor it was impossible to notice the black tarp, slathered over with a mixture of black paint and coal dust and hidden behind a coal pile.

Stewart needed about 440 gold bars, or a bit less than six tons, for their cut of fifty million dollars. This was actually fifty-five million, but no one was counting. He wanted the extra five million as a special present for someone.

Finally the last EAST dump trailer pulled out of the wooded area. Each driver had taken a different route as soon as possible. One truck went for Indiana, one into Illinois and another toward Missouri.

All states had a common border with Kentucky. Some routes were longer than others and actually required driving away from Chicago, their final destination. But it was all part of the plan. Stay separated. The cops wouldn't catch them all together.

It was 3:45 on Monday morning. The Mafia soldiers were exhausted and anxious to leave. Adrenaline, coffee, and sandwiches had kept them going but now weariness was apparent in all of them.

Five of the ten mobsters had left, each driving one of the EAST dump trucks. The two men who had caused the diversion up at the depository also left in one of the two automobiles. The small, armor proofed truck from which they had fired the rocket was left behind. It would be too hot to take up on the highway.

Stewart knew that left just three men; Grimaldi, Big Guy, and Slim, the one who liked guns. He had been moving away from all of them as their numbers dwindled down. He remembered clearly Cason's advice that the Mafia will have a twist at the end.

Something you won't expect. He had been working his way toward the mine cut that went back to the opening into the cave.

He was also watching Grimaldi, now in deep conversation with Slim, gesturing and holding his hands out. It looked to Stewart like he was explaining something. He backed further away. He was a good seventy feet from them when he realized Big Guy was not with them. His skin crawled with goose bumps as he spun around.

Chapter 55

Stewart's helmet lamp revealed Big Guy walking toward him from the mine entrance where the giant Toro now sat, quiet and empty, after delivering its last cargo of gold and disgorging it into an EAST dump truck.

Stewart missed seeing him go down to the entrance. The man had hitched a ride in the Toro's cab with the driver and the cab is on the opposite side of the big ore hauler from where Stewart had been working.

Big Guy's lamp light glared brightly back at him. Stewart judged him to be one hundred feet away. He was cut off. He could not escape that way.

Suddenly he heard Grimaldi's voice. Stewart's head jerked around, 180 degrees, like a puppet on a string.

"Hey, Paul." Grimaldi called out. "Whadda ya doin' down there. You did a hel-luv-a job. We couldn't have done it without you. I wanna shake your hand." He had a big smile fixed on his face.

Stewart just froze. That statement was completely out of character for the Mafia boss. He hadn't smiled for the entire weekend. Stewart knew that everything he had done was expected of him or else. He was getting his requested share. And on Friday he had promised Grimaldi that he could deliver the goods as planned.

Stewart knew enough about these criminals that they don't go around thanking people for anything. These men don't waste time. The score was not over until they made their escape.

So this must be the twist that Eddie had warned him about. The change the Mafia would make in the ending. And the change definitely involved him. He saw another head light start to move towards him. It was Slim walking his way. It was a slow determined stride.

"Thanks Tommy," Stewart said. "But we all need to get out of here. I'm going to my truck."

Now Grimaldi was walking behind Slim. "You have to stay behind." He said it in a matter-of-fact way. "Nothing personal you understand. I wish it could be different. But this heist is gonna get real hot. They need to find someone here. A trail that won't lead to us."

They both continued to walk. Stewart turned to look at Big Guy. His light bobbled along. He was still coming from the other direction. Stewart was only fifteen feet from the perpendicular mined out cut that lead to the cave.

He yelled his statement at them. "You're going to tie me up. I go to jail and you get away. Is that it?"

321

Stewart was actually angry at them. This wasn't fair, he thought. Then reality hit him hard. These men don't know about fair. They do what's good for them.

"We need a body, Stewart," Grimaldi continued. "Live people can talk. It's strictly business. We're not mad . . . you did your job. Now we have to finish ours, okay!"

Stewart had not expected a twist this big. Even though Eddie had warned him that they might kill him, he thought that would be for messing things up. Or if they didn't find gold. But he wasn't prepared for this turn of events.

He had to take charge. They were in his domain. He was a caver. They were outsiders. Again, he thought, *Fight back. If you're going to die, make them pay.*

He spun around and ran to the mined out cut. He sprinted down the thirty feet to where his gold had been dumped in a pile and dropped to his knees. His head lamp shining, he groped around until he found the object wrapped in black oilskin near the opening to the cave below.

He reached up with one hand, turned off his head lamp, knelt down behind the gold bars, and waited. The Mafia men had to cover more than fifty feet from both directions in the main shaft to get to the cut. They got there just as Stewart dropped for cover.

They came around both corners simultaneously. Their three helmet lamps glowing brightly down into the mined out room. But lights diffuse quickly into the blackness and thirty feet was a long distance in a dark mine to see clearly.

They all stopped instinctively. They had expected to see a light from Stewart's head lamp. Unfamiliar with working below the earth, they just assumed the light would be there. They had not thought about turning off their helmet lights for the past three days. It was like breathing or the dawn coming. It was supposed to be there.

But here in this underground mine cut there was nothing but darkness. Stewart peeked over his metal barrier, a barrier made entirely of pure gold bars. Slim and Big Guy had guns in their hands.

They continued to walk slowly forward. Stewart watched their lamp lights move back and forth trying to locate him. "Come on, Stewart," Grimaldi said impatiently. "Let's get this over with . . . you're just making it worse, okay."

When they were only fifteen feet away, the twelve gauge shotgun roared to life. Slim flipped backwards and dropped like a stone. The full force of number four express load pellets caught him center chest. Stewart didn't hesitate. He had used a pump shotgun for years as a boy growing up on a farm hunting game birds and rabbits.

In one smooth fast motion, he pulled back on the pump action which threw the expended shell out of the chamber, then slammed it back forward which rammed another live round from the magazine into the firing chamber ready for action.

The Mafia men didn't waste time either. As soon as the shotgun fired they didn't wait to see what happened to Slim. They returned pistol fire at the spot where the flame from Stewart's weapon had appeared and ran for cover, firing ineffectively with one arm extended behind.

But Stewart had ducked behind his golden shield. The bullets of return fire bounced off the gold bars and the wall of coal behind it. The two mobsters raced back around the corner into the main shaft.

"Son-of-a-bitch had a shotgun hidden and we walked right into it." Grimaldi yelled. Then he spotted one of the smaller tractors sitting there with its bigger headlight shining brightly.

He jumped into the driver's seat, started up the engine, and fumbled with the gears until he found the lever that raised the bucket up in front of his upper body and face. He could still rise up in the seat to see or fire over the top of the scoop.

"Let's go back and finish with that bastard, okay."

Big Guy walked in back of the tractor as it rounded the corner into the mined out room. This time they remembered to turn off their helmet lamps. Behind the tractor's head light with their Beretta nine millimeter automatics raised, they were ready. The tractor rumbled down almost to the solid wall of coal at the end of the cut. They stopped right in front of the pile of gold ingots.

"He must be lying down behind it," Grimaldi said. "Walk off to one side and look while I keep him covered." The Capo stood up with his gun pointing above the golden treasure.

Big Guy stepped away from behind the tractor. He moved slowly and kept behind the light as he went to the side wall. "Beats me, Tommy, but he's fuckin' disappeared."

He took his eyes off the coal face as he stepped carefully back toward the tractor over the uneven mine floor.

"It's not possible," Grimaldi started. "He's got to be ———."

The sound of the shotgun in such close quarters would scare any human. It boomed out three times in rapid succession. The first round of steel shot hit Big Guy in the side. He sagged down fast with a groan of pain.

The second round blew out the tractor's light. The third was a guess. An estimate in the dark. But all Stewart had to do was raise the shotgun slightly. That's where Grimaldi's face and or the tractor blade would be.

After the mobsters had run around the corner, Stewart had picked up the black tarp and slipped down behind it on the ledge in the cave. He was able to stand on some small boulders and lean against the rock wall with just a corner of the tarp open enough for him to peek out. It was all he needed.

Now the total absence of light closed in around Stewart like an old friend. Many nights he sat in some cavern after supper in the complete tomb-like blackness and welcomed the sense of quiet and peace that it afforded him. Only the occasional drip of water had sometimes broken the silence.

But Grimaldi was out of his element. *It's black as shit in this coal mine,* he thought. He heard the groaning of his henchman lying on the mine floor. He couldn't turn on his helmet light. Stewart was a fast shot and he'd be dead in five seconds.

If he backed out sitting on the tractor, Stewart would come after him. If he got off and ran back toward the main shaft Stewart would turn on his light and blast him. He had to make a deal.

"Stewart." He yelled. "Whadda' want, okay?"

The answer came from a voice that had changed. It was also flat and deadly. "I want to kill you."

"You probably could. Maybe."

Big Guy groaned. "I'm sittin' up boss. I've got my gun. Let him come."

Stewart heard them both but kept silent. Instead of answering he let his actions speak for him. The capo heard the distinctive sound of live shells being shoved into the magazine of a shotgun. It made a series of sharp metallic clicks.

Stewart had used four rounds. He punched each one home with extra force for effect until the weapon held six shells again.

Grimaldi was sweating heavily. He was running out of time. This Stewart guy was near them but for some reason, invisible. He didn't like the odds or the business sound of the shotgun being reloaded by someone who knew real well how to use it.

"Here's the deal." Grimaldi spoke out loud. "You let me take my men out of the mine on the tractor to my car. We're gone . . . you won't hear from us again. No reprisals!" He emphasized the last two words.

Finally Stewart spoke. "Trusting you is not a healthy habit. How do I know you'll stick to this deal?"

"You don't. But if I'm found dead my boys will know who did it. Some other family member will try to get to you for killing a capo. But letting me live after I tried to kill you. Then I owe you one. That's how it works, okay."

Grimaldi continued. "Something else too. I know you and Fast Eddie ain't goin' talk about this job. You got as much to lose as we do."

There was a long silence. *It actually makes sense,* Stewart thought. *I couldn't live with myself if I jumped out and killed two more men anyway. One was enough, even in self defense. Besides, Paul Stewart is going to disappear forever by tomorrow night.*

"I agree. You've got the deal." Stewart yelled out.

Grimaldi turned on his head lamp. The capo dropped his gun in the tractor's scoop and started to help his men. Suddenly Stewart had a new thought. A new direction for this whole caper. It just came to him out of the blue. He looked at the Mafia boss and thought. *Now I've got a twist coming your way!*

Chapter 56

With no hesitation and the confidence of a man defended and surrounded by a SWAT team, Grimaldi got out from behind the tractor's protective bucket, turned on his helmet light, put his back to Stewart, and helped the wounded Big Guy onto the tractor seat.

He turned the vehicle around and then stopped beside the body of the Slim Man. Agilely he got out, picked up the dead man, put him in the bucket on the front of the tractor, and drove off. He never looked back. Absolute trust can be beautiful.

Stewart quickly turned on his helmet light and looked at his watch. It was 4:15 Monday morning and time was running out. He still had work to finish.

From his hiding place on the cave's ledge, he climbed up into the mine, lifted the tarp and fixed it with tie clips so it would be out of the way. He pulled on a pair of latex gloves as he ran to the other small tractor out in the main shaft.

Until now, he hadn't touched anything that would leave a finger print. It started right up and with the bright light turned on, he drove into the mine cut where the gold bars lay waiting.

In fifteen minutes he had scooped up the heavy ingots and dumped them over the ledge from the coal mine into the cave where they slid down onto the high shelf.

He replaced the coal dust covered black tarp. Then he hand picked some coal and carefully stacked it up against the tarp. The opening was only three feet high. Not too much to cover.

The Mint Police would be checking every square inch of the mine floor. But they would not be looking for an opening into a cave. In this poker game, that was his ace in the hole.

He backed the tractor up to the main shaft where he picked up four sections of rails from the old track used by the coal car. He had pried them off the mine floor earlier in the week before the Mafia arrived. He had meticulously worked that area so it would look like it had been done a long time ago by rubbing coal dust and dirt into the fresh pry marks and rail ends to give it a look of untouched antiquity.

Again he steered the tractor to the coal covered tarp and dropped the sections of track right up against the newly laid coal. Stewart knew they would use metal detectors, but this should fool the operator. The iron rails will disguise the reading from the gold below the ledge. He got off the tractor and strategically placed a few more pieces of coal in front.

Then he drove the tractor down near the mine entrance, stopped fifty feet back in the shaft, turned off the tractor and his helmet light and just sat there. He waited for his eyes to adjust to the darkness around

329

him illuminated by the glow of the half moon outside. He listened for any human sounds. He heard nothing. It was still dark at five in the morning.

He walked softly out past the entrance and stood behind a tree. He noticed the other small tractor that carried Grimaldi and his men was parked along side the giant Toro and the small truck used for the diversion up at the depository. Grimaldi's Cadillac was gone. No one was waiting for him.

But there was a lot of noise and activity up at the gold depository. *Good. They could not have heard the gun shots echoing inside the mine shaft.*

He jogged at a steady pace through three hundred yards of oak scrub and pine woods to his cave system now owned by the National Park Service. He slowed to a walk as he came to the parking lot and glanced around to be sure no one else was there.

He saw his truck where he had parked it last night at nine thirty. He left it here to keep it away from all the big vehicles that moved around the mine entrance yesterday. As an extra precaution he had removed the license plate, threw it in the cab of the truck and locked the door.

Replacing the license plate, Stewart drove through the new attraction's landscaped driveway onto the secondary road that led to the main highway. Access was blocked off by the Kentucky Highway Patrol at the entrance ramp to State Road 31W.

He pulled off on the road's shoulder, turned off his head lights, and watched. They were checking driver's licenses and license plates of all vehicles that came out of this secondary road. He was sure some of the EAST dump trucks made it onto the highway before state police set up the road block.

Stewart made a U-turn, switched his lights back on, followed the secondary road away from the highway towards the Radcliff Industrial Park, and turned off on a right fork that took him to the Camp Carlson Army Travel Camp, a recreation service for military personnel.

Stewart had given each of the Mafia soldiers a Golden Access Pass to enter the camp grounds. All kinds of motor homes, vans, station wagons, and other recreational vehicles were moving in and out, both at night and during the day, so a dump truck wouldn't be entirely out of place.

The back side of Camp Carlson opened onto State Road 60. There were no road blocks there. Stewart then drove west, away from Fort Knox, Radcliff, and route 31. He would drive a loop, some forty-five extra miles, to get back to Elizabethtown.

At six in the morning he pulled into a 7-11 Store. Just two cars were parked at the front door and one at the gas pumps. Only one person on duty inside. The telephone was located in an outside booth away from the store. He parked there.

He sat in the truck listening to his tape recorder while writing down information. Then he used the pay phone to dial up the Louisville office of The Federal Bureau of Investigation.

The telephone was answered by a recording that asked the caller to leave a message. They would return when the office opened at 8:15 AM. Stewart knew the time and date of his message would automatically be added. That was important.

He felt even better about not speaking to a live person. No one would interrupt or ask questions. Now he used a high pitched voice that spoke in short, jerky phrases.

"The gold depository . . . at Fort Knox . . . has been robbed. Five, quad axle . . . twenty five ton dump trucks . . . carry the gold. First one left . . . Radcliff at one thirty . . . this morning."

He gave them truck descriptions; make and model; the company name on the cab doors; license plate numbers, and the fact that each truck was routed through a different state to arrive at Chicago.

He did not mention the Mafia or give any names. He specifically left out any reference to Grimaldi. If the police stopped his car, they would find one wounded and one dead man. He would claim it was a drive by shooting.

Then with great emphasis he added. "I'm risking my life . . . to be a good citizen. I am not a . . . part of their group . . . but they will know . . . who informed on them if information leaks . . . to any news group that . . . the FBI had an informed source . . . who disclosed these details."

He hung up the phone. He knew they could trace his call to this location, but that would not be a danger to him. He wore latex gloves so that fingerprints could not be lifted from the telephone or the booth. Voice imaging would not help them either.

Once again, Richards alias Stewart, revealed his naiveté. The FBI would be concerned with capturing anyone involved with this unprecedented robbery, including him. They would want to take credit for solving this case ahead of any other law enforcement organization and grab international newspaper headlines plus the admiration of the television newscasters around the world as the premiere protector of the United States Government, its assets, and the public.

If by some slim chance, they didn't need to reveal the fact that they had received a tip before anyone even knew that the famous Gold Bullion Depository at Fort Knox had been robbed, they might honor his request.

The FBI knew the importance of protecting its sources of information. Otherwise tipsters or informants would disappear and go elsewhere. But this robbery could be an exception to the rule. This would be too big an investigation with too much at stake not to play it for all its worth. They needed all the good public relations they could generate.

Right now Stewart desperately needed a cup of coffee, but he didn't dare go into this 7-11 Store where someone might recall seeing a man driving this particular type of Ford truck who used their pay phone at this hour on this Monday morning.

It wasn't very likely. But Stewart was taking no chances. He climbed back into his pick-up and drove to a McDonald's a few miles away near the entrance ramp to the parkway.

Driving along in the early morning light traffic, he shuddered involuntarily. He wondered how Grimaldi would handle this. Somewhere during the process of fact finding and information researched about this incredible event the press might learn that a tipster called the authorities before the theft was discovered. Grimaldi would know it wasn't his men. That left just one other person who knew about it . . . Paul Stewart.

Of course, if the FBI, with the cooperation of local and state police, did their job efficiently and could apprehend several of the trucks in the next few hours, the Mafia Capo would immediately know it was Stewart.

He hadn't planned it this way from the start. He had wanted to lash back at the unfairness of the federal government; whether it was at their attorney, Jay Cohen; the National Park Service, the Mammoth Cave National Park, Bank One, or even the University of Kentucky. They all had turned on him.

From the time he first thought about how it could be done, however, he had always been uncomfortable with the theft and the enormity of it. Being kicked and beaten by the government at every turn he took was unfair, but it was not breaking the law.

But Grimaldi had planned to kill him all along. So this was Stewart's twist in the plan. He wasn't going to let them get away with this robbery. And he knew this choice of action might cost him his life. They would come after him for a second time.

He pulled his truck into a three car line at the McDonald's drive-in window to order a big breakfast and a large coffee. Right now he needed the energy from food and the kick from caffeine to keep himself awake for the rest of the trip back to his Lexington mobile home. He parked away from other vehicles in the McDonald's lot and ate while he thought more about the consequences.

Chapter 57

Stewart munched slowly on his food as his mind covered the list of probabilities he now faced. Grimaldi would take this as a giant double cross. Now he would like to kill Stewart for a different reason. He hoped and prayed that Grimaldi would be captured, held without bail, tried, convicted, and sentenced to a long jail term.

If I end up in court, I should get a greatly reduced sentence for calling the FBI to help solve the case and recover the gold. Stewart stopped in mid-chew. He just realized what the mob would do to him as an informant if he spent one day in jail.

Another thought flashed into his brain as his jaws remained motionless. If the authorities didn't catch him, even with all the care that he and Eddie had taken, the Mafia might still track him down.

Oh my God. Eddie. Stewart swallowed his food whole. *I've forgotten about Eddie. It's us not just me who they'll track down. Now it's both of us.*

This major change in the plan he had not discussed with Cason. He would not understand why you would carefully plan and successfully pull off such an intricate and spectacular heist and then give it back.

For sure he would never have agreed to double cross the Mafia, even if they had tried to kill him in the mine too. That would be craziness. Much too big a risk, too much mister nice guy, and much too stupid, Cason would have told him.

When Eddie comes back they'll find him, make him talk, and then kill him. Then I would be the next dead man, Stewart thought. He continued to agonize over the many directions this real life or death chess game could take in the next few weeks.

But if Grimaldi went to jail, Ochopinto's consigliore might prevail on the mob boss to keep his family away from Kentucky. Stay clear of any further involvement in the crime. Although revenge was a huge motive in the world of organized crime, in this case it wouldn't be worth it. The cost might be too great if the FBI finds out that the Chicago Mafia was involved.

And they would be watching them carefully, keeping them under extreme surveillance. Their attorney would strongly insist that they shouldn't be tainted any further with the biggest crime in history.

The warmth from the coffee and hot food was having its effect. The let-down was beginning. He was coming off an incredible high. Stewart had just been through hell and had come back.

The adrenaline was backing out of his system, his nerves were letting go of his mind and body, relaxing a grip that had held him like a vise for the past three days while he was in the company of tough and murderous men.

He had just experienced a horror in the coal mine with the Mafia. He had killed a man in a gun fight, even though it was in self defense. And he had stolen money.

I'm an ordinary guy. I was a college professor. A teacher of young students. I had a simple, uncomplicated life; married with two wonderful children and I enjoyed exploring underground caverns to marvel at some of God's most beautiful designs. Now everything is turned upside down.

In one day he had broken two of God's commandments: *Thou shalt not kill; Thou shalt not steal.* And Stewart had committed them both. As a Christian person, he would have to live with that for the rest of his life.

But in defense of your life, doesn't that justify killing? And the commandment about stealing. If you try to give it back. Doesn't that count? I'm trying to fix that part, God. I've already called the authorities.

Stewart anguished about these thoughts. And he didn't have the answers. He would have to seek guidance in church and pray about it. Stewart shook off his melancholy and started up the truck. He pulled back into light traffic as he got on the Bluegrass Parkway heading east toward Lexington eighty-nine miles away. He concentrated through the drowsiness on what he still had left to do.

Today he would inform his landlady by telephone that unexpectedly he had to move out. He would leave an extra months rent to keep her happy, and give her a forwarding address of General Delivery in San Diego.

This would begin the process of eliminating and removing anything to do with Paul Stewart. Now he had to make the man disappear fast. Tomorrow he would get back into the computers at UK and have his records indicate that he had quit on Wednesday, the following day, and had given that same forwarding address.

He would need to do everything just right in the next few days. Maybe it would save them. But he knew how relentless the Mafia could be when they were double-crossed.

It was 6:45 AM. He turned on the radio and pressed the first pre-set button that automatically tuned to WUKY at 91.3, the University of Kentucky's music and National Public Radio news station.

The local newscaster had just started. "It appears to be a random act of terrorism by persons or groups unknown. According to the local sheriff's office, there were at least two people involved when the unmarked truck backed up to the gold depository gate, opened its back doors from inside, and reportedly fired some type of rocket launcher."

The radio announcer continued. "One guard sustained a shoulder wound and a facial cut from flying metal shards that were blown off the fence gate. We have been told that he is now in stable condition at the base hospital.

"The second rocket exploded against the depository doors, broke them inward, but did not penetrate into the building. No one has yet taken credit for the attack or made contact with the authorities. That's all the informa ——."

Stewart turned off the radio. He took a ball point pen and made notes on a pad about what he still had to do before he got some sleep. His short list included:

Pack all clothes; throw away all items marked with the name Paul Stewart; take all personal items, and burn all photographs of himself in the mobile. Then leave everything else.

He planned to put everything else in his truck today and drive back to his duplex and again become Floyd Richards. He would replace the license plate he had been using since the Mafia arrived. Then he knew he had to get some sleep or he would begin to make some serious mistakes. But first a hot bath and then shave off the beard and mustache.

Later tonight before closing time, he would drive to the public library and assume yet again another identity. Peter Stryker would have to email Elonzo Cassidy. Only he didn't know yet what to tell him.

Chapter 58

The Unites States Mint Police Force was established in 1792. Not many people have heard of them but they are one of the oldest law enforcement agencies in the nation.

They are responsible for the protection of over one hundred billion dollars in the treasury or other assets stored in facilities at Philadelphia, San Francisco, West Point, Denver, Fort Knox and at their headquarters in Washington, D. C.

This means the protection of life and property through the prevention, detection, and investigation of criminal acts which includes collecting and preserving evidence, and making arrests, involving the enforcement of both federal and local laws.

Doctor William F. Fanzio has been the Chief of the Mint Police since 1985. Under his watch there had been no real problems or major crimes and he had intended to keep it that way. But with a phone call at two in the morning local time in Washington, D. C. on that particular Monday in late October, all of that was about to change.

"Say that again, Major." The sleep was blown out of his head as the chief listened to the incredible report.

"I don't care who wants to look inside. You know our position. Under no circumstances is any member of an outside law enforcement agency allowed inside that depository," Chief Fanzio said. "That includes the FBI too . . . understood?"

"Yes, Sir." The Officer-in-Charge at the Fort Knox depository responded. "I'll get some more off duty personnel in here right away. We'll get the vault open for a visual check as soon as possible."

"Report back to me on that right away."

Then Fanzio told him that their CI Unit, criminal investigative squad, would be arriving later that day and they would handle the case and any required contact with other law enforcement agencies.

"Oh . . . by the way, get those front doors fixed ASAP."

"But that means tradesmen will have to work on both sides of the doors . . . sometimes inside."

"Put a guard on 'em. Just like you do when the security systems are repaired or updated. And stop the panic . . . you're not thinking clearly, Major."

Fanzio shook his head in disbelief and hung up the phone.

His wife was awake too. "What's the matter, dear?"

He told her and then added. "This rocket attack must have rattled the Major's brain."

The chief lay down and tried to go back to sleep wondering why some idiots would try such a stunt. He thought of the old metaphor. *It's like trying to rob Fort Knox. It can't be done. I guess they hadn't heard.* Secure in that knowledge, he finally dozed off.

But the alarms inside the vault that went off were a nagging worry for the Officer-in- Charge.

"It's probably due to vibrations from the rocket attack." The Captain of the Guard offered.

"Then why didn't that recent earthquake set it off?" The major asked.

"I didn't think about that," was the captain's wry response.

"Well, that's why every employee with a partial combination to the vault door is here now. All except one. I hope to hear back from the base hospital soon." The major glanced at his clock. It was 2:45 AM.

Chapter 59

Although a separate organization, years ago the Bullion Depository Officer-in-Charge made an arrangement with the U. S. Army to have its employees treated at the base hospital.

"We're all part of the federal government," he originally told that hospital administrator. But in the attempt to try and save money, it actually resulted in even longer delays on this crucial Monday.

A new, young resident physician was the only doctor on duty in that wing of the Fort Knox base hospital that early on Monday morning when the Officer-in-Charge had anxiously telephoned.

"But he's not available right now." The nurse on duty told him. "The doctor is currently attending to a patient. He will have to call you back."

"Well this is a damn emergency." The Officer-in-Charge yelled.

"That **is** just what he's attending to now!" The nurse yelled back. "A patient in the emergency room.

He's one of your employees . . . a guard at your depository gate."

"Well have him call me ASAP." He slammed down the telephone in disgust.

Thirty minutes later, the resident physician finally returned the major's call who explained what he needed.

"We have to open the vault. Can't you put her in an ambulance and bring her over here now?" Then he added. "We'll take her down to the vault in the elevator."

"This is an impossible request. I don't have the authority to make such a decision. First, you want a patient who just had an operation for acute appendicitis on Saturday taken out of the hospital in the middle of the night prior to her release on Tuesday.

"Second, you demand that our medical personnel wait outside your building while you move her all over the place. That's not possible. She must be attended to by some one with medical knowledge at all times under such conditions even if it were allowed."

And thirdly, he told the major that this would be countermanding United States Army medical regulations. The young resident doctor tried to sound very official.

"Then get me the person who has such authority." He demanded. "You do understand the severity of our situation?"

"Yes, Sir, I do. I'll try to track down the attending physician, Lieutenant Colonel Colger. But he might have to consult with the hospital Chief of Staff. That would be Colonel James Brighton."

"Have one of them call me immediately."

The Officer-in-Charge hung up the telephone. He was caught up in a spider web of government bureaucracy at its finest which would certainly help to create the mother of all heists.

The famous and often referred to "Murphy's Law" was now in full effect. Almost any branch of the federal government was known for its procrastination and the inability to act with any urgency. Add to that the snail's pace at which hospitals respond to any request that contradicts the orders of the attending physician, and recognizing that this involved an army hospital at this hour of the morning, the situation was impossible.

The Officer-in-Charge was forced to watch time move inexorably, as one hour after another slowly crawled around the face of his desk clock. He made and received several telephone calls from the base hospital during the next two hours.

Finally at 5:45 AM, an army ambulance was bringing that one employee who mentally possessed a piece of a special number so desperately required to open the twenty ton vault door. From the hospital to the depository she was accompanied by that same young resident physician who rode with her in the back of the vehicle.

The powers that be at the hospital had finally been contacted and after much gnashing of teeth and arguing, a compromise had finally been reached with the Officer-in-Charge at the gold depository. The resident doctor would go into the building walking along side the patient-employee on the gurney.

But he was required to wear a blindfold that would be acceptable to the Captain of the Guard. And he was told he could not remove said blindfold unless the patient, for whatever reason, began to require some medical attention.

Emphatically, the captain said, "There's no way you're going to see her portion of the vault combination when she dials it."

The physician would be allowed to hold onto the edge of the gurney so he wouldn't trip or fall and would be told when to step up, down, sideways or whatever. The thought of such a procession was definitely comical.

When the ambulance stopped at the depository gate, there was a gaggle of radio and television crews, and other members of the news media who were video taping, photographing, and recording the entire event for posterity.

Armed depository guards and members of the Mint Police met the vehicle and helped keep the press back as they shouted questions at the girl who lay prone on the gurney when it was pulled out of the ambulance.

With bright television camera lights blinding her, flash bulbs popping, and microphones being shoved at her face, it was like a rolling interrogation. The young girl was terrified.

The questions were fired at her from all sides. "Who are you? Why are you here? What's your name? Why are you so important? Why would they bring you in an ambulance? How come you're on a stretcher? What kind of medical problem do you have? Are you going to die?"

She was told not to answer any questions, so she just put both hands over her face and waited to get away from them. Once inside the building, she was so unnerved from the experience that she immediately needed to use the restroom to relieve herself.

This normal body function and simple request caused another delay. The young resident doctor wanted to help her off the gurney and into the women's restroom. He would wait just outside the door. That however would require the removal of his blindfold.

Wherever Mr. Murphy was now he had to be smiling. His law held fast. "If anything can go wrong, it will." And in this particular case, it would definitely continue to get worse.

"I'm here to assist the patient!" The physician blurted at the Captain of the Guard.

Snidely, the captain responded. "But urinating is not a medical procedure, doctor. One of our female employees can help her into the bathroom."

"But none of them have medical training." He shot back. "She is still hooked up to an IV drip, but it's attached to the gurney. I have to disconnect it and then re-attach it when she comes out of the rest room. I certainly can't do that with my eyes closed, Captain!"

Finally by 6: 30 AM, an entourage consisting of the Officer-in-Charge, the Captain of the Guard, other employees, more guards, the girl on the gurney, and one physician had taken the elevator downstairs to the vault room. It took two trips in the small elevator. They joined two other depository personnel who possessed the other pieces of the combination to the vault door. The whole group stood back ten feet from the vault door behind a steel wire imbedded glass enclosure that also had a door made of the same material.

This prohibited anyone from seeing or secretly taking pictures of any part of the vault door combination as each employee, one at time, stepped forward to dial in his or her memorized secret number.

The girl on the gurney possessed the last section of the combination. She was pushed through the wire imbedded glass doorway toward the steel door by the young physician, whose blindfold was freshly adjusted and majorly tightened by the Captain of the Guard.

The doctor gritted his teeth. He wouldn't give the captain the satisfaction of admitting to pain. But it felt like his head would implode, which was the intent of the pissed off captain.

The female employee was giving navigational instructions to the physician as the four wheeled gurney slid across the polished stone floor. "More to the left, Doctor. Now a little to the right . . . slide it closer. Okay . . . hold it right there." She dialed in her number.

The door's locking device, six huge piston sized solid steel rods, was heard to retract back into the thick steel door itself. Then an electric motor hummed as the giant door swung open wide back against the wall.

The alarm systems had been disabled, and the Officer-in-Charge followed by the Captain of the Guard were the first to enter the vault room where they began a visual check. They did not notice anything out of the ordinary during a cursory look at the first row of storage compartments.

The fine gold bars were piled up in stacks in the two level concrete and steel vault which was further divided into numbered compartments. Each stack contained the same number of ingots.

United States Mint protocol required that they start with the lower level and check inside several compartments on a random basis according to a sequence of numbers. Each compartment also had a door.

They had been at it for thirty minutes. Everything was in order. No discrepancies were noted. As they turned the corner at the end of the corridor to check the next row of compartments on either side, they stopped dead in their tracks.

"What the hell is that?" The Officer-in-Charge gasped. There was a gap, a two foot wide hole that ran for twenty feet straight along the front of the next five compartments.

"It looks like the hole goes back under the doors on all these compartments." The captain answered.

The Officer-in-Charge opened the first affected storage area. Along the corridor on this row all the small rooms were four feet wide by ten feet in depth. As the thin metal door swung wide open, his face turned waxen. For several seconds he said nothing. Then his voice exploded.

"Jesus Christ Almighty. There's no gold in here. No damn floor either!"

"That hole's deep too." The Captain of the Guard added looking over his shoulder. "I can't see bottom."

The captain recovered quickly and unlocked the next four compartment doors that had a gap in front. The major was right behind him along with two other employees pulling the doors open. All compartments were empty.

"The only thing these locked doors are protecting is a freakin' hole in the ground." One employee said. "It's all gone down into some black pit looking thing."

"Maybe it's a sinkhole." The major said hopefully. "The gold could be down in there."

"Bull shit." The captain hollered. "This ain't no sinkhole. It's two sides of a rectangle. Look at the edges. It's been cut with a saw blade of some kind. This gold has been stolen!"

"It's not possible," said the Officer-in-Charge. "I can't fucking believe it. Fort Knox has been robbed!"

Chapter 60

Chief Fanzio's office was in U S Mint Headquarters located at 801 9th Street NW, Washington, D. C. It was 8:30 AM east coast time on Monday when Chief Bill received his second telephone call that same morning from the Officer-in-Charge at the Fort Knox Depository.

This was the frantic, stuff has hit the fan type phone call. It would be the worst telephone conversation that Fanzio had ever received since he took office. The major tells his chief what they discovered; the hole in the vault floor, the coal mine, and all the heavy equipment left at the mine entrance.

Fanzio was stunned for a moment. Then slowly, "Jesus, Mary, and Joseph. This can not have happened!"

"That's right Chief. We couldn't believe it either. The Captain of the Guard put several heavily armed Mint Police down in the big hole with flashlights. They're still searching. It's a large old mine down there."

Fanzio tells him that the CIS, criminal investigative squad, will be leaving for Lexington in the next hour on one of their planes to look into the rocket attack.

"Now I'll let them know the real problem," the chief adds.

"News like this is going to get out soon. The press has been outside since the rocket attack last night. We won't keep this robbery quiet for long."

He emphasized to Fanzio that this wasn't just some small time burglary. This was a very professional heist that took the coordination of a lot of men and equipment.

"All the law enforcement in the area has been here . . . plus two car loads of FBI are due here shortly. The team you're sending can't handle all this. We need some outside help here, Chief."

Dr. Fanzio thought for a moment. "Let the FBI investigate the mine entrance, the tractors . . . and on up into the mine. This is a federal crime, so have them coordinate with the other agencies since the opening is not on Mint property."

"But what if they want to climb up from the mine into the vault?"

"Absolutely not. That's all on or under our property. Get some guards to block it off two hundred feet from the hole in the vault. I want our team to check over that area."

Fanzio continued to spout instructions, adding that he would send six more Mint Policemen immediately from other duty posts to scour the whole length of the mine for any trace of that gold.

"I may even fly out today . . . but first I've got make some more phone calls."

Fanzio immediately called the Director of the United States Mint. She told him that before any public statement could be made she was required to inform the Secretary of the Treasury and that he would want to call the President of the United States.

"I hope you don't need me for that. I need to be at the crime scene immediately. Too much can go wrong quick."

"By all means. As chief, you need to go to Kentucky and personally take charge of the investigation. This crime will test your Mint Police to the limit, Bill. And your ability to deal with the press."

That afternoon, Chief Fanzio, with several of the other promised Mint Police, were on a government plane that he had to requisition away from a congressman who wanted to use it with his wife to fly to Central America on a so-called junket, which the dictionary aptly describes as a journey or festive social affair made by an official at public expense.

"If the FBI hasn't done it already, cordon off the wooded area around the mine entrance," Fanzio said over his cell phone to the senior member of CIS. "I don't want people trampling all over the crime scene."

Then he spoke with the Officer-in-Charge and went over another list of items and information required for the telephone call he had to make tomorrow morning to inform the mint director about the severity of the theft.

"I don't care if you have to stay up all night taking inventory." He hollered. "I need to know exactly how many ingots were stolen."

He leaned back in his passenger seat and stared out of the window as he thought about the enormity of the problem. He ate a sandwich, popped in two Mylanta Gel Caps, a Pepsid, and chased it down with a glass of milk. His ulcer was letting him know how it felt about this whole mess.

Tomorrow he would give the mint director all the information she needed for an official announcement by 10:00 AM Washington time. Then daily updates would be routine as things progressed.

It would be their problem in Washington, he thought, about how to convey this information to the public and the press with the most damage control possible. He was sure a top official would make an announcement by tomorrow afternoon or at latest, the next morning.

Along with the FBI, Fanzio knew he would be the source of information for many officials back in Washington, as well as for all the press who were now setting up camp around the Fort Knox area. *This is definitely not going to be fun,* he grimaced.

In order to reduce the worries and concerns of the public, administration policy makers decided that neither the President nor his press secretary would include any mention of this crime in either a public address or a press conference. Hopefully this lack of any recognition would reduce its prominence in the news.

Instead the announcement would come from the Secretary of the Treasury at a small news conference as an addition to a more important discussion of current fiscal policies. However that approach definitely did not work.

The press was bored with the speech until he informed them about the theft with a kind of a paper rustling, "Cough, cough, oh by the way, the Fort Knox Gold Depository was robbed yesterday. The loss is estimated at over one billion dollars."

Those in attendance must have been wired to 110 volts of electricity. The slouching bodies, the drooping heads, and those reading a mystery novel sat straight up like the Road Runner searching for Wiley Coyote.

That announcement fired the imagination of newsmongers around the world. All of the major television networks; the local and national radio commentators; the newspaper columnists, and news magazine editors couldn't talk about or print stuff fast enough. And one of those lovable tabloids printed the following, reader grabbing headline.

Communist Trained Groundhogs Eat U S Gold Reserves

On a scale of one to ten, current federal monetary policies came in fifteenth. While the news media provoked the public with scare tactics about acts of terrorism, or that a new crime wave has struck at our nation, the administration did counter with facts to assure countries around the globe that the loss represented less than one percent of the nation's gold reserves.

But the witches stirring the brew of irresponsible reporting went so far past reality that the President finally had to make a statement.

"The United States remains fiscally solvent. I can assure the American public and the world at large that our treasury is safe, and that these criminals will be brought to justice soon."

However, no matter what he said the press continued relentlessly with huge headlines that played to the public's imagination. As a result the stock market took a big drop during the next several days.

Additional support for the administration came the next morning when the Attorney General of the United States, joined by the Director of the Federal Bureau of Investigation, held a briefing to inform the press.

They told the television audience that "such a crime, a crime that strikes at the stability of this great country and threatens our ability to protect our government's assets would not go unpunished."

Further, they promised the American public that these perpetrators would be caught, tried in a federal court, and sentenced to the fullest extent of the law. With that statement the two men took questions from the press.

Chapter 61

On Monday night after the robbery, Paul Stryker, using a computer at the Lexington Public Library, sent an email to Elonzo Cassidy.

Business plan went well. Ours is secure. At curtain closing, the twist was in for P. S. - but G. missed - G. now wants P. S. and you. I will assume old ID again - F. R. - Have plan in mind - will contact soon.

Richards couldn't explain by email why he had called the FBI. *It was best to let Eddie wonder why Grimaldi wants us dead,* he thought as he drove home. He knew sure as hell Cason wouldn't call him to ask why.

Richards had arrived back at his duplex earlier that day; lugged his suitcases inside; dropped them on his bedroom floor; took a hot shower; shaved off his beard and mustache, and fell in bed and was quickly fast asleep.

The alarm rattled him awake at 7:30 PM. He dressed quickly, drove toward the library, but stopped at a fast food restaurant to get a quick bite, and arrived before closing time to send his message. He hadn't seen a newspaper or watched television since Friday and by Monday night the awful domestic disturbance at the Barakat residence was old news.

When he returned to his duplex, he now had time to check the postal drop box at the street. It was stuffed full, mostly junk mail. Inside his home, he found a bunch of telephone messages. Almost all were inconsequential, but one was from Doris. Her voice was different. She sounded very weak, but the fear in it seemed to be gone.

"I'm away for a few days," she said. "The children are fine. I'll call again soon."

Richards just sat and looked at the telephone. He had too much to do over the next few days to get involved with Barakat again and he didn't know where to reach her anyway. He had no idea that she had called him from the hospital. She would be in there for several more days.

The first EAST dump truck left the coal mine at 1:30 AM; drove to Louisville on SR 31W; picked up Interstate 65 heading straight north past Indianapolis towards Gary, Indiana, at the southern tip of Lake Michigan, and finally west into Chicago near the

Midway Airport where the truck pulled into a large warehouse at 7:30 AM.

The driver made it in six hours and didn't exceed sixty-five miles per hour. The FBI didn't retrieve the message about the robbery until 8:15 that morning, and as a result, no law enforcement agency had been alerted. But that wouldn't be the case with the rest of the giant dump trucks.

The other four trucks were also going to Chicago, each to arrive at a different warehouse at five distant addresses around the Windy City. Grimaldi was not going to store all this treasure in one place.

Each driver drove a different route through states adjacent to Kentucky, and due to the more circuitous routes, some would take longer than others to arrive and exposure on the highway would be greater. It was a trade off. A precaution against all of them being caught together.

At eight fifteen Monday morning, the various messages recorded over the weekend were printed out and disseminated to different agents at the Louisville Field Office of The Federal Bureau of Investigation.

One message was immediately hand carried to the Special Agent in Charge who was having morning coffee with a new recruit downstairs in the cafe on the first floor of the building. They were watching and discussing the only news item on all the major television networks. The attack at the Fort Knox Bullion Depository.

"That is a federal crime and falls under our jurisdiction. Since you're interested in our terrorist unit, you'll get your feet wet on this one," he said to the recruit as he saw his secretary coming through the door.

"She won't let me have a minute's peace." He smiled at her but she didn't smile back.

She handed him a folder marked for *his eyes only*. "This is not going to be an easy week," she said. But her comment belied the excitement in her voice.

He read through the anonymous telephone message left early that morning. "I don't think this is a crank call . . . too much exact detail . . . and his personal request for anonymity?" He looked up at them both. "That tells us he's involved, but he's had second thoughts."

As they left the cafe, the agent was cranking. "We've got a car down there now, but we're getting nowhere with their guard force. Get me the person in charge at the Gold Depository. I want to verify this message." He said to his secretary.

The telephone call took fifteen minutes before the agent could get through to the Officer-in-Charge, who had just finished talking with Chief Fanzio.

"Were you also robbed this morning . . . besides the attack at the gate?" The Special Agent asked.

There was a long silence at the Fort Knox end of the telephone. "We just discovered the robbery an hour ago when the vault was opened. How would you know about it?"

"I can't disclose the source, but you've just verified that the information we received earlier is correct. Tell your chief that an APB will be sent to all states that border on Kentucky. They're using trucks."

Chapter 62

The Louisville Field Office of the FBI sent an All Points Bulletin to every law enforcement agency in each state that had a common border with Kentucky which included Tennessee, Missouri, Illinois, Indiana, Ohio, West Virginia and Virginia.

The list included other FBI offices, the highway patrol, sheriffs' offices, and police departments within that state, its counties and towns.

Due to the high profile that this case would create, and the need for immediate attention to information already received, the clearance to initiate action from a Field Office came that morning during a telephone conversation with the FBI Director in Washington, D. C.

"I've got all the information on the trucks needed to put out the APB and time is of the essence, sir. If I forward the material to your headquarters office we could lose another couple of hours and the trucks might disappear off the highway by then."

"Copy my office and keep me posted daily." The director responded. "I've got some congressional oversight committees that will want to talk to me real soon."

Chief Fanzio was on the telephone with the Special Agent in Charge by nine that morning and was given an almost complete update regarding information from the telephone message left earlier.

None of this information could be announced or made public. It was too early. The investigation was only starting and it had to be kept confidential. Neither the FBI nor the Mint Police Chief would disclose this to anyone without a need to know designation.

At the moment, that included every politician in Washington, D. C., most of whom would jeopardize the investigation in an attempt to garner attention for themselves.

By 9:00 AM, every available vehicle in the service of any law enforcement agency in those affected states was getting on the highway. Small fixed wing aircraft and helicopters were already in the air to follow the routes considered to be the most probable used by the trucks.

Color pictures of an EAST dump trailer were faxed and in the hands of every search unit. The very size of a dump trailer that could haul twenty-five tons and the unusual rear quad-axle feature would set the vehicles apart from most trucks on any highway.

The second trailer was routed on SR 60 north using back roads to Interstate 64, west through Indiana to Mount Vernon, Illinois, where it turned north on I-57 through Champaign and Kankakee to Chicago. The driver left the mine at 1:55 AM but the route would take eight hours.

The search units were heavily concentrated on every road around the west and south side of Chicago. If the Windy City was the final destination, coming in from either direction undetected would be very difficult.

At nine o'clock that morning, seven hours into the long grinding drive, the big EAST trailer had just crossed I-80 and was approaching Calumet Park, just outside Chicago, when an Illinois State Highway Patrol car raced past.

The truck driver involuntarily squeezed the steering wheel, leaned back in his seat, held his breath for a few seconds, and then started to breath again when the patrol car continued on ahead.

Suddenly the car braked dramatically as the officer turned on his light bar across the top of the sedan and allowed the truck driver to unwillingly catch up.

The driver was so involved staring up front that he missed looking in his rear view mirror as the second Highway Patrol Car slid along side, holding its speed steady with the truck's cab. Then this patrol officer also turned on his top twirling lights, plus a screeching siren.

This jolt of sound and color scared the truck driver back to reality. He was getting busted. He glanced in his big outside rear view mirrors and saw two more patrol cars racing up behind him. Quickly, he stepped on the fuel pedal.

For a moment he thought about forcing them off the road or running them over in his giant rig when he heard the whump, whump of rotor blades overhead.

Next came the sound of a bull horn that blared down at him.

"Pull over and stop the truck now!" The insistent voice said.

The helicopter unit informed the driver about his next problem if he didn't comply. The use of tire sticks thrown out ahead of his truck would rip most of the tread completely off the wheels. Trying to escape on the remaining rims was not a good option.

"If you don't stop, we will fire automatic weapons through the roof of your cab. You have ten seconds to comply."

It was over. The second truck and the driver were captured. That left three more still on the highway carrying gold bullion worth over six hundred million dollars.

Chapter 63

The third trailer left the mine five minutes late at 2:25 AM and rolled down 31W away from Radcliff to Lexington on the Blue Grass Parkway. Then north on I-75 to Cincinnati, taking the secondary road number 27 out of Ohio into Indiana at Richmond. He drove along the state line, then west through Fort Wayne and picked up route 30, a four lane highway that would take him across Indiana to Chicago.

As a single driver moving at five miles an hour over the speed limit, stopping twice for food, including one diesel fuel refill, he would take almost nine hours to cover the 523 miles.

Seven hours and thirty minutes into the trip, the truck was three quarters of the way across Indiana passing through Grovertown when he crossed an intersection where a sheriff's car from Starke County had just arrived.

The Deputy Sheriff was stopped behind a pick-up truck, waiting for heavy traffic to clear. He glanced at the All Points Bulletin facsimile picture of the truck that he had received in his car. His department had just installed the new equipment.

He was planning to cross over route 30 and head north to the Town of Koontz Lake for a mid-afternoon rendezvous when his cell phone rang. He answered it, listened for a moment, and then responded.

"I know I'm late, Essie . . . but I've been south of here down at Ralph Odum's farm. Some damn kids last night tearing around his barn again on those all terrain RV's. They shore did wreck his vegetables."

"You want some pussy or not, Henry? We only got thirty minutes left on my lunch hour. See you at number four. I just finished cleaning it . . . got fresh sheets on the bed." Essie hung up. She had used the one black telephone in the little two room resort cottage at Koontz Lake Lodge to call the Deputy Sheriff.

"Shit . . . she's pissed off good." He said out loud. *It'll be five minutes of bitching before I can get my cock in her mouth to shut her up.* Henry put his cell phone down on the car seat next to him and glanced back up to see if traffic had cleared.

At that instant, the huge EAST trailer roared across in front of him, diesel smoke pouring out of twin stacks behind the cab. The Deputy Sheriff sat up quick, eyes squinting, as he counted off the four sets of axles on the rear of the big dump truck.

"Gawd aw-mighty, damn! There's that sum bitch now." He hollered out loud again. He wheeled his patrol car, tires squealing, around the pick-up in front, punched the gas pedal to the floor, and launched his vehicle down the highway after the big trailer.

As soon as he got close enough to verify the license plate, Henry grabbed at the microphone hanging on his radio and called into headquarters where calls were relayed to all law enforcement vehicles in the area.

Within minutes, units of the Indiana Highway Patrol came off of I-65 and with the help of other sheriff department vehicles, a road block was set up thirty miles further west on route 30 near Valparaiso.

A lumber truck was commandeered and parked sideways across the two west bound lanes. Oncoming vehicle traffic was allowed around it as a dozen more law enforcement vehicles were parked blocking access across the median strip. All officers were out of their patrol cars with shotguns and automatic weapons ready.

Henry was right behind the truck in his sheriff's car. *Crime might not pay, but pussy sure does,* Henry thought. *If I hadn't been trying to fuck Essie, I'da never seen this truck.*

At the moment that Henry had that thought in his head, the EAST truck driver slammed on his air brakes and the big trailer's tires squealed and smoked simultaneously. The thick cloud of acrid smelling burned rubber and brake lining filled the air and covered Henry's car as he tried to brake and swerve away from the back end of the heavy trailer.

The right front of the Starke County Sheriff's car plowed into the left side of the EAST dump truck as they both slid sideways to a stop. The driver of the truck jumped out of his cab and came back to see Henry slumped over his steering wheel. He had blood running down his face even though the air bag inflated quickly and then collapsed as required.

The Mafia henchman jerked the door open, pulled the unconscious body out of the patrol car onto the road, jumped behind the steering wheel, and with the wrenching of metal, backed away from the trailer, wheeled around across the median and headed back east.

Because the EAST truck was turned almost perpendicular to the road, law enforcement officers two hundred yards ahead couldn't see the driver jump out and get into the sheriff's car. But they did see it drive off in the opposite direction.

Several Highway Patrol Officers and sheriff's deputies left the roadblock and raced their cars towards the big trailer. But with no knowledge of how many men might be in the truck or if they were armed, they had to be slow and cautious.

It took time to stop; get out with weapons trained on the huge dump truck's cab high above them; yell warnings; find the unconscious deputy and check his condition; gingerly approach and pull open cab door with guns at the ready, only to find no one there.

The Mafia driver had gained some precious time. With the patrol car radio active he could hear everything being said by law enforcement over the airways, and he knew exactly the route he needed to take.

After two miles he turned north on state road 49; drove the next nine miles at a wild speed with the rack of lights on top still blinking to Interstate 80/90; doubled back to the west, and ten miles later he was in Gary, Indiana, where he left the sheriff's car in a covered parking garage near the Greyhound Bus Depot.

He bought a ticket to Chicago just three minutes before the bus left. He pulled out a cell phone, pressed in a number and left a short message.

"This is number three . . . left truck at Valparaiso road block . . . escaped in a patrol car." He cut off the transmission. He didn't need to say any more.

The truck driver arrived in the outskirts of the Windy City twenty-five minutes later where he got off at the first bus stop and disappeared. He was lucky. In his case the long arm of the law was a little short.

The cell phone that had recorded the message was on the front seat of Grimaldi's Cadillac. But he had his own problems. The Mafia Capo had stopped at a convenience store to gas up the black sedan; buy more coffee; Gatorade; a six pack of cold water, and snacks for himself and the Big Guy lying down in the back seat.

He had to stop much earlier to buy bandages; ice, an ice chest, and some zip lock bags to make cold packs to put on Big Guy's shotgun wounds to stop the bleeding from the many punctures. He sprayed Bactine on the man's entire side to keep down infection.

They couldn't stop at a hospital, clinic, or doctor's office. The injury would have been reported to the police, plus Slim, the dead Mafia killer, was in the trunk. Not easy to explain either.

When Grimaldi did return to the car and retrieved the message he cursed out loud. Then he pulled back into traffic heading into Chicago where he could get help for his men. He had seen dozens of law enforcement vehicles on the road and knew that the crime had been discovered.

The first telephone call from the driver of truck number one was perfect. The man had safely reached his destination in Chicago when he'd driven the truck through big rolling doors that opened into one of Ochopinto's warehouses where the gold would be secure.

Just before the capture of the second EAST trailer, the driver had telephoned as he braked the big rig to a stop. He tossed his cell phone out of the passenger side window over a guard rail down a steep grass embankment before he was taken out of the truck at gun point.

Grimaldi was pissed and puzzled. *Now they've captured two trailers. How the fuck could the cops have known what trucks to stop?* His face darkened as he thought about it. None of his men would rat on him.

There was just one guy, okay . . . that fuckin' professor. This time he's dead!

Chapter 64

It was just past 3:00 AM Monday when the fourth EAST trailer left the Fort Knox area to run a gauntlet to Chicago that no one at this hour even knew about. His route took him constantly west on 31 to I-264 to I-64, where near Mt. Vernon, Illinois, he stopped for donuts, coffee and a cigarette.

Then with a short jog north on I-57, the driver went west again on I-64 to just outside St. Louis, Missouri where the truck headed north on I-55 through the center of Illinois. The Mafia henchman had been driving for seven hours when he pulled off the road near Springfield for food and fuel. The time was just past 10:45 AM.

He had stopped at a Flying Jay truck stop which offers everything any vehicle driver could want from hardware and books to groceries and hot meals. He took on a load of diesel and moved the rig over to a parking place away from the fuel pumps.

371

His cellular telephone buzzed in the drink cup holder where he kept it. He picked it up and said. "This is number four."

"The police got number two and three. They've been tipped off. Where are you?"

"Just stopped to fuel up and eat. I'm three hours from home." The EAST driver answered.

"Be real careful." Grimaldi said. The transmission ended.

The driver stepped down from the cab and stretched as he carefully glanced around checking all the vehicles in the lot before he walked to the entrance of the building. He strode to the restaurant section and ate a big meal with two cups of coffee as he surveyed everyone inside.

He turned in the books on tape for another western mystery, bought more cigarettes, and rented a shower room. He locked the door behind him, placed his clothes and purchased items on the bench, stepped into the shower stall and adjusted the water temperature.

His eyes were closed as he let the warm water cascade down his body. This would be the wake up he needed for the balance of the trip. *Just another two hundred miles to go.* He leaned against the shower wall letting the water wash away his fatigue.

With the water running hard, the shower stall curtain closed, and room door shut, he couldn't hear a thing outside. He toweled off, dressed again, and stepped out of the shower room into a circus of confusion both inside and outside the Flying Jay.

Highway Patrol officers, local police, and sheriff's deputies were searching everywhere for him. But they didn't know who "him" was, what he looked like, or his name.

He glanced outside the building and saw that the EAST dump truck was surrounded by law enforcement officers, plus a helicopter was just landing in a field next door. It looked like FBI personnel who were stepping out.

The public address system blared instructions to everyone inside or around the Flying Jay building, requesting that all drivers and passengers return to their vehicles and wait to be identified by an officer of the law.

The entrance to the truck stop was blocked by official cars and no vehicle would be allowed in again until the entire place was emptied of all the public. The Flying Jay employees were to be gathered together in the restaurant for identification by the manager.

There was a blockade at the parking lot exits and those vehicles leaving would be searched, including the trunks of cars or backs of trucks. This search was going to be very thorough.

He stepped past people exiting the restaurant and through the windows saw that law enforcement officers were stationed behind the building also. And he couldn't escape across the street or to the Burger King Restaurant next door either.

As he turned back with the flow of people leaving or waiting in line to pay for their meal ticket, he searched around inside the building. He glanced down the hallway that led to the restroom area and saw another man start to exit a shower room stall.

From the way he was dressed, the Mafia soldier sensed he was also a truck driver. As he moved fast towards the stranger, luck played its hand. The man turned around to retrieve a forgotten item hanging on the back of the door.

He was half way leaning into the room when he was shoved hard back inside and slammed against the wall. The soldier went in with him, quickly shut the door, and as the man tried to get up he caught him with a solid punch to the solar plexus. For the second time he went down with a thump and gasped for air.

As his head came up he was staring at a big pistol that was jammed into his nose. "You give me quick, straight answers and I won't kill you . . . understand?"

"Okay, okay. Just don't shoot me!" The wide eyed man said as he looked up. But he only saw a big pair of reflective sun glasses and the brim of a baseball cap pulled down to his assailant's eyebrows.

"Gimme the keys to your truck."

The man hesitated and the gun barrel started up his right nostril. It hurt bad.

"Here. In my jacket pocket." The man pulled out the keys.

"Describe your truck real good and where it's parked. Then I'm gonna knock you out and take this room key with me. If you're lying . . . I'll be back in thirty seconds and slit your throat." A long switchblade snicked open two inches from the man's eyes.

The Mafia driver slugged the man on the head with his gun barrel and he slumped down for the third time. He shut the door behind him which locked automatically and then put the key in his pocket as he walked out through the front door.

The crowd had thinned dramatically. After a three second look, he walked quickly to the described truck.

The man was a contract hauler with his own cab and today he was hauling a flat bed full of recently harvested, yellow colored hay bales. It was the only trailer of its kind in the parking lot.

He walked up to the truck, stood casually leaning against the cab door, and lit a cigarette. He smiled under his sunglasses at the approaching Highway Patrolman and offered his fake driver's license. It was a Tennessee license with a nice picture of him bearing a false name and address underneath.

"What's all the fuss about, officer?"

"We're looking for the driver of that big EAST trailer over there. Did you see him leave that truck or know what he looks like?"

"No. Just stopped for a quick meal. Gotta' get this hay upstate today."

"I need to look inside." The officer opened the cab door and glanced inside. He stepped up and looked into the back of the small cab.

The Mafia driver eased his hand towards the pistol in his jacket pocket and waited anxiously. He hoped the officer wouldn't see any other pictures or question him further. He got lucky for the second time. The officer handed his license back and signaled toward the exit driveway where other law enforcement officers waved the hay truck forward.

He drove back on the interstate and immediately took the next city exit. It was only four miles into Springfield where he parked the flat bed truck as soon as possible. He walked until he hailed a cab which took him to the nearest car rental office.

Using his fake identification and a similar credit card, he rented a Ford Taurus and drove fifty miles to

Bloomington, where he returned the car. He had seen the Highway Patrol Officer write down his false name and address on a legal pad that included every other driver released from the Flying Jay parking lot.

He guessed they found the locked shower room door during a search of the building twenty minutes after he left and got a description of the hay truck and its license plate from the owner of the cab who should be nursing a sore head. They would find the hay truck in Springfield quickly and canvass the transportation companies in the area.

In Bloomington, he took a cab to a different rental agency, and rented a second car using his own identification and drove a different make of car to Chicago. Incredibly, he was the third Mafia driver who got away, but more stolen gold was back in the hands of the federal government.

During his drive to Bloomington, he telephoned Grimaldi who had arrived in Chicago. The Big Guy was getting medical treatment from a doctor on the Mafia's payroll who would not report the gunshot. Funeral arrangements were being made for Slim.

"This is number four. They grabbed the truck near Springfield at a Flying Jay. I was inside the restaurant but got away."

"Come by my office in the morning. I wanna hear all about it." Grimaldi hung up.

Then he left a message for Frankie and Bruno to show up in the morning also. They had just returned from Kentucky and they knew Paul Stewart.

Both of them had heard his voice, and both knew what he looked like. Bruno had worked with Stewart

on the scaffolding cutting up into the vault. Frankie
had lived with him during the job.

Chapter 65

The last EAST trailer to leave Kentucky was making good time. Grimaldi called the driver as soon as he knew his other trucks had been captured.

"This is number five."

"This is *G* calling. Where are you?"

"I'm in the middle of the state." Grimaldi knew he meant central Illinois.

"Two and three didn't make it. They have information on all units . . . they got number four where you're heading . . . better change route, okay."

"I understand . . . but end up in the same place . . . right?" The Mafia Capo confirmed his question.

It was a warehouse on the northwest side of Chicago. Grimaldi hadn't changed that plan. But even if the driver was more careful and watched for the police, it would not change the fact that the All Points Bulletin initiated Monday morning by the FBI was the biggest and most extensive highway search for a group of vehicles in history.

The trucker now drove north on Interstate 39 which took him through La Salle, up near Rochelle, but he avoided I-88, a toll road, where employees working for the Interstate Highway Commission could have been informed about the trucks.

Instead he picked up 38, a principal highway which paralleled I-88 and headed due east through De Kalb to route 59, where he turned north into Arlington Heights. He was in touch with Grimaldi again when he arrived in Chicago and told him he was twenty minutes from the warehouse.

"They're expecting you." Grimaldi said. "They've rolled the doors open . . . drive it straight into the back of the building."

The driver was extra careful in the returning noon time lunch traffic. He stayed within the local speed limit, slowed at all traffic lights, and even stopped if the light just turned yellow. He didn't want to chance a crossing even if he could comfortably get through the intersection. That worked for him.

It didn't work that day for a twenty-five year old girl, an office worker by herself in a 1996 Toyota Camry returning late from lunch and putting on lip gloss looking in the rear view mirror that was turned toward her face. She didn't see the traffic light. It could have been the size of a refrigerator hanging there and she still would have missed it.

Doing thirty miles an hour, her car slammed into the huge EAST dump trailer as the truck rolled through the intersection under a very green light. The truck driver saw her Camry only two seconds before it hit his right front wheel and bumper.

He tried to swerve slightly to the left, but only managed to compound the problem when his trailer side-swiped the entire left side of a United Parcel Service truck that was sitting in the left turn lane of oncoming traffic.

The Camry bounced like a bloated tick off a rhinoceros, spun around and smacked into some parked cars on the right side of the street. The seat belt kept her from being seriously hurt. But her upper lip and the inside of her left nostril were colored a beautiful cherry red.

The EAST driver did not stop. He pushed down on the floor pedal and poured the diesel fuel into the huge engine. It responded and smoke spouted from the twin exhaust stacks as the driver ran late through the next yellow light while he held down his air horn to warn other vehicles that he wasn't going to slow up. Nobody argued with this giant street monster now gone amuck.

He was only twelve blocks from his destination. After driving carefully for ten hours, the driver was determined to safely deliver his payload of over two hundred million dollars in gold bullion. He damn sure wanted his bonus of one million bucks.

But now lady luck turned a cold shoulder. Two police cars were stopped side by side at that very intersection, where four of Chicago's finest, two in each patrol car, were conversing with windows down on that cool October day as the truck driver sped through the now red light right in front of them.

Seconds earlier, one patrolman asked the adjoining two, "Did you hear those crashes?" He didn't need an answer. One vehicle involved in the metal melee now zoomed across in front of them. In unison the two patrol units laid rubber as their cars turned in hot pursuit.

"Jesus Christ!" One officer yelled into his radio mobile. "That's one of the big EAST rigs everybody's been looking for." Sirens were turned on and car top rack lights were emblazoned as the chase was on.

Just two blocks later one patrol car was struck broadside. The pursuit vehicle, with all the noise and lights it had available turned on, ran a red light right behind the first patrol unit which was following the monster truck.

The driver of the psychedelic painted van was jamming as he entered the intersection. He had the windows up with the heat on and special boom boxes spewing out rap music at a decibel level that a deaf mute could have heard. The jet black sun glasses he wore didn't help his vision either. That took one patrol car out of action.

"Some bitch hit me five blocks back," the trailer driver said to Grimaldi. "I didn't stop and two cop cars were on my ass . . . one got hit."

The Mafia boss was sitting in a black limousine two blocks up the street from the warehouse anxiously waiting for his fifth and final truck to arrive. He knew better than to wait inside the warehouse. If everything went as planned, he would visit his gold a little later.

He had more men in a second car parked behind him. He jumped out of the passenger side and yelled for those soldiers to pull their car out in front of the police car when the EAST truck raced by.

The mobsters almost hit the back end of the truck in order to whack the right front side of the patrol car and knock it into vehicles coming up the opposite side of the street. But the two officers had phoned in for back-up at the beginning of the chase and the law was converging from all around.

The truck shot into the warehouse as the rolling doors were closing. When they slammed shut, the man waiting inside and the EAST trailer driver went out a back entrance and ran off. They knew not to be caught with the truck if the police found it. Incredibly, this fifth driver also escaped, never to be found by the authorities.

One of the policemen climbed up on the hood of his damaged patrol vehicle and watched the truck disappear into the building. His partner was trying to write down the license and description of the car that pulled into them.

But the experienced Mafia driver spun his car around after the impact and sped off in the opposite direction illegally passing a car in front to hide his license plate. He succeeded in doing just that.

Grimaldi watched the whole event go down right in front of his eyes. He couldn't believe it. He had the pot of gold at rainbow's end snatched out of his very hands. In just two minutes, five more police cars were all around the warehouse and the officers were breaking into the front door near the two, twenty foot high rollers that had just closed. The capo knew this truck was lost too.

The warehouse was owned by a dummy corporation. At a later date their consigliore would state. "My clients don't own that EAST dump trailer; they don't know the driver; the driver had no permission to enter their property; and the driver chose their warehouse at random, trying to escape from the police."

Of course it would soon be discovered that members of the Chicago Mafia owned the warehouse, but nothing could be proven since the owner of the truck was never identified, the current license plate led to a junk yard, records from the truck manufacturer indicated the trailer was delivered new to a dealer who sold it to a Canadian company that four years later sold it for cash. But the recent buyer used fictitious names and addresses.

As Grimaldi's limousine drove carefully away from his parking space, he was cursing out loud. He ground out each word with great emphasis.

"Stewart . . . that dirty . . . rotten . . . double-crossing . . . shit." He shook both fists in the air as he added. "You're gonna pay for this real soon."

Chapter 66

By late in the day on that seemingly interminable Monday, reporters from various city newspapers learned from police sources that there was an All Points Bulletin out for five big trucks, but only a few people knew why.

The news of the robbery at Fort Knox was not made public until Tuesday afternoon, after Dr. William F. Fanzio, the Mint Police Chief, had finished his report that morning to the Director of the U. S. Mint.

Once the announcement was made the media started hearing about giant trucks that had been stopped in states surrounding Kentucky, all the way up into northern Illinois and in the city of Chicago itself, where the fifth trailer was seized during a police raid on a warehouse.

Reporters and television mobile units were at the final capture scene quickly and the public was witness to Chicago FBI personnel working in and out of the warehouse. The huge building was brightly lit, inside and out, all night long, and law enforcement personnel guarded the EAST trailer in shifts.

"This morning," the television reporter with the mobile unit said, "The United States Mint Police have arrived and they've taken charge of the truck. As you can see, they are all dressed in black caps and uniforms with gold insignia."

He went on to say that in fifteen years of news casting he had never been witness to, or even heard of, this branch of federal police before. But it's obvious that thousands of gold bars from the robbery at Fort Knox are in that truck."

Now that the news was public, Chief Fanzio held a press conference in Lexington, Kentucky on Tuesday afternoon to announce the capture of four trucks. This announcement was premature for purposes of the investigation, but he turned the meeting into an advantage that even he didn't realize at that moment.

"Each of these four, twenty-five ton capacity, EAST dump trailers carried gold stolen from the United States Bullion Depository at Fort Knox." He went on to give credit to all the law enforcement organizations involved that helped to capture the huge trucks.

"But there is still one missing vehicle," he added. "We suspect that truck is hidden somewhere in Chicago, since all the other trucks were caught in Illinois heading north. Anyone having information leading to the arrest of the persons involved in this theft or the location of the stolen gold will be given protection by the federal government."

There was another meeting being held Tuesday morning. Capo Tomaso Grimaldi had already caught hell from the Chicago Don, Louis Ochopinto, on a safe unlisted telephone at Grimaldi's headquarters.

From his suite in a Paris hotel, removed from the crime scene as requested by his trusted family consigliore, the Don had seen the television report of the fifth truck captured in Chicago on Tuesday morning. He was not happy that only one truck arrived safely.

An hour later, Grimaldi met with two men. "That fuckin' Stewart's gonna pay. We should have killed him in the mine but the smart son of a bitch got the jump on us, okay."

He pointed a finger at Frankie and Bruno. "You two catch a flight to Louisville and drive back to Lexington. You know what he looks like and where he lives, so this should be easy. You kill that fuck, okay. I wanna' hear about it real soon."

In Switzerland, Eddie Cason saw the same television news that Don Ochopinto watched in Paris. Last night he already had received a disturbing email message from Peter Stryker that was bad enough. *Grimaldi wanted them both dead. What the hell is going on?*

He doesn't bother with the email now. He calls Richards at his duplex. It had been a long day and night for Paul Stewart on Monday and now, on Tuesday, chameleon Floyd Richards was trying to get some desperately needed sleep.

"You did what?" Cason yells into the telephone. "Jesus . . . God All Mighty." Cason blurts out sitting on the motel bed. He rocks back and forth in anguish while Richards tells him in detail what happened in the mine and how he had called the FBI as soon as he left the area.

Cason didn't speak for several seconds. Old thoughts flashed through his mind. In prior times and for a great deal less money, even without the death threat, he would have hung up and disappeared, never to return.

The old Eddie Cason would have withdrawn the whole five million American dollars from the Swiss bank and fled to South America, South Africa, or South Anywhere. But Cason had changed. He had found a new life and a real friend in Richards, and Eddie liked himself, this new person he had become over the past year.

He even smiled as he spoke. "I'm coming back, Floyd. We are going to live or die together in this mess. Did you drop the film off yet?"

"I put it in the night drop at the Kodak place. It should be ready today."

"Don't go near it. I'll grab the next flight back and pick it up myself. Leave the ticket taped under my mailbox . . . and look out, Floyd. Grimaldi will send people that know you."

Chapter 67

By Wednesday, the four captured trucks were in the hands of the U S Mint Police. Each truck was assigned two drivers and a twin guard escort. Protocol required that the Mint Police drive the lead car in front of each truck and FBI personnel followed in a vehicle behind the captured dumper.

All four EAST trailers would rendezvous at Fort Wayne, Indiana, where the entourage of vehicles was increased to three Mint Police vans and three FBI units, leading and interspersed between each truck. From there the caravan drove through northern Ohio, Pennsylvania and on into New York.

The media was absolutely giddy, televising the whole event from helicopters above, to rolling video vans, while a phalanx of photographers dutifully recorded where they stopped along the route.

Reporters with microphones extended asked the men their preference in urinals, high or low fixtures, and what food each consumed for lunch or dinner, and bed or pillow choices at the motels reserved at night.

Of course it really got dicey when at midnight one snoop recorded via video a vicarious vision through the slats of a motel room's window blinds when a United States Mint Policeman on his knees mounted a female FBI agent from behind.

Everyone agreed that such reporting was a slight invasion of privacy, but at least the photographer didn't catch one of those gay moments in law enforcement. The resulting pornographic video was a best seller, affectionately entitled, "Bullion Bully porks Fed's Fanny."

Then to add to the media hype and viewer interest, the highway patrol in each state got into the protection act adding additional patrol cars and motorcycle guards. The latter would race up and down the long procession, weaving in and out between vehicles to keep everyone awake.

The major national television networks would provide an update each evening as the procession of gold laden trucks and law enforcement personnel drove to New York.

The entire world was watching and listening to this unparalleled result of an incredible heist gone awry. But the administration only told the public that it was superior law enforcement techniques that resulted in the same day capture of the four, or as newspapers printed it in London, *Lorries loaded with loot.*

Now viewed by a global audience, the United States government insisted that everything would be done in accordance with international standards. And considering the fact that a great deal of gold owned by foreign governments was stored in other banks in this country, required the President to rebuild confidence in both his administration and the reputation of the United States Treasury. *As safe as Fort Knox* would be restored as a statement and a symbol of national strength.

The London Bullion Market Association maintains a world wide good delivery list of acceptable refiners of gold, several of which, both private and government owned, were in the United States. But the closest and one that was operated by the federal government, was the U S Assay Office in New York.

Most of the gold ingots had been scratched or gouged by either the two smaller front loaders or cut and even bent by the giant Toro ore hauler that had scooped up the bars from the mine floor and then unceremoniously dumped them from a considerable height into a steel truck body.

On arrival in New York under heavy guard the damaged ingots would be counted as each truck disgorged its cargo at the refinery loading dock. Then they would be transported to the smelter to be melted and poured into new ingots. Additional gold would have to be added as many bars were no longer the correct weight.

Once cooled, the Bullion was individually wrapped, packed, and this time carefully transported by truck back to the depository at Fort Knox. Again under the same total law enforcement supervision and vehicle escort.

The New York stock market only rebounded partially, about sixty percent of what it dropped even though eighty percent of the gold had been recovered. One event should not have had any influence on the other. Unfortunately, moronically programmed computers, instead of intelligent investors, worried about the possible results of this calamity.

The one EAST truck driver captured was taken to the Cook County Jail in downtown Chicago where he would be held until he could be arraigned for a very long list of federal crimes.

After arraignment, which would happen in a few days, the Mafia henchman would be transferred to Joliet, a federal prison outside of Chicago, to await trial. Grimaldi couldn't allow that to happen. There would be too much pressure on him to talk about his boss, the crime family in Chicago, and who was responsible for masterminding the heist.

The Warden at the Cook County Jail instructed his guards to keep a sharp watch on this important prisoner and never let him out of their sight. Consequently, he was incarcerated in a single cell separated from the normal row of prisoners. He went through the chow line with a guard at his side and ate his meals at a table by himself, away from the other convicts. In the exercise yard, he was kept away from all inmates.

The next morning, a lifer was approached by a visitor to the prison. The man had been convicted of a double murder and sentenced to life in prison without the chance of parole. He'd been behind bars for three years. He never did know who his visitor was, but the visitor knew he had a wife and two little kids. The wife came to see her husband the following day.

"Someone called me yesterday . . . sounded like a white man. Said twenty five thousand dollars in cash has been deposited in a new account in my name . . .

said I had to tell you right away. What does it all mean?"

"It means I'm lookin' after you, baby. Don't tell nobody about it. You use it . . . for you and the kids."

The next day there were a lot of men in the shower. The maximum allowed. A guard stood at the opening into the bathing area where two long rows of goose neck shower heads came out of white painted walls on either side. There were no stalls, no curtains, or any separations between the showers.

He had his eye on the EAST truck driver, but the man was forced to use a shower far down the row. The hot water got turned on hard all up and down the shower room on both sides. A fight broke out near the guard to get his attention. Steam suddenly filled the air and vision was impossible.

A groan of pain came from down the shower line. The guard suddenly realized what was happening and blew his whistle for back up. Naked men started running out, blocking the guards as they pushed into the steamy room.

As they worked their way down the shower row, water on the flooding floor began to turn pink in color. It became very red when they found the body of the truck driver with a sharpened table knife sunk deep into his chest. He was very dead.

Chapter 68

Bruno and Frankie tried to book a flight out of Chicago to Louisville on Wednesday, but there was only one flight with stand by opportunity. They drove to O'Hare airport and waited. At flight time only one seat was available on a stand-by basis, the others were already taken.

Using false identification they paid cash for a flight the following morning when both of them could travel together. On arrival in Louisville, they rented a car and by 2:30 PM they were at Stewarts' mobile home in Lexington. No one was around so they forced the door open and found all the furniture there, but no clothes or personal items.

Frankie used the phone to call the Department of Forestry at the College of Agriculture. "Is Professor Paul Stewart there today?"

The receptionist checked her records. "No. He is not teaching a class today . . . not even this week."

Frankie asked. "Is he still a professor in that department?"

"Wait a minute." It was ninety seconds before she came back on line. "No. UK records indicate he resigned from the college on Tuesday. He did leave a forwarding address."

"All right . . . I'll take it." Frankie answered.

It was Friday before they could get in touch with his landlady at the mobile home park. She gave the two men the same forwarding address that UK had reported, General Delivery, San Diego, California.

Frankie called Grimaldi in Chicago. "It looks like Stewart had this skip planned from the start. Two sources say he's left town."

"Check out Eddie Cason's place. See if he's home yet. If he is, you make him tell you where Stewart is now. And something else bothers me. Why he wanted that dentist busted up. Something's strange about that. If Cason's not back from Europe, you'll have to find out about that dentist and his wife. Background stuff, okay."

On Thursday, Eddie Cason had already arrived back in Lexington and called Richards from the airport. "I've got to get some clothes and stuff out of my mobile home and bunk in at your duplex. They know my address. When they come back they'll be looking for me too."

"It would definitely be better if the two of us stuck together for the next week or so," Richards responded. "We might have a better chance."

Cason walked to long term parking, loaded two suitcases in the passenger seat, revved up the engine on his black, Syclone sports truck, and left the airport.

Whatever happens, it's good to be home. This was the first time that Cason ever felt that way about any place. Before, wherever he was, he just had an address there. It wasn't home, he had no family around, it was just a place where he slept when he was working a con. Here in Lexington he had family, his sister Karlene, his niece and nephew, plus his good friend, Floyd Richards.

As soon as Cason arrived at his mobile home he checked under the mailbox at the street. Scotch taped underneath was a ticket to redeem some photographs. He quietly entered his home and checked around. Nobody had been there yet, but he knew they would be coming soon.

He packed up some more clothes in a duffel bag, grabbed some personal items, including the pictures of Karlene and her family, and left. Most of his clothes were already in two suitcases in his truck.

Cason drove right to the Kodak store and picked up the photographs. One batch of twenty-two photos plus a duplicate set. He ordered two additional enlargements of both sets and addressed two nine by twelve inch brown manila envelopes.

He tipped the girl a twenty dollar bill and asked if she would put the right postage on them when she put the new photographs in the mail. She smiled coyly. She was glad to help the good looking man with the engaging, dimpled smile. Then he drove to Richards' duplex to plan what they should do next.

*   *   *

In one of the Italian restaurants in Chicago where Grimaldi frequently dined, two Mafia men familiar with the heist were holding a conversation. The driver of the truck that successfully made the trip to the Windy City was talking to one of Grimaldi's top Lieutenants.

"When am I gonna get my million bucks?" The driver asked. "Grimaldi made us a promise in Lexington." The annoyed man held his arms out, palms up. "If we got the stuff to a Chicago warehouse, we got paid a big bonus."

"Listen, Joey. You just delivered the stuff. And right now he's got other problems." He held his right hand up like a stop sign. "Don't worry, you'll get paid . . . but don't push your luck or you'll end up like Rossi . . . real dead."

"Whadda' you mean, dead?"

"He got caught by the cops . . . went to jail. We knew he'd make a deal to get a reduced sentence. So he got taken out yesterday."

He gave the driver a hard stare and waved a finger in his face. "We'll let you know when to pick up the money." The Mafia Lieutenant turned and walked toward a table in the back of the restaurant.

The driver had trouble saying anything. It was just as well. He went to the door and stumbled out onto the sidewalk. He was caught up in an overwhelming sense of loss. Not one other person in the mob knew that Rossi was his first cousin and best friend. Certainly not Grimaldi or his top men.

Italian families were very close, and he had grown up with Rossi. As kids they lived just two blocks away from each other. They had gone to school together and knocked around at nights or on weekends having fun with the girls or working odd jobs for allowance money.

Their two families spent a lot of time together over the years. Dinners, ball games, movies, and vacations. And none of them were involved in crime. Just good working people with ordinary jobs. The Rossi and the Paladino families.

But when young Paladino had been offered the chance to work for the mob, he took it. At first it was all small stuff, running errands or handling pick-ups of money or drugs, whatever his immediate boss told him to do.

He had no illusions about becoming a Capo or even a boss. And he was a devout Catholic. He wouldn't even dream about killing someone. Then he drove cars or trucks or helped with pre-arranged thefts of freight from the docks, or to heist cargo flown into the airport. He was just a soldier. That's all he wanted out of life. To make a living for his wife and family.

He had brought his cousin into the mob business a few years back and Rossi had helped Paladino do stuff that his boss said was all right. They would give him a chance to make it with the family. He took the same kind of jobs that Paladino did. No rough stuff. They agreed not to ever mention to anyone in the Mafia that they were related.

Joey Paladino was staggering down the street towards his van. He couldn't believe it. *Grimaldi had his cousin killed for no reason. Just because they thought he might talk. They didn't give him a chance . . . didn't even talk to him about what to say or do in prison. Just killed him.*

Paladino drove home in a stupor. What would he tell his family? They didn't know about it. The Cook County Jail information officer hadn't called the Rossi family yet. He was frantic. Not only for the loss of his cousin, but he thought they might kill him too. He didn't like that forefinger in his face, the look on the Lieutenant's face, or the death threat.

The Mafia is known for its greed and violence. That usually works to keep their members in line. But once in a while, it works in reverse.

Paladino remembered the newscast by Fanzio, U S Mint Police Chief. He saw the announcement on national television later that anyone who had information leading to the arrest of the people responsible for the crime or the whereabouts of the gold would be given protection by the federal government.

Well. They're going to have to do a lot more than that, Joey Paladino thought.

Chapter 69

Barakat's mother and father hired a good criminal attorney who stated that his client did not attack Mrs. Barakat that night before the Lexington Police arrived at their house where they found him beaten and lying unconscious on the living room floor.

His attorney claimed that the same men who almost killed his client also tied up and beat his wife. He offered the police documentation for the record.

"Here is a signed statement taken at the hospital bedside of Dr. Barakat, who is still suffering and in great pain."

I was so relieved that the criminals had not raped my wife and that they had not beaten her too severely as compared with my own innumerable life threatening injuries. I never laid a hand on her.

It was the dentist's word against the word of his soon to be ex-wife. There were no witnesses to the contrary, so the Kentucky State prosecutor for Fayette County could not file charges against Dr. Kalid Barakat, even though there was considerable hearsay evidence to the contrary, but no factual proof of his abuse.

But his criminal attorney was smart enough to have the house signed over to Doris as part of the divorce agreement plus twenty-five thousand dollars.

Doris Barakat was released from the hospital on Saturday. She returned to the home that she would soon own. She called Richards at his duplex. He answered the phone. "It's good to hear your voice, Floyd. How have you been?"

He was surprised. Not only that she called but the quality of her voice. Doris sounded like she had a new lease on life. "I'm really tired," he said. "Been really busy."

"Barakat's gone . . . for good." She blurted out. "I've got so much to tell you. Maybe we could have lunch next week sometime."

Richards was still so exhausted from the past week and now worried about staying alive, he couldn't really quantify her statements. He explained that he was in the middle of some business with Eddie Cason that required all of his time and he would be unable to see her for awhile.

"How are the children?" He changed the subject.

Doris wouldn't be able to pick up Karen or Robby until the paperwork found its way through the court system. It would be another week or more before she could take them home, although she would be able to visit them every day.

"They're fine, but you can't talk to them right now. I mean . . . I really need to talk face to face, Floyd. Please give me a call soon."

As he hung up he had no idea what she was talking about. He had avoided talking to anyone at the college or in his neighborhood. But he knew that he couldn't see her or take the children for the next few weeks. He didn't want to get them involved in his problem.

The whole situation had turned back on Eddie and him. It was his fault that they were in this mess. It was one problem to be sought by federal and local law enforcement for their involvement in a major crime.

But it was much worse to be hunted down and murdered by professional killers who knew exactly who you were and wanted revenge for a double cross. This was way too hot. Richards felt like he had fallen into a giant cauldron filled with boiling oil. And he and his friend Eddie were going to cook.

Chapter 70

Monday morning, one week after the break-in at Fort Knox, Chief Fanzio was still in Lexington set up in a temporary office with an assistant, a telephone receptionist, and a secretary. They were handling a myriad of telephone calls from agents with the FBI, the Mint Police from different states, various Washington D. C. politicians and high ranking government officials.

Most of the conversation the first week was about *The Great Gold robbery,* as it was referred to now by television and newspaper reporters. He was very pleased with the progress to date but still worried, as he informed the Director of the U S Mint.

"My men tell me that each of the four trucks captured carried nearly the same number of ingots."

He explained to the director that they had used very sensitive metal detectors to scour the mine, plus a visual search under high intensity lights.

"Incredibly, we've found some two hundred bars strewn about in the coal mine that they didn't even bother to take . . . thank the Good Lord," he added.

He explained that most of the gold was found within one hundred feet of the hole under the vault, and about fifty bars were strung along the main, center shaft where the overloaded tractors, moving as fast as possible, had bounced them out onto the mine floor.

"The ingots were just left there," Fanzio reported. "But we're still missing more than two hundred million dollars in gold. That means a fifth truck must have arrived safely in Chicago."

He told her that the FBI, our Mint Police, and local law enforcement are undertaking a major search in the city. That completed his Friday telephone update.

Fanzio was recording the activity during the last few days which would be typed and forwarded by special courier to the Mint Director's office in Washington, D. C. Email and facsimile transmission were too easily compromised.

The report included his opinion, a reference to the fact that a major criminal organization must be involved, since one truck was found in a warehouse in Chicago, purportedly owned by the Mafia.

On the morning news, coverage had turned to the capture of the four giant dump trucks, and how much gold had been recovered in one long day, as announced by Chief Fanzio.

Suddenly his office door burst open. His secretary interrupted the dictation. "There's a stranger on the telephone. He would not identify himself, but claims to have information about the theft."

Fanzio quickly punched the button on the blinking line as his secretary closed the door behind her. Joey Paladino was using a throw-away cellular telephone purchased for cash with no requirement for name, address, or any identification.

"You were on television last week," he began. "You talked about protection for certain information. Is that still true?"

Fanzio was recording their conversation, but it would not lead to anyone or to any place other than a Chicago area code and an unregistered cell phone number.

"Yes . . . that's still true. What's your name?"

"Don't be a smart ass," the voice said. "Now here's what I want."

Paladino laid it out for the chief. He had worked on his demands over the weekend by himself. Using the best English language at his command, he wrote everything down on paper which he would burn after he ended the communication. He read the following from it.

I drove the missing truck. I can lead you to the gold. I want a reward. Ten million dollars deposited in a Swiss bank account in my name. I want me, my wife, and kids put into the witness protection program and relocated to Australia. I want it in writing from the Attorney General himself to include a promise that I will not be charged with any prior crime or tried in

any court for my part in this robbery.

"I'll have to discuss this with my superiors. If will take several days."

"The longer you wait the sooner that gold will disappear. They're gonna ship it over seas and melt it down to remove government markings. Then they'll sell it."

"How can I contact you with an answer?"

"I'll call tomorrow. And just so you know this is legit, the hole in the vault floor was cut exactly twenty feet by ten feet and nine feet above the ceiling of the coal mine." Paladino stopped the transmission.

Chief Fanzio set up an immediate conference call with the Director of the U S Mint and the Attorney General in Washington. Once everyone was on line, Fanzio told them about the call and then played back the recording for them to hear.

There was a request to play it again. Afterwards, his boss asked. "You're on top of this, Bill. What is your take on the validity of the call?"

"Only our Mint Police and the gold vault employees know how big a hole the criminals cut in the floor. That information has not been made public."

The chief's voice rose up an octave. "And most importantly, my crime squad just reported to me on Saturday that these professionals cut through nine feet of coal, rock, and concrete. This guy is for real."

"Can we delay him a few days so both the Chicago FBI and the police can search for the truck before we negotiate his demands?" The Attorney General asked.

"I don't want to take that chance," Chief Bill sharply replied. "This driver has no doubt been offered a substantial reward for a safe delivery. But something has gone wrong for him . . . something has triggered his immediate need to distance himself and his family from the mob."

"They just murdered the only driver, the one witness we were able to apprehend," the Attorney General admitted. "And they did that the third day the suspect was in the Cook County Jail."

"There's your answer," the chief shot back. "That was the trigger for whatever reason. We could lose the gold by waiting a few days. You can't imagine the pressure this man is under and the grit it took to call me!"

"I've already talked to the Secretary of the Treasury about the possibility of a reward request from someone," the female Mint Director interjected. "And we both agree with that position."

The woman set the tone with some tough rhetoric. She was not going to allow the Attorney General and the FBI to screw this up and have their pride get in the way because of their principles about not giving in to extortion or bribery.

"I can't emphasize this enough," she continued. "All of us want that two hundred million dollars in gold bullion back in Fort Knox as soon as possible. What we're talking about here is re-establishing the reputation and the security of our nation's gold reserve."

406

"You want Chief Fanzio to start at five million?" The Attorney General suggested.

"No. Absolutely not," she insisted. "Meet his demand when he calls tomorrow. Five percent is cheap. It's the cost of doing business."

"Now," she added with finality. "May I inform the Secretary of the Treasury, who wants to inform the President that we are in agreement on this decision?"

The conversation was over. The Attorney General knew it was not within his purview to argue about Treasury policy. But exonerating a crook and the offer of a pardon was totally within his jurisdiction.

However, he knew that time was of the essence. He did realize it was possible that a delay could result in the loss of the entire hoard of missing government gold. Then he would have to explain to the President and the Congress why he chose to disagree with the prevailing position taken by the Secretary of the Treasury, the Director of the U S Mint, and its Chief of Police.

The Attorney General didn't want to risk hanging himself in front of the American public and catch the ridicule of the press. He started on the required documents to meet the deadline.

Chapter 71

Frankie and Bruno spent all day Monday finding out about Doctor and Mrs. Doris Barakat. They already knew Barakat's home address, so they drove by the dental office. It was still open as people were coming in for appointments made earlier in the month.

Doris was there at the office and she had taken charge. She was a new person. The office staff was glad to see her back. Last week with both Barakats in the hospital, one of the hygienists had called another dentist who traded off with their office when one of them had a problem. He was there. His partner would handle their own patients.

Within a short period of time, the partners would buy the practice from Kal Barakat at a big discount, considering the circumstances and the fact that these two dentists were keeping the business open and operating without pay.

The two Mafia soldiers checked with a credit bureau and found out that Barakat still had a small mortgage on his house that was paid up to date. The credit report had been updated in August and it listed his wife including her former name, Mrs. Floyd Richards. Next they requested a report on Floyd Richards.

"Well . . . look at this!" Frankie said to Bruno. "Her ex is a college professor with the geology department at UK . . . sound familiar?"

"Grimaldi don't like them *cowincydeuces,*" the heavy set, thick browed Bruno managed to say.

"That's what I like about you, Bruno. You talk like Yogi Berra."

Frankie called the college and found another coincidence. "This guy quit the college too."

He wrote down the address of Richards' duplex and they drove there that night at dusk. Nobody seemed to be around. A Ford pick-up truck was parked under some maple trees on the pine straw next to the worn, wooden steps.

Frankie snorted. "That's the same color truck Stewart drove." He got out and walked around the duplex and wrote down the license number on the pick-up truck. He slid back inside the rental car and closed the passenger door.

Bruno started the engine as he spoke. "It's six o'clock. I'm hungry . . . let's get some chow. Then we'll come back."

"Hold it." Frankie held up a hand as they saw a car approaching. It slowed down and turned in at the duplex. They watched the red pin-stripped, black Syclone sports truck drive up by the steps and stop. The driver stayed in the vehicle. The horn honked twice.

Frankie looked through binoculars as Richards came out of the door down the steps and into the Syclone.

"He looks kinda like Stewart. I mean he's the same build. Gotta hat on so I can't tell if he's bald. Too dark to see his eyes . . . they should be real blue. And this guy's got no beard or mustache." Frankie snorted again.

"A guy can shave, ya know," Bruno grunted as he waited for the truck to pass them by. Frankie gave him a disgusted look as Bruno automatically made a U-turn and followed at a safe distance.

At a stop light Frankie wrote down the license number. They followed the Syclone across town to a house where the truck parked in the driveway. The pictures of Eddie Cason that were secretly videotaped in Chicago when he came to see Don Ochopinto were in Frankie's hand. Bruno parked their rental car just past the house.

He had to turn off their head lights to keep from being so obvious a tail. Now it was so dark outside that they couldn't see the driver as he got out of the vehicle. When the knock on the front door was answered by his sister, Karlene, Cason's back was toward the street. They still couldn't make him.

Frankie and Bruno left. They had the last name off the mail box and the address of the people their suspects had gone to visit. They would check the telephone listing in their motel room or a cross reference directory with that address to get a phone number and a full name.

It was a warm family reunion with Karlene Owsley and her family. They all sat down in the living room and sipped beer or wine. Typically feminine, Karlene wanted to catch up on their activities. Her husband as usual didn't say much.

"What's the matter with you two?" She said in a friendly way. She looked at her brother. "You've been out of town and Floyd's been out of touch."

Cason said, "I've been in Chicago checking out some opportunities for both of us." He couldn't tell her the truth. Those opportunities might bring a deathly touch.

Thirty minutes later they sat down to a big dinner. During the course of the meal Richards had to give vague answers about what he had been doing too.

"What's with the buzz cut, Floyd?" Karlene asked. "You've just got stubble coming out on top now."

"Must be cold on the dome," Cason's nephew said teasing.

"I tried the bald look for awhile. It didn't suit me," Richards said casually.

During coffee and desert, Karlene dropped a bomb.

"It was terrible about Doris and that dentist. Who would have thought such a thing could happen to people we know?"

Richards had his cup of coffee half way to his mouth. It stopped moving as his head came up with a look of total surprise.

"What are you talk ———." Richards stopped in mid-sentence. Quickly he glanced around the table. Cason spoke up fast.

"Floyd doesn't like to be reminded of that, Karlene . . . former wife and all."

The conversation quickly switched to other topics; the unseasonably cold weather, and what was going on at the Mammoth Cave National Park where Karlene worked.

They made some excuses to leave an hour after dinner. Once in the Syclone, Richards blurted, "What happened, Eddie? Why didn't you tell me about it?" He was clearly annoyed.

"I figured you knew about it, Floyd. I mean . . . you were here and I was the one in Switzerland."

"I was in the mine all that weekend and last Monday. I was too nervous and tired at night to watch television or read the paper." He explained.

"I asked Ochopinto to do me this favor when I was in Chicago. I didn't know for sure if it went down until I called Karlene the day I got back. She told me everything she knew about the robbery and the Barakats. But they didn't touch her. You ask Doris when she calls again."

"I guess you saved her life, Eddie. I thank you for that. But it may cost us ours."

"I thought that the minute I got your last email. If you hadn't told the FBI, Grimaldi would not be after us."

"That was my fault. They'll track us down through Doris," Richards admitted.

Chapter 72

When Joey Paladino called the temporary office of the Mint Police in Lexington at ten o'clock on Tuesday morning, he got his deal, everything he had asked for on Monday. But then he felt like this could be a trap. It was too good to believe.

"How do I know it's not a set-up and you'll nab me when I show up?"

"I am not lying to you," Fanzio stated. "Some things you just have to take on faith . . . plus we darn sure want that gold back." The chief tells him the telephone number and the address of the office of the U S Attorney in Chicago.

"They've got a fax waiting there for you from the Attorney General in Washington. It's what you wanted from him. They'll fax it to you."

"I don't have a fax machine."

"Then they'll send it to your bank. You can pick it up there and read it."

"Nah. You wouldn't be telling me this if it ain't true. I'll take your word for it. So whadda you want from me? And what about my family?"

"I've just received instructions from a United States Marshall with the Witness Protection Service located at the same U S Attorney's office. You may take your wife and children there now and read that fax."

Fanzio explains to Paladino that agents from the Chicago FBI office will meet him there and that he will remain in their custody when he leads them to the bullion missing from Fort Knox.

"If it is not there, then you will not get the ten million dollar reward. But gold recovered or not, you will be detained for your testimony as a federal witness in the prosecution of the persons responsible for this major crime. This is all in the fax."

"Okay. My name is Joey Paladino. "You've got a deal. I'll be at this attorney's office in two hours with my family."

Three hours later he was in a federal conference room in another building eating sandwiches and drinking coffee with agents of the FBI. Paladino had supplied them with the warehouse address and they pinned a large city map of Chicago on a cork board wall and were discussing how the raid was going to go down in the next forty-five minutes.

The FBI had been informed almost immediately after Chief Bill Fanzio had made the deal with Paladino and they had already set their plan in motion. Fanzio insisted that three U S Mint Police would be in attendance when they raided the warehouse.

The Federal Bureau of Investigation could hardly refuse. They also informed Chicago's Police Chief who assigned six, two man patrol cars to the operation under the direction of the FBI. He wanted some credit for the capture too.

The FBI had a parking garage under the building so that all vehicles could be loaded and men put in place without any witnesses. Joey Paladino piled into one of the vans along with several agents.

In twenty-five minutes the caravan of law enforcement personnel was near the warehouse in an industrial section of the Windy City getting a last minute report from a helicopter that was circling the building at a distance with two agents using binoculars to look for activity on the ground.

"I copy that," the FBI task force leader answered the helicopter pilot.

He then gave an order to the task force. "Code Red . . . I repeat, Code Red. We are going in. Air support says no suspects outside the building. Get fixed and report back."

The FBI vans and cars took their positions around the building while the Chicago Police vehicles blocked the streets. When in place, each unit checked in with the task force leader.

He gave the signal and a dozen armed agents plus three Mint policemen stormed the front door which collapsed under gunfire. Once inside they spread out as the task leader announced their identity with a bull horn. It was fairly dark in the warehouse at three o'clock on an overcast day. The only light came from a row of small dirty windows thirty feet up along two sides of the building.

They all stood still. Sneakered feet could be heard quietly padding on the cement floor at the other end of the long warehouse. Then a sound like a garage door closing softly, followed by a whirring noise.

They didn't dare turn on any flashlights. That would make them an easy target. The FBI had quickly discovered during a records search earlier that this building was owned by the same company that owned the other warehouse across town, whose owners were reputed to be members of the Chicago Mafia.

That information plus the fact that Joey Paladino told them he worked for Tomaso Grimaldi, a capo in the Louis Ochopinto crime family was enough reason that the authorities put together an overwhelming force with major fire power.

However it was anti-climatic. One agent found the electric power source and flipped the switch. Light disclosed what had been shadows and forms seconds earlier. There were crates and boxes piled high in a circle around the incredibly large, but until now missing, EAST dump trailer.

No one was around. But cigar and cigarette smoke hung heavy in the air. The small crates were either full of gold ingots with the wooden tops nailed down tight or open on the floor partially packed. They found that the truck still contained the majority of the missing bullion.

It had been slow and heavy work by a few trusted men who would have required a lot more time to unload and repack twenty-five tons of gold in heavy wooden boxes, pack them into other trucks, and drive to the port for loading one more time into large container bodies for shipment overseas.

The Mint Police immediately cordoned off the whole area around the boxes which virtually surrounded the truck. A small fork lift nearby held one crate ready to stack on top of several others. The engine was still running.

"What's happened to the guys who were just here?" The task leader yelled. "Search the whole building . . . search the loft. I see some rooms up there."

Then speaking into his hand held two way radio to the police outside. "Look for men leaving the building. They were just here."

Searching outside, FBI agents found video cameras recently installed, but hidden high up under the four corners of the overhanging roof. Inside they found one big monitor with a screen divided into four parts that hung across the middle of the dump truck that could be easily seen by the men unloading the gold.

The agents hadn't noticed it at first. The monitor had been turned off. Searching further they found a big freight elevator that went down one floor below street level to a large basement. That was the sound they heard when they burst into the warehouse.

It took the federal agents and the Mint Police two more days of difficult searching to find out how the men escaped. What they finally discovered was that the building had originally been a brewery when it was first built over sixty years ago.

The distillery had big mixing and fermenting vats on the first floor and the large wooden casks of beer that were drawn off were stored in the basement. Across the street the owners had a retail outlet that was very popular during the Second World War and on into the fifties and sixties.

There was so much traffic and movement between the distillery and the restaurant and the beer joint, that the owners got a permit to dig a tunnel under the street that connected the two buildings.

The Mafia had covered the tunnel with an old, huge empty cask that could be rolled to one side electrically to conceal the entrance. The men had escaped through it undetected. Again, the long arm of the law was just too short.

Chapter 73

Also on Tuesday morning back in Lexington, Frankie and Bruno were collecting information on vehicles from the automobile licensing division at the Fayette County Courthouse. The Ford pick-up was registered to Floyd Richards and the Syclone to Edward Cason.

"It's too much of a coincidence again, Bruno," Frankie said. They had spent the day following Richards. It was three in the afternoon and they watched as Richards met his ex-wife and their children at a McDonald's restaurant.

This was the first day that Karen and Robby were reunited with their mother and their father, whom the children hadn't seen for several months. They leaped into their daddy's big arms and he picked them both up and swung them around in sheer joy. He smothered them in hugs and kisses.

Doris had just picked them up from school for the first time since Family Services had taken them away from the Barakats and put them in a foster care program. But this meeting requested by Doris with her ex-husband was a cool one.

Richards had been deeply hurt by his former wife and there was no hug or kiss or handshake. Just an emotionless, "Hello," from Richards.

Doris understood where he was coming from, but now she wanted back into his life, to be with him together as a family again.

She had received advice from her divorce attorney, a woman with a Lexington law firm that did their share of pro-bono work with the public.

"Don't push it," she had told Doris. "You're the one that left. If you really want him back you'll have to give him a lot of space. You've been sleeping with another man . . . no doubt you've hurt his pride. Basically your actions told him he wasn't good enough in several areas of married life."

"I guess I'd be asking him to forgive and forget. I know that's asking a lot. It would be for me if things were reversed."

"Time heals all wounds is an old expression," the attorney said. "But in the area of the heart, I just don't know, Doris. Everyone's different. In my experience I know this . . . give him lots of time and attention."

And watch his reactions to everything carefully, she told Doris. Then when you sense time is right, turn on the affection, then the love and then the sex. Those emotions occur frequently when you are dating or you're engaged, but after the wedding as time goes by . . !"

The attorney left that sentence hanging as she leaned back in her swivel chair and spread her arms out.

"When the kids come along you have to balance all their care and activities with work. Then somehow, those fun, touchy, feely things between you and your husband seem to slip out of a marriage."

"Yes. I guess I started to look elsewhere," Doris conceded with a frown.

The two Mafia soldiers watched the family enter McDonald's. They saw the parents go through the line to order food while the kids ran out into the enclosed play area.

"Look at dose kids slidin' down that yella' curvy thing. Havin' fun, huh?" Bruno said with a simple, but honest smile.

Frankie glanced sideways at Bruno. He knew his elevator didn't go all the way to the top. He was child like. His emotions could run the gamut quickly from rage to laughter.

Mentally short changed, it made him emotionally unstable. He couldn't deal with problems in a normal way.

But two things you could always count on with Bruno. He was honest with his friends and true to his boss. Dependability, that's why he was valuable to the mob. And not only was he put together like a tank, but in the eyes of any commander, he was the ultimate, perfect warrior. Like a robot, he would do whatever he was told. He would save you or he would kill you, and do either one without a second thought.

Frankie had the binoculars up to his face every time he could focus on Richards. Once he told Bruno to take a look.

"I can tell by the looks on his face," Bruno offered. "He don't have no beard or mustache and his hair's growin' out, but that's Stewart." He handed the binoculars back to his friend. Question answered. One long look was enough for Bruno.

Out of the mouths of babes, Frankie thought. He didn't want to say that out loud. He liked Bruno and he didn't want to hurt his feelings. He might have understood what he meant.

Richards stepped into the play area and watched his kids. *God in Heaven, I've missed them.* He just stood there and stared as they played. Once they saw him looking, they would yell out, "Hey Dad, watch me! Are you watching?" He gritted his teeth to stop the tears that welled up in his eyes.

Doris studied Floyd carefully. She wanted to get inside his head and know what he felt every moment she was with him. *But that next moment will be up to him. I'll wait for Floyd to ask next time. I hope the kids will be the glue that can pull us back together.*

Frankie studied Richards too. It was more like predator watches prey. He looked at the structure of the face and head, not the "looks" or expressions that Bruno talked about. His was a youthful observation, but a good one.

The bright blue eyes were gone too. They were contacts, Frankie was sure. His gait was just like Stewart's, who walked in a lazy way, easy like, but powerful. Bruno's right . . . no doubt about it . . . that's Stewart!

Doris hoped he wouldn't ask to have the kids by themselves too many times in the future. He already said he'd like to have them for a weekend again. But not for a little while. *I wonder why he is holding off seeing them. That's not like him . . . He was really mad at Barakat when the visitation was stopped.*

She watched her ex-husband bring the kids back to the table. They were on either side of him holding his big hands. *He's a solid guy. I was so immature.*

But Doris had lived though a lot in the past twelve months. She had aged about twenty years emotionally; and although she was still in her late twenties, her face had aged from the beatings.

I hope he can see past that. I do love him. I pray I'll have another chance. This time she was determined to be better than a good wife. She'd be a great wife first, and then a mother second.

The reunion was over at four thirty. They said their good-byes. The parents were quite formal, while the kids showered their dad with love. Robby was not ashamed to squeeze his dad or give him a buss on the cheek.

A rental car followed Richards' truck as he stopped off to take care of some errands; laundry; dry cleaning; drug store, and pick up some groceries. Cason was coming over to have dinner and eventually they would talk about their life threatening problems and if the two of them would ever get to enjoy their finder's fee, the gold ingots below the coal mine floor, lying on the cave's ledge.

"Looks like the police haven't found that last EAST truck," Richards said as they grilled some hamburgers over charcoal. "Maybe Grimaldi will ease up on us."

Four hands hovered over the grill as the two men stood close to it. It was very cold outside.

"Forget about it, Floyd. Even if four trucks got through, you cross the mob . . . you pay." Wistfully, he added. "Only I'm gonna pay with you."

Richards looked at his friend. That was the one thing he didn't think through. He didn't mean to get Eddie in this fix.

"Maybe I should call Grimaldi," Richards offered. "I'll tell him you didn't know I was going to call the FBI. You meant for Grimaldi to keep the bullion . . . that's what you thought the plan was all along. And you were in Switzerland . . . you had nothing to do with it."

"It's a nice thought, Floyd. But it's too late. I'm a loose end. They know you're my friend . . . that I might say something to the authorities if they only whack you. Grimaldi couldn't chance that now."

It was ten o'clock. The two close friends had finished dinner with a few Coors Light Beers along the way as they talked and planned on into the evening. It was real dark outside now.

The two mobsters had been sitting in their car watching from a distance. Once they saw Cason arrive in his Syclone and the grill was started, Frankie and Bruno went off to eat and call Grimaldi.

"Yeah . . . it's him for sure, Tommy," Frankie said into his cellular telephone. "He changed his looks pretty good, but Bruno says it's him too. And his buddy, Fast Eddie Cason, has been with him ever since we got here."

"If you two are sure, then you do them both. Understand? We can't leave any witnesses. They were both in this together from the start. But now we're gonna finish it. Both of them okay!"

"I hear ya, Tommy. Both . . . now . . . tonight." Grimaldi cut the transmission.

Chapter 74

Frankie and Bruno had been waiting in their car for over an hour, turning the heater on and then off, sipping coffee and munching donuts. To them it was just another day on the job. Nothing to lose an appetite over.

They had to wait for the right time when most people were already home and the darkness would hide them and their car from prying eyes. Frankie had already smeared wet dirt over some of the numbers on the car's license plate just in case.

It was wind still and unusually cold for October. The night was doubly dark. Both moon and stars were covered by cumulous clouds heavy with moisture and it had been coming down for the past twenty minutes in thick, wet flakes of snow. Frankie nudged Bruno. It was time.

He started the engine and slowly pulled into the little driveway next to Cason's Syclone. They wanted to get away fast once the job was done. Bruno stood by the car, while the taller Frankie walked around the building trying to look in the windows.

The other half of the duplex was vacant. Frankie noticed that it was dark inside and there were no cars parked near it. He saw what he was looking for and trudged back through the thickening snow with his felt hat pulled down and his jacket collar turned up against the cold.

"They're in the living room," Frankie said. The big men walked the few steps over the snow covered pine straw and their shoes made prints when they quietly climbed the wooden stairs.

They pulled on thin leather gloves. Simultaneously, .22 caliber revolvers appeared in one hand while the other hand attached a short barreled Harley silencer to the weapon. Afraid that airline security would spot them in their luggage, Grimaldi sent the weapons to their motel in a carefully packed box by overnight fed-ex the day after the men flew down.

They stood at the door for a moment, pistols hanging from one hand like an appendage on that arm, peering through the sheer, white curtains that covered the glass in the door. Their targets had not moved into the kitchen area.

Frankie tilted his head and signaled at the door. Bruno backed off, took a run at the duplex door and it burst open with a loud bang against the wall. The two killers ran straight ahead into the small living room.

Richards had been relaxed, sitting in his favorite recliner with his legs straight out resting on the kicked up ottoman. He struggled to get up.

The two Mafia soldiers had their pistols aimed and ready to shoot, but Cason was nowhere in sight. That saved Richard's life for the moment. The two intruders stood still and glanced quickly around for the other victim.

"Come on out, Eddie," Frankie yelled, "or we shoot your friend . . . Paul Stewart . . . or is it Richards?" His face hardened as he stared at him.

Richards stuttered their names as he held both hands up in the air. "Frankie . . . Bruno." He looked from one to the other. "Listen guys . . . I'm the one that told the FBI. Eddie was in Switzerland. He didn't even know I was going to call them."

"Shoulda thought about that sooner, professor," Frankie answered. "Now it's too late. The man wants you both dead."

"Please . . . let him go, Frankie." Richards was pleading now.

Cason was in the bathroom. He had finished draining the beer and was combing his hair while he continued to listen to the recorder. He heard the door smash open and knew what was happening in the duplex. The mob had found them.

He pressed the reverse button, waited two seconds, hit play, quickly hit reverse again and this time found what he wanted. They were yelling for him to show himself.

"Easy. I'm right here . . . I'm not armed. I'm coming out."

He held the tape recorder in one hand and slowly stuck both arms out into the lighted hallway to prove he didn't have a gun. One finger pressed the play button and voices broke the sudden silence.

Everyone could hear Richards speaking, then Grimaldi, who was clearly giving instructions to the driver of the first EAST dump trailer to leave the coal mine.

"That's Tommy's voice," Frankie bitched. "They've been taping us."

"You bastard!" Bruno growled. His face turned red. Veins stood out on his forehead. He was angry. They tried to hurt his boss. He was ready to kill.

Cason peeked around the hallway corner into the living room as he pressed the stop button. With hands over his head he walked slowly towards Frankie and Bruno.

"Look at the photographs on the kitchen table," Cason added. "You're in them too Bruno . . . standing up on the scaffolding with that circular saw."

He had no way of knowing it, but Fast Eddie Cason had just made the wrong remark - - - to the wrong person - - - at the wrong time.

Bruno didn't appreciate the subtleties of this new development. He just raised his gun arm and pulled the trigger. But Frankie understood the problem and he knew Bruno. By instinct, Frankie managed to reach out and just graze Bruno's hand. The revolver made a soft, pumph sound as the bullet slowed slightly through the sound suppresser.

Fast Eddie got slowed down too. But the shot hit him in the shoulder instead of the forehead. Bruno didn't lack for talent when it came to aiming a weapon. By all rights, Cason should be dead.

The .22 caliber pistol is the weapon of choice for a killer. It's used to shoot someone in the front or back of the head, but the bullet is small and it lacks power for a body shot. Cason staggered back two steps against the wall and sank to the floor groaning in pain and holding his shoulder.

"Hold it, Bruno," Frankie yelled. "Calm down and keep them covered."

He looked at Richards. "I suppose you got more tapes and pictures some other place?"

"We do," Richards answered meekly.

"I gotta look at those pictures."

Frankie was confused as he stepped into the kitchen. He had been told by Grimaldi to kill both of them tonight. No excuses, no exceptions. But he knew that this could be a real problem for the crime family. He saw the packet of photographs on the kitchen table, but he never got the chance to open it.

Frankie's cell phone vibrated in his jacket pocket. He stopped in mid-step. This had never happened to him before either. His number was unlisted just like the throw-away cell phone that Joey Paladino had used that very morning in Chicago to make his deal.

"Shit," Frankie said. "This whole thing is gettin' fucked up."

He pulled the small phone out of his pocket and looked at the number on the digital screen. He didn't recognize the number. He wanted to hit the end button, kill the two targets, and get the hell out of there. No one could blame him for that. He would have done what he was told by Grimaldi.

But again his instinct told him otherwise. Something in his subconscious nagged at him. He needed to answer that damn phone. Frankie punched in the button and said, "Yeah."

Chapter 75

A voice he didn't quite recognize or expect asked. "Have you made the contract yet?"

"Who the hell wants to know?"

"Louis Ochopinto. I'm in my apartment with our consigliore."

"Jeez, boss. I didn't know it was you. We were just about to do 'em when they played a tape and gave me a packet of pictures."

"I just saw the photos this afternoon. That Fast Eddie's got brass ones. He sent them to me! I hadn't heard about a tape . . . what's on it?"

"He only played one part. You could hear Grimaldi talking to the first truck driver, Joey Paladino."

"That fuckin' weasel! He told them where to find the truck. The Feds hit it late this afternoon . . . got it all back. Paladino's family is packed and gone. Now these pictures and they got tapes! It's gettin' too hot. We don't need two dead guys in Lexington that's gonna lead to us. Get outta there now. The contract is off."

"We're leaving, boss. Anything else?"

"Bring the evidence. You tell those two fucks . . . they're living' lucky for now. Tell 'em if those photos or tapes ever show up again, they're both dead. You tell them that's a promise from the don!"

Under Bruno's watchful eye, Richards helped Cason to a kitchen chair, gave him four extra strength Tylenol, and tried to stop the bleeding. Frankie stood over them. He repeated the Don's words exactly.

Then added, "You're two lucky ass holes. You got balls too, professor. I don't know how you did it. We frisked you over every day during the job. Come on, Bruno. We're leaving town for now. Don't make us come back, professor. I was gettin' to like you."

The two mobsters took the evidence and left. Richards peeked out of the door and watched them drive off. He went to a kitchen cabinet, got the bottle of Wild Turkey, and poured two tumblers half full with no ice.

"Here, Eddie. Drink it down. We both need it." Very slowly, Richards sank his weary body into another kitchen chair. They were both exhausted from fear and stress. He lifted the glass to take a sip when Cason stopped him.

He still had that Fast Eddie dimpled smile and the blue eyed sparkle. "Here's to us, buddy. We had the last twist!"

Richards grimaced at Cason as they clinked glasses in a toast. "You're irrepressible, Eddie."

Cason mimicked Frankie. "I hope that's good, professor." They both took a long swallow followed by big sighs.

They used a couple minutes to finish off their drinks and catch their breath.

"We have to get you to the emergency room . . . that bullet's going to infect you."

He helped his friend stand up and get into a heavy winter jacket. Richards took something out of a drawer and turned back to Cason. He had a big wooden handled ice pick in his fist.

Cason was startled. The color left his face again and his knees got wobbly. "What's this, Floyd?"

"Oh, sorry. I didn't mean to scare you. I've got to stick a hole in your coat."

Cason had to sit down again. "Sweet Jesus, Floyd. I didn't expect you to kill me."

Richards reached inside Cason's shirt and pressed the bloody bullet hole against the lining of his jacket. He took the ice pick and shoved it through the center of this new bloody stain. Then he did it again from the outside, wiggling the pick around a little to make a bigger hole.

"There's always a cop at the hospital," Richards said. "When we tell the emergency room personnel it's a bullet wound, he'll be on us to write it up. Here's what we tell them."

Richards explained that they had just stepped outside to drive to an all night diner. "It's eleven at night. You were just opening the truck door when a car stopped at my driveway and some kid yelled out.

"We couldn't understand what he said. You turned toward him, a gun went off and you were hit. A drive-by shooting. The car raced off . . . I was helping you down in the snow. We couldn't get the license number; it was dark and still snowing. End of story."

433

He helped Cason down the steps and into his truck. By now the four Tylenol and the booze had mellowed him a bit. Everything went as planned at the Central Baptist Hospital downtown.

Cason was immediately put on intravenous fluids which included a pain killer and he was out when they wheeled him into surgery. The bullet was easy to get out.

Richards did the police interview and a squad car followed him back to his duplex. He had remembered to trample the snow around Cason's truck by the driver door. The snow hadn't quite filled it in yet. The neighbors were roused out of bed but they couldn't offer the police any help. Saw nothing and heard nothing.

"One twenty two caliber pistol shot wouldn't make much noise," the patrolman offered when he got off the phone. "That's what they just took out of your friend."

They looked around outside some, but Richards didn't offer an inside search. In a few minutes the squad car left.

Richards was not a liar. That was not in his nature. He was not raised to tell stories and it went against his religious teachings. But no way could he and Cason tell anyone what really happened. He may have set a record in the world of crime and punishment. He had gotten a second reprieve from the Mafia. And he and Eddie wanted to live a lot longer.

Chapter 76

When the caravan of trucks and tractors originally arrived at the coal mine, Richards, alias Stewart, had started the tape recorder in his pocket. The first detail he recorded was the vehicle types and their license plate numbers. He knew that might be key information later on.

Then at the end of each day, when he went back to the double wide mobile home he rented as Paul Stewart with Frankie as his baby sitter, he took the used tape with him and hid it. The next day he would bring a new tape. Then if one were lost or ruined, he wouldn't lose all of the information.

Weeks before, during one of their planning sessions, Cason said, "Remember Maxwell Smart, the funny detective on television who talked into the heel of his shoe."

Richards spent an hour drilling holes in and cutting out a small chunk of the heel in one boot from the pair he planned to wear in the mine. He made a plug from the outside edge of the boot. He could use a spot of

435

glue to hold it in after the little tape was secreted inside.

"You're taking a big risk, Floyd . . . taking photos and recording voices during the heist."

"You told me they might twist the deal at the end, Eddie. This is insurance. I hope we don't need it."

From Friday at noon until early on Monday morning, Stewart and the Mafia had spent almost three days working in the mine. They checked Stewart twice every day, frisked him before he went in and when he came out.

But it was Grimaldi who gave Stewart the idea when he instructed his men on that first day. "You can piss three rooms away from where I'm standing if you can't wait. But you damn sure better crap in that portable shit house we brought. I don't wanna smell your stink where we're working, okay."

Following those instructions, Stewart made several trips to the portable outhouse every day. But using a pen knife, he would pop out that day's fresh tape or put it back in his shoe heel before leaving at night.

The tape player was kept in the mine too. The mobsters used a mined out room near the work area as the place to take a break. They had brought canvas folding chairs to sit in and plan or talk; eat or drink; but only water, sodas or coffee; to smoke, or just close the eyes to rest. Boards on boxes were the tables for sandwiches and snacks.

Bruno saw it and said, "Hey . . . this is just like a food court at the mall." The name stuck.

The drilling and cutting, or the coal and rock dropping to the mine floor made a terrible racket. So the "food court" was where Stewart talked to Grimaldi or the others. And at the end of that mine cut, some twenty feet further away up against the coal face in the dark, was the outhouse. Chemicals kept it odorless.

And unless you walked there with your helmet light shining you couldn't see it. But for the loose boweled members of the group, it was nearby.

Stewart hid the tape player on top of it. A molded niche there was the perfect place. Even mobsters never touched anything inside or outside one of those things unless it was the door handle or the lock inside. He didn't need a microphone. With the sensitivity turned up high he could pick up any conversation.

He hid it that Friday afternoon when he was using a stop watch to time the big Toro tractor running back and forth from the vault area to the mine entrance. He was directing everything and saw to it that the chairs were placed opposite the food tables in the twenty foot wide mine cut, not too far from the outhouse. He would use his helmet light in the toilet's privacy to replace the tape and turn it off when he wasn't there.

The photography was more difficult. He had two helmets. Both were yellow hard hats with a standard light built into the front. All the other men wore the same yellow helmets also. Stewart had specified the type of helmet to buy on the purchase list of items he had given to Grimaldi.

He wore the same helmet in and out of the mine every day, which is when they would check him over. Once inside, it wasn't hard to wander around checking on the work in progress, the tractors or whatever.

437

He kept a second yellow helmet hidden in one of the many mine cuts off to each side of the main shaft under a piece of black tarp. He would make a switch. It was always black as death throughout the coal mine. So it was easy to see helmet or tractor lights coming.

The second helmet had an implant. It was a nine volt micro coin camera. A spy tool. But it could easily be purchased over the Internet in a variety of sizes. So named because it was no bigger around than a silver quarter, just an inch thick, and hidden inside the helmet in some extra webbing. It would be easily overlooked if someone else picked it up.

The lens opening was positioned in a tiny hole, impossible to see since it was set a quarter of an inch below the helmet light, which provided the brightness needed to take the picture, triggered by a minuscule remote Stewart kept in his pant's pocket.

The camera made a tiny click, but with all the men stomping around, the tractor's diesel engines rumbling, or the saws cutting into the ceiling, that was not a concern. Stewart didn't even use up one roll of film, so that was not a problem either.

He had told Eddie Cason early in the planning stages, "Yes, I know it's the Mafia and they're extremely dangerous. But we're not going to be in their turf in Chicago. Instead, they're going to be underground in our territory, our black coal mine. They're not cavers or miners. That will be my big advantage."

He patted a worried Cason on his shoulder. "Remember, Eddie, Grimaldi is depending on us to set the parameters for the job."

Chapter 77

A few days later, once his shoulder stabilized and the pain had subsided, Richards helped Cason move back to his mobile home. They could not believe how lucky they were to be alive and just how close they came to death.

Cason said, "Lady Luck threw us the dice and said 'roll them, boys, they're all sevens and elevens.' We had some super run, Floyd."

They had made a great team together. Each contributed his own special talent to the caper. But it wasn't over yet.

"You know what I've still got to do, Eddie. And you'll be all right with that?"

"Yeah. It's not what I would have done a few years back, but I understand where you're coming from."

Chief Bill Fanzio had spent the last two weeks in Lexington and he was about to close down his temporary office. He was very pleased with the

439

recovery of all five EAST trailers. The Mint Police in Chicago had escorted that last big truck with all the gold put back in it to the U S Assay Office in New York.

That accounted for the last two hundred million in gold ingots. About one billion dollars worth of bullion was back in the United States Treasury. But the tally of the content of all the trucks had come up short of what was missing from the vault.

There was still a significant shortage. His personnel at the Fort Knox Depository and the Mint Police had searched everywhere inside the mine and all around the entrance.

"We still can't account for some four hundred and fifty bars." The chief was talking to the Director of the U S Mint in Washington, D. C.

"In dollars, how much is that?" She asked.

"Over fifty five million dollars. In cash or diamonds you could hide it easy . . . but we're talking over six tons of bullion."

"You've still done a great job, Chief. That's about five percent of the total," she said. "Two weeks ago we would have settled for a ninety-five percent recovery in a heart beat."

"Thanks, Hillary, but somebody has that gold. Somehow there must have been another small truck involved."

"We can't pay you to explore the cave again, Floyd. We're still short of funds."

"I understand that. But I still haven't heard back from all the applications sent to other colleges for a teaching position."

Richards was talking with the Superintendent of the Mammoth Cave National Park who also had charge of developing the new cave system.

"So while I'm collecting unemployment compensation, I thought you would let me continue to map the caves and tunnels . . . no cost to the government of course. I'm just itching to go underground again."

"I can't see the harm in that, Floyd. After all, you did discover that cave."

"Oh . . . I'd like to take Eddie Cason with me. It's safer to work in pairs. It'll be good for him. The doctor says he needs to exercise and keep working that shoulder."

"I read about that drive by shooting in the paper. I thought those things happened in New York or Chicago . . . not Lexington. Sure, take Eddie with you."

Richards and Cason rented a motel in Radcliff to spend as much time as possible underground in the cave. They saw the nearly completed one story building at the end of the parking lot. In the near future at advertised times for different tours, park employees will guide the public through various sections of the cave to view the Indian relics; take the stalactite and stalagmite trip, the wet tour . . . stream and waterfall, and other cave wonders.

A stairway with railings had been built down to the actual cave opening in the sinkhole that Richards had discovered. But it had been greatly enlarged and additional stairs were needed to get to the cave floor.

Electrical outlets were visible as they would be needed by tour guides to light up the pathway that was still in the process of being cleared down into the many caverns.

The partners walked past workmen when they entered the cave and thirty minutes later squeezed through the crevice behind the big boulder that dropped down to a series of tunnels and caverns that led to the coal mine. Since they had never mentioned this lower cave system in any of their weekly reports, and they were the last explorers on the payroll, no one knew about it yet.

In less than two hours, they reached their dream cavern. Richards had the equipment necessary to climb back up on the ledge where he found the gold bars still there, just as he left them, piled in among chunks and pieces of coal from the broken mine face.

He put two gold ingots in a canvass bag and lowered it down to Cason. He repeated this until Cason had four bars at 27.5 pounds each for a total weight of 110 pounds which Richards would carry out, and three bars for him that weighed 82.5 pounds. His shoulder still bothered him and he was smaller in stature than Richards.

Every morning they went into the cave system weightless and labored hard every night to carry that gold out. For comfort, the weight had to be distributed more evenly, so they both placed a bar in special tough pockets made of webbing that hung on each side of their hips off a waist belt and the other one or two in a backpack.

Finally after six days the last of the gold they needed was hauled out. They made sure they emerged from the cave well after the workmen had gone for the day. The construction manager left on those lights already installed for the workmen. Richards promised to switch them off.

It was exhausting work, but the two men had hauled out eleven hundred pounds of gold, forty ingots worth around five million dollars. On the last day, Richards also carried out two pieces of coal.

The other 400 bars worth about fifty million dollars were left on the cavern ledge. They would be dealt with at a later date, and certainly, Richards and Cason had no plans to haul them out.

Chapter 78

Back in Lexington, they stored the gold in Cason's mobile home. He wouldn't have any visits by children, ex-wives, or the more numerous friends that Richards had developed over the years at the University of Kentucky.

For the next two days they carefully packed ten wooden crates, four ingots in each, which weighed in around one hundred and fifteen pounds per box. The crates went in the back of Richards' Ford pick-up truck covered by a securely tied down tarpaulin.

The two of them drove to Chicago where they used another fictitious driver's license, provided by Cason's former jail mate, to send the crates using Consolidated Freightways, a well known trucking company with offices throughout the United States.

"I want to insure each crate for five thousand dollars," said Anthony Paparazzo, alias Eddie Cason, who had a legitimate address in Chicago, but of course no one by that name lived there. The apartment was vacant at the time. Mr. Paparazzo also produced a calling card with the name of a metals manufacturing company in Chicago.

"What's in the crates?" The clerk asked.

"Bars of steel and lead coated in brass. It's an alloy that will be used in a nuclear power plant," Paparazzo answered.

"They're not hazardous material are they?" The clerk asked with a worried expression.

Paparazzo assured him that they were not hazardous yet and paid him in cash for the delivery plus the insurance. Richards and Cason only hoped that their description of the cargo would eliminate any thought of theft.

"The shipment should arrive three days from now," the clerk advised.

The two partners spent the night in a motel on the south side of the Windy City. The following morning, Cason made a telephone call to Lexington, using a pay telephone in a booth.

Chief Fanzio's secretary burst into his office with about the same message she had the first time.

"I can't believe it, but someone's on a pay phone. I had to guarantee the operator you would take the call and listened to the coins drop in the box. Again, he won't give his name, but says he has information about the missing gold."

The chief gave some instructions before he picked up the telephone. He had it recorded and put a tracer on the call immediately. The two men in Chicago hoped he would do just that.

"I want to be anonymous. This will be my only telephone call," Cason said in a robotic voice, void of inflection. He told Fanzio that a shipment of crates containing Fort Knox gold would leave Chicago this morning. He gave him the name of the sender, the freight company, the name and address of the recipient plus the expected day of delivery. Cason cut off the transmission.

The chief made a telephone call to his Washington, D. C. office and requested that two Mint Policemen contact the freight company and serve notice that they would meet the shipment in transit immediately and accompany the crates to their destination with the trucking company personnel.

He then called another U S Mint office and requested that several armed Mint Policemen meet him at the airport two days from now and gave them flight information.

His men were waiting at the luggage area at the required time and whisked him away to a downtown address where they arrived early on purpose.

They snacked and sipped coffee across the street at a Starbucks cafe. Fanzio had kept in touch with the men that accompanied the shipment of ten crates. They were due at the same address in thirty minutes.

The nervous driver parked the Consolidated Freightways truck at the curb in front of the big building. His passenger was a Mint Policeman sitting in the cab with him. His assistant driver rode in one of two black Mint Police vans that parked behind the truck.

When the back of the truck was opened, Fanzio said, "Deliver four crates now. Leave the others in the truck."

The drivers unloaded the crates onto dollies and accompanied the chief with two Mint Policemen into the large building's lobby and took the elevator up to the seventeenth floor where the addressee was located.

Chief Bill opened the huge walnut double doors next to the brass name plate on the wall which read, *Cohen, Brooks, Belzberg and Murray, Attorneys at Law.*

The surprised receptionist stood up as the five men, with the crates on freight dollies, filed through the doors.

"May I help —-?"

The chief interrupted before she could finish. "These are four of ten crates addressed to a Mister Jay Cohen, attorney for the National Park Service. Is he here today?"

"Well, yes . . . but he is in conference at the —-."

He flipped open his badge under her nose. "You need to inform him immediately that the Chief of the United States Mint Police is here and I have some questions."

She watched two grim looking Mint Police with side arms in their belt holsters step up behind their chief.

The receptionist disappeared immediately. In thirty seconds she was back with a broad smile and said to everyone, "Please follow me."

The whole bunch paraded down a hallway lined with cubicles that housed desks and seated secretaries, who stopped doing everything except to watch wide eyed and silent. Mean looking guards in uniform with guns and badges most prominent did not bode well for the esteemed counselor-at-law. They were led into a large conference room, very empty except for one Mr. Jay Cohen and his secretary.

Fanzio gave the orders. "Get him to sign for it," the chief said to one driver. "Leave the crates here. Then wait with the receptionist out front."

Jay Cohen didn't like to be surprised or out of control in any situation. Slowly he read the delivery receipt, signed it, and handed it to his secretary.

The chief spoke up again. "If you will, miss, make a copy for Mister Cohen and bring the original back to me."

"Now wait a minute!" Cohen said. "I have no idea what this is all about. You must have me confused with somebody else."

"I certainly hope you're right, Mister Cohen. But we've had an anonymous tip about this whole shipment. Let's look inside these crates . . . that will answer a lot of questions. You mind if one of my men opens them?"

Cohen saw that one Mint policeman was all set with a crow bar in his hand. The attorney nodded at his secretary to make the copies and said, "Go right ahead. I'd like to get to the bottom of this too."

The top boards were quickly pried off and the bubble wrap opened up. Gleaming bars of gold shined up at the assembled group. Cohen stared at the ingots in disbelief and then at the chief. The lawyer was mute.

"The tipster, who called from Chicago, also told us that this shipment was your legal fee for services rendered as consigliore, or counselor, for the Philadelphia Mafia. Would you care to comment?"

Cohen glanced at the chief and then at his secretary who just returned with the original delivery receipt for Chief Fanzio. She wasn't about to miss out on anything.

Finally, totally exasperated and at a loss for words, Cohen blurted, "This all has to be a huge mistake."

"You can see the mark of the U S Mint on all that bullion plus the shipment was addressed to you. Those are not mistakes, Mister Cohen. They are hard facts. Judging from what's here and the other six boxes still in the truck, that's about five million in gold. Who in their right mind would send you that for no good reason?"

"This is craziness, Chief Fanzio! Why would I have the gold sent here where my whole staff could see the boxes? What was I going to do? Open them all and take the gold home in my briefcase?"

"Don't be sarcastic with me, Mister Cohen. You're the one who arranged for the National Park Service to take over that new cave system which goes under state road 31 west. And so does the coal mine. Now this payment is sent to you. A big coincidence, don't you think?"

The chief never gave attorney Cohen a chance to respond. "You're under arrest as an accessory to a federal crime. The gold theft at Fort Knox."

He turned to his two policemen and said, "Cuff him . . . he's coming with us."

Chapter 79

Richards and Cason drove the pick-up back to Lexington. On Saturday morning they were at Cason's home to carefully discuss further plans. Finally they were relaxing over a beer and Cason pointed the remote at the television and turned on the eleven o'clock news.

"As a further development in the incredible gold robbery from Fort Knox, Jay Cohen, a prominent Philadelphia attorney, was arrested late Thursday as an accessory to the crime. He was held in jail overnight and made bail Friday morning."

The announcer added, "This strange turn of events simply adds to the mystery of who actually committed the crime of the century."

Cason's face sparkled with a big grin. "Yesss! That gold we lugged out was so heavy and it was so much trouble to send it to that damn attorney. But it sure was worth it!"

Richards smiled back at him. "Well, Eddie. It was kind of a personal thing for me. He's been so nice to us over the past year; I just thought we ought to throw him a bone. Every dog needs to eat."

"Pay back can be so sweet," Cason said. "Especially when we can see it live."

They watched as Cohen, looking haggard and unshaven came down the steps from the courthouse with his criminal attorney and ran smack into a herd of raucous news-hounds, television and newspaper reporters with microphones held out in front like a barricade, blocking the humiliated and embarrassed attorney.

"Now I'm going to crack another beer and watch it all over again. We can listen to him whine and explain his problems to the press." Cason had pushed in a blank video tape, and punched record.

On Monday, Fanzio's secretary, for the third time during the investigation, popped unannounced through the door into his office.

"Well this time I've got a name, Chief. Floyd Richards is on hold . . . he wants to know if there is a reward for finding some of the missing gold?"

"This is the damnedest case . . ." His voice trailed off as he grabbed for the telephone. The secretary smiled at her boss as she left him to listen to one more amazing conversation.

"Mister Richards. This is Chief Fanzio. Can we meet?"

"Yes sir. I was hoping you would ask."

"Can you get to my office this morning?"

"Yes . . . I live here in town. Everybody in Lexington knows about your office. I'll be there in half an hour. Oh, by the way . . . here's my telephone number."

Richards hung up the telephone. He was in his duplex with Cason. The last part of the plan was now in motion.

Fanzio walked into his assistant's office. "Get the team on this fast. Find out everything you can about Floyd Richards . . . here's his phone number. I wanna know what he eats for breakfast."

The office staff for the U S Mint in Lexington had grown considerably during the investigation. They had been flown in from other U S Mint offices around the country.

When the big, pleasant looking, almost shaggy haired Richards walked into the office, everyone saw an affable looking, neatly dressed professor with an over the shoulder book bag. He smiled and said good morning as he offered his hand to the chief.

Richards was led into Fanzio's office where he sipped on an offered cup of coffee as the three men sat down. The crime squad leader had joined them.

"I'll start at the beginning since you don't know much about me yet," Richards offered quickly.

"You understand we'll need to record this conversation," the chief stated.

"Go right ahead . . . saves time later," Richards added.

He proceeded to chatter like a magpie. They got his whole history; divorced with two kids; asked to leave his professorship at UK for reasons he didn't quite understand; lost his cave system to the National Park Service, and he was currently unemployed.

They stopped him several times to ask for more background information. Richards told them all the things they would have found out anyway, but side stepped on a few facts. He hoped they would think he was forthright and not holding anything back.

"So, since I'm broke and haven't heard back from my applications to other higher institutions of learning about a position as a hydrologist or geologist, I've been exploring that new cave system again and found something very surprising."

He hesitated as he glanced from one to the other.

"Would you care to share that information with us?" Fanzio asked.

"Well, ahh . . ." Richards stammered and looked uncomfortable. Then he appeared to gather his courage and put on a serious face. Richards, or Stewart, or Stryker . . . he was becoming adept as a chameleon.

"First I'd like to know if you would pay a reward for gold that is still missing? I feel that ten percent of anything recovered would be fair to both me and the government."

"How do you know any is still missing?" The investigator asked.

"Just from what I've heard on television and your own press releases."

"That's an assumption on your part," Fanzio stated. "No exact figures have been released."

Richards looked from one to the other. He grimaced, raised his shoulders and turned his palms up in a condescending gesture. "Well, I've been wasting your time."

Richards stood up to leave. "I thought I'd found a clue here, but I guess not."

"Hold on, Mister Richards." Fanzio said. "We appreciate your coming here. You have to understand that everyone we've dealt with so far regarding this robbery has been a criminal, or very evasive and extremely difficult."

"I wouldn't want to be anything like that. I'm just offering a straight forward proposition. Of course, I would need a written agreement . . . signed by either the Director of the U S Mint, or the Secretary of the Treasury."

The two Mint Policemen glanced at each other. Fanzio said, "Obviously, you've given this a lot of thought. So I must assume you have found something."

Richards didn't speak. He just sat there looking at each of them . . . waiting.

"Oh. We didn't answer your question," Fanzio said. "I'll have to discuss this with the Director. Rewards are outside of my jurisdiction."

"You have my phone number. Just give me a call. Let me know," Richards said, as he got up to leave again.

"Ahh . . . Mister Richards," the investigator said. "You were going to share something with us?"

"Of course. I have it in my book bag." He unzipped the bag and placed two pieces of coal on Fanzio's desk.

"During my exploration, I found this coal in the cave. No one takes heavy stuff like this into a cave for heat or light."

Richards didn't wait for questions or remarks. "This came from that same coal mine that led to the depository vault. I took careful compass and depth readings. I was only fifty feet from the surface. Over geologic time, part of the coal mine collapsed into the cave."

"Then my men could go in there and find that cavern too. Why do we need to pay a commission to you?" The chief asked.

"It's a large cave system . . . much of it unexplored. Even using expert cavers you would never find it. The few pieces of coal that were in there to mark the cavern are gone or on your desk."

"Well. Now we get down to it. You're not so innocent after all, Mister Richards. This sounds like extortion," the investigator remarked.

"Mister Richards," Fanzio stated. "Evidently, you've found some missing gold. But you need to understand, if a bag of money fell out of an armored truck and it had the bank's name on the bag it wouldn't belong to you. You see my point?"

"Perfectly. I know it doesn't belong to me. It has the mark of the U S Mint on it."

Richards leaned forward, looking directly into Fanzio's eyes. "I've read that the ingots were dropped out of the vault, so it still belongs to the treasury. I didn't take it. The gold can stay right there . . . forever."

"You seem hostile, Mister Richards," the investigator said. "As a citizen of the United States, don't you feel an obligation?"

"I used to think that worked both ways," Richards answered.

He looked at Fanzio again. "There are no free lunches, Chief. I'm suggesting a business deal. You have to understand. It's not a case of my returning it to you. The gold is still on your property . . . or under it.

You have the opportunity to get back ninety percent of it, or none of it. That's a good offer."

The chief gave his investigator a knowing look. A look that indicated the deal was on the table. This meeting was not going to go anywhere else. It was done and over.

"Okay. We'll be in touch, Mister Richards. Thanks for coming in."

Chapter 80

Richards reviewed the meeting with Eddie Cason. They decided to sit and wait. Make no further contact with the government. Let them come back to Richards. They had agreed that Eddie would stay out of the public spotlight. One of them exposed was enough.

Usually any arm of the government is slow to make a decision and then even slower to act upon it. But not in this case. Chief Fanzio quickly initiated a lot of discussion between the Director of the U S Mint, the Secretary of the Treasury, law enforcement officials, and employees at the Mammoth Cave National Park System.

The Park personnel informed them that this new discovery appeared to be fairly large and complex. They explained that after two hundred years of exploration, they were still finding new tunnels and caves at Mammoth.

"Without having any clue where to look, it would take years to find that one cavern that leads to the coal mine," one expert caver and spelunker told them. "Or more likely, you'll never find it in your lifetime."

Again the Director of the U S Mint settled the question when she was on a conference line with the Secretary of the Treasury and Chief Fanzio.

"Suppose this man does know the location of the missing gold," she began. "And furthermore, he is the only one who knows, and tomorrow he gets murdered or dies. What do we have then?"

"Nothing. And we've probably lost the fifty million," responded the Secretary. "We have to pay him for the recovery. Based on what we know about him, he has not broken any laws."

On Friday of that same week, Chief Fanzio called Floyd Richards. "Come by my office, Mister Richards. I have a letter for you signed by the Director of the U S Mint."

Richards read the agreement and was satisfied with its content. "Do you have to reveal my name to the press?"

"Unless you're in the Witness Protection Service, the press has a right to splash your name and your reward all over the news." The chief realized that Richards was uncomfortable with the forthcoming deluge of publicity. He studied Richards closely.

"You worried about that?"

"Somewhat. I just don't want my children at risk . . . kidnappers, that sort of thing."

But Richards was worried that the Chicago crime family would come after him again for picking up a sizable reward, while the Mafia chiefs were facing major problems.

But Ochopinto and Grimaldi were so deep in it, neither one wanted to make the slightest ripple, much less a wave. Everywhere they went, criminal attorneys were at their elbows, speaking for them or telling them what to say.

Both of them had been indicted for having arranged to rob the Fort Knox Bullion Depository. This time the government's star witness, Joey Paladino, was in hiding, guarded twenty-four hours a day by U S Marshals.

Two days later, several members of the Mint Police, including Fanzio, entered the cave system with Floyd Richards. The chief wanted to see everything for himself.

Two and one half hours later, Richards was helping the chief climb up the rock wall to the ledge where they indeed found the missing gold, along with the disguised entrance to the coal mine. The supplies that Richards had left there during the caper had been removed earlier.

The bullion depository personnel retrieved the gold from inside the coal mine using a tractor with a long scoop on the front plus some hard work by men on the cave ledge below.

When the Director of the Mint held a press conference and announced that all the gold had been finally recovered, television and newspaper reporters had a field day. Under the Freedom of Information Act, she had to reveal who found this final cache of gold ingots and the fact that he was paid a handsome reward.

"Mister Floyd Richards is a real patriot," She said. "He could have kept all the gold for himself."

The following week was very hectic for Floyd Richards. He didn't want this kind of exposure; interviewed on television; newspaper articles written about him; met with the Mayor of Lexington, Chief Fanzio, and the Governor of Kentucky at a dinner. The two politicians didn't want to miss out on the publicity.

By the end of the week, Richards was worn out. He had to be careful about what he revealed. He didn't want to make a mistake, so he tried to play the whole episode down. His two children were excited, and as young as they were, they too were interviewed at school. They were so proud of their dad.

Officially, the chief was complimentary too. But after another week of investigation by his Mint Police and the FBI, he called Richards for yet again another meeting.

Chapter 81

"We've done a whole lot of checking on you over the past week, Mister Richards. Officially, we appreciate your help in the return of this final portion of the Mint's assets. That aside, I've got a lot of concerns about you and what you haven't told us."

The chief went into detail. He told Richards that he believed the Mafia did supply the man power; the sophisticated diversion at the gold depository building early that morning; the ability to break up through the floor of the vault, and the money to buy all the expensive dump trucks and mining equipment.

"But the Chicago crime family doesn't wander around poking in caves or mines. You however make a living doing that. You had the knowledge, the ability, and the opportunity to discover the coal on that cavern floor during some earlier exploration of the cave system that led up to that ledge and subsequently the coal mine."

Richards just sat in front of Chief Fanzio. He kept quiet and expressionless, but very impressed with the depth of their investigation and the deductions that the Mint Police Chief had drawn from the many recently collected facts.

"You were the mastermind behind this whole scheme. You and your good friend, Edward Cason, only recently released from jail, and who no doubt has contacts with the Chicago Mafia."

The chief was on a roll. He banged a fist on his desk as he continued to explain that the Mafia didn't bother to hide those gold bars on that cave ledge, disguise the opening with such care, and place six original iron rails in the mine to create a false reading on their metal detectors.

"Unfortunately, we can't prove any of it." He leaned over his desk as he continued to glare at Richards. "Certainly the Mafia won't involve you. That would prove their duplicity in this crime."

He explained that the Lexington Police department provided information about his ex-wife, Doris, and her abusive husband. That an anonymous phone call led the police to a grisly scene at their home where Dr. Barakat was found beaten, no doubt by professionals, during the same weekend the robbery took place.

"Another coincidence, I guess," the chief stated.

Then checking his notes, he told Richards he knew what the National Park's attorney, Jay Cohen, had done to him and his cave partner, Cason, over the past year.

"It must have given both of you great satisfaction to send that bullion to Cohen and watch me arrest him."

The chief told him that the person who sent the gold from Chicago to Philadelphia didn't exist. A false lead. Another anonymous tipster called the next morning to implicate Cohen. Subsequently, it was determined that neither he nor his firm ever had any involvement with the Philadelphia crime family.

Fanzio leaned back in his chair as he looked up. "Frankly, you're a paradox, Mister Richards; a model citizen all your life; except this last year when the two of you with the help of the Chicago Mafia arranged to steal a billion dollars in gold from the most secure depository in the world, and then tip the FBI so we could get it all back. Incredible!"

Further, he told Richards that the two of them had walked a tight rope, like a high wire act, balanced on one side with miracles and luck, and the other with brains and planning. The chief shook his head in disbelief.

"Then your friend Eddie Cason got shot. That was no drive by shooting, Mister Richards. You crossed your Chicago friends . . . and they sent serious people."

The chief sat forward in his chair again. "I couldn't even begin to imagine how you two got the Mafia to back off at the last minute. That's the miracle! And a puzzle."

Richards finally spoke. "You should write a novel, Chief . . . that's some story. I'm just a college professor looking for work."

"What galls me most," Fanzio said, "is that we had to give you a reward." The chief sat up, arms out straight on his desk. "That's called pouring salt on the wound."

Richards changed the subject. "The newspapers and the television networks report there's a lot of public interest in seeing the caverns and the mine."

"Yes. The Treasury Department and the Mint have been deluged with letters and phone calls from around the world."

"I guess the National Park System will be very busy." It was more of a question.

"No," the chief answered bluntly. "Mister Cohen made a lot of nasty comments about the Mint Police when he was arrested and jailed. So we investigated a little further." The chief leaned back again in his chair. This time he had an amused look on his face.

"The coal mine is almost totally on Mint property and current records indicate the cave system is mostly under both Fort Knox and our property. In his rush to get the new caverns for the National Park System, it appears that Cohen only did half a job."

He told Richards that Cohen's agreement with Fort Knox to allow the park system to take guided tours under the base was sent from his Philadelphia office to Army headquarters at the Pentagon in Arlington, Virginia. Concurrently Cohen told the park system to build out the project and that the paper work would take care of itself.

"But he badly lacks protocol," Fanzio emphasized each word. "He by-passed the base commander. A general no less . . . went right over his head. Being neighbors, however, we have always had a fine working relationship with the general and his personnel at the fort."

"Would you stop your recorder, Chief? Let's have this off the record."

Fanzio punched the button and sat back to listen.

With little expression on his face, Richards explained. "I know some people that might pay the

464

Treasury Department five million dollars up front for the lease rights to advertise and market both the cave system and the coal mine together. Take over the project."

The chief's face went blank. That really stopped him. For a few seconds, he couldn't move or speak. So Richards just continued.

"A monthly operating fee would also be paid. Of course it would depend on the traffic. Perhaps a minimum of ten thousand, maybe up to twenty thousand a month in addition."

Richards started pacing around, deep in thought. "This will be a huge public attraction. The parking lot and the building at the cave entrance would have to be enlarged, plus the land around the mine entrance would need to be purchased."

He glanced over at Fanzio, who was totally astonished. Richards added. "I'm sure a good attorney could talk Mister Cohen into a reasonable price for the improvements since the National Park System won't need them anymore."

The chief recovered. "You son of a gun!" He muttered. "This is what you wanted all along. The Treasury Department would get all of its money back . . . plus an ongoing fee from the two of you."

Now he was on the edge of his chair. "One thing we can't figure . . . Cason's trip to Switzerland. He needed a real passport in his own name to deal with any Swiss bank. Plus the airline ticket . . . that's how we knew he went there."

Chief Bill stood up as his mind raced ahead. "But that was before the robbery. He did go there to deposit money, didn't he?"

Now Richards allowed a small grin. "That was not Mint money, Chief. That was an advance, you might say."

The chief held up one hand like a stop sign. He closed his eyes and dropped his head on his chest. Slowly he said. "Please . . . I don't even want to know about it."

About the Author

The author lives with his wife in Winter Park, Florida, or Edwards, Colorado, where they are visited by four grown children.

A graduate of the University of Virginia with a liberal arts degree, he served in a top secret cryptographic unit of the U. S. Army during the Korean crisis organizing intelligence from codes deciphered by the National Security Agency.

He moved to Florida, retired early and has written in three different genres. *The Final Plan,* a Nazi espionage thriller, *The Second Creation,* where science fiction portrays a battle between the Anti-Christ and the Biblical prophecy of a second coming, and his third novel, *The Coal Mine Caper,* about robbing Fort Knox is the crime of the twentieth century.

Printed in the United States
69265LVS00001B/2

9 781410 709578